MALEDICUS

Charles F. French

MALEDICUS

The Investigative Paranormal Society

Book 1

Edition 2016

ISBN-13: 9781533425430
ISBN-10: 1533425434

Editor: K. D. Dowdall

Cover Design: Judy Bullard
www.customebookcovers.com

Interior layout: Maureen Cutajar
www.gopublished.com

*To my wife Liz, without whom I would never
have committed to being a writer.
My thanks and my love.*

Acknowledgements

I have many people to thank for their help with this novel. There are a myriad of readers who have made useful commentary among the many drafts of this book. I will try to list them all: Dean Jane Hudak, Lisa Lewis, Lara Signe Hoover, Richard Loeb, John Roccaro, Ray Santiago, Carmen Santiago, Katie Altpeter, Madison Cannon, Paola Mosquera, Dr. William Feeney, Kate Ferullo, Haley Wolf, and Tricia Sloan. To all, thank you!

Thank you to Professor Barbara Pavlock who gave me the correct Latin for the name Maledicus.

"There are more things in Heaven and Earth, Horatio,
than are dreamt of in your philosophy."

HAMLET
A PLAY IN FIVE ACTS BY WILLIAM SHAKESPEARE
First Published in 1603
London, England

"All that is necessary for evil to succeed is
for good men to do nothing."

EDMUND BURKE
SPEECH TO ELECTORS OF BRISTOL
NOVEMBER 3, 1774
As cited in "The Works of the Right Honorable Edmund Burke"
First Published in London, England in 1899, Vol. 2

ONE

LUCIUS ANTONY CAIUS
ROME, ITALY, XL ANNO DOMINI

Lucius Antony Caius exalted in his good fortune. He was in complete control of his destiny, of his place in the world. Not for him was the belief in the three sisters of fate—they would not measure and cut his string of life. Caius, also known as Maledicus, as he was called because of his odd lisping voice coupled with the grating sound of sandpaper grinding on coarse wood and with his evil personality, believed he controlled his world. And his evil persona caused others to fear him. He didn't look like the image of a strong Roman—he was short and fat, with little hair, but he was as dangerous as the most powerful General.

I will be emperor one day. Anyone who stands in my way I will destroy. All of them have no purpose other than for my use and pleasure.

As a trusted advisor to Emperor Caligula, Maledicus served Caligula in secret ways, giving Maledicus a myriad of fringe benefits for his services. Often invisible to the public, he was able to insinuate himself into almost any group and was capable of gaining power over others by knowing their weaknesses, their foibles, their sins, and their degradations.

Maledicus was also a procurer. He delivered people to the Emperor. He paid attention to what the Emperor wanted, and he, Maledicus, was able to arrange for the sadistic use of them by Caligula. He knew Caligula's perversions, so Maledicus presented the Emperor with victims, often girls who were Caligula's distant cousins in poorer families: sometimes Maledicus' thugs kidnapped them, sometimes through extortion, by giving themselves to the Emperor for his perverse pleasures.

Maledicus listened to the whispering of Roman officials and the members of the high Roman families. His status in Caligula's inner circle gained him entry to every family and every place in Rome. He installed well-paid spies and made an example of the first informant to betray him by arranging a particularly brutal murder. That man's naked, disemboweled body was left sprawled in front of his home with "TRAITOR" spelled in blood on his torso. He made use of his network of thieves, liars, cheats, and criminals to keep the Emperor informed of the movement within the Roman populace.

As long as he remained a valued asset and did not interfere or cause a problem for the Emperor, Caligula overlooked Maledicus' own dark pleasures. Compared to Caligula, Maledicus considered his own sins to be small. Caligula was a beast, a syphilitic who infected the Empire with evil and disgrace during the few years that he reigned. Although Maledicus believed his superiority to Caligula, he had the good sense never to utter those thoughts. Many Romans despaired at the direction of the Empire, but for Maledicus, it was heaven. He was a perfect match for Caligula's Rome.

After an official state feast, Maledicus returned to his home in ecstasy. His good fortune was vast. The feast itself was one of enormous proportion with many courses served with the most exquisite foods available in the Empire, each course more elaborate than the previous: ostrich eggs and roast, caviar, eels, figs, olives, and wines in abundance were among the many delicacies. The invited guests in attendance included: slaves, male and female, chosen exclusively for their beauty. Maledicus, as was his custom during these events, did not participate. Following the feast was an elaborate orgy held for the Emperor's pleasure. Maledicus would have opportunity to indulge himself later, but now he needed to work, so he watched and listened. He would learn much while the others debauched.

Two days earlier, one of his spies brought important information to him. The young man, a clerk who worked in the estate of General Aurilieus Cassius, came to him. Maledicus invited him into his home and gave him wine. "Relax," he said with his best smile stretched across his face. "You are safe here." *You are for now anyway, but what pleasure I could have listening to your screams.*

"Now what do you have to tell me?"

"I was working on my copying of papers in the scriptorium when I heard whispering, and I immediately remembered that you had told me to pay attention to such things."

"Good boy," Maledicus said in an almost kindly tone and patted his hand. *Such soft hands...they would be so easy to tear apart.*

"I could only hear bits of what was said, but," the boy said and paused and looked around in fear of being overheard.

"No one can hear you in this home. I assure you."

"I heard words like 'plotting against the Emperor' and even 'assassination'."

Maledicus smiled again, paid the young man, and dismissed him.

Such whispers, true or baseless, was the ore that Maledicus could mine into a powerful blade of iron, struck against enemies. The others forged into a powerful phalanx able to overrun any obstinate foe.

I hate Cassius. He is a definite problem. Maledicus knew that the General despised him, so this information about Cassius was a useful weapon. Knowing Caligula's paranoia and intense distrust of the General, Maledicus would present the rumor as fact to the Emperor, and that insinuation would seal Cassius' fate. He would die a traitor's death.

During the orgy, Maledicus instructed a particular girl, Dulcia, one whom he had used before and knew was the type Cassius preferred, young, dark haired and nubile, to ply the General with wine, and after sating him with alcohol and sex, to whisper to him, to pry out any secrets the man might have.

Cassius always enjoyed his time with this girl because she would do anything he wanted sexually. Unlike his wife, a very proper Roman Matron, this girl indulged any sexual fantasy he wanted. In fact, she encouraged him to try new ways.

Dulcia reported to Maledicus later that night. "Did you enjoy yourself, my dear?" he asked and smiled. "I hope the good general was up to your abilities."

She lifted her beautiful head and licked her lips. "I love playing with him."

"And did he do more than spill his seed, I hope?"

"Much, much more, Sir. He cannot keep his head when he drinks. Then he is like a baby in my arms."

Cassius had a weak spot—he was not a strong drinker. Sexually spent, with his head lolling and slurred speech, he bragged of his plans to the naked girl whose head rested on his chest. "I'll be the one who changes Rome. I'm the best suited for it. From an old royal family, and I've proven myself in conquest. I'll take that sick excuse for an emperor down." He smiled and kissed the girl again, but he never remembered saying anything to her.

Within 15 minutes, the General was snoring gently at her side. Dulcia disentangled herself and went to the room in which Maledicus waited for her report. Maledicus rewarded the girl with a sizeable payment and sent her on her way.

The girl reported General Cassius to Maledicus that indeed, Cassius had been in the planning stages of a coup. This information was more than Maledicus could have hoped for. Cassius was the very image of a great Roman soldier, tall, strong, square-jawed, and with a searing ambition to be much more than merely a general. Cassius saw himself as a future Caesar. His weakness, however, lay in his inability to judge with whom he should engage in pillow talk. Even though he was not above indulging his own desires, Cassius was disgusted with the Empire's civil and moral decay.

Of course, he saw no inconsistency with his participation in these orgies. They were, he reasoned, the proper reward and tribute for a Roman general such as he, whose work and life had been devoted to the expansion, preservation, and honor of the Empire. Additionally, Cassius saw himself as a true Roman, of impressive lineage and strong conquests and therefore above the mass of ordinary men, who needed special restrictions and discipline to lead proper lives. He was a leader of men, and as such, expected extraordinary rewards for his actions.

Cassius, however, thought Caligula was leading Rome into disaster. He considered Caligula to be a mere politician as well as a member of a corrupt family, not someone fit to serve as leader of the mightiest Empire the world had ever seen. Caligula's profligacy sickened him – once proud Rome was replacing conquest and military discipline with depravation and decay.

Rather than rejoicing in conquest and expansion of the Empire, multitudes cheered their vicarious pleasures at the Coliseum and its showy violence and indulged in too many luxuries. Rome was in danger of becoming a fat and lazy society that would fall victim to its internal stupor and disease, unless someone who was strong enough could change its course, someone like Cassius.

Maledicus was patient. He had seen that Caligula had guided his very young cousin Albelia into his private chamber. As he watched the Emperor with his arms around the slender shoulder of the girl, moving her and whispering to her, Maledicus saw Caligula turn to him and wink. He knew that Caligula would enjoy using and corrupting this girl and that he would have to wait for him to finish taking his pleasure before they could speak. Maledicus waited on a bench outside the room, under the watchful eyes of Caligula's guard. Yet, they knew him and understood that he was a trusted advisor. *Fools, one day I will replace this idiot of an Emperor, and then I will show the world what a truly powerful Emperor is.*

He listened to the sounds coming out of Caligula's chambers: the older man's moans of pleasure and the girl's cries of pain, doubtless she had been still a virgin upon entry to that room. Finally, the door opened, and the girl, draped in only a thin sheet ran from the room.

"Send Maledicus in," rang out the Emperor's voice.

Caligula lay on his bed covered on from the waist down. A film of sweat covered him; he had obviously enjoyed himself with the girl.

"May I approach, Sire?" Maledicus knew how to play the obsequious fool.

4

Caligula nodded. Maledicus went near to the Emperor and whispered the news to him. "You are in danger, Sire."

Caligula may have been insane, but he was clever and paranoid, which made him very dangerous. They set a trap. "Let the fool think that he will be successful," Caligula ordered. "Let my centurions know when and where they should be to take them."

"I will do that, Sire."

Maledicus prearranged a meeting with Cassius and the conspirators. "I am one of you," he told them. "The empire is in danger of falling into disrepute and decay, and we must do something about it."

After he saw their agreement, Maledicus excused himself to visit the lavatory, and he wiped his brow with a black scarf, the signal to the centurions who quickly invaded Cassius' home and took the men into custody.

They were all publicly condemned as traitors. Caligula personally issued the punishment order, "Because of the severity of their crimes, and their threat to the safety of the person of the Emperor and the security of the Roman Empire, I order their deaths by crucifixion." They suffered this horrible and excruciatingly slow death over a span of several days. Their bodies, taken down from the crucifix, tossed like garbage into the fields for carrion to eat. These men would have no honorable burials, a horror, an anathema for Roman citizens.

His work done, Maledicus was granted his Sire's leave to return home, where he could be who he truly was. Those who thought him merely an unfortunate, but useful, citizen had no idea of his capabilities. He had been at the trial and the executions, and finally he had returned to his villa. As he entered, he nodded to his guards then ordered wine from one of his attendants. The young man scampered to obey. Maledicus sat in one of his comfortable chairs, drank the wine and nibbled on grapes, all the while content with what he had accomplished. He had much to look forward to.

In the villa Caligula had given him, Maledicus had a subbasement fitted for torture, degradation, and murder. He had men loyal to him who would bring victims for his use and then dispose of their bodies. Men, women, and children were all fodder for his obscene delights.

While Maledicus brutalized a wide variety of people, male and female, young and old, slave and free, he preferred above all else to use, corrupt and kill the innocent. The fear and screams of the blameless children gave him the most pleasure. Their torment filled him with the most overwhelming belief in his own power and invincibility. He tortured them, killed them, and wallowed in their gore.

So, when asked what he would like for a reward, Maledicus replied – he wanted the Emperor's cousin Albelia and her family. Caligula was finished with her, so he easily granted the wish.

Delivered to Maledicus' house of horrors in chains included the young girl, her mother, father, younger brother and sister. The girl's father had a gag on and could say nothing. All he could do was glare at Maledicus with hatred in his eyes. As the soldiers ushered them into Maledicus' sub-basement, the mother turn to him and begged on her knees, "Please don't hurt us. Please don't harm my children. I'll do anything you want. Anything. Please don't harm them."

"Dear woman, please don't worry. You have nothing to fear. This is merely a formality." He reached out, caressed her face and smiled. *Stupid bitch, I will make you watch the others' torments and save you for last.* "Do you really think I would hurt children?"

Their screams, although unheard above the sub-basement, lasted for hours.

Food for the carrion.

TWO

Roosevelt Franklin, a retired history professor, had lost his beloved wife Sarah to cancer several years earlier, and he had not stopped grieving. Death had also claimed two beloved people from his closest friends, Samuel and Jeremy. The three retired men needed to know if there was life after death. Therefore, they formed a ghost-investigating group.

"Gentlemen, I believe we have legitimate activity," Roosevelt said in a quiet, calm voice. The IPS, the Investigative Paranormal Society, was on a case.

Roosevelt didn't look up; rather, he continued to gaze intently at the two instruments on the battered coffee table directly in front of him. The table showed signs of heavy use by an active family, with scratches and gouges in the wood, and a few permanent stains from what looked like ink, paint, and glitter. It fit well into the living room in which Sam and he were sitting, a well-used room in a modest single home owned by a Mr. and Mrs. Kaufmann in a working-class neighborhood on the east side of Bethberg, Pennsylvania. The furniture was worn, but comfortable, with the stains of several spills from children's glasses indelibly marked into the fabric. Pictures of children and various family members adorned one wall, while a large television sat in a place of honor against the other wall, directly across from the family's large sofa.

Roosevelt glanced at the digital thermometer: The temperature in the room had dropped 10 degrees, from 60 to 50, in just over 2 minutes, and both men shivered.

"Roosevelt?" Sam also was watching his instruments: a digital voice recorder and a handheld digital video camera, all recently purchased and of the newest and highest quality available; Sam had positioned these shiny toys in front of him. Sam sat on the other side of the table, catty-cornered from Roosevelt, who held up a finger to Sam signaling him to wait for a moment.

The two men looked like complete opposites. Roosevelt was tall and lean, with white hair combed straight back. As he typically did, he wore one of his tailored English style wool suits complete with vest, this one tan and made from lightweight wool for the heat. He insisted it was comfortable, even in the hottest summer conditions, although Roosevelt's friends doubted him. Roosevelt enjoyed the old-fashioned feel of the outfit; he said that it suited him because he was, indeed, an old historian. Additionally, he agreed with the sentiment of the knighted designer Sir Hardy Amies who said, "A man should look as if he had bought his clothes with intelligence, put them on with care, and then forgotten all about them." Roosevelt wore his clothing with simple elegance and grace.

Sam was the opposite. He dressed in whatever he felt comfortable and cared nothing for the opinion of other people on his appearance. He wore blue jeans nearly worn through in places, which he loved because they were comfortable. A black slightly oversized tee shirt, and battered work boots completed his favorite look. "Look at me," he said when Roosevelt tried to convince him to dress a bit nicer. "I look like what I am: an old, retired, small-town cop, a short, pudgy, bald guy, and I really don't give a shit if anything I wear impresses anyone." He sat in an easy chair, with an unlit cigar in his mouth. He knew he couldn't smoke in someone else's house, but he still liked having one to chew on.

"Jeremy, is everything working?" Roosevelt asked in a muted voice.

"Yes guys, everything is fine." Jeremy, the third member of their group, sat at the folding table in the foyer of the modest Cape Cod style house. Jeremy, a small, slightly built man of 70, kept his gray hair short and neatly cut. He wore a gray, pencil thin mustache and was dressed in brown slacks, loafers, and a light blue polo shirt. He wasn't far from the others, but they still used new walkie-talkie phones to communicate. While Roosevelt thought this somewhat silly, Sam and Jeremy were delighted with the newest additions to their gadget collection.

"Only the finest stuff for our operation!" Sam said earlier.

Jeremy sat and watched the flat screen monitor. As the member who was most adept with computers, he had become the de facto equipment manager. As he looked at the screen, a haze of some kind appeared on it. He leaned forward to assure himself that it wasn't something on the outside of the monitor. He checked carefully to be certain that the equipment was functioning normally. His friends had often teased him about being an old guy who was so technically proficient, but now his skills with electronics were proving to be very valuable. He was certain – something transmitted onto recording.

"Guys, I have a question." He spoke into his walkie-talkie. "Are you seeing anything?"

"No. Should we be? Is something here?" Sam had been watching the room as Roosevelt kept a close eye on his EMF, Electro-Magnetic-Field meter, and his digital thermometer.

"Yes, I'm getting something. At first I thought there might be a problem with the monitor, but I checked it. It's fine. So, yes, I am seeing something."

"Jeremy," Sam growled. "D'ya think you could be a little more specific? What the hell are you seeing?"

"Samuel," Roosevelt looked up at Sam briefly and then back down to his meters. "The readings have gone up significantly on the EMF. I had a base reading of .5 in this room, and now it is reading 25." One of the theories in the field of paranormal investigation stated that a high EMF reading might accompany the presence of paranormal activity. Certainly many other causes for EMF activity existed, but a consistent base reading that suddenly spiked was reason for attention. They had previously checked the entire house to determine an EMF baseline reading, keeping careful notes of the readings from each room of the house. The living room where they were now sitting and the basement were both clean, showing only a .5 on the meter. A jump of only one to two points would be very important; this increase was significant.

Sam started to speak, but Roosevelt signaled him to be quiet. "Shh," he hissed and looked up. "Did you hear that?"

It sounded a little bit louder than a faint whisper. They always used digital audio recorders in an attempt to record EVP activity, Electronic Voice Phenomenon, spoken communication that was theoretically beyond the ability of living human beings to hear, but, for some reason, could be recorded by the electronic equipment and then later verified in a research and evaluation session. This sound, however, they both heard.

"Yeah, I sure did, Rosy. What the hell do you think that was?"

"It sounded to me like a voice. At least I think so. And Samuel?"

"Yeah?"

"Don't call me Rosy." Roosevelt grew annoyed.

Sam grinned. He knew how much his friend detested that nickname, so, of course, Sam loved to tease him with it. Roosevelt preferred the sound of his full given name – he called everyone by their full names. He felt that it was appropriate and more dignified, especially for men of their ages. Sam disagreed.

"With any kind of good fortune, Samuel, our digital voice recorders will have captured what was said."

The temperature plummeted another ten degrees. "Samuel, the thermometer is now reading 40 degrees. I think something is going to happen. Please be ready."

"Damn, it's cold in here. Should've brought a coat. But it's been so warm this year, even in December, you wouldn't think we needed one."

The weather had been unusually warm, and people talked about Indian summer even at the beginning of December—some were now beginning to take the talk of global warming seriously.

"You can handle it, Samuel. Remember, you are the tough guy of the group."

—Leave me alone!—

Both men heard the voice; it was raspy, and while not loud, it was significantly more audible than before. In their previous investigations, they had never heard anything like this.

"Son-of-a-bitch!" Sam felt the rush he used to experience on a stake out when he finally had something on a perp. Even though he had been retired for over ten years, he still missed the thrill of the chase.

"Samuel, I think we have finally got something!"

"Guys, are you ok in there?" Jeremy continued to monitor the activity on the computer.

"Yeah, we're fine, Jerry."

Jeremy ignored Sam's teasing. He, like Roosevelt, wanted to be called by his full name, but he refused to acknowledge Sam's baiting.

"Well, keep your eyes open. Something's on the monitor."

"What's the temp now? Seriously man, it's freezing in here."

"Samuel, it is now 35. That is a drop of another five degrees."

"Well, fuck."

—I said, leave me alone!—

"Guys?" Jeremy's voice was a bit tremulous. "Um, you have company, I think."

Roosevelt looked up from the meters. "What do you mean? What are you getting?"

Jeremy's monitor showed a mist swirling and forming into a shape somewhat like a human being. There was something close to a face, and it looked like it might be scowling. "Uh, it doesn't look friendly…Can't you see it?"

"I cannot see anything." Roosevelt didn't understand this. While the digital audio recorders were intended to pick up what could not be heard, the video recorders were used to substantiate whatever they witnessed visually. The IPS counted on having verifiable data, as well as having personal experiences, to back up any recorded evidence.

As an historian, Roosevelt had long argued that most historians made a serious mistake by not acknowledging the importance of oral accounts of history as well as that in written documents. He preferred to find evidence in any way or form he could and then evaluate each piece itself. He encouraged the IPS to use the same approach in exploring the supernatural world. Verifiable support for claims of paranormal activity must be found. Now, if something was being recorded on the visual recorder, but they couldn't see it during the time of the recording, then it was similar to EVPs. Perhaps they had discovered a new paranormal phenomenon.

"Guys, it's getting clearer. I can see what looks like a body and a face. You can't see anything?"

"Nope," Sam answered.

"Nor I."

"Well, it's definitely there. And it looks angry and nasty. I don't like this at all."

Sam didn't like the touch of fear he heard in Jeremy's voice. It wasn't Jeremy becoming frightened that bothered him; it was the idea of something scaring his friends that did. He rose and began to cross over to Roosevelt. As Sam began to walk, something shoved him from behind. He stumbled, but he didn't go down.

"What the fuck?!"

Seeing the anger on Sam's face, Roosevelt was immediately on his feet and put his hands on Sam's shoulders to steady him.

"Samuel, are you okay?"

"Yeah, I'm just getting a little pissed off."

"I understand, Samuel. So am I." He stepped around Sam and spoke directly at the place where Sam had been standing. "Do not ever do that to him again. Do you hear? I do not let anyone hurt my friends. If you want to try that again, do it to me."

"Rosy, don't do that! Don't target yourself."

They could both see something begin to appear in front of them…it was without a distinct form, like a mist rising from a lake in early morning, and it shimmered slightly.

"There it is! It's very clear now on my monitor. Roosevelt, Sam…do you see it? Well, guys, do you?"

"Yeah, we do…" As Sam answered, the mist slowly coalesced into the outline and shape of a man, a phenomenon they had never before witnessed. This might be a full body spirit, the kind of apparition often thought of as the ultimate find of the paranormal investigation world. With curiosity and excitement rising, Roosevelt leaned forward to look at the phantasm more closely. As he did, it moved as if it had an arm, and Roosevelt's head snapped as if he had been slapped hard. Sam grabbed Roosevelt to steady him, looked at his friend, and saw Roosevelt's face turning red. He didn't realize that Roosevelt had felt his left arm start to go numb and tightness had begun to build in his chest. Sam only knew that he wanted his friends away from here. They could plan another way to get rid of this thing. Sam was willing to face it alone if need be.

"That does it! C'mon Rosy, it's time to split and get some backup."

Jeremy ran into the room. "Guys, let's get out of here!"

Roosevelt nodded slightly. "Okay, but we will be back to handle this. You are a bully, and you have frightened this family long enough." His voice rose in intensity. "We will be back to deal with you."

"Let's pack up—now!" Jeremy's voice was sharp and clear. Roosevelt and Sam turned to Jeremy and stared for a moment. They rarely heard their low-key friend give orders. Typically Jeremy maintained a quiet demeanor, not one given to inspiring obedience, but this time they listened to him.

—Get out of here!—

Now the voice was distinct and loud. It sounded like a grumpy old man who might have been yelling at children walking on his lawn.

They began to collect their equipment from the living room but intentionally left one digital video recorder and one digital audio recorder behind – turned on and recording. They would return later and perhaps find more evidence for this haunting, and they definitely would deal with this foul-tempered spirit. Roosevelt would call in some outside help, someone he was sure could dispel this cranky and perhaps violent ghost. This thing was the kind of thing that Father Bruno would be happy to help with; the good Father had experience eliminating nasty ghosts.

They stopped in the foyer and quickly packed the rest of their equipment. As they did, Roosevelt turned away from his friends. He reached into his inner jacket pocket and took out a small medicine bottle. He secretly placed a nitroglycerine tablet under his tongue. He didn't want to let the others know that his heart was pounding, and his chest was tight.

Sam, however, noticed. He took Roosevelt aside and, in a very quiet voice, asked, "Are you okay?"

"I'm fine. I'm fine. Let's finish and get out of here."

—Leave!—

They left.

THREE

To a stranger walking into Helen Murray's house was like entering into an unorganized museum or perhaps a Victorian era cabinet of curiosities. A high school history teacher by vocation and an archeologist and historian of the arcane by avocation, Ms. Murray was so passionate and unpredictable in her teaching approach that she captured the imaginations of her charges. "History is the story of people, of us. You are all living history right now. You are the ones that will be making history. If you hate history, then you hate your own stories."

She was often seen dressed in period costume, and she would bring in artifacts she had collected. It was not unusual for Helen Murray to come to school in a Roman era toga, an antebellum gown, or a Victorian dress.

Helen saw herself as an active historian as well as a high school teacher. She had summers free, which gave her the opportunity to explore her passions fully for at least two months every year.

Helen Murray was in her early forties and unassuming in her dress and appearance. She was thin, not shapely, with long straight salt and pepper hair with just a hint of a curl, which she kept parted in the center. When not in costume to illustrate a lesson, she dressed conservatively at school and wore jeans and comfortable, serviceable clothing—old battered but comfortable leather coats and worn sweatshirts. Her skin, always tan, was leathered from her many years working outside in the sun during the summers. She had a mysterious sex appeal—it radiated from within, the kind that often made men of an intellectual sort give her second glances.

Helen had her friends, and she socialized as a member of a weekly book club and with a few fellow teachers, but in her core soul, she protected her heart. Having had her share of romances, and her heartbreaks, she kept potential lovers at a distance. She did not want to open herself again to the possibility of the intense pain of losing a partner in romance. Whenever a fellow began to intimate that he wanted exclusivity, she would gently break off the relationship. Helen was a very good judge of people, and she wished no drama in her life, so she never became involved with the kind of man who might become dangerous. She would tell her girlfriends: "Any desire I ever had for the bad boys ended when I was in high school. I don't need to mix danger and romance."

Helen Murray had enjoyed the quiet nature and rhythm of her life, the steady movement of school year to summer to school year, until recently.

Helen's younger sister Jessica, and then only living sibling, had been her closest friend. Even though they were very different in their desires and approaches to life, their bond had been closer than that of most sisters. Jessica had deeply wanted a family, so when she found a man whom she loved and who loved her in return, she was ecstatic. Jessica had a long history of finding men who misused her, so Helen was thrilled with her discovery of Andrew, a gentle, loving, and responsible man.

Yet, Jessica's new romance did not lead to immediate fulfillment for Jessica; she and her husband shared a dream of a house full of children, but years passed without any. Jessica and Andrew had both consulted numerous doctors and tried everything they could, with no results. Finally, years later, when in her late thirties and having given up hope of ever having a child, Jessica became pregnant. This great joy extended past the ecstatic and astonished couple to include Helen. When the child was born, they named her Helena, which moved Helen to an elation that made her speechless, a truly rare condition for a woman who always seemed to have a way with words and something important to say.

The sisters' parents had died several years before Helena was born, their brother Anthony had been killed much earlier, and because Andrew, an only child, had also recently suffered the loss of his parents, Helena was left with neither grandparents nor any close relatives in the area. Helen was the baby's only extended family, and she doted on the little girl, buying her clothing—from thrift stores because she knew the little one would outgrow them almost immediately—many toys and stacks of books, which she would read to the infant, and then later to the toddler who sat contentedly on her aunt's lap. Helena's huge brown eyes focused with rapt attention on her aunt's face as she read to her. Helen wanted to instill in the child her own deep and abiding love for words, stories, and books.

Change can occur with the sudden horror of a lightning bolt crashing into a home and causing it to burn. Such a thunderclap hit Helen's family. Helen had taken the then 2½ year old for the weekend, so her sister and brother-in-law could have some needed private time together and Helen could have a weekend with her beloved niece. The little girl was so well behaved she gave the lie to the belief in the "terrible twos". All children are different, Helen maintained, and she refused to categorize her niece according to unfounded expectations of behavior. It was not that the little girl was spoiled; she was not. Both Jessica and Helen believed in loving discipline. They knew it was important for the child to learn that she was not the center of the universe and that she could not have everything she wanted. Helena was a happy and energetic little girl.

Helen's phone rang at 2 A. M, the nightmare hours, when everything that is wrong and everything else that might go badly seems to be amplified, the time that many people spend sleepless, staring at their ceilings as they worry about their lives.

Helen's sister, Jessica and brother-in-law, Andrew were killed in a car accident, returning from an evening at a local jazz club to a nearby bed and breakfast where they had been staying for their getaway. The man who hit them had been drinking at a local bar. The bartender had cut off the drunken man, after six beers. However, an empty bottle of Southern Comfort was discovered on the floor of his pickup truck. Andrew and Jessica were driving through an intersection when Billy Bernard, blew through a stop sign in excess of 90 MPH. The front end of Bernard's Ford pickup rammed into the little Volkswagen Gulf, like a battleship breaking up a fishing boat. The screeching sound of metal on metal was like a giant hand with claws ripping through the side of a metal building. The truck instantly crumpled the side of the car, ramming into it and crushing Jessica immediately. Bernard had lost all control over the truck, and it pushed the little car across the road, finally pinning it against a telephone pole. Andrew died with his head smashed like an overripe melon against the pole.

Bernard walked away from the accident without a scratch. He got 5-7 years for vehicular homicide.

That terrible night had happened three years earlier. The couple, who had been practical and prepared for life and death, designated Helen, as Helena's guardian should anything happen to them. As a result, the transition to Helena living with her aunt was legally relatively easy. Because the child was so young, she adapted to the circumstances quickly, not fully understanding what had happened. She missed her parents and cried a great deal in the first few months, and called for her Mommy and Daddy, but she slowly recovered, and with the resilience of youth, she began to adapt to her new life with her beloved aunt.

15

For Helen, however, this situation was anything but easy. She had to deal simultaneously with her despair at the loss of her beloved sister and brother-in-law and with her love of and devotion to her niece, for whom she was now the sole family. Helen was the one who arranged the funerals and stayed together, emotionally, for the sake of her niece. If she hadn't had Helena to care for, she wasn't sure she would have made it.

Helen would often awaken in the middle of the night shaking from terrible and, sometimes, unclear and incoherent nightmares. She often dreamt that her sister and brother-in-law would appear to her, clearly dead, with gray and rotting skin, like out of a Hollywood zombie movie. They asked how Helena was—*are you taking care of her? Do we need to come back?* Sometimes, they would accuse her of interfering—*She is our daughter—you are the one who should have died.*

Helen dreamt of cars crashing and people killed horribly. She would hear the sound of steel crushing and the screams of people in terrible pain.

Those dreams were soon replaced by others, in which she saw Billy Bernard standing over the open caskets of her sister and brother-in-law and smiling. With a rotting face and one eye hanging down from its socket, he would turn, take a pull from a bottle of Jim Beam, and laugh at her. *"Hey honey, it's not so bad anyway. At least, I made it."* Then he offered her a drink from the filthy bottle of booze.

Helen would wake from her dreams soaked in sweat and shaking in anger. Her breath came in shallow gasps as if she were enduring an asthma attack, something she had never before experienced. When she finally got her breathing under control, sometimes she broke down into tears. Other times, she fantasized about breaking into prison and killing Billy Bernard.

She spoke with her minister about her anger, and he helped a bit. She also attended counseling, but the therapist was more interested in being sympathetic than actually offering advice on how to deal with her emotions. She stopped after two sessions.

Trying to deal with her emotions herself, Helen did whatever she could to keep herself together. She kept herself completely busy, so any time that wasn't devoted to caring for her niece was filled with work. She took extra classes and tutoring, anything to keep her mind occupied. And she taught Helena, played with her, and read to her. Nothing could keep her mind from sometimes thinking about Billy Bernard. *I want to close my hands on his neck and slowly choke the life out of that bastard.*

Despite Helen's struggles with her anger, it was something she kept hidden as Helena thrived and grew.

16

The years passed quickly as Helen settled into her new life of caring for Helena as her now more-than-aunt. She found an excellent daycare for her niece while she worked as a teacher. Later, when the little one began school, she spent only a brief time in daycare after school, until Helen was finished with teaching, and could pick her up.

As any good parent would, Helen made sacrifices and changes to her routine and life. She no longer planned long historic and archeological journeys in the summer. Rather, that time was spent together with Helena. She took Helena on short trips and adventures. Helen was delighted with the girl's innate intelligence and burgeoning curiosity about the world. Helen planned, when the girl was older, on taking her on excursions to Europe, but for now, smaller expeditions were fine.

Life had seemed to settle in a routine and a semblance of normalcy for aunt and niece, until Helena mentioned seeing "the bad man."

FOUR

As he did every morning, Roosevelt woke up and reached for Sarah, only to be dismayed when he realized she wasn't there, that she was, indeed, gone, and he would have to make it through another day without her. That was the worst part of every day, having to face another waking period without Sarah.

After rising, Roosevelt always put on the thick maroon robe Sarah had given him as a birthday present ten years ago. The feel of it made him smile. He walked across the bedroom to his dresser. There he picked up his wife's picture, taken a few days after they were married, and kissed it. He whispered, "Good morning, my love," before gently replacing it on the dresser.

He opened the curtains, looked out at the Pocono Mountains and smiled. His home was just outside of Bethberg, PA, located south of Stroudsburg, PA and north of Bethlehem, PA, and he had a magnificent view of the old mountain range. No matter how he might have been feeling, this view always lifted him. He loved the mountains and the variations of leaves on the trees, especially in the fall. But even in the winter, when the leaves were gone, except for evergreens, he still saw beauty in them. Some mornings he would see a hawk flying, and then he would smile his wide, slanted grin.

After looking outside, he found his way to the bathroom. Even though he was fully awake, his body was always reluctant to move in the morning. He patiently tried to produce a morning stream, and he cursed his ever-growing prostate, *Nature's joke on me*. Roosevelt appreciated the irony that he kept losing muscle and strength with age, but the one thing that kept growing was something he wished would shrink. His doctor kept a close eye on the situation—there had been no indication of prostate cancer—and had put him on pills, but they had little effect.

Finally finished, he plodded into his kitchen he kept neat and clean in honor of Sarah. Roosevelt was not by nature a tidy man, nor was he a complete slob, but complete order was not his way. The kitchen had been Sarah's domain, and she had built it with a French country décor. It was bright and cheerful, and it made him smile.

Roosevelt was an adequate cook; his wife could have been a professional chef if she had chosen, but she preferred to do her cooking for her husband and friends. "I don't want to turn it into a business and risk losing my love for it," she told Roosevelt when he had encouraged her to start her own restaurant. Instead, she had set her artist's soul free in her kitchen and in her culinary creations. She made him dishes that he had no idea how to cook, and he would never attempt them. He had not eaten any of her special dishes since she had died. He could have ordered them at fine restaurants, but he honored her by not eating them at all.

He now cooked simple, basic dishes, and he had recently begun to indulge in less healthy foods: he loved cheeseburgers and French fries, especially fries covered in cheese. He had stopped worrying about the effects on his health. He would soon be seventy, and he thought that it wasn't going to hurt him now. If it did shorten his lifespan, then he was that much closer to seeing his beloved Sarah again.

The next stop for the morning was coffee. Roosevelt had been drinking coffee since he was sixteen. Then he felt that it made him look like an adult, when in actuality, it had made him look silly and exactly what he had been, an awkward teenager trying to appear grown up. But he had acquired a love for the dark brew. He always began the day by grinding a full pot's worth of French Roast beans into a near espresso powder. He used this to concoct a strong and very rich pot of coffee, which he always drank black. He drank one cup and then took his daily assortment of pills: for his heart, for his high blood pressure, for his prostate, for his arthritis, and a variety of vitamins. He deeply detested having to take them, but he had promised Sarah he would take care of himself, so he did just that. *Other than my heart, my blood pressure, my arthritis, and my prostate, I am completely healthy.*

After finishing his initial cup of java, the rest of the coffee he drank throughout the morning, Roosevelt always took a long, steaming hot shower. The hot water loosened his stiff muscles and joints. He then shaved completely and always with a steady hand, which was important because he detested what passed for razors today. He insisted on using his father's old straight razor. He had an old stropping belt, and he kept the blade in near perfect condition. This razor was still the finest shaving instrument he could find. He did know that if his hands ever began to shake he would have to stop using it, but until then, he would keep it and shave with it daily.

The last part of his morning routine was breakfast. Roosevelt made himself a meal five mornings out of the week, and the others, usually Mondays and Thursdays, he would meet with the other members of IPS at the Bethberg Diner for breakfast. He tried to keep the meal he made for himself light: oatmeal, or a couple of scrambled eggs.

Then he was ready to face the day.

One more day of survival, one more day without Sarah.

FIVE

ROME A.D. 40

Maledicus, like some other sociopaths, believed he was transforming, that he had a nearly godlike ability to absorb the life force of others into him and increase his own being. He held completely with the destruction of each life he took, that he incorporated those souls into himself, and those ingestions fed his very spirit and made him into more than a man. He saw himself metamorphosing into a god. He would achieve apotheosis. Soon, he felt that he would be unstoppable.

Maledicus was growing more overt in his crimes. Since the discovery of the most recent plot against the Emperor, he believed that he had established himself as indispensable to Caligula; he was the watcher, the eyes that the Emperor needed even as he indulged himself in his puerile desires.

Soon I will be more powerful than the Emperor himself. I can become Emperor, and then no one will be able to stand before me. I will be God of Rome. All will worship me. All will kneel before me. I am invincible and immortal, already a God.

Maledicus was convinced of his apotheosis.

Maledicus was certain of his coming Godhead.

Maledicus was wrong.

Caligula, in his growing insanity and paranoia, had begun to suspect Maledicus was becoming too powerful and he might be trying to usurp the throne. Several attempts to assassinate the Emperor had already occurred, and he feared the inevitability of more.

Caligula had some of his own spies watching Maledicus. The Emperor loathed the fat little man, but he also respected his ability to gather and use information. Maledicus could be, Caligula realized, a truly formidable foe if his ambitions pointed in the wrong direction.

21

Caligula consulted with the one person whom he trusted more than anyone else in the world, his sister, Drusilla. Despite having given her in marriage to a Roman of high standing, Caligula had her moved to his own royal palace where she lived as if she were his lawful wife in all ways.

"My beautiful sister," he whispered to her one evening in bed, "What do you think I should do about Maledicus? Do you think he is a threat?"

"My dear brother," she said, leering at him and running her tongue over her teeth. "The little toad is beginning to worry me. Haven't you seen what he has been doing recently?"

He kissed her deeply and then asked, "What has the little fat abomination been up to?"

Knowing her brother would be enraged by jealously, she said, "Why brother, he has been watching me. I think he desires me for his room of horror."

Drusilla had been worried about the power Maledicus was gaining as an advisor to her brother. She saw what he was able to do with his whispers and insinuations to Caligula. Even the strongest of families were not safe from his campaign of rumors and fear. She heard about the terrible things he did when he had people brought to his "special room." Even to one as jaded as Drusilla, Maledicus' actions were shocking. She saw her own behaviors as beyond reproach, because she was, after all, the favored sister of the Emperor. But this disgusting little cockroach was feeding his desires, not merely on the expendables of society, the slaves and criminals, but he was targeting and using men, women, and children of the ruling class. And he seemed to be aiming higher and higher with his choices of prey.

"Dear brother, he frightens me. He watched me all evening, even after I arraigned to have a beautiful young slave sent to distract him."

"Really, well, you are beautiful, my sister."

"Yes, I am." She smiled and traced one long fingernail down her brother's chest. "But if he is willing to stare at me publicly, then he must be planning on doing something about his desires."

"Mm," he mumbled. He loved the touch of her hand. "Yes, that would be bad."

"And my beloved, if he can come after the preferred one of the Emperor, then surely he sees himself as above you." She rested her head on Caligula's chest and remained silent while he thought. She knew what she had set in motion.

"Drusilla, do you really believe that he is a threat to me?"

"I do," She said as she kissed his chest. "I wouldn't have brought this to your attention if I didn't."

Caligula considered the situation. While he distrusted most people instinctively, he believed his sister, this sister above the others, understood him and loved him. He thought she was the one person in the whole Empire who truly cared what happened to him. If she was concerned about this procurer of his, then he would be alarmed also.

He set more spies upon Maledicus.

One soldier, Magnus, a particularly vile man, a large and vicious fighter with a horribly scarred face and a temperament to match, whom Maledicus used as muscle for his needs, was soon in the Emperor's employ. "You will watch and report to me. Do you understand? If you do well, I will reward you beyond anything you can imagine. If you fail me, you will be crucified."

Magnus understood that he had an opportunity. He thoroughly enjoyed his work for Maledicus, anything that allowed him to use his sword or hands to kill amused him, but now he had the opportunity to serve the Emperor. He would not fail; this was his chance to have everything he wanted.

Magnus reported on the increasing carnage of Maledicus. One story, in particular, interested Caligula. Maledicus was keeping two soldiers in his chamber of horrors and was torturing them slowly. At the height of their screams, when these strong men were begging for mercy and a quick death, he made them call him Emperor. Then he killed them.

Caligula seethed and set his trap for Maledicus.

SIX

The IPS rotated where they held their meetings: once a week at each of the three primary members' homes and gathering for other meetings, in the mornings, at the Bethberg Diner. This one was at Roosevelt's house, and they were convening in his library, a fitting place for a man who styled himself as an old-fashioned British country gentleman.

While certainly a proud American, Roosevelt always thought of himself as an Anglophile and one who had been attracted to the order and dignity he associated with this kind of life. The walls of the room, lined ceiling to floor with deep walnut bookcases, were overflowing with volumes of varying sizes and conditions. Some books were standard hardbacks, some were very old, some were very handsome leather bound editions, and others were tattered paperbacks. Some were small, and some were folio sized, but they all suggested by their wear and tear, were well read. If a visitor scanned Roosevelt's shelves, he saw a wide range of offerings: from many books of historical study to literature to science to the world of the esoteric. It was clear that in this room, books were for reading and not for display. Roosevelt was a snob about many things; he drank only the best single malt scotches, smoked only the finest cigars, and dressed in hand tailored soft wool suits, but he was not a snob in the way of many a book collector. He was a lover of books not for the potential monetary value of a rare first edition but for the wisdom, ideas, satires, themes, and stories they contained. He loved the texts not for their decorative appearances, but because he loved to read.

"Books, gentlemen," he often said, "are not defined by the quality of their bindings, but by the substance of their words." Anyone who made the mistake of admiring his "collection" immediately knew, by this not so gently delivery, and very seriously intended, admonition. Roosevelt considered one of his tattered paperbacks as important as the most expensive hand-bound leather and gilt edged tome.

Roosevelt was also not a snob about homes—in his opinion, a home should be comfortable and welcoming, and it should have books. Everything else was extraneous.

An old, large, dark walnut wooden table stood in the center of the library, scarred from the strong usage of time. With papers, books, and pens, including an old quill pen and ink reservoir, scattered about its surface, the table projected a feeling of solidity and strength. This was a table, used often and hard and was there for practicality, not for show. Around it were several large, comfortable brown leather chairs. A medium size humidor, with a cherry wood exterior, sat on a table in the room's far corner. Inside was an assortment of cigars of very good quality available to anyone in the room.

Roosevelt wore the tan wool English suit he always did for their meetings. He preferred to present a level of formality at the proceedings. He did not see these gatherings as simply a gentlemen's nightclub or a night out. These were serious matters in which they were engaged, and he preferred to dress as he did when he was still an active professor of history. He had decided to wear tailored wool suits nearly forty years ago after rummaging through an old chest in the attic and finding a photograph of his grandfather, who had emigrated from England in the early 20th century. Roosevelt had deeply loved his grandfather, who had been one of the main influences in his life and one of the few members of his family Roosevelt could tolerate: his grandfather had helped develop Roosevelt's love of reading and of the outdoors. He frequently surprised the youngster with books, often science fiction and adventure, and he was the one who taught Roosevelt about camping, fishing, and hunting. When he saw his beloved Grandpa in the perfectly tailored suit, he decided that he would emulate his idol.

It was seven in the evening on a crisp night in December when the primary members of the IPS gathered around the walnut table. Roosevelt had a Madura Churchill sized CAO cigar and a crystal glass with two fingers of 12-year-old Macallan. Samuel also had a cigar and a glass of Buffalo Trace bourbon, while Jeremy sat with a cup of Earl Grey tea. He didn't drink, not since David's death. As always, Jeremy hid his discomfort of being around alcohol well; even his closest friends who knew he was an alcoholic did not know that the first thing he did when entering a room was to scan for whatever booze might be there. He told Roosevelt and Sam it didn't bother him if they drank, that he was under control. But that was a lie; every day he fought the urge to drink.

The three friends were enjoying an after dinner conversation before they began their meeting. They had convened earlier, and Roosevelt had cooked a meal for the three of them: filet mignon, roasted potatoes, and stir-fried vegetables.

During a quick after-dinner-and-before-meeting conversation, Sam had asked how Roosevelt had managed to be stuck with the name he had.

"My parents had a wry sense of humor about many things, but especially when they named me. Certainly many people were given patriotic names that have reflected their country's heritage, and as an historian, I do appreciate that gesture: George Washington is common in the United States and William Wallace in Scotland, but I ask you gentlemen, Roosevelt Theodore Franklin? They must have realized how odd that sounded. Now, I am very proud to have been named after one of my heroes, President Theodore Roosevelt, but with the inversion of the order and the added confusion of my last name, it was a bit of a trial growing up."

"Yeah, but it must've given you character. I bet you had your share of fights over it."

"Yes, I did, and I managed to win most of them. My parents' investment in boxing training for me paid off well."

Roosevelt looked and carried himself as what he was: an almost elderly gentleman, a professor, and a retired officer from the Unites States Marine Corps. His silver gray hair, cut short and impeccably neat was his style. He was lanky, 6'3" frame, bent with age, yet he was still in excellent shape, although recently diagnosed with a heart condition. His doctor had told him it was essential he continue to exercise, eat well, and take his medicine. He was 68 years old and weighed what he did when he was thirty, a fact that made him very proud. He was a somewhat vain man, especially about his fitness. However, his pet habits, his cigars, and his beloved single malt scotch whisky, did not go over well with his doctor. Roosevelt knew he could not control how long he lived; he wanted to be healthy but not at the expense of giving up his favorite indulgences.

Samuel was not in good condition: he had a large belly, and he didn't care about staying fit. He frequently ate fried foods and sweets—his favorite meal was a huge California cheeseburger and French fries with gravy, accompanied by a tall glass of beer, and finished with a large slice of chocolate cake. "I don't chase after crooks and bad guys anymore. I hope that ghost hunting doesn't need any running." Sam didn't add the real reason he didn't care what shape he was in was the guilt he carried from his son's suicide.

Jeremy was slight, slim, and in good condition, even though he seemingly never did any real exercise. He was, however, secretly very proud of still being in good shape, but to him, this was a very personal issue, not to be discussed even with his closest friends. He maintained the exercise regimen of calisthenics and using a stationary bike that he had done for so long with David. So, a bit later, when the topic of exercise came up, he deftly changed the subject to why they were conducting their investigations.

"Really guys, why do you want to do this? Why do we go running around looking for evidence of ghosts or whatever? I think it is important to think about. I know I want to."

"We are searchers, Jeremy." Roosevelt puffed out a circle of smoke and admired the expanding ring before it dissipated. "I think that we are doing this work because we want to know answers to the questions that humanity has been asking since its beginnings: What are we? Why are we here? Do we have souls? What happens after death?"

Each man was quiet. Roosevelt leaned back and looked away. He puffed deeply on his CAO Brasília Churchill. The end glowed cherry red and then faded to a white ash. He held the smoke in his mouth, savored the rich tastes, and then released it slowly.

"Perhaps Hamlet was wrong when he called death 'the undiscovered country from whose bourn no traveler returns.' Perhaps we can meet such a traveler and find out what lies in that 'undiscovered' country."

"Why Rosy," Sam said with a huge smile. "Damn, that was fuckin' profound."

Roosevelt shook his head and tried to keep from smiling. He was unsuccessful. "Yes, it was Samuel, and do not call me Rosy."

Samuel laughed his deep, rumbling belly laugh.

"Seriously, Samuel, we are philosophers in our own way. We want answers to deeply difficult questions. Think of the word philosophy itself."

"Love of wisdom." Jeremy was smiling at his interjection. Roosevelt raised one eyebrow.

"Well, damn, Jerry." Samuel sipped some of his bourbon and grinned.

"But I would love to have," Jeremy added after sipping some of his tea and looking at the glass of bourbon, "some of that wisdom. I thought we were supposed to get smarter as we got older."

"Well Jerry, it looks like you and me didn't. Sorry, pal."

"Yes, I know, Sam. You're right I suppose, because I do spend too much of my time with you two guys."

"That's because you love us so much, Jerry."

Shortly, Roosevelt called the meeting to order.

"Gentleman, our last three investigations are complete."

"Our first case was at the Rheinhardt's place. While it was interesting, I think we can say with one hundred percent certainty that there was no paranormal activity of any kind at their home."

"None," Sam added, "unless you call squirrels and mice running around in rafters and fucking bats in their attic paranormal."

"They were disgusting, but definitely normal." Jeremy shuddered at the thought of the vermin, and Sam smiled at Jeremy's reaction.

"I informed the Rheinhardts that what they need are good exterminators and not paranormal investigators," added Roosevelt.

"In any case, they are relieved to know that they have not a haunting but an infestation of rodents. Case closed."

Jeremy looked up and became serious. "It wasn't a waste of time. We got to have more experience and an opportunity to work with some new equipment." As their technical manager, Jeremy was always delighted to acquire and use new electronic and digital equipment. He might be a senior citizen, but he could keep up with the technical knowledge of the most advanced youngsters. "We worked with the new EMF readers and our new night vision goggles and the infrared camera."

"True, it was the infrared camera that got the pics of the rodents. I could've used stuff like this when I was on the force. It would've made some of the detective work a lot fucking easier."

While the IPS was a relatively new group, they had managed to find a number of cases to investigate. They advertised their services on their website and other social media, which Jeremy designed and maintained. They also placed ads in the local newspapers and used word of mouth. They operated as a non-profit organization, and they never charged a fee or accepted any donations for their services. On all of their advertisements and their website, they had this motto: "We are searchers for truth, not seekers of profit. We will assist you."

"Of course," Jeremy said and laughed. "We didn't expect some of the calls we got. I thought everyone would be serious."

"Yeah, Jerry, we definitely got to get better at screening calls," Sam said and laughed.

Jeremy's face reddened. "It wasn't my fault!"

"No indeed, Jeremy, it wasn't." Roosevelt tried to smooth his friend's ruffled feelings. "But you have to admit that whole thing was…ah…interesting."

About two months ago, they had received both a message on the website and a frantic phone call from a group of college students who were worried that their fraternity house was haunted.

"Yeah, we got ourselves all worked up…thought it might be a real case, something with a real ghost in it."

They loaded Sam's van with their equipment, went to the frat house, and knocked on the door. At first everything was quiet.

"Maybe they are too frightened to stay here," Roosevelt suggested.

"It could be," Jeremy said and rang the doorbell again.

Sam was getting suspicious. Then they heard the sounds of moaning and groaning, a cliché straight out of a bad horror film. Looking up, they saw frat boys covered in sheets like they were dressed for trick or treat.

Jeremy swore, which was unusual for him. "Goddamnit! They were fucking messing with us."

Roosevelt said, "Don't get upset, Jeremy. It is not worth it." Then he grinned just a little. He didn't usually hear his very correct friend use profanity.

Then Sam grinned. "Not to worry, guys. I got this."

He went to the door and banged hard on it. Using a loud voice that rang with authority, he yelled, "Open this door now, unless you want serious trouble!"

They heard the sound of whispers from behind the door. Someone opened the door just enough to peer out.

They saw a large hand holding police identification up to them. "Open up, now!" What they didn't know was that it was stamped with "retired" on it, but Sam had covered that detail, and they were too drunk to notice anyway.

They heard the sound of scurrying to hide underage drinking and probably drugs. The door opened and a not completely drunk kid looked at them. "You're a cop?" he asked.

"Well, boy. It's good to see your parents spending a ton of money on your education ain't gone to waste. Fucking right, I am. And I don't like having a joke like this played on me or my friends. Understand, bright boy?"

The kid's face turned paler than the bed sheet he had been hiding under. "Yes, Sir," he mumbled.

"What did you say? I can't hear you!" Sam barked like a drill instructor on Parris Island.

Jeremy looked over at Roosevelt. He didn't think Sam should be misrepresenting himself, but Roosevelt just gave a small shake of his head, indicating not to say anything.

"Yes, Sir!" the boy answered louder.

"So, let's be sure you got this straight. You tell your buddies never to mess with us again, or I'll be back, and that time with my friends on the force. Got it, bright boy?"

He kept repeating yes sir over and over. They turned and walked back to their van, got in, and drove away, all the while maintaining their air of seriousness.

Then Sam pulled the van over to the side of the rode.

"What is it?" Jeremy asked, completely concerned.

Sam and Roosevelt looked at each other and broke out into laughter. Sam's laugh was like a booming series of thunderclaps and Roosevelt's like rapid-fire machine gun. Jeremy simply sulked. He thought they had not acted professionally.

After that incident, they learned to screen the requests more carefully.

Both Sam and Roosevelt smiled at the memory of the second "case."

"Gentleman, our last two investigations are complete. Let us deal now with the most recent, the Kaufmann case. That house certainly caused some excitement. Therefore, I believe that we can say that it is our first verifiable paranormal activity that we have encountered and that we have documented. We all had personal experiences, somewhat more than we would have desired, but we still were able to deal with it.

"To recap, after we left the house, I put in a call to our friend Father Bruno, who agreed to bless the house. I also asked Karen Miller, our local medium to visit the place. She said that she had contacted the spirit, which was the ghost of an elderly, somewhat cranky and confused gentleman."

"Wow," Sam said. "That sort of sounds like us."

"Well, I hope not. Miller said that the reason the spirit became aggressive is that the spirit is in the state of mind he had when he died…the man was suffering from Alzheimer's disease."

"The ghost was senile?" Jeremy asked softly.

"Yes, he was. Miller said that she was able to calm him and to help him on his way…to, as Jeffries says, move into the light."

"Shit, I hope that doesn't end up being us one day."

"I agree, Samuel," Roosevelt added. "For good measure I asked our friend Father Bruno to bless the house which he did. The Kaufmanns have said that they have had no further activity. So, that case is closed. Good work gentlemen." Roosevelt raised his glass, and Sam, clinked his glass and Jeremy his cup.

"So," Roosevelt said, "moving along. Are there any new cases for us?" Roosevelt was constantly on the lookout for new and challenging problems to explore.

Jeremy looked up at his friends from his notes. "We have been contacted by three potential clients, one…," Jeremy added in a hushed tone because he disliked offending anyone, including those who were not present even to be aware of the potential offense. "One is, um, a bit shaky. There is an unfortunate fellow who I know indulges in too much cheap wine. He has been trying to cut back by going to A.A. meetings. I have seen him there at a few recently, and he claims that he has been seeing shadow figures wherever he goes."

Sam and Roosevelt understood where Jeremy had probably received this inquiry. Jeremy had gone into a deep depression after the death of his partner, David, and he had slipped into heavy drinking. He managed to stop with the help of attending A.A. meetings and through the support of his closest friends. At least, Jeremy hoped he had finished with drinking, but he worried about relapsing every day.

"You talkin about Downtown Mikey?" Downtown Mikey was a poor soul known to many in Bethberg as an old alcoholic who had finally lost his job and home. Lately he was seen sleeping either on a cardboard box or in shelters.

"I think it is more likely, Jeremy, that the spirits he is seeing are coming from the DTs, not from the ghostly realm," Roosevelt said gently.

"I know the fellow who runs the shelter, Jeremy," Sam added. "I'll talk to him and see if we can do anything about getting Mikey into rehab."

"Thanks, Sam."

Roosevelt sipped his whiskey and puffed his cigar. He had noted a while ago that Jeremy was capable of being around his friends if they were drinking without any problems. He hoped that he was not causing Jeremy difficulties, but life was hard.

"And the other two cases?"

"One is in a small Mennonite Church in Virgin Town." Virgin Town was a tiny village deep in the heart of Pennsylvania Dutch and Amish country in central Pennsylvania. "The minister claims that there have been sightings of an apparition and that disembodied voices have been heard."

"Are they scared?" Sam asked. He was always concerned when people were frightened by their experiences. He enjoyed removing their fears, especially when claims of the supernatural could be easily debunked.

"Not really." Jeremy sipped his excellent tea. "The minister is more intellectually curious about these phenomena, as he said in his email."

"Well, I think we can agree that this case is a possibility. How about the other one?"

Jeremy looked at his fellow investigators. He saved the most important for last. "This one, I think, is the one for us. Guys, it's, I believe, possibly, the real thing."

Sam and Roosevelt exchanged a glance. They knew that Jeremy tended to exaggerate his claims about the paranormal.

"I know exactly what you two are thinking." Jeremy looked at them with a pained expression.

"Well, Jerry, you got to admit that you thought there were ghosts in our first cases. Do you remember?" Nothing more than squirrels and mice in the walls…no ghosts." Sam laughed again.

Jeremy looked down. "Man, really guys? This isn't right. You guys don't take me seriously."

Roosevelt looked at Sam and shook his head, all the while suppressing his smile.

"Ah, c'mon, Jerry. You know I was just kidding and I can be a dick sometimes," Sam said and held out his hands palms up.

"We are both sorry, Jeremy. We do value your opinions. You know that," Roosevelt added. "Please continue, Jeremy."

"There is very good reason to look into this case, guys. I'm not exaggerating, as you two like to claim."

Seeing the hurt look on Jeremy's face, Roosevelt added, "Go on, Jeremy. We want to hear it. You know we value your judgment. We simply cannot resist teasing you sometimes. Please, tell us."

Mollified, Jeremy sipped his tea. "I received both a phone call and an email on this one." Jeremy had set up a phone and answering machine dedicated to the IPS in his office in his home.

"The woman who called is one Helen Murray, a history teacher at Bethberg High School. She's a single woman who is raising her young niece Helena. Apparently, the little girl is named for her. Ms. Murray's sister and brother-in-law were killed in a car crash, and Ms. Murray became the girl's legal guardian."

"How old is the kid?" Sam asked.

Jeremy consulted his notes. "She is, um, five and a half. Helena has been living with her aunt for several years, all without any indication of paranormal activity, except for recently. That is why Ms. Murray contacted us.

"The other day I conducted a preliminary interview with her. Her tone, during our brief conversation on the phone, was urgent, guys. So, I thought I would talk with her further and present my findings during this meeting."

"You did well, Jeremy."

Jeremy had sat across from Helen in her comfortable Craftsman style home. He was drinking tea she had served while speaking with her. "How long have you been in this house?" he asked as a way to begin his interview with her.

"I grew up in this house and lived here until I moved out after college. Then my parents died, and I always loved the house, so I purchased my sister's share and moved in, some ten years ago."

"Did everything seem to go well then?"

"Yes, life was normal. I had my work, and I decided to do renovations on the house. I loved the place and had fond memories of it from growing up there, but I wanted to make changes and to put my own touches on the place."

"Renovated?" Sam asked, as he interrupted Jeremy's recounting of the interview. One theory in the world of the investigation of the paranormal claimed that renovation sometimes triggered supernatural activity. Perhaps because spirits were upset with the changes in the places they considered their own homes.

"Yes, she did extensive renovations, but without any apparent paranormal activity."

"Why then, are we interested?" Roosevelt wanted Jeremy to get to the core of the matter.

"That is exactly what I wanted to find out," Jeremy added and continued with his recounting of the interview.

"When did you first notice any kind of activity?"

She thought carefully for a moment, then, she said, "Last spring. Of course, much had changed around here anyway."

This essentially discounted the renovations as an issue. It seemed to have been far too long for any reaction to them.

"Aunt Helen?"

We both heard a little voice calling to her, and she smiled. "I'll be right back."

"She returned in a little while with a beautiful little girl who had been taking a nap. The girl sat on her lap for a few minutes, then got up and walked over to me," Jeremy said.

"Your teacup is empty. Would you like to have more?"

"Well, she had such a serious expression of concern on her face that I was utterly charmed. You both know that I am not usually taken with children, but this little one immediately caught my heart."

Both Roosevelt and Sam smiled.

"We had tea with Helena. The child was named for her aunt, and then after letting her go to the park with a neighbor who also had children, we continued our conversation."

"I began to notice small things at first," Helen said. "Items being moved when no one was home. Helena was at pre-school, and I was teaching. Then

33

sometimes, when I was at home, I began to hear thumping noises and knocks. I initially attributed them to the sounds an old house makes. Of course, the logical problem with that explanation is that I had never, not even as a child, heard them before."

"Did anything else happen?" Jeremy asked.

"I began to feel like I was being watched, although I never saw anyone." She paused, took a sip of her tea, and she frowned.

"Please go on," Jeremy added gently.

"Things got strange, and I became very concerned when Helena told me she had seen a man in the house. At first, I was very upset. I mean, had there been an intruder? But Helena didn't seem to be bothered at all, and I found no evidence of any kind of break-in, so I wondered if this might simply be an invisible playmate. But…"

"But what, Ms. Murray?"

"Please, call me Helen. What bothered me most was soon after this, Helena got frightened. One night she woke up screaming and came running into my room to sleep in my bed with me. Now, I know this is not unusual, but one night, it took several hours before I could calm her."

"Was that the end of it?"

"No, unfortunately not, since the night-time incidents continued, I thought that I should take her to a child psychologist and see if she was having residual trauma from the loss of her parents. He said that she simply had an over active imagination. Then…" she added with a laugh. "He said that maybe she suffered from ADHD. I know Helena as well as if she were my own biological child, and she does not have ADHD. I completely discounted the psychologist's suggestion of putting Helena on medications. Helena is a bright, intelligent, and creative girl. She is a very frightened little girl. She has seen the man several more times. I need to know what is going on. Can you help me?"

"Something in that house is frightening the child. That much is clear," Jeremy stated.

Roosevelt raised his left eyebrow in a sardonic arch. Sam observed without comment but with great interest. This was one of Roosevelt's tells, which was especially useful when they played poker; it usually signified that Roosevelt held a hand of serious possibilities. He slowly lowered his eyebrow.

"So, we seem to have an unusual and interesting case: unusual in that the haunting seems to have appeared with no prior reason for it, and interesting to us all, indeed, urgent, because a child is frightened and perhaps threatened."

They sat for a few minutes, then, Roosevelt stood. "The world has changed a great deal in the time that we have lived gentlemen, in its outlooks, in its technology, in its mores and values, but, we, I am deeply relieved to say, have not. I know you men; I know your worth. So, are we in an agreement people? Is this the next case for the IPS?"

"Agreed," Sam, answered.

"Agreed," added Jeremy.

"I would like to propose a toast, gentlemen." Roosevelt raised his glass, Sam his, and Jeremy his cup. "To our success and honor gentlemen."

"To success, and honor," said Jeremy.

"Success and honor," finished Sam.

SEVEN

Patrick Franklin sat at his desk with his head held between his hands. The room was dim, lit only by a small lamp on the desk. His head ached, and he desperately needed to get some real sleep, but his desire to read what was on the tablet in front of him outweighed his body's needs.

A tall, slim man with broad shoulders, and short, clipped graying dark hair, he was dressed in comfortable jeans and a blue Marine Corps sweatshirt. His body ached from the intense workout he had pushed himself through a bit earlier in the evening. Patrick was a devoted student of various martial arts, which he often used to try to calm the energy in him whenever he was in a state of turmoil.

He dressed in a loose fitting sweat suit for his workout and bowed as he entered the dojo he had constructed in the basement of his home. The room was well lit, with a padded exercise mat covering the 20" by 15" area of the floor. He had constructed an archway of bamboo that defined the entrance to the dojo. When going through either way he always bowed—showing respect to this place of study was part of his makeup. In one corner of the room hung an old, well-worn hundred and fifty pound heavy bag, a speed bag and a timing bag. Along the far wall in a series of wooden holders were a Tanta, a Wakizashi and a Katana, as well as wooden bokken used for practicing kendo sword strikes. Along the right wall were sabers.

Patrick had achieved the level of 3rd degree black belt in MCMAP, the United States Marine Corps Martial Arts Program that focused on the trilogy of character, mental, and physical disciplines in creating a Marine Warrior Ethos. He believed that all of the martial arts eventually moved towards a synthesis in which they became one way, a synergy of disciplines, of one warrior using many weapons, an idea that deeply resonated with him, reflecting his Renaissance attitude, to be skilled in as many aspects of life as possible.

As Patrick performed the techniques, he concentrated on breathing Zen style, in through his nose deep into his belly and slowly out through his mouth. After completing this practice, he donned a pair of old leather boxing training gloves, and he battered the heavy bag. He ignored jabs and simply worked the bag with hooks and crosses until his shoulders screamed and his arms ached and felt like they might fall out of his shoulders. Satisfied with his punching, but still wanting more, he picked up a bokken and practiced kendo sword strikes for another 20 minutes. Then with the Marine Corps saber, he practiced classical sword fighting. When he was finished, he was nearly exhausted. Sweat poured down his face and over his body. He then slowly bowed at the archway and took a long, steaming hot shower.

Prior to his workout, Patrick had felt that there might be contact. It was similar, but not the same, as the aura some sufferers of epilepsy receive as a warning they are about to suffer a seizure. Patrick believed there was nothing sensory, no jagged light, no smell, no feeling on his skin, only a presentiment that something would happen. It was like the feeling of not being able to recall some memory, but knowing that it was on the edge of awareness. He felt on the brink of communication with his brother Michael.

Patrick opened a display case that was mounted over his desk. In the long walnut cabinet was Michael's Marine Corps Officer's sword. When his brother died, Patrick had chosen to keep the sword as a tangible reminder of Michael's life. Patrick carefully removed the weapon and sat in his large, leather office chair. He pulled the sword from its scabbard and held it in his right hand.

Patrick carefully placed the sword on the large desk, took out a yellow legal pad, and held a pen in his right hand. Then he tried to use a meditation both Michael and he learned during kung-fu training to empty his mind. He sat in a comfortable position, breathing slowly and felt himself begin to enter the state he needed.

Several hours later, Patrick woke with great difficulty. He felt like a vise encompassed the top half of his head. The feeling was a sensation of tightening and then releasing with every heartbeat. The pain was excruciating, but he tried to focus anyway. Patrick knew he had not fully achieved the desired meditative state; instead, he had slipped into a kind of trance and had lost all sense of awareness. It was in that state that his brother could communicate with him via automatic writing. The physical hand holding the pen and marking the page was Patrick's, but the force behind the writing and the handwriting itself belonged to Michael.

Patrick put the desk light on its lowest setting to reduce the glare and began to read . . .

I know that there is a reason I am here. I know there is some task I must accomplish—how I know this is unclear, but I do know it with complete certainty. I also do not yet know what that task is, but I am also aware that you, my baby brother, are part of it.

Patrick smiled at the "baby brother." Michael emerged from their mother a mere ten minutes before Patrick, but it was enough for him to claim bragging rights as the older sibling. He called himself Patrick's big brother, and in many ways, he had been. They were fraternal twins, and Michael was the larger, more agile, and stronger of the two. They were both very intelligent, but Michael said that Patrick was the geeky kid brother that he had to watch out for. As a child, Patrick was scrawny and weak. He was determined to fight his own battles, but when he tried to defend himself against larger bullies, he usually came home bruised or with black eyes. Michael admired his bravery and let him fight first, but then he would enact his own vengeance on Patrick's foe. Patrick tended to be the little kid for his age, and bullies found him to be a natural victim. Michael soon corrected these kids about his brother being a target.

As older teenagers, as Patrick began to gain a level of physical maturity, they studied Martial Arts together, first Tae Kwon Do, then Kung-Fu, then boxing, and Patrick eventually was no longer the scrawny kid who needed to be watched over by his brother. They were both talented at fighting, but Michael's innate abilities allowed him to progress faster and further than Patrick.

When he was 17, Michael earned black belts in Karate and was a skilled amateur boxer. Michael successfully competed in the Golden Gloves tournament as a light-heavyweight boxer. Patrick had also fought in the same tournament, but he had not reached the same level of achievement as his brother. Patrick was coming progressively better, coming into his own. During his youth, Patrick, was almost as big as Michael. Nonetheless, his "older" brother never ceased to call him little brother or baby brother.

Patrick idolized Michael the way that younger brothers often admired older siblings. He was Patrick's hero as both his older brother and as his twin.

I must be patient. That is easy enough because there is little for me to do except contemplate my situation. A bit of irony. Wouldn't you say little brother? I was always the one who wanted action. True, I did love philosophy, but I always claimed that philosophy without practical implementation of ideals and beliefs is nothing more than mental masturbation.

That is, of course, why I determined that I must not be a hypocrite. I fervently believed, and I still do, in Donne's admonition—"No man is an island, entire of itself".

You know that I entirely rejected as silliness and narcissism the claims of the so-called post-modernists that there is no truth, that nothing is verifiable. I know that such claims are the results of a self-absorbed, spoiled, and soft society. They don't even realize that their claims originate in existentialism. You see, I still enjoy debating philosophy little brother.

Patrick was a voracious reader. At the age of seven he read at the tenth grade level. He had a very high I.Q., and his reading interests, by the time he was in high school, were eclectic: history, science, the classics, Shakespeare, and philosophy. He also showed himself to be a natural polyglot and studied French, Latin, and Spanish through high school. He breezed through his work and earned academic accolades: honor roll, National Honor Society, and he was named Valedictorian of his class. Michael, while not as academically gifted as his little brother, was, nevertheless, an excellent student, whose favorite study was philosophy. He used to joke with Patrick that they were an odd pair—where would you find teenage brothers who argue over Kant and Plato rather than who is going to take out the garbage?

I wish that this were true communication Patrick. I know that it is one way and that it must be very difficult for you. You are not going crazy and I am truly writing to you. I will keep in contact as the purpose for this becomes clearer to me. I wish that I could talk with you again, or at the very least be able to read something from you. I must hope that you continue to go through with this, no matter how difficult. I love you baby brother, and I will do anything I can to help. Never forget that.

Patrick sat at his desk and stared at the writing—his head ached and tears ran down his cheeks.

He closed his eyes and thought, *Am I insane?*

EIGHT

THE IN-BETWEEN

Caligula knew in two weeks Maledicus was going to be delighted with a gift he was delivering. The Emperor had called him into his private chamber and told the fat, sweating man the information he had given several months ago about one of the prominent families in Rome had born fruit. "This was extremely useful, Maledicus. Because of your watchful eye, I can now eliminate another potential threat. Now, I would typically order the execution of this entire family on the crucifix, but I'll give you a gift of them. I'll have them taken in chains to your palace."

Maledicus was delighted. This family was of the highest-ranking he will have had the pleasure to enjoy their agonies and deaths. *It will give me the greatest growth yet.* With the power he would gain from them, he would be close to being able to move against Caligula himself. *What a delight that would be—to have Caligula, bloody, defiled, and dying, begging for his life, calling me, Maledicus Emperor of the Roman Empire.*

Magnus, along with several of his carefully picked soldiers, transported the frightened family to Maledicus and herded the father, mother and three children into the chamber of horror.

Over the span of several hours, the room filled with the blood and viscera of this unfortunate family.

Unknown to Maledicus, this was the last time he would be able to commit his atrocities. Caligula had ordered his execution. Because Caligula, in his own paranoia, saw this family as a threat and he wanted them disposed of, the Emperor told his men to wait until Maledicus was deep in his enjoyment and then to kill everyone: Maledicus, his servants, and his victims.

Within a few minutes of when the soldiers began to use their swords, everyone in the palace of Maledicus, including the procurer himself, lay dead.

Soon, almost immediately, Maledicus was in a place he didn't know. The In-Between was beyond time and space, defined only by what the souls who occupied it perceived. Like an enormous train station, it was a locale of arrivals and departures of souls to further unknown destinations.

When Maledicus entered into the In-Between, in an eruption of murky light and sound like the belching of an unhappy ogre, the demons immediately noticed him.

In Maledicus, they knew that they had found a deep vein of evil to mine for demonic treasure. When Maledicus' spirit first emerged into the murkiness of the In-Between, each spirit, demon or otherwise, immediately acknowledged what Maledicus was, a potential demon. Maledicus was surprised and enraged. He believed with absolute certainty that he was immortal and invincible. The shock of his mistake about his earthly powers caused him untold rage.

This is wrong! I am immortal and cannot die! I am supposed to be the Emperor of Rome!

Maledicus, spent what seemed to him to be a near eternity—was it five minutes, five weeks or was it fifty thousand years? Time was impossible to chart here. Maledicus was somewhat resolved over his existence in the In-Between, but acceptance did not mean acquiescence. His rage did not dissipate; rather, he was able to bring it under control eventually, even as it grew stronger. The power of his wrath attracted one of the dark demonic tendrils towards him.

Fascinated with this almost pure spirit of malevolence, the tendril observed him—his fury and his confusion, and it was delighted. The anger was titillating and delicious. Demons knew that time was unimportant and completely misunderstood by the newly arrived—Maledicus was an interesting curiosity almost immediately upon his arrival, the demons knew him for what he was: pure evil.

This demonic tendril, in particular, delighted in the taste of lost souls that had not achieved great notoriety and had festering evil that desired murder and desecration; for this demon, who sought Maledicus, was a great connoisseur of the palate of evil, and this was his favorite flavor. Maledicus was the spice that gave the feast of suffering, its most exquisite appeal.

When Maledicus, was in Rome, he had experienced great shock and fear. He had never believed that he could die, and when he realized that he was going to perish, he panicked. What would happen to him?

When the Roman short swords slashed at him and thrust into him, tearing his body apart and letting his offal spill onto the floor in front of his soon-to-be corpse, he felt his life fading. Then with seemingly no time elapsed, he was in this new place—the one he came to know as the In-Between. The name itself was odd for him. He did not know why it came into his mind, or what it meant, since he had no concept of heaven, hell, an afterlife, or reincarnation. He had simply existed and assumed he always would.

He seemed to float sometimes without any body, and other times, he would appear to walk in a full corporeal state, dressed in his familiar Roman toga. Yet, he never felt anything physically. There seemed to be no logic to time, no set ordered passage, no night or day to define his existence. While he had been a sadistic monster, Maledicus had also been a Roman citizen, who moved in a very logical and ordered world. Where he was now was the complete opposite; this was a state of seeming chaos.

Eventually he managed to bring his rage under control, to that of a volcano ready to erupt, but still in stasis. His internal lava always threatened to blow, but it never did, always simmering just below the point of explosion. With that control, he became an observer. Maledicus realized if he were to be able to conquer this situation, he would have to understand it and not simply react like a child with a temper tantrum. He would have to react as he had conditioned himself to do in Rome in times of danger—with calm, logic, and understanding of the situation. He settled himself and watched. As a living human, he had gained invaluable information on prominent Romans by watching and gathering information. He was able then to turn that knowledge into power, especially by carefully dispensing it to Caligula. With each donation of intelligence to the Emperor, he grew in power and status. He would do the same, or as close to it as he could, here. There are others here, he reasoned, who can benefit from information.

He sometimes saw other spirits appear. These newly arrived, though, would never see him, but he delighted in their inevitable confusion and despair. He observed as their spirits simply popped into the In-Between, looking as they had in life. At first Maledicus marveled at their different clothing, but then he realized he was simply seeing the superficial changes in human decoration. Maledicus saw spirits, looking like people, but in unusual dress that he could not identify. He seemed to understand inherently that they came from time-periods other than his own. Some were in great fear.

I wondered what they did in their lives to make them dread the consequences. Indeed, they do give me the slightest spark of entertainment. Watching their fear was like watching the throes of a dying animal.

That was of no consequence to him. To Maledicus, it was their fears, their cries, and their anguish that was important. It was the closest thing he had to the sadistic pleasure he had experienced on Earth in the tormenting, torturing, and murdering of innocent people.

Their fears and screams had fed his psyche in the same way he had satiated his enormous appetite for food in the many feasts he hosted. He had amazed even the most voracious of the Romans with his capacity for consumption of food. In the In-Between of heaven and hell, Maledicus, could not glut himself on either food or the infliction of pain on others, but he still had some satisfactions.

Maledicus was briefly amused, but it was too transient for any lasting satisfaction, like nibbling on a grape, enjoying the juice and texture, while knowing that in the next room, a lavish feast awaited him. He watched many of these spirits entrap themselves in their anguish. Maledicus would derive great joy and laughter at the discordant and vibrantly powerful sound. He observed them searching for a path or a way out of their confusion, and he would whisper to them, *"Over here, come this way."* He would then burst into laughter as he led them farther astray. Some were so confused and disturbed they would cry as if real tears could emerge from their non-corporeal eyes. Some howled with despair as he led them away from the light and into a soupy fog of incomprehension. Their pain was delectable.

Maledicus also saw things that perplexed him. He also witnessed some spirits who appeared calm. There seemed to be other souls greeted by other beings, whose great joy was disturbing to Maledicus as they vanished in a blinding light that was anathema to him. Its brilliance blinded him. It ripped at him and threatened to tear his spiritual form to shreds just as the Roman swords had cut into his belly and hacked him into pieces. That pain had been horrible. He knew the soldiers could have dispatched him quickly and painlessly, yet it was obvious to him they were told to cause as much physical torture as possible.

Had he not suffered so much, he might have laughed at the delicious irony of the situation. Yet, how was it possible to feel pain here? Not him, not Maledicus, as he now realized, his mortal body had been vulnerable. He now came to believe that his current form was invulnerable, indeed, immortal! Nevertheless, of all the things he saw in this place, the ones who caused the blinding flashes of light were the most obnoxious, the most horrific to him. He instinctively understood that they, and that detested illumination, represented the greatest threat to him. Maledicus shrunk away from them, feeling rage and shame.

Why am I here? What force allows me to see such terrible things? The light is horrible! Am I cursed? Is this infernal nothingness my punishment? Yet, he said with much bravo, who would dare punish me?

Maledicus sulked. It was inconceivable that he was not able to do as he wished and that he had been so mistaken about the way of the universe. When he was alive, he rejected all consideration of souls and afterlife. He believed that all the simpering philosophers and mystics were frightened weaklings, unable to grasp the pleasures of the physical world.

They were all fools anyway—where are the gods sitting in judgment? I see no Jove. I see no Elysian Fields. Just this—I am caught in an eternal field of mud.

NINE

DECEMBER 9

Roosevelt looked at his wife's picture as he sat on the edge of his bed. He kissed the picture and cried.

September 1988—It was the happiest day of Roosevelt's life, even more than that of his wedding day. Roosevelt thought that while the wedding was wonderful, too much of the event was a public performance for the benefit of their families and friends. Along with their status as members of the upper class came expectations. Their wedding was not as he would have wished: a small ceremony with the two of them simply expressing their love for each other; rather, it felt like an affair of state.

It was held in Saint Patrick's, New York City's greatest cathedral, and several thousand were in attendance. Roosevelt had been prepared to keep his own family's wishes at bay, but he acceded to his fiancée's request that they satisfy her family's expectations. He was not a shy man, but he was very much a private man. Roosevelt believed deep expressions of love should not be overtly public. He would rather have excluded his family completely from the ceremony because he could not stomach most of them. He despised their sense of entitlement and the sheer laziness that accompanied it. They would often rail bigotry and nonsense about the laziness of the working class and the poor, but most of his family simply lived on the massive inheritance accumulated by the work of their industrialist forbearers. While he disliked much of the history of his family, at least the previous generations had not been idle high-society parasites, looking only for the next party or indulgence as most of the current generations were.

Roosevelt loathed their lack of knowledge about the world and their need to satisfy every desire they had. They possessed neither intellectual curiosity nor ambition to create something nor a desire to contribute to the betterment of the world. They were, in his opinion, the worst example of what too much

45

money and power simply being handed to people could create – a people utterly without merit. He would rather be with anyone else than almost anyone in his family, with the exception of his twin nephews, Michael and Patrick. Like him, they also had little use for their family, who were later horrified when the young men chose to be officers in the Marine Corps. The family did not see the military as an appropriate life choice for someone of their status. *Damn them all.*

This was not a time, however, when Roosevelt would cause friction, not for his beloved Sarah.

He did have to admit though the whole affair seemed to be straight out of a fairy tale, even though he thought he was a little bit old at 48 to be starring in the role of Prince Charming. Still, his wife did look like a fairy tale princess in her gown. While she was not a young girl, Sarah was ten years younger than Roosevelt. She, too, had not been married before, and she had been the image of a blushing radiant bride. It was with joy he watched her walk gracefully down the aisle. By looking into her eyes, he was able to keep the audience out of his mind. Only his bride mattered.

Both Sarah and Roosevelt emerged unscathed from the potential arguments and tension during the reception. They had glided from table to table and played the perfect host and hostess to their guests. They were treated as though they were a newly married couple of nobility in England, as if they had just inherited a title of great power and prestige – accomplished by the joining of two powerful families. This, however, was not in the newly wedded couple's minds or plans. After the wedding, they would set their own course, in what would seem to both of their families, a backwater of a place, far from the high society of New York and Boston – Bethberg, PA, a small old, former industrial town north of Bethlehem and south of Stroudsburg.

The two following days, during their honeymoon, Roosevelt considered his happiest and his best. While he had agreed to the manner of the wedding, he had been absolutely firm that no one except Sarah and he would have any say or influence on the honeymoon. As a mature man who had never before been married, he was determined to make his wife as happy as he could and to experience as much happiness as possible. Rather than going to the Riviera as so many with their status did, they rented a car and drove into a remote section of the province of Quebec to stay at a log cabin he had found years earlier during a fishing excursion. It was quiet, secluded, and beautiful. On their way, they stopped at a nearby village to purchase food and necessities.

The log cabin was a ranch style with a country kitchen and a living room with a cathedral ceiling and a large wood fireplace. The home was set immediately on the shore of a large lake. Surrounded by evergreens in a dense forest, the land had an idyllic feel. Rising behind the trees on the north side of the house was a mountain, which shielded them from the business of everyday life.

None of their family and friends knew where they were. They had simply said they were going to a private honeymoon getaway. Roosevelt was determined that nothing would interfere with their time together. He knew such moments would be rare in life. For their family and close friends, it had become a kind of parlor game to try to identify where they were going. When Roosevelt found out about this attempt later, he was amused, both at their incessant curiosity and at their complete inability to find the answer. He also laughed deeply when he found that the two places considered most likely were Paris and the Bahamas. He knew that demonstrated most of the so-called friends knew very little about them. Only two people suspected the kind of place they would go to: Sam and Bruno.

The couple had already arranged their escape from their families' expectations of their lives by taking work in the small Pennsylvania city. When they returned to their everyday lives, they would be out of the social orbit they both shunned.

Roosevelt and Sarah were two people deeply engaged in the world: he was a Professor of History at Bethberg College, and she was a surgeon at the Bethberg Medical Center. They loved their work and lived busy professional lives, but they also loved getting away from the world both had known as children. The newlyweds did not desire luxury. They cared neither for a five star hotel with the finest amenities nor for a top rated restaurant with elegantly prepared and presented cuisine. They both laughed at the idea that food was first "eaten with the eyes." To them, that was simply a sign of snobbery and foolishness. They both preferred hearty and honest food and basic and comfortable lodgings. To them, coffee they brewed in the morning in a cast iron camping style percolator, and drank while sitting on the cabin's front porch and watching the sun rise over the lake while sitting and cuddling together in the chilled Canadian mountain air outweighed any so-called civilized luxury. This was a side of Roosevelt he had shown to neither his academic colleagues nor to his family. This freedom from the hectic life of society was something he revealed only to his wife.

On their first day at the cabin, the need to sleep and to recover from the long drive comprised their first day. The first evening together, however, was the closest he had ever felt towards anyone. When he was younger, he had scoffed at the romantic notions that many had, but now he believed completely that he had found his soul mate. He had never before felt as he did now, complete with his wife. He was always comfortable with himself and confident in his abilities, and he never felt incomplete, but now he understood he had not realized what he had been missing. He had not grasped the sheer sublimity of the love he felt for Sarah. When they were in each other's arms, making love, no one and nothing else existed.

Later, he would look back and realize that others in the self-absorbed postmodern world could not understand the deep nature of their love and connection, but he had dismissed them anyway as silly and self-serving narcissists who refused to find value in love; indeed, their silly philosophic ideas explained nothing and were, he would explain to his horrified academic colleagues, merely self-indulgences expressive of a soft and egotistic society, like the moaning of a teenager that "you just don't understand me." He loved tweaking their smug noses. Roosevelt believed in truth and meaning, but that the journey to find it was the point of life. The point of education was the search for, not the gaining of, truth. He realized as he lay in bed holding his sleeping wife, that while he had experienced war and horror in his life, nothing, not even that trauma, could be stronger than the love he experienced for Sarah.

The second morning, the day he considered as immeasurably perfect, he woke first, kissed his sleeping bride, and went to the stove and brewed coffee. He made it strong and deeply satisfying.

He came back to the bed—their bed of love and lovemaking—and he sat next to her. "Good morning, my wife."

She opened her eyes, smiled, and stretched—an image that would remain with him the rest of his life. She was never more beautiful than at that moment.

"Good morning, my husband," she replied. "It feels so good to say that."

He handed her a mug of the steaming coffee. "Careful, it is hot." After sipping a bit, she slipped out of bed, and donned a robe. Together they went to the front porch and sat on an old wooden bench.

The sun rose about one half hour later, and Roosevelt had poured them both a second cup of coffee. As they sat and watched, the emerging sun slowly burned the morning mist off the lake. With his arm around her and Sarah snuggled into his body, he felt as happy and content as he ever would.

"Look," he whispered and slowly pointed, after placing his mug on a barrel that served as a table. "Do you see that?"

"Yes, my God, it's beautiful."

Soaring about the lake, searching for food to scavenge or fish to hunt was a huge bald eagle: its wings, stretched out, steady and flat, catching the updrafts and staying aloft with seeming effortlessness. As they watched, neither saw the magnificent creature ever flap its wings. It flew as if it knew that the air was its dominion and as if it were proud to fly by them. It flew as if it knew it was king of the sky and nothing could ever challenge its control and domination. It flew as if it were a masterpiece of nature's paintbrush, a moving, living, piece of art.

Sarah turned to Roosevelt and kissed him deeply. "Thank you for bringing me here."

"Thank you for being my wife. I would not have, could not have shared this with anyone else."

The rest of the perfect day was simple: Sarah and Roosevelt made love, cooked meals for each other, and basked in the beauty that surrounded them. They were happy and fulfilled . . .

As Roosevelt looked at the photograph of Sarah, he cried.

How do people handle tragedy in their lives? How do they cope with the death of a loved one? How do they put together the pieces of broken lives? How do they find meaning in a world stripped of the person who had been their touchstone, their love?

In our society, there are grief counselors, counselors at funeral homes to "help with the passing of a loved one" and psychologists available to try to help people deal with deep loss, but ultimately, everyone must face the darkness on their own. Some have success in confronting it, and some have failure. Some take refuge in a bottle and descend into their own private hells of self-induced oblivion; some find comfort in throwing themselves into volunteer activities to help others so that they move outside of themselves and their specific pain. Some simply give into the loss and begin to fade away, like some of the spouses who have lost longtime husbands or wives, and they then begin to die the day their spouse died, only to follow their mate in a year or two. Some make the effort to survive and move on in spite of the magnitude of their suffering. Others simply put the pieces of their now fragmented existences back together one by one. They search for routine and attempt to instill a sense of normalcy back into their lives.

There are no true guidebooks, no ways that are proper for everyone, no answers that will erase the pain for all. Everyone must face their grief individually and somehow survive or perish.

Roosevelt had decided to survive, mainly because he had promised Sarah several years earlier that he would.

Sarah was dying and had not wanted to spend her remaining time in a hospital. Since she had very little time left, Roosevelt and Sarah had decided to have her return home and receive hospice care. At this point, she had been ill for four years and the adrenal cancer had ravaged her to the point where she was no longer the robust and healthy woman she had been. Her frame had always been athletic, and she had scorned women who tried to be too skinny—she found them to be silly and sheep to society's expectations. But after the years of the effects of the disease and the various treatments, she was now only 85 pounds, and she seemed to be little more than a skeleton covered with decaying and papery thin skin.

When the diagnosis had first come that she had an adrenal tumor, a very rare form of cancer, they had both been deeply frightened, but with recent developments in treatment options, they had maintained hope she had a good chance for long-term survival and perhaps a cure. The doctor had told them of the seriousness of the illness. He also added that given her otherwise excellent health and good frame of mind, she would stand a reasonable chance in fighting the disease. They had immediately begun a highly aggressive treatment including chemotherapy and radiation and additional drugs. And Sarah had maintained a positive outlook no matter how much pain she suffered.

At first the results were promising. Sarah's cancer quickly went into remission, and she began to recover her strength. She lost her hair, and Roosevelt, in a demonstration of support for her, shaved his head, which made her laugh.

"Please, Roosevelt, please grow your hair back. I love you for doing that, but baldness…doesn't…suit…you!" She fell back on their sofa laughing. At first he had been offended, but then watching her laugh like that, he began to also. They held each other and continued to shake with laughter. Finally, when it slowly stopped, he looked at her.

"I promise, Sarah. I will start letting it grow immediately." They kissed, and she stood and took him by the hand. She led him into their bedroom, and they made love—very gently.

Soon after her return home, Roosevelt took her on a buying spree for scarves: long, short, simple, expensive, cotton, silk, refined, bandanas—everything they could find in a myriad of colors. "These are not to hide your head my love, but you love scarves, and you love colors, so here is a reason to indulge—and I want to do this for you."

The first three years of her illness were like riding on a hilly country road with a storm approaching. The clouds would gather and drench them with torrents slamming down and lightning flashing in the sky. Then suddenly, the rain would break, and the sun would peek out, revealing a deep blue sky with a hint of a not-quite-formed rainbow. Then they would crest the road and go into a long descent, and the end, obscured with fog. They never could quite see the end of their country road.

The treatments kept the disease at bay for a few months, like a wall of a medieval castle resisting an army's siege. Then, inevitably, the attacks began again, and the disease launched boulders over the castle's walls. The illness never completely moved into remission, nor for the first few years did it hit with its full power.

What did happen was that each part of the journey, each ascent and descent increased in duration and effect on Sarah. In the second year of her sickness, Sarah had to give up her position at Bethberg Medical Center and later her volunteer position in the local Boys and Girls Club as an art teacher. The strain of managing the classroom had become too much for her. Not the students though. She was astounded at how considerate these very energetic and often rowdy youngsters had become when they learned of her illness. They had loved her, and they, too, feared for her. They showed their love on her last day in the classroom, when they presented her with cards they had made, ranging from simplistic to complex in terms of talent, and she was moved her to tears. The students cried also. Even the tough boys who radiated both strength and fear, the boys she hoped to influence to avoid the dangers of the street and to stay in school and get an education—even they cried for their beloved teacher.

Knowing she had to leave both her life's profession and her beloved avocation was a wrenching experience for Roosevelt. He knew how serious this disease was. He knew ending her career as a surgeon had been difficult, but leaving the classroom had broken her heart. Because they had never been able to have any of their own, these kids had become her surrogate children.

In the end of the third year, over Sarah's objections, Roosevelt moved their bedroom from the second floor of their house to the first floor. Sarah had maintained that it would cause Roosevelt too much inconvenience to change where he had worked for so many years, but he shrugged off her concerns and simply moved his office/library to the second floor. He could not bear to watch his beloved wife struggle to go upstairs at the end of the day. She had resisted the change, but he had been firm in his decision. While Roosevelt had typically acquiesced to her wishes, this time he did not.

"Well," she said when she looked at the new bedroom and considered its possibilities, "I always thought you kept this room too dark." He smiled at her gentle teasing. Roosevelt knew she would be delighted with the chance to redecorate this room. She would definitely fill it with brightness. And he indulged her with anything she wanted for the room, no matter how unusual.

Her taste was eclectic: she loved many forms of art, bric-a-brac, knickknacks, antiques, and almost anything with brilliance. If anyone had seen the room and had attempted to define a guiding, unifying theme, they would have been defeated. But Roosevelt knew it showed her love of color and her joy in life.

Sarah was determined to be frivolous and silly for his sake. She had already come to terms with the idea of her death, and she was comfortable with it. She had no fear of her demise. Her vaguely Protestant upbringing had long ago been supplanted with views closer to Deism than anything else. She believed that no one official religion could truly claim to have the real answers to the mysteries of life. She would say to Roosevelt, "God is in everything and is everywhere."

What would happen after death? Well, if she were correct, then she would wait for Roosevelt to join her, and if she were wrong, then the truth would be revealed to her. She was confident they would meet again. Their connection in life had been too strong to end by something as tenuous as death.

But for her beloved Roosevelt, she was deeply concerned. Sarah knew how much he worried about her, and she knew he was not comfortable with his own views on mortality. She knew he was trying to look brave for her, to hold up the strong, confident front so she would be able to lean on him. But Sarah saw in his eyes what he tried to hide. She saw the tears he barely kept under control; she perceived the fear he tried to keep secreted from her; she knew he wished he could trade places with her, and it was killing him that he was unable to protect her. She saw he was frightened and frustrated.

So, she tried to bring color into his life.

Shortly before her death, she made him promise, "knowing you will continue my beloved Roosevelt, that you will enjoy life as best you can, and that you know I'll be waiting for you, I don't want you to hurry to meet me, my beloved husband."

He laid his head next to hers on the hospice bed and cried.

"I know you will never break a promise you make to me."

She managed to turn to him and hold his face in her shaking and fragile hands.

"Look at me, my love, please."

Roosevelt blinked away his tears and looked at his wife's thin and ravaged face.

"I love you, Roosevelt."

"And I love you, Sarah." He gasped a sob.

"You must promise me to survive and to go on. You must do this now, I don't know how much time I have left, and I will be very angry with you if you don't. That is all I ask of you."

His heart was breaking, but he couldn't deny his wife this request. Even though he had no desire to continue without her, he acquiesced. "I promise, my love."

The next day, Sarah died.

TEN

THE IN-BETWEEN

As Maledicus meditated on his circumstances, various demons were studying the depths of his former existence, like miners exploring a new, untapped vein hoping to find valuable ore. The vein they were looking at would be malleable into a new form, a kind of spiritual alchemy.

One ancient demon, formed long before the emergence of this universe, an amalgam of other smaller demons, paid Maledicus particular attention. When this demon, known as THEY, saw him, it rejoiced. Here was such matter as could be molded into something darkly magnificent. THEY had found a kindred being, one it could make into a similar form. This Maledicus would seem to be part of the multitude of THEY, but would exist separately as it tested him, watching to see if he could eventually merge. THEY would give him the illusion that he was part of the legion, but he would only be a weak representation of its actuality. THEY never simply pulled any spirits into its mass. First, came the creation of the art form, in its own likeness, and then the observation, watching to see how well the new demon would function as an extension of the negative force. In several millennia, if the fledgling demon proved strong enough, then THEY absorbed him truly into its being, but for now, it would offer him transformation into a new form, which he would think was complete communion with the great demon.

THEY moved like a swirling, dark, storm cloud, pulsing with colors never seen by the eyes of living human beings, surging around Maledicus. THEY surrounded him but did not contact him. The form never stopped undulating, moving erratically with extrusions emanating and retracting. It seemingly had mass, but it had no solidity. Its form was inconstant; its metamorphosis was constant. Swirling masses of gigantic worms hissed and retreated in it. Most spirits, even those of the most evil humans, when confronted by THEY, were horrified, but Maledicus was delighted. He had never seen such beauty.

Sublime, It is like a god. It is like me. I can feel it, Maledicus thought.

"Yes," THEY answered. "You are similar. THEY have been watching you, studying you and come to you with an offer."

Inky forms spread closer to Maledicus, like the jets from a prehistoric, giant squid. These shapes were threatening, but also very comforting, to him. Tendrils slowly reached around him, caressed him, and gave him comfort.

"Do you want to join with THEY? Do you want to be one of the privileged ones? Do you want to have true power? You knew a portion, a small example of power in your life, and you rejoiced in it." THEY's voice was sweet and gentle, like the sound of one of his slaves as they whispered into his ear, knowing that they had to please him or suffer the terrible consequences. The voice seemed to kiss his ears.

Maledicus, however much he enjoyed the attention, was not easily seduced.

My power was not small. I was counselor to the Emperor. I had his ear. I gave him what he wanted, and he gave me the power to do as I wished, to be the Emperor of the Roman Empire!

"Yes, that is true," the demon responded. "THEY was delighted with you. THEY had hoped that you would replace that sniveling, syphilitic fool by becoming Emperor yourself. What you could have accomplished: it would have been a symphony of horror!"

Maledicus saw what THEY perceived. THEY revealed itself to Maledicus, and he saw what might have been: a terrified Empire bowing before him, giving him everything, worshipping him as Emperor, as God. He saw rebels crushed and crucified by the thousands, a massive expansion of the Empire in all directions, a vast number of new arenas filled with the most terrible of entertainments, slaves and captives taken from conquering and put to death in novel and terrifying ways. He saw the blood of thousands of the slain paint the floor of the coliseums crimson. He felt the fear that hundreds of thousands, if not millions, of people would have felt towards him, an empire to do with as he wished, all under his control. This glory might have been.

"Yes, it might have been. In other universes, it has been, but there you were killed first. Yet, you still have potential to be great. You can still join, to choose a position of power rather than to be punished, to become truly immortal."

For the first time, Maledicus began to wonder if his time in the In-Between was limited. Was he in peril? After all the time he had spent there, he had assumed that this was his eternal fate, but he realized that he might have been making the same mistake he made in life, to ignore potential danger and to assume invincibility. He would not do that again.

THEY said, "THEY have observed you and have found you to be worthy of joining. This offer is not given lightly. This offer is rarely made, and no one is ever forced to accept. You must accept of your own free will, but you only have this one opportunity. Only those, truly worthy, will have this one chance to achieve greatness. If you do not accept this offer, then THEY will leave you forever, will find others to whom to make this offer, and you will then deal with the light. It is entirely your choice to make. Let THEY enter you and you will understand."

Show me, Maledicus thought. He felt the demon's words echoing through him as if a giant drum beat inside him. Even though he had no physical body, the sensations were as real as if he had been corporeal. He felt the inky jets enter and communicate with him. He learned and understood the totality of this magnificent and horrifying offer: he could either join with THEY and receive the continuing pleasures he craved—to torment others, to plague, to cause havoc, chaos, and terror, to corrupt and destroy innocence, in short, all he had done in life and along with that, an eternal existence with enormous power. He could have all that simply by accepting the demon's rule. Otherwise, he would stay within the vicinity of the light, to that blinding, painful light that terrified him. THEY let him perceive that in the light, he would learn of action and consequence, of knowledge and understanding, of reparation and repentance, all of which was repugnant to him. It made him quake with outrage. It made him tremble with fear and shame. It was for the weak to admit mistakes or to amend behavior. Maledicus despised the weak.

Using the voice he could hear only within himself, Maledicus shouted, *"Yes, I accept. Take me with you, and make me one of you! Give me this power!"*

Instantly, the whirling mass pulled Maledicus into it. Maledicus instantaneously became part of this entity. He screamed and felt himself change for eternity; his spirit was no longer his own, and his soul was no longer human in any way. THEY took Maledicus, ingested him, tasted him and delighted in what it felt. The mass, satisfied with its meal, vomited him out. The corrupted human spirit had entered THEY and been regurgitated as a new part of the entity, but still separate, to be tested and observed to see if he deserved permanent absorption into its totality. Like a butterfly that had emerged in pure beauty from the chrysalis, his transforming now complete, from the potential of human evil to complete demonic malevolence. He had become a demon, fated forever to exist in the In-Between. Now as part of THEY, he was capable of contact with and desecration of the world of the living.

The mass spoke to him, "You will have a purpose Maledicus, specifically on Earth. Be patient and learn. THEY have chosen your way and will give you the conduit that you need to perform your beautiful art. You will have access to Earth through the form of a statue, a tiny, unimportant artifact that no one will attach any importance to, but which will serve as your tunnel to the physical world."

Maledicus' form pulsed and undulated now. He no longer seemed to be a human form. As he moved, an armed tendril that stunk with decay emerged and moved into the world of the living.

I have true power! Maledicus thought.

"Maledicus, remember, you have power only because you are part of THEY!"

ELEVEN

Jeremy deeply missed the antique store David and he had owned and run. He stood outside and looked at what had been the display window of their store. Now a toy stop, it held a bright assortment of playthings, including a large red train display the owners kept running constantly, even when the store whether the store was opened or closed. The town's small children loved the train, and while it did appeal to Jeremy, the lack of antiques in the window always caused him a dart of pain.

Surpassed only by his love for David, the store had been Jeremy's focus and passion in life for several decades. Without David, it had lost its meaning. Since David's death, Jeremy was unable to keep the same passion for the shop. While before, it had stood as a testament to their binding love, now it seemed more like a grave marker, and Jeremy preferred to remember his partner as he was when he was alive, not as he looked when he died.

Jeremy and David had lived together as partners for 30 years. They were both cultured and discreet; they had come of age prior to the generation that had created the movement for gay rights. While they didn't live a closeted existence, neither man deluded himself into denying his orientation, nor did they make public disclaimers of whom they were. They chose not to make a public declaration of their relationship. Neither man had any inclination to deny the truth of their orientation to anyone who knew them, but as gentlemen such topics rarely arose and neither man was given to public political statements. Certainly, as the gay rights movement began and gained momentum in other parts of the country, David and Jeremy supported the younger generation, but they did not actively participate in any protest. It was enough that they were accepted by the cultural, artistic, and intellectual community of Bethberg, and they were happy in their lives.

"Our friends know," Jeremy said to any challenge made to him by others.

In those days, when David and Jeremy first shared an apartment in Bethberg, many of their friends referred to them as "confirmed bachelors". It was an old-fashioned phrase, but to many, Bethberg itself was an old-fashioned community. The gay rights movement had not been publicly declared in the area, but also it could be argued that the women's movement, the civil rights movement, and the anti-war protests never really materialized there either. It was not an inherently conservative place politically; rather, it was very slow to embrace open and accelerated change of any kind. But for those who moved in the circle of artists and intellectuals, small as that might have been in Bethberg, acceptance of sexual orientation was a given but not to be discussed.

The Bethberg intelligentsia had embraced Jeremy and David, but the men were also aware of the dangers existing for them in some parts of town, in which approval would not be forthcoming. They avoided the people who secretly or openly spewed hatred towards gays, the kind of unthinking bigots who unfortunately might exist anywhere. In Bethberg, there was not an active chapter of the KKK. Neither did the kind of militia that was common in many parts of rural Pennsylvania. However, that did not mean Bethberg was free of homophobic people. Danger was always a possibility for David and Jeremy.

Jeremy met David at an art exhibition at the New York Museum of Modern Art, and they made an instant connection; in fact, they called it love at first sight. They had both had several prior relationships, but never before did they feel anything this strong so quickly or that their souls had connected. David was quite a bit older than Jeremy was and had lived in Greenwich Village in the city. He was a successful art critic and dealer, but he had grown tired of the pace of New York and had been seriously considering moving out of the city to a less high-paced area. When David fell for Jeremy, he knew that he wanted to spend the rest of his life with this younger man. When they moved in together two years later, David was 50, and Jeremy was 35.

"It was fine living in New York City when I was younger, but I need to slow down now," he told David. "I used to absolutely thrive on the pace, the drive of people and the sheer exuberance of this magnificent place, but it is beginning to take a toll on me now, and I know it is time for me to bid adieu to my beloved city."

Even though he desired a slower paced lifestyle, there was nothing slow about their romance. It was deep and passionate, and David swept Jeremy off his feet. Soon it was clear to everyone who was close to them both men were deeply in love with each other. Whenever they were together, they had a difficult time not touching each other in some way, even if it was just a simple caress. They frequently looked deeply into each other's eyes—no one else existed for them when they did. They had become each other's soul mate.

That they lived in places over an hour and a half away from each other was no deterrent for their romance. Since David was tired of the city, he moved to Bethberg to be with Jeremy. They pooled their financial resources and their accumulated knowledge of art, history, decoration and business and created an antiques business. They purchased a large, dilapidated Victorian home and renovated it to its proper glory. When they were finished, it did, as Jeremy remarked, "rival any grand Queen Anne in the upscale neighborhoods of San Francisco. David, my love, we are the proud owners of our very own beautiful and elegant painted lady."

They also bought a store in the downtown and opened their business. Soon their store with a very simple name, "Antiques in Bethberg" was one of the finest antiques locations in Northeastern Pennsylvania.

The store itself, they renovated to exhibit items tastefully. "We are not running a flea market," David insisted. They were able to offer items from the unusual for collectors such as fine Victorian pocket watches to Edwardian and Renaissance Italian furniture. One of the benefits both would laugh about was the need to travel to investigate and procure items. They both loved their journeys to Europe and into Italy in particular to find more objects to sell in their thriving store.

It was through their antique business that Jeremy came to know Roosevelt. Roosevelt and his wife Sarah loved looking at and shopping for fine antiques in as many places as possible. They rambled through yard sales to flea markets to auctions to high-end antique stores. They often traveled around the country looking for items, and they were delighted to find the assortment and quality of antiques that Jeremy and David's store offered. Within a few months of its existence, "Antiques in Bethberg" became a regular stop for Sarah and Roosevelt.

Over a period of several years, they came to enjoy their visits to the antique store more for their conversation with David and Jeremy than for the actual purchasing of antiques. The two couples began to have dinners once or twice a month. David may have been ready to leave Manhattan, but he sorely missed the sophisticated New York City dinners that featured good food and lively, intelligent conversation. Those Manhattan dinners they replaced with the meals they now shared with their new friends.

Not long after Sarah first became ill, another tragedy struck the close-knit group of friends. While attending an opening of a local artist's oil paintings at a new gallery in downtown Bethberg, David turned to Jeremy and said, "I don't feel well."

Jeremy looked up from an abstract expressionist style painting he was admiring to see his partner's face – ashen and covered in sweat. Jeremy immediately went across to him.

"David. What's wrong? Do you want to sit down?"

David was trying to say something, but all Jeremy could hear was a sibilant rasp. David looked into Jeremy's eyes, moved his lips in a silent whisper, trying to tell his beloved partner something.

David fell over dead.

Jeremy later learned that David died by a sudden and massive brain aneurysm. In a few very brief moments, Jeremy's well-ordered and comfortable life disintegrated into chaos. In less than a few seconds, Jeremy lost the love of his life, his partner, his companion, and his best friend.

The loss was devastating for Jeremy, and he fell into a nearly non-functioning state. Sarah and Roosevelt stepped in and tended to Jeremy and to their affairs. David had no living family, so Jeremy and David had both listed Roosevelt as executor in their respective wills. Roosevelt insisted that Jeremy stay with them for a while, and Sarah and he arranged the funeral and the wake.

Later, when he recovered to a degree, Jeremy learned of Sarah's illness, and he threw himself into helping her. Towards the end of her battle with the cancer, Sarah asked Jeremy to promise that he would watch over Roosevelt. Even though Jeremy knew that Roosevelt was a proud man, he agreed and stuck to his promise. Both men quietly continued to lean on each other.

Jeremy never, however, came to terms with not knowing what it was that David had tried to tell him before dying. He also deeply regretted not being able to say goodbye and not being able to say one more time to David that he loved him.

Jeremy sold the store and tried to move on with the rest of his life but always kept his heart to himself. He quietly rebuffed well-meaning friends who suggested, after some time, that Jeremy try to date again. Jeremy knew that after finding his true partner, that there would never be anyone to replace David.

TWELVE

DECEMBER 9

Sam sat alone at the bar at McGuigan's Pub, with a beer in front of him, staring at the television set. A boxing match flickered on the old black and white TV. Sam only appeared to watch the action so no one would talk to him. An old acquaintance had approached him before, but Sam had simply ignored him.

"What's with Sammy?" the retired firefighter had asked the bartender. "He acted like I wasn't even there. Jesus."

"Don't let it get to you, Mike." Mitchell the balding, elderly bartender lowered his voice and spoke into the other man's ear. "It ain't nothin' personal. But you know how he gets sometimes. Just let him alone. He'll be ok in a couple of days."

Sam didn't hear any of their words. He was deeply involved in the memory of a conversation he had had in this same place quite a few years ago before he had retired from the police force.

"Have you ever wanted to get into someone's head? To really be able to hear what they're thinking, to know what they're feeling?" Shortly before his retirement, Sam had asked these questions to a friend of his on the police force. They sat at a corner table in the dining section of McGuigan's, a small Irish pub in Bethberg. While it was not a cop's bar, it was a place where many police officers and fire fighters went for a brew and food. They tended to go on the off times and avoided the Friday and Saturday night crowds, when McGuigan's featured Irish music and bands, and a younger crowd dominated the place. The cops usually went on other nights or the afternoons. Still, even on the busiest nights, there seemed to be at least one or two off duty officers having a pint. A benefit for the owners was that the presence of off-duty cops tended to keep out the rowdier types. Other than a door checker for keeping out underage drinkers, McGuigan's bar needed no bouncers. The food ranged from basic bar burgers to more elaborate fare based on traditional Irish bar food, such as Shepherd's pie. The beer on tap featured, among others, Harp and Guinness.

"Sam, that's one hell of a question." Sam sat at the table with Steven, his oldest and closest friend on the force. A six foot, three inch, 240 pound former college football linebacker, Steven made a powerful image. His ebony skin and brown eyes reflected his deep intelligence and compassion. These traits had served him very well as he rose to be the first African-American Captain of the Bethberg Police Force. Steven had been through a great deal of trauma with his family, but he had always remained one of the strongest and best people Sam knew. Steven's parents had died together in a car crash only a few months ago, and he had been the one to handle everything. His siblings were far flung, so it was left to Steven to oversee everything. His oldest child—Sharon—suffered from an ongoing battle with cerebral palsy. The young woman was now in college, but her body was showing signs of rapid deterioration. No one knew how long of a life she might have or how quickly her condition might deteriorate, and it tormented her father. Even though he knew it was not possible, Steven would gladly have switched positions with his daughter and given her his health. He was, nevertheless, deeply proud of her spirit, courage, and intelligence and supported anything she tried to do with her life. Sam was also very proud of her, because he was the girl's godfather. When Steven had asked him, Sam had been surprised, because it had been many years since he had been inside a church. He agreed, and to his surprise, took the task seriously, to the point of rejoining the Church and even helping with Sunday School. The shared responsibility of Sharon brought them closer even than being police officers did.

Steven looked at his friend. "What's on your mind, Sam?"

Sam had served on the Bethberg Police Force a long time. He had gone to the Police Academy after having been in the U. S. Marines for four years. He made it through the Academy easily and joined the Bethberg force immediately after and had long ago passed the coveted 20 year mark. When many considered retiring to move on to something else, Sam stayed. He was a cop and had intended to remain one until he stopped working. He had risen to Sergeant through hard work and determination. Along the way, he had decided to get a college degree going part time while staying on the force. It was a difficult task, juggling family time, work time and school time, but he persevered and earned his B.A. in Political Science. He then was promoted to Lieutenant and became a full-fledged detective. Initially the job was not a great deal different from that of the regular officers, but times changed in Bethberg as they did in the rest of the country. Murders became regular events, and he gradually developed into the main homicide detective. Now, after nearly 40 years on the force, Sam was seriously thinking of retirement.

Sam sat and stared at his half-finished pint of Guinness. Steven knew better than to push Sam. Even though Sam was nearly ten years older than Steven, they were as close as brothers could be. Steven knew that Sam would eventually answer him, that when Sam got this quiet, something very serious was bothering him.

"A lot actually, well, maybe, just one thing. Damn, I could use a smoke now." Sam had quit smoking cigarettes, for the most part, around ten years ago, but he still smoked on occasion. He longed for the calming feel of the smoke in his lungs.

"Here." Steven held out a pack of Marlboros and a gun-metal-steel colored Zippo lighter. Sam took a cigarette, lit it, and flipped the lighter shut, which always made a satisfying clink. He inhaled deeply, savored the smoke, and released it slowly through his nostrils.

"I've been thinking a lot recently. I wish I could get into someone's head."

"A woman?" Steven raised his right eyebrow into a pointed arch. Sam hadn't dated anyone since his divorce years earlier, and Steven had wondered if Sam would ever date anyone else.

"No, it ain't a woman," Sam growled. He took another deep drag. "I've been thinking about Josh."

"Oh." Steven realized that he should have understood sooner than he did. Josh was Sam's son, and he committed suicide many years ago. He was Sam's only child and seemed to be an intelligent, well-adjusted kid. His friends, were involved in high school activities, and planned to go to college.

One day, when Sam was at the station, he received an urgent phone call from his wife. He could barely understand her—only that he should come right home. When he got there, other police officers and an ambulance were there, something he was used to seeing at other people's homes, not his. His home was a place where normalcy and happiness. It was a guarantee he believed in and where safety and protection from the world's problems were givens. He panicked. He turned off his car. He jumped out. He ran into his house.

"Mary? Mary? Are you OK?"

Two young cops tried to stop him, but he pushed through them. His wife, curled up on the floor, was crying. He looked at her and then at the other police officers, who avoided his eyes.

"Mary?" he asked softly as he knelt down and tried to take her in his arms, but she wrapped herself into a tighter ball. "What is it? What happened? Did someone hurt you?" If someone had hurt her, he would find them and kill them. She only shook her head. Then she let out a low moaning keen. That sound suddenly amplified into a full wail. Then it hit him—Josh.

He stood abruptly, fear pumping through him like a balloon overfilled with helium, about to burst. "*Oh god, oh god, not Josh, not my boy, not Josh.*"

He knew from Mary's reaction that this was bad, very bad. He had seen similar reactions too many times before from survivors in murder cases. He turned to one of the cops. He grabbed him by the uniform and pulled him aside. He looked into the young man's eyes. "Tell me, now!"

The young cop stammered. "He, he's in the garage." Sam released him and ran through the house and into the garage. The EMTs had turned off the car, an old Chevy Caprice that Josh loved, and they had opened the outside garage door. Even with fresh air moving in, the fumes were still thick in the small room. As Sam moved to the car, he saw Josh slumped over the steering wheel—dead.

Sam collapsed to the floor. He would later learn that Josh had left a note saying only – "I'm sorry. I have to do this." Regardless of the following investigation, they never found any reason for his death. No one, including his closest friends, who were just as shaken by his suicide as Josh's parents, had any idea why the teenager had killed himself.

Sam was ordinarily a strong man. He had been a marine; he had experienced the horror of war and had survived. During the war, enemy soldiers fired on him, and he had killed several VC and saw them die not far from where he had stood. As a police officer, he had seen deaths from car accidents, suicides, and homicides, and he had survived. He had been responsible for the prosecution of several very dangerous criminals, including a beginning serial killer and a drug lord who had ordered several hits, and he had felt righteous about their jail time, also about placing them on death row. He had stared down a shaking junkie with a "Saturday Night Special" gun was pointed directly at him, and he had survived. Once, a gang member shot him in the stomach, and he survived, but he almost did not survive the death of his son.

One night, several months after Josh's suicide, Sam had been sitting in his car on the ridge of Old Smith Road, which overlooks Bethberg. He took out his .45 automatic, chambered a round, and put the barrel to the right side of his head. He had come to do this, to put an end to his pain. He had previously tried to drink himself into oblivion, but that didn't work. He would simply wake up hung over and with Josh in his mind. He thought that doing himself was the best option. Sam sat rigid, with the gun to his head, for about 30 minutes but eventually and slowly, he lowered the gun. *I'm a coward. . .* he thought.

Sam took another drag from the cigarette. "I've been thinking about Josh a lot lately. You know, what kind of man he would've been. You know… he was a smart kid, really smart, a lot smarter than his dad. He probably would've been a doctor or a scientist or something."

"But not a lawyer," Steven smiled.

"Yeah, definitely not a scummy lawyer. You know, he was a good kid. Shit, if he had been fucked up on drugs like some of the kids we see now, or involved in some of the other bad shit that we are seeing, like gangs, or whatever, I'd have found out…and I would've understood, at least, what happened. But, man, he wasn't into any of that shit."

Steven looked at him.

"He wasn't." Sam pointed a finger at him. "Don't you fucking think that! I'm not some idiot, some moron who thinks that my kid won't do anything wrong. I know what kind of trouble kids can get into—serious shit. I checked, and I looked hard. I looked way outside of the official department policies. I found nothing. Nothing. Believe me it would've been easier to deal with if I had found something. I would've known what trouble he'd been in. I would've had names to go after. Nothing man, there was fucking nothing. My boy was clean."

Steven held up his hands, palms out to apologize.

"Man, it's all right. You know we're good. I just wish I would've been able to find an answer. Now all I got are questions, and a big fucking hole in my heart." He stubbed out the cigarette and accepted another from Steven.

"So," he said after lighting up. "I wish I could go back in time and find out what he was thinking, what he was hurting about and help him. A dad is supposed to be able to help his son. You know, I never was able to help…"

Steven looked down as Sam wiped his eyes with one of the bar napkins.

"Ah shit, look at me….I look like some kind of baby …blubbering."

"It's ok, Sam. If anyone says anything about this, rags on you about this—I'll take care of them. I know you're a big boy, but Man, I got your back."

"Last call, Sam." The bartender's voice pulled him out of his memory. "Huh?"

"Last call. It's time for you to go home and get some sleep, Sammy."

"Sure, I'll try to do just that." Sam pulled a twenty from his wallet to pay for his beer.

"Put it away, Sammy. They're on me."

Sam nodded and went out into the night.

THIRTEEN

1890

The dig had progressed much better than had been expected. Dr. Peter Boswell, one of the world's foremost experts in Ancient British Archeology and History, was supervising an excavation at an obscure location in the down land section of England. Much of his recent work in Neolithic culture focused in the Cranborne Chase region. He was having great success and was determined not to overlook any possible finds. One very interesting potential lead had come to his attention in an unusual way.

The man who owned the small house had contacted the University of Cambridge, and the message was forwarded to Dr. Boswell, since he was already in the area, and the Department was eager not to let such opportunities slip away to competitors. Dr. Boswell, one of the University's most renowned and admired scientists, was always keen for any information he could use. The homeowner, one Mr. Taylor, had contacted the University after he made an unusual discovery. He had been trying to repair his house's leaky basement. When he was digging out a section of floor that seemed to need reworking, he discovered that a small, sub-basement existed. In that sub-basement were various ancient Roman statues and relics.

Dr. Boswell would not have been surprised if he had discovered the site had been disturbed or looted. It was not an uncommon problem. Mr. Taylor was certainly not, by any standards, a wealthy man. Dr. Boswell, himself from an aristocratic background who, indoctrinated with that class' expectations about those beneath them, viewed anyone of the working class to be less than honorable. Boswell privately admitted to himself, however, that few of his own class were above chicanery or deceit. He had, through many years of dealing with both academics who wished to forward their careers and collectors who were often less than honest in their dealings, come to view his fellow man as less than truthful. He knew that a find like this might have tempted many men to gain considerable financial remuneration from the black market sales of the discoveries. Many private collectors were willing to pay substantial amounts to add to their private museums or curiosity cabinets. Dr. Boswell understood the way of the world and the use such collectors had. He understood some of his own research went into unusual and arcane areas; therefore, finding leads for his work often involved unscrupulous people. He was certainly willing to deal with anyone who could help his work, but he had no illusions about their intentions. When he reached the site, Dr. Boswell was startled and impressed; it seemed to be in good order and relatively undisturbed. The only sign of any problem was minor scattering of debris from Taylor's initial digging of the basement floor. Indeed, the site, other than minor damage, was unblemished.

In deference to Taylor's privacy, and to recognize his honesty in the matter, Boswell paid for (through the University, of course) a separate cellar entrance to be constructed. Taylor was delighted because it would leave him with another functional entryway, one that was, in fact, larger and more accessible than what he previously had.

The archeologist and his team were able to enter, do work, and leave with minimal intrusion into Taylor's life. Likewise, they did not have to worry about Taylor interfering with their work.

Boswell was also impressed with the man's knowledge of what he had found and of the history of Britain. For a working-class man, Taylor was well informed. *Good for him, knows more than most of his ilk,* Boswell thought. The professor arranged a small stipend to be paid to Taylor "for his inconvenience in the matter." To Bosworth the money was insignificant, but to Taylor, the extra hundred pounds was like a fortune. In rendering the money to Taylor, Boswell didn't mention the find might be worth at least one million pounds Sterling. Even if the amount was considerably less, it would still be of a substantial monetary value. Taylor should be satisfied with what he received Boswell reasoned. After all, this was being done in the name of Great Britain and Science.

Henry Turley was an expert at buying and selling esoteric and arcane. He kept a storefront in London that advertised he was a dealer in antiquities and fine items. The merchandise in his shop was for the most part, was completely legal if very expensive. They were the sort of items many Victorians of wealth loved to collect to display: paintings, statuettes, clocks, and bric-a-brac collected from the estates of forgotten and collapsed families, all which suggested value and artisanship. He would sell nothing that was not of some worth; the key to his success was making certain that his upper-class custom-ers always left feeling that they had acquired an item of some significance and wealth.

He never wanted anyone to check on his stock and claim that he was selling junk, so he assiduously checked on each item's significance, history, and provenance. This part of his business was successful; it was to this inventory he referred when dealing with the government. Everything in his ledgers was clear and above-board. His secretary was an older gentleman who had done such work for twenty years, and Turley used an accounting firm that was old, conservative, and honest to tend to his financial books that the government saw. He was the very image of the honest, if somewhat naïve, businessman. He never had any problem with the tax people, and he spoke of the British government with respect and reverence. The gentlemen who came to his store knew he was trustworthy, and he never overcharged for his items. Thus, Turley's reputation as a decent and scrupulous businessman was well established and in this business he earned a solid, but not spectacular, living.

Turley's other business, however, was far more interesting and much more lucrative. This endeavor was a carefully guarded secret he revealed only to a select clientele who were interested in purchasing items of the occult, the unusual, and sometimes, the illegal. Mr. Turley was a well-educated man. While he had not attended university, he had been a remarkable autodidact. He had read the equivalent of a doctoral degree in history, focusing on the occult and the unusual and he was aware of the Rosicrucian's, Freemasons, and many aspects of spiritualism history. This interest not only fueled his passion for knowledge but also led him to develop his secondary business. He had made many acquaintances with fellow searchers, and he had quietly become a man who could acquire and sell that which others could not or would not. Because of the nature of these transactions, everyone kept them secret, and in this business, Mr. Turley kept his own books, which were carefully kept locked in a vault.

His other shop that Turley, had paid handsomely for, was in a sub-basement of his primary store. He had insured the confidences of the workers by providing them with a much larger than normal pay, and he continued to employ them, in secret of course, on other tasks. Because he had purchased the property, his little "store", he kept private. Turley wanted no one outside of his specific customers to be aware of it. In its present condition, gaining access to the sub-basement door required the moving of a carefully arranged pile of chaos sitting directly on top of it. The storage room itself gave the impression of being in a state of unfinished clean up. Much of the junk and debris Turley had accumulated over the years assembled into a seemingly uncoordinated yet carefully constructed pile on the floor. No one would ever see a door under it, with a specific design forming arcane symbols he changed monthly made from the rubbish. What seemed to be chaos was, indeed, a carefully planned order. At this point, a pair of entwining serpents, a very ancient symbol of knowledge, could be determined if one knew where to look at the pile. The symbol was indistinct, but there, nevertheless. It took Turley about one-half hour to move enough to gain access to the door, but the secrecy and security was worth the effort.

Turley kept the inventory of this sub-basement a secret: fine statuary, relics, occult items, art, vases, coins, skulls, and other esoteric. These objects will fetch him a tidy sum of money. From his careful saving and the eventual sale of his main store, he knew he would soon be able to retire and live the quiet life of a modest country squire in Switzerland. He had previously kept the money from the sales of these items in that subbasement, but he had grown increasingly uncomfortable with that arrangement. When he had accumulated a substantial sum, Turley quietly made an excursion to Switzerland, a little holiday, he had said to his regular customers when he closed his store for two weeks two years previous. There he opened a numbered account and deposited his money. He enjoyed that the Swiss banks respected privacy, and he felt living there would be a good option for him. He had always been attracted to the sublime grandeur of the Alps. At his age, Turley believed the time was coming when he would be able to enjoy the relaxation he deserved in the remaining years of his life, so he was always looking for opportunity to enhance his financial circumstances.

Therefore, when Mr. Taylor entered his public store with the small Roman figurine and several ancient gold pieces, Turley instantly understood their value and that some of his more discerning clients of esoteric would be especially interested in owning the statue. Mr. Taylor showed Turley the item. He stammered, "Sir, I been told you might be the man to talk to. You might be interested in it."

After questioning Mr. Taylor intensely, Turley realized this idol had come from a recently discovered archeological dig, and that legalities of the purchase might be an issue. Further, he had never met nor heard of Mr. Taylor. If such a situation arose before, he would inevitably send the would-be seller away. He preferred not to take chances on buying the special items from unknown people. Turley was ready to dismiss Taylor with a scolding about selling illegal items, but when he looked at the little idol again, he hesitated. There was nothing particularly unusual about it, except that it suggested an unknown

Roman god, probably a household god, one of the many Lares that served to observe and protect the houses in which they were placed, but it seemed different…the face was, in itself, well…evil. This one was different, not so much in its appearance – it was simply a Roman man in a toga, but in its feel – a suggestion of menace, a hint of aggression seemed to emanate from the little statue. Turley, fascinated by it, broke his self-imposed regulation.

"Please allow me to examine this item more closely." Turley smiled at the nervous Taylor and held the statue up to the light, then placed it on his desk and examined it with a large magnifying glass. "I will buy it if you are reasonable about the price."

Taylor nodded and indicated he was very willing.

Turley purchased the idol and the gold pieces at a substantial price, one that surprised the nervous seller. Taylor had not haggled; in fact, he had nearly fainted at the amount of money he was being offered. Turley wanted Taylor to be contented with the sale but also to be silent about the transaction. He made it clear if anyone found out about the matter, Taylor would be at risk of legal prosecution. "If the government were to hear about this, they would come after you first, and I doubt you have the money to hire the kind of attorneys that I do, Mr. Taylor." Taylor's eyes grew wide at the implied danger.

Turley also hinted that he had other means of securing Taylor's silence. Turley knew that no one could ever prove where the idol came from, but he wanted to add a touch of fear to the transaction, so that Taylor, if tempted to talk about it, would know that he risked being visited "by very large, and very unpleasant men who would then rectify the situation." Taylor had no way of knowing that Turley never did such things, but it added a nice touch of drama and security nevertheless. Taylor agreed completely to the terms of the sale and assured Turley he would never mention it to anyone. Both men were pleased. Taylor left with a considerable sum of money, and Turley knew he could sell the statuette for an even larger sum. He already had a particular buyer in mind for the idol.

A few months after buying the idol, Mr. Turley sold it to a man who lived in the highlands of Scotland. He was a man of leisure, who had inherited a minor noble title, a considerable estate, and a massive fortune. Sir Peter Ross came from a family that claimed it had descended from the Tudor line. Whether they had or not was entirely unclear as it is likely that the Ross family, like many other merchant families in the Elizabethan period, had purchased noble titles, but Ross fashioned himself after the image of King Henry VIII. Ross was a very large man, both in height and weight. In his youth, he was a muscular fellow who excelled in all sports. With his broad shoulders, massive chest, and height of 6'4", he had been an impressive physical specimen. Now in his sixties, he had grown considerably: at 450 pounds, he was large; he was rotund; he was corpulent; he was fat. He did not have a double, he had quadruple chins, and the only space between his legs where they did not touch was at his ankles.

He seemed to be more of a living blob of flesh than a man, yet he was still relatively healthy. He amazed his doctors, who continuously warned him about his habits of consumption. He would laugh at them and say, "I will outlive the rest of you." As far as the doctors of his time could determine, he was still a healthy man. They had no way of measuring his cholesterol levels, of seeing that plaque was rapidly blocking the flow of blood in his arteries, and that a heart attack or stroke was likely in the near future.

Despite his size, Ross still dressed impeccably, but his tailored suits required more wool than did most suits for two other average sized men. He indulged his desires, all of them, in great quantities. He tried to follow his hero, Henry VIII, in feeding his passions. Additionally, he was a student of the dark arts. While he did not practice any, he loved collecting truly unusual occult items and very rare books about these subjects, and he was willing to pay a great deal of money to indulge his desires.

Ross sat in his specially designed, enormous, leather chair in his library, one that could have served as a sofa for two other people. As self-indulgent as he was, Ross was not given to self-delusion. He knew how large he was, so he had special furniture designed to fit his bulk. He had commissioned a local furniture maker to build a fine sitting chair to accommodate his girth. The man had done a wonderful job. The chair was handsome and very strong. It never groaned or shifted under Ross' weight, so the man had received a substantial bonus in addition to the agreed upon price. When pleased, Ross was grandiose in his gratuities.

He sat in that chair, drank a large snifter of excellent cognac, and puffed a Cuban Churchill sized cigar. As he did, he admired his newest purchase, a small idol he had procured from his visit to London. Ross surprised many by not letting his size keep him from traveling – he simply paid for the size of train compartment or special carriage that he needed. Life was for living, and indulging, not hiding away.

As always, Turley had something to interest him in the special shop. While, on the surface, seemingly an ordinary household Roman god, Ross suspected the statue was a representation of something much more significant. When Turley contacted him and told him about the idol, Sir Ross became immediately interested. Turley informed the corpulent buyer he had the figurine verified. It was a rare discovery, in a recent archaeological, found in the remains of the domicile of one Maledicus. Maledicus was one of the worst degraded and vile men in the corrupt reign of Emperor Caligula. He had been one of the procurers of victims for the Emperor's pleasure, and rumored to be involved in magic and demonology. There are those who believe he was banished to England where he was later murdered or he had been murdered in Rome. That part of the history was unclear. Other than that, very little was known about him.

This tantalizing information was enough for Ross. He paid a handsome sum for the little idol and returned to his estate with it, where he later sat examining the curious thing.

The statue itself, he was sure, was an image of some kind of devil, and not a protective household god, a Lars. It was not a devil in the tradition of the Judeo-Christian religions, certainly not of the Horned God, which most Christians saw as the image of Satan, but which Ross knew was Cern, the Celtic God of fertility. The horned god was part of ancient agricultural religion and seen as positive in the pre-Christian Celtic mythology, so Ross was reasonably certain that it represented something else. This statue suggested something much older, perhaps Sumerian. He wasn't sure, but he would certainly investigate it thoroughly.

He had no doubt, though, that it was evil. It seemed to exude malevolence, which, of course, he knew was impossible. As fascinated by the occult as he was and with as much time and effort as he had spent investigating it, Ross found no evidence for its reality. True evil was a manifestation of man—Ross was certain of that; the occult was fascinating but not real—human beings and their ways were the true evils of the world. He would argue that point with anyone.

Ross took a large swallow of cognac and picked up the statue. After holding it up before his eyes, and turning it in the light, he began to wonder if he had been mistaken. It now seemed to be quite ordinary. Any trace of Sumerian or Babylonian influence seemed to have vanished. It had been only a trick of the light and his fascination with his find. It was just a statue, and he was happy to own it and to add to his collection. Somewhat disappointed, he sighed, a motion that shook his bulk like the tremors of a small earthquake. *I have studied the dark arts,* he thought, *and this is nothing more than a minor, if interesting, piece of art. I will continue my search for the truly unusual again tomorrow.*

That night Ross had vivid and disturbing dreams: of things that Ross never dreamt: of a man using and debasing men, women and children; of a man committing torture and murder; of that same man looking into Ross' eyes and laughing. The people screamed in fear and pain, as their flesh, ripped and torn, spewed blood everywhere. Ross tried to close his eyes, but he couldn't—he was compelled to see this horror, even as it made him scream and whine in terror.

Maledicus reached out to Ross, who tried to move but couldn't. He was immobile. His entire body felt encased in metal, held in the grip of a giant's steel glove. The man held Ross' head between his two hands and squeezed. Pain coursed through his body. Ross wanted to beg and plead, but his mouth was as immobile and useless as the rest of him. He seemed to have shrunk to a tiny body, crushed in this awful man's grip. He could feel and see his head squeezed like a rotten melon, threatening to burst open. He could only mew in fear.

Ross' eyes opened, and he sat upright in bed. He was breathing in short, shallow gasps, unable to fill his lungs. He was hot, and his head pounded with a pain beyond any headache he had ever experienced. He felt like a giant vise with sharp metal teeth was being shut on his head. Sweat poured down his face. He felt his left arm going numb, and what seemed to be an anvil on his chest. He tried to reach for the cord to summon his butler, but he was unable to move. His eyes bulged almost out of his head as arteries burst in his head and his heart seized with a massive attack.

He was dead as he fell back on his bed.

FOURTEEN

DECEMBER 9

Helen read to Helena every night as she put her to sleep, her regular routine. The child loved books, and as most children, had her favorite stories to hear. Many nights she loved an old book that Helen had from her childhood, *Katie the Kitten*. Helen had adored this book, and she was amazed that she still had an old copy that was not completely worn out.

Recently, Helena had been entranced by the Winnie the Pooh stories. Regardless of what Helen might read to her, the little girl seemed delighted by the nightly ritual.

Helena lay in her bed with her fairy blanket pulled up around her, while Helen sat in a chair next to her. Not only did the little girl love hearing the stories, but this was also one of Helen's most cherished times of the day. She could finally put aside work and other mundane cares and simply focus on being with her beloved niece.

Helen read about Pooh, Tigger, and the other characters from the beloved children's series, and Helena was entranced, her big dark eyes shining in delight.

When Helen finished, Helena, sat up, smiled and said, "One more time, please?"

Helen smiled and relented. "Okay, honey. But just once more, and then it's sleepy time for you. Now lay back down first, and let's get you completely tucked in."

She helped the little girl slide back down in her bed and pulled the blankets up to her chin. "There. Now you'll stay warm and comfy all night."

She read softly and in a few minutes, watched as the little girl closed her eyes and fell asleep. Helen reached over and turned out the little lamp next to her bed. She left on only the night light by the floor, so the child would not be in total darkness.

Then Helen went to the kitchen, prepared a cup of Earl Grey tea with lemon, and into her living room and sat in her favorite reading chair. This time was for her alone now.

Normally she would read a book of history, but today she was enjoying one of her favorite mysteries, what she considered her desert reading. Work had been stressful, and she just needed some time to relax.

About a half hour into her reading, a sound made her look up. Her emergency hearing was as well-tuned with Helena as if she had given birth to the child. She put her book aside on the side table and stood, just as the little girl came walking into the room, holding her worn green blanket and sobbing.

The girl ran to her, and she knelt down and scooped her up. She sat and held her as the child cried.

"Shhhhhh. It's ok. I'm here. Nothing can hurt you." She spoke softly to the child and held her close.

"But the bad man, Aunt Helen. He scares me."

Helen felt her body go frozen. Was someone in the house? It didn't seem possible. Not wanting to let her niece alone, she rose and went into the room. But there was no one there. Helen checked carefully and tried to reassure the girl that no one was there. She did see though that several items had been moved, including the book where she had put it before turning the light out. Perhaps Helena had done that, but it seemed unlikely.

After sitting with Helena and making sure she fell back asleep, Helen decided it was time for her to go to sleep. When she returned to the room, she saw her book on the floor, and she was sure she had placed it on the small table. Something just wasn't right here. She had to admit…she felt something also. She was frightened. She didn't know why and she didn't like this feeling.

Not at all.

FIFTEEN

DECEMBER 10

Jeremy had contacted Ms. Murray earlier by telephone and arranged for the IPS to conduct an initial investigation that weekend. Ms. Murray would meet them on Friday afternoon at her home, and she and her niece would spend the night at a local motel. Jeremy promised her the IPS was insured against any damages and they would only be in her house for one night for the preliminary investigation. He also tried to calm her fears; he assured Ms. Murray they would do everything they could to help.

Arriving before the others, Jeremy spoke with Helen. "We'll set up our equipment after we have met with you. We'll stay until you return in the morning. After we complete our investigation, it'll take a few days for us to examine the recordings and such for potential evidence. We'll then contact you and meet about our initial findings." He looked at the woman, who despite being quite formidable, was showing obvious signs of stress and worry. Her eyes were marked by dark circles, and she held her mouth in a tight line. Jeremy was worried about her. "Is that ok, Ms. Murray?"

"Yes, it is." She looked at him and gave a hopeful smile. "And I thank you very much. We're both frightened and getting more afraid every day, but my niece is especially scared. I hope you can find what is going on and have an idea of what we can do about it. I need answers, and I need this to stop."

Jeremy looked at her. "Did something else happen?"

"Yes, Helena mentioned a bad man who was in her room. Now, I monitor carefully everything she sees on television, and there was no reason for such a thing to have occurred to her. I felt something. I know I sound ridiculous, but I did, so I decided to contact you."

Jeremy nodded. He understood the fears of someone who was bullied or

77

intimidated, and he hated that feeling. He looked down at the walking stick he was carrying and immediately thought of David.

Jeremy and David had been in their antique store one evening early in their time together after having moved to Bethberg. They had gone from the relative comfort of New York City where it was possible in those days to live ordinary lives without much concern for how anyone viewed their homosexuality to the small city of Bethberg, where such ease of living was not always possible. It had been the 1980s and not yet a more open and accepting time.

Jeremy, with his mouth agape, had been staring at David.

The older man laughed the deep belly laugh that Jeremy had come to cherish in his soul mate. "I think that I may have shocked you, dear boy."

"Uh....yeah...you could certainly say that." Jeremy sat down in a desk chair and looked at what David was holding.

"Well, at least, I think you are now sufficiently recovered from your surprise to look at me more normally."

"But you never said that you...."

"That I am a collector of weapons, an old queer like me, would have such things around?" He smiled and held up the pearl-handled 1880 Remington double-barreled derringer. The little steel gun engraved throughout, shone as if it were brand new.

"Not only redneck backwoodsmen and so-called real men keep weapons my dear boy. This particular piece is an absolute thing of beauty—a true work of art. It is a shame that too many people see these pieces as merely tools of violence."

Jeremy began to interrupt, but David held up his palm, halting him.

"Yes, I do know that it is a weapon, and that is its primary purpose. It is a very effective way of dealing with one's enemies, but most useful, of course, at very close range. Hence that is why it was a favorite tool for gamblers."

"Do you have enemies?" Jeremy sounded almost like a little boy when he asked the question.

David smiled a crooked, tight grin, the one that suggested he knew more than anyone else, and which often irritated Jeremy. *Here comes the lesson,* Jeremy thought and kept quiet. It was better to let David have his say than to create an argument.

"Jeremy, unless you are a saint, and perhaps even then, everyone has enemies. I am definitely not a saint – are you?"

"You know I'm not, especially after last night." Jeremy grinned.

"True, dear boy, true. You're definitely not a saint, and I'm so grateful for that. But, my love, you are too trusting, and there are many who would hurt either of us simply for who we are."

"We should be safe here. No one has bothered us, and we have many friends."

"That's true, but it's still always a risk. Believe me on that point. And you do trust too easily."

David saw the hurt look in Jeremy's eyes. At times like this, Jeremy seemed even younger than he actually was. "Now trusting can often be a marvelous thing. If you were a cynic, we would not be together, but, my love, you also need to realize that there are very dangerous people out there. It does seem to be safe in this pretty little town of yours."

"Of ours!" David saw tears begin to form in Jeremy's eyes.

"Of ours. . . of ours, Jeremy. I only say that because I will always consider myself first to be a New Yorker. But even if it seems to be safe here, I will never let my guard down, never again. I refuse to let anyone hurt you or me. I will not let that happen again."

"Again?" Jeremy got up and walked over to David.

"Let me have some of that excellent Scotch that Sarah and Roosevelt gave to us as a house-warming gift, and then I'll tell you." David reached into a teak liquor cabinet and removed a bottle of 25-year-old Macallan. He poured a healthy drink neat, into a fine Wexford crystal whiskey glasses. "I hope a time comes when we don't have to conceal in any way what we are and how we love, or have to disguise ourselves as 'confirmed bachelors.' But, unfortunately, today, we do.

"I have always loved traveling, Jeremy. I began my adventures as a young man out of college. I had inherited a not inconsiderable sum from my grandfather, so I had the luxury of being able to see the world without having to worry about a career."

"It must've been wonderful."

"It certainly was. I was able to conduct a world tour, the kind of thing that was then in vogue, especially for artistic young men. Well, I enjoyed myself enormously. I will spare you some of the details Jeremy, because I don't want to cause you any jealously, but let's say I was young, fit, attractive and very horny." David laughed that deep laugh.

"It was when I explored the good old U.S.A. that I ran into problems. Have you ever wondered, my dear boy, where my crooked nose came from? I wasn't born with this." David pointed at the severe bend in his nose. "It used to be perfectly straight. And these scars by my eyes, they did not come from boxing.

"I was in the West, magnificent country, beautiful beyond my ability to describe. The people, on the whole, were friendly and welcoming. But not all.

No, not all. One night I was in a bar in a small town in Montana, and I had had a little too much to drink. I saw a cowboy, and he was just a magnificent specimen, and I knew he was gay. I could see it in his eyes.

"As we were leaving the bar, a few other cowboys decided to have some fun. They confronted us outside. My new friend turned on me, called me, "a queer boy" and said I was hitting on him. The truth is that I was, but he also wanted the same, only now he was too frightened to go along. So he turned on me."

Jeremy swallowed a gulp of tea.

"You know that I am a capable fighter. I was a boxer in college, but it was five against one, and I took two of them, knocked them out, but the others got in their licks. They certainly did." David finished his whiskey and poured more. "Hence the way my face is now."

"I love your face, David."

"Thank you, my love, but I wish you could have seen me before. Anyway, they beat me unconscious, broke my arms, stole my money and left me for dead on a side road on the way out of town. I suppose I was lucky that they didn't simply kill me. I have often wondered why they didn't. Luckily a local rancher found me and took me to a hospital. I did recover, but I learned a lesson about trusting too easily and always having a weapon with me. That is why I always, without fail, at least take my walking stick with me."

Jeremy gaped again. "I thought it was because of your limp."

David laughed. "No, Jeremy, I can walk just fine without it. That limp is simply from arthritis. But look at it." He picked it up and tossed it to Jeremy. The stick was heavy, made from oak and had a silver handle, formed into the shape of a wolf.

"I always thought you had this because you love the old Universal horror movies, particularly *The Wolfman*."

"Well, that does make it interesting. It's very much like the one that Claude Rains used to kill the Werewolf at the end of that movie, but that isn't why. It's heavy, solid, and a formidable weapon. Do you see the dent on the back of the wolf's head?"

Jeremy examined it and nodded.

"Two very big, very stupid, and very aggressive idiots try to attack me several years before we met. This time, however, because I was prepared, it was they and not me who had to go to the hospital. I loathe stupidity, and I detest bullies. And I will never let us be attacked or hurt."

SIXTEEN

DECEMBER 10

Since David's death, Jeremy had taken to carrying the walking stick with him, as a constant physical connection with his partner.

He held the stick tightly in his hands and looked into Helen's eyes. This haunting seemed to be another kind of bully, and it wouldn't be allowed to continue.

"Ms. Murray, we will do anything we can. We will not stop until this is taken care of."

"Thank you again. I hope you find some answers."

Jeremy thought, *so do I Ms. Murray. So do I.*

Within a half-hour of this conversation, the entire team had arrived and had finished setting up their equipment: digital cameras had been placed in several of the rooms in the house along with digital voice recorders. The individual investigators also carried audio recorders and mini-digital cameras with them, as well as an assortment of other paranormal investigative equipment: special thermometers, electromagnetic field gauges, a thermal camera and a full spectrum still camera. They would try to capture anything they could on still photographs as well as digital video recordings and in EVPs, or electronic voice phenomena: voices that were recorded that they might not have been able to hear with their own ears. Samuel, Roosevelt, and Ralph, the owner of the Bethberg Diner and who occasionally assisted them on investigations, were moving throughout the house while Jeremy manned the central control area: a large folding table that had several computers and monitors placed on it so that the entire operation could be watched. Jeremy, as the electronics specialist, was the natural choice to spend most of the time at the control area. All the investigators stayed in contact with small walkie-talkies.

Paranormal investigation groups tended to fall into two distinct types—those who used psychics and mediums and relied heavily on feelings and those that preferred a scientific approach. The IPS fell between the two categories, but as Roosevelt said, "We are doing this to ask questions about life and death, to learn answers, and to help others—their motto in Latin was 'Comperio et Adservio' (to learn and to aid), when needed, we will utilize any tool or resource that we deem useful. And that includes mediums, psychics, and priests." Whatever direction a specific investigation might take during its course, the IPS always wanted to begin with a scientific approach.

They placed the control table in the small foyer of the house, where Ralph was sitting. He was new to the group, so he was, for the moment, operating under Jeremy's watchful eyes while Samuel and Roosevelt went throughout the house.

Roosevelt and Sam were in the little girl's room—painted bright green and decorated with unicorns, garden fairies, cuddly forest animals, and rainbows—a bright testament to a cheerful, happy child. That something was scaring the little girl deeply concerned the group.

"Is anyone here with us?" Roosevelt asked and then waited for an answer his machine might record and found later when they reviewed their potential evidence. By its very nature, an EVP meant a digital documentation of a voice or a sound that existed out of ordinary human perception, nevertheless, captured by their equipment. To Roosevelt, an EVP was usually the most compelling evidence that they acquired. He distrusted the potential for human error and manipulation that was possible with photography. He trusted Jeremy and Sam implicitly, but he still preferred the audio recordings as the best evidence of paranormal activity.

"Do you wish to communicate with us?"

The two men stood diagonally from each other, Sam by the head of the girl's bed, and Roosevelt near the door to the hallway.

"You know, something is scaring this little girl. Is that you? 'Cause I don't like anyone that scares or bothers kids." Sam paused for effect as if he were questioning a criminal. "You got me on that? 'Cause if you're trying to scare this kid, we're going remove your ass from this house. Bank on it, pal."

Roosevelt looked at his friend and saw the visage of the cop who he had been: interrogating a suspect he thought had harmed a child. Roosevelt knew that Samuel would stop at nothing to protect a child.

Roosevelt continued, "If you are not here to bother the little girl, then tell us who you are. But I do have to add that my friend and I do not accept the frightening of children, so if that is what you are trying to do, you will have to deal with us. Do you understand?"

The two men stayed in the bedroom for about an hour, trying to communicate but with no apparent results. They had already covered Ms. Murray's bedroom, so the only place left on this floor was the office.

"We've covered this room pretty well. There's one more room up here. Do you want to get Ralph involved more?"

"That is an excellent idea, Samuel. I suggest that you go to the living room and do a session with Ralph, and I will cover the office."

"You sure you're okay up here alone?"

"Yes, my dear Samuel, I am fine. If anything happens, I will let you know, and I am sure that you can be here in a moment to help me."

Sam smiled. "You got it, Rosy."

A few minutes later, Sam was sitting with Ralph in the living room of the modest Cape Cod home. Sam was relaxing in a recliner that had seen better days, and Ralph sat diagonally across from him on the end of a long, comfortable sofa. Everything about the room suggested a warm, cozy place, designed for living and comfort rather than ostentation and display.

This was the central room in the house, where Ms. Murray made a happy place for her niece and herself. Scattered about the room were numerous stuffed animals and toys; Ms. Murray was obviously not a stickler for making sure everything was always put away. Many bookshelves hugged the room, and books ranging from colorful children's books to heavy historical tomes filled the shelves. A vase of flowers sat in the middle of the old wood coffee table, itself marked by time with scratches, scars, and the marks of heavy use by children. All in all, to Sam, this was a happy room or it should have been.

"Is anyone here with us?" This was the question they used to begin an EVP session. "Do you want to talk to us?"

Sam looked over at Ralph, who was sitting stiffly, obviously nervous. "You ok, Ralph?"

Ralph was a big man, well over six feet tall and with a quite a bit of weight on his frame. Normally a very cheerful fellow, his customers at the diner loved to talk with him and hear his stories. Now he was subdued.

"This ain't what I thought it would be," he said softly.

"That's because you're new at this. It gets easier as you get more experience."

Ralph looked uncertain if he should believe Sam. "C'mon, it had to be easy for you. I mean, you're a cop…a detective. You must've done, I dunno, hundreds of stakeouts."

"Yeah, I did. And it's similar in a way. You always spend a lot of time simply waiting and observing. It can seem boring, but it ain't. But what we do is different from police stakeouts. In all my work as a cop, I never went looking for anyone who was dead, only for those who made people dead. This…can take some getting used to. And remember, it ain't like we got a lot of experience doing this ourselves, but we're here. Anyway, give it a try. Ask something."

"Like what?"

"Anything that comes to mind. Man, in the diner, you can't stop talking. Here you seem like a shy teenager asking a girl to the prom."

"All right, all right." Ralph blushed. He was embarrassed at his nervousness. "So, like Sam asked, is anyone here with us?"

Sam was about to say something when he stopped and held up one finger to Ralph, signaling him to be quiet. "Did you hear that?"

"What? I didn't hear…"

"There, I knew I heard something. I heard it again." Sam listened intently. While his eyesight had been deteriorating with age, his hearing had remained acute. He would have sworn that he had heard a very soft sound, almost like a sigh or a whisper.

"Is that you? Are you trying to talk to us? If you are, speak up."

They heard nothing.

Sam spoke into his walkie-talkie. "Rosy, you talking at all?"

"Samuel, no I am not. I have been sitting and observing. This house is small, and I did not want to contaminate your EVP session. Did you hear something?"

"Yeah, I think so, but it's stopped now."

"Jerry, did you hear that buddy?"

"Sam, I didn't hear anything. But maybe the equipment picked up what you heard."

"Right."

"Samuel, I will begin a session up here, but let me know if you do hear anything else. We can certainly coordinate our efforts."

"That's fine, Rosy. We'll be quiet."

"Thank you, Samuel." Roosevelt put his walkie-talkie back in his coat pocket and looked around at the office in which he was sitting. Like the other rooms in this house, it was small, but it was crammed with items: standard office equipment on an old wooden desk, simple but strong, one that Roosevelt admired for its inherent quality. Ms. Murray's computer, printer, and monitor sat on it, along with various papers; she was obviously working on an academic project. Several books were stacked, not neatly, on the side of the desk and framed pictures of her niece and of a young couple, who

Roosevelt assumed were her deceased sister and brother-in-law, sat on the other side of the desk.

The room's walls were lined with bookshelves from floor to ceiling filled to over-flowing with volumes of well-read books. These were not for display to impress anyone. Roosevelt was deeply impressed, both with her attitude towards books and with her selections. As an historian, Roosevelt saw that her choices also reflected a serious interest in her studies. She had a wide assortment ranging from prehistory to the 20th Century the apparent focus of her studies was on Ancient Rome and mysticism. *Interesting*, he thought. *Typically, mysticism would be an interest for someone who was a student of the Renaissance, but she obviously found connections with the Era of the Roman Empire.* He scanned some of the titles: Gibbon's *The Decline and Fall of the Roman Empire*, Plutarch's *Lives*, Cornell's *The Beginnings of Rome*, Heather's *The Fall of the Roman Empire*, Suetonius' *Lives*, Livy's *The Early History of Rome*, Saint Augustine's *The Confessions*, Dio Cassius' *Roman History*, Le Glay's *A History of Rome*. Roosevelt smiled. *Ms. Murray was certainly a serious student.* He looked at some others: Fowler's *The Religious Experience of the Roman People*, Cumont's *Mysteries of Mithra*, Clauss' *The Roman Cult of Mithras: The God and His Mysteries*, Schafer and Kippenberg's *Envisioning Magic: A Princeton Seminar and Symposium*. Roosevelt raised his left eyebrow – Ms. Murray could have been a professor if she had chosen. Her reading certainly suggested a deeply serious, studious nature.

It was not only books and journals that filled her shelves, but also assorted small statues and coins, memorabilia, and photographs from her archeological journeys during her summers off from teaching high school, and small paintings adorned the tiny room. The room had the feel of a Victorian cabinet of curiosities. Certainly this was her sanctum sanctorum, her place of study, where she could be herself completely.

Roosevelt pulled out the desk chair and sat. "EVP session…Roosevelt in the office. Is anyone here with me?"

He gave time for any unheard answer to be recorded.

"Is there more than one entity here?"

He walked around the small room so that he would give anything that might be there a chance to respond from a different location, in case it might favor a particular part of the room. Plus, his knees and shoulders were aching, perhaps warning, as they often did these days, of an oncoming storm. He felt better if he moved around.

"Ms. Murray and her niece are very good and sweet people. I wonder why anyone would want to bother them or frighten them. Are you aware that you are scaring them, that you are causing the little girl distress?"

Roosevelt glanced at the books again and considered a possibility.

"If there is someone here, and you are frightening them by mistake, then perhaps we can help you. Perhaps you are unaware of the effect you are having. Are you trying to ask for help? Do you want to move on?"

Roosevelt felt the air near him go cold. He took out his thermometer and saw the temperature had dropped by a full ten degrees. He placed the thermometer on the desk, directly in the line of the digital video recorder so its readings, would be captured and verified by the camera.

"Is someone here now?" It was a theory in the community of paranormal investigators that when a cold spot appeared, an entity of some sort might be present and potentially manifesting itself, and that the cold resulted in the being drawing heat to itself for energy. This theory, like so many in the field, was unproven, but it provided a workable paradigm, especially for serious investigators. Since there was so little in the way of scientific guidelines by which to function, they had to make use of whatever seemed to be sound theories about how to proceed. They realized they might be creating new ideas for science in their investigations by the way they performed their inquiries.

"If you have something to say, then this is your opportunity." Roosevelt felt movement, a slight feeling like a gentle breeze blowing during a warm spring morning. He sat in the desk chair and waited.

"As I said, if you need help, we can try to assist you. However, and I want to be very clear in this, if you mean harm to Ms. Murray and her niece, we will do everything we can to remove you from this home. Do you understand? We do not tolerate intentionally frightening innocent people."

Roosevelt thought he heard something, but he was unsure. His hearing had recently begun to deteriorate, and even with his hearing aids, he had still lost some aural capacity.

As he prepared to stand, he smelled something odd and disturbing. He reached for his walkie-talkie. "Samuel, can you come up to the office for a moment?"

"Sure Rosy, is everything ok?

"Yes, I am fine. Please come up."

A little while later, Sam entered the room and looked at Roosevelt, who held a finger up to him to be quiet. Then… "Samuel, am I imagining it?"

Sam shook his head no. Roosevelt and Sam had served together in combat as Marines during the Vietnam War, and in one of the most intense battles, they had fought a seemingly unending army of V.C. soldiers. During the battle, American planes had released napalm onto the V.C., creating a conflagration of burning human and vegetation. The smell of napalm combined with smoldering flesh and trees was something they would never forget. As Samuel and Roosevelt stood silently in the small office, the two men both detected a hint of that terrible smell in the room, much like a distant whiff of the horror of the Vietnam War.

"Shit. That can't be, Rosy. It ain't possible."

"I know, Samuel, but I do smell it."

"Son of a bitch."

Then, as quickly as it came, the scent departed. It was gone.

"That was…ah…certainly unusual, Samuel."

"Yeah, it was, man. I don't know what the hell that was, but I don't like it."

"Samuel, I think we have done what we can for this evening. Let us turn on the lights and gather our equipment. We will talk to Ms. Murray and let her know we have to evaluate our evidence and then discuss the next step."

"Sounds good to me."

They reconvened at the control table.

"Hey guys, any luck?" Jeremy added.

"We are not sure. There were a few possibilities, but we will have to see with the evidence. Did you see anything on the monitors?"

"Nada, guys. It was as slow as could be."

"Well," Sam said. "Maybe if there is anything here, it just didn't like us or didn't want to come out and play with us."

"True," Roosevelt added. "It would not be the first time that spirits have not shown on cue. Unfortunately, we cannot schedule their appearances."

"Yeah, Rosy, but I think that we can still do a little more until we decide our next step."

"What do you have in mind?"

"Let's leave a couple of cameras and voice recorders here. Maybe we can catch something?"

"Jeremy, the equipment is your domain. What do you think?"

"I like Ms. Murray, but I don't have the inherent trust in people that you do Roosevelt. This stuff is expensive."

"I think it is for the best, Jeremy."

"Jerry, shit, it's just money." Sam laughed. "Let's fucking do it. Maybe we'll catch something."

Jeremy sighed. "Ok."

SEVENTEEN

JANUARY 1968

"**M**ove! Move! Move!" Lieutenant Roosevelt Franklin screamed at his men and pointed at the ridge above them they were supposed to occupy and hold from the advancing Viet Cong troops. It was a narrow strip, along one edge of the mountains leading up to higher mountains. They were stationed at the base at Khe Sanh, fighting to hold this position against an attacking force of V. C, which itself was part of a much larger military thrust known as the Tet Offensive.

The Tet Offensive, started on January 31st, was a massive attempt by the North Vietnamese to regain control of the area known as South Vietnam. The Communist government of North Vietnam had ordered a near country-wide attack on the south. To the soldiers based at Khe Sanh, near the border separating the two countries, the battle was not smoldering embers but one of raging flames.

Roosevelt and his men scrambled to get to the protective ridge so they could find some semblance of cover from enemy fire, seemingly coming out of the surrounding mountains and trees. Already, during this fighting on this day, several of Franklin's men, all of whom were from Eagle Company of the 3rd Marine Division, had been killed.

Franklin, a newly minted second Lieutenant, was brave, but also lucky to have one Sergeant Wallace in his unit, a battle hardened soldier who had served in the Battle for the Chosin Reservoir during the Korean War. Roosevelt was grateful to have such a man with him and was not shy about asking his opinion on what to do. Roosevelt had enlisted in the Marine Corps after completing his undergraduate college education, much to the dismay and disbelief of his family. "Fighting in this war is for others to do, the minions of the world, the people who will serve you, not for you. You belong to the movers of society not the scum who have to fight its battles," they had told him. Despite his youth and facing the wrath of his family's formidable patriarchs, Roosevelt's innate sense of decency and fairness gave him the courage to oppose his family and to enlist in the Marine Corps.

He saw it was entirely unethical that someone, who came from wealth and privilege, should be able to avoid serving when those young men who came from the inner city or the country had no choice when they were drafted but to serve or go to prison. Roosevelt knew with his family's connections, he could avoid the draft, by entry into the National Guard, the wealthy man's draft dodge. He knew it was a safe way to look like his was doing the honorable thing. But Roosevelt despised the sense of entitlement his family embraced, and he was guided by the actions of his hero Theodore Roosevelt. He did not agree with the reasons for the Vietnam War, but he would not capitalize on his ability to avoid service. If other young men had to go, then he would also.

After announcing his decision to his distraught family, and particularly enjoying the purple face of his father as he nearly choked on his foie gras as he heard his son's choice, Roosevelt went to see a Marine Corps recruitment office and signed up. After boot camp, the Corps had another newly coined Second Lieutenant, one of the positions in battle in Vietnam considered most likely to be killed quickly. Typically, these ROTC soldiers came to the war expecting to find it as it was taught in their classes, and many died quickly as they learned that the reality of fighting was vastly different from its theory.

Roosevelt, though, had no desire to die needlessly out of ignorance; he had no intention to simply be another statistic, to be counted among the American dead. So, he watched, listened, and acted on whatever useful information he managed to gather. He understood he was not ready to lead his soldiers, so he had to learn what to do as quickly as he could and to depend on those around him who did. He soon realized that his unit's courage and battlefield knowledge was exemplary.

"Over there—follow me," yelled the sergeant, and scrambled up to the ridge. This battle was unusual. Typically, the soldiers would branch out into small units, for search and destroy missions. Yet, the entire camp was under attack, so this resembled a traditional battlefield action. They were able to make their way to a small abutment that served as a natural shield. On the other side of the hill dropped down into a small valley bordered by a mass of trees and a rising mountain. This backdrop served as an ideal place for the enemy to use for hiding, sniping, and a concealed place from which they could launch attacks. It did have a severe disadvantage for the V.C. From their location at the top of the ridge, Roosevelt's men were able to dig in and fight with the small advantage of shooting downwards at the approaching enemy.

Roosevelt's men, tired from their previous search and destroy mission, were exhausted. They had been in the field for two weeks and had just returned to camp before the attack had begun. They were exhausted and filthy. Each man felt as if he were carrying the load of the world on his shoulders. Each marine had carried at least sixty pounds of gear, with a variety of equipment: an M-14 rifle, a pistol, several grenades, a backpack, sleeping roll, canteen, pot, and rations, rounds of ammunition, sanitation supplies, shovels, and other assorted gear. Some also had mortar launchers, mortar shells and tubes, bazookas, binoculars, radio equipment, and maps. Some had personal items such as books, souvenirs from combat – often grisly like an ear cut off dead Charley – and some had reminders from home, letters and pictures. Some had good luck charms.

The soldiers felt that they were trapped in a sauna. The temperature was 90 degrees, with near 100 percent humidity. Even though it should have been colder this time of year, the weather itself seemed to be against the American and South Vietnamese troops. Roosevelt's men had barely had time to return to camp before the Tet Offensive had begun. Roosevelt's mission had been a success—they had found and eliminated a small group of V.C. who had been operating very efficiently as snipers. The Americans managed to return with only a few wounds, no fatalities, and drained of energy, soaked in grime and sweat and in deep need of rest. All they wanted was to shower and sleep.

Instead, they had to fight almost immediately.

The alarm sounded as soon as the sentries realized they were under attack. The flares of incoming missiles and mortar fire lit the dark sky. Soon the ground shook as explosions raked the immediate area. Roosevelt gathered his men, and a Major came to him and ordered him to defend the upper ridge. Roosevelt felt adrenalin flow through his body, filling him with energy. Despite his exhaustion, he felt wired and ready to fight again.

When the battle began, it seemed to have been in several places at once. Communication had broken down quickly, so very few units knew what the others were doing. They only knew that they were under fire.

"Guess we're not going to get any R and R," Roosevelt said to his sergeant.

Wallace looked at him and growled, "Fucking Gooks. C'mon, Franklin – get up there and keep your fucking head down!"

Roosevelt's men quickly moved to the ridge and took cover. Roosevelt thought going out there was probably a stupid idea, but it was a direct order.

If the enemy launching the mortar barrage knew they were on the edge of the ridge, his men would have been an easy target. But they stared at the shells flying over them. They then watched as what seemed like a horde of V.C. came quietly out of the darkness of the jungle at the edge of the mountain.

Roosevelt's men set up positions and began shooting. One of his men had an automatic machine gun scattering fire down on the advancing V.C. At the open of the firefight, the Marines had the distinct advantage, shooting downhill on their enemy. The enemy seemed to keep coming.

Roosevelt's unit was holding the ridge against the onslaught. The machine gun that had been set up to Roosevelt's right at about ten yards was cutting through the advancing troops like a scythe through hay. Only in this field, the hay seemed to regenerate as quickly as it was mowed down. The V.C. soldiers seemed to spring quickly out of the earth fertilized by the blood of their fallen comrades.

Immediately to his left and right were privates, Sam Sadlowski and George Bruno, men who would become two of Roosevelt's closest friends throughout his life. They were in crouching positions behind the ridge and shooting down on the enemy. His other men stretched out along the ridge, almost like a row of archers defending an enemy castle from a siege of a foreign army. Except, these were not rocks and arrows sent against them, but the deadly fire of the V.C. and the grenades they tossed up the hill.

One of the grenades detonated to Roosevelt's right, not close enough to harm him, but enough to cause some hearing damage. He looked over and saw the marine who had been manning the machine gun was dead. Bruno also saw this and slithered over to the weapon quickly. With another soldier feeding the ammunition, Bruno opened fire.

"C'mon, you fuckers! C'mon, you pieces of shit! Eat this, motherfuckers!" If it hadn't been for the battle, Roosevelt would have been shocked at the outburst, because Bruno was one of the most proper soldiers he had ever met. He rarely, if ever, swore, but now, caught up in the battle, he felt like an ancient Roman soldier fighting for the glory of the Empire.

The Marines were doing a good job of holding their own, easily killing many more of the enemy than taking casualties themselves. But they were losing men, and they were beginning to run out of ammunition.

"Do not just shoot at anything," Roosevelt yelled. "Make every bullet count."

Sam, normally, a loquacious and jovial man, was quiet and hypervigilant as he squeezed off round after round from his rifle, bringing down an enemy soldier with nearly every shot.

Roosevelt saw Wallace ranging along the edge of the ridge, checking on the soldiers. As he moved back towards Roosevelt, a bullet caught him in the head and spun him around like a doll. Wallace collapsed. Roosevelt began to rise to go to the dead man, but Sadlowski grabbed him and pulled him to the ground. "Stay here, Sir! Unless you want to die even faster than we all probably will." Roosevelt stared at the private.

"Sir!" Sadlowski added, and Roosevelt let out a short burst of laughter.

Roosevelt before had been complaining silently to himself about the heat, but now he had forgotten about it. He ignored the sweat pouring down his neck and back and the jungle rot he could feel spreading in his boots, but it would be better to feel that than to be dead. He grabbed a grenade, pulled the pin, and then tossed it.

For a short time, the enemy had stopped advancing. The mortars the Marines had set up and were firing seemed to have a substantial effect on the V.C. soldiers. An almost eerie silence held the air for about 30 minutes, and Roosevelt and his men continued to watch, alert and focused.

Then they saw another group of enemy begin to move up the hill towards them.

"Jesus Christ," Sam said. "Look at them." He added softly, "They don't end, the fuckers just keep coming."

It was true. Another wave of the enemy emerged from the forest.

Both sides resumed firing. A grenade killed two marines to Roosevelt's left, and the power of the enemy assault was more intense this time. Even more V.C. seemed to be coming their way. But the Marines held their ground.

Roosevelt looked at the advancing enemy and was terrified. He wished the sergeant were still alive. Jesus Christ, how much was he supposed to do?

"Semper Fi, you sons of bitches!" Sadlowski yelled, and threw a grenade down the hill. The remaining Marines on the hill fought quietly and intensely. With the level of the Marines' fire, the V.C.'s advance was slowed, but it wasn't stopped.

"Rosy, listen. Do you hear that?" Sam looked over at Roosevelt. He was the first to hear the sound of planes approaching. Soon the enemy heard it also. The pilots had been radioed the placement of the enemy troops, and they moved in and barraged them with gunfire and bombs. Even though the bombs were exploding on the other side of the ridge, the ground shook like a volcano was exploding under their feet.

The planes were dropping both bombs and napalm on the enemy. As the napalm hit the ground and the V.C., it seemed to explode into a living, pulsing inferno. The sickly sweet smell filled the air with noxious fumes, imbuing itself into Roosevelt's and the rest of his men's memories for the rest of their lives. They listened with horror to the screams of the wounded and dying enemy.

When the planes left, the initial wave of enemy troops was reduced to about ¼ of their previous strength. Soon, the Marine fire dispersed them, and they successfully held their ridge, at least for that day. But the battle for Khe Sanh would continue for many months. Roosevelt, Sam, and Bruno would survive this battle and the Vietnam War, but they would never forget it.

EIGHTEEN

DECEMBER 12

When the IPS reviewed the potential evidence amassed during an investigation, even in just one night, it was a long and tedious task. This meant sitting together at folding tables with monitors, cameras, and recorders and carefully and painstakingly going over the entirety of what they had recorded. Since they had so many cameras and recorders activated for the entirety of their time at the Murray residence and for a time after they left, they had over 35 hours of material to examine. They understood the extreme importance of focused and dedicated coverage, and made no assumptions that any recording could be skipped or merely glanced at because they never knew where a potential piece of interesting or pertinent evidence might be found. It was possible after viewing three hours of a digital recording in which nothing happened, that a two-second segment might show the appearance of an entity of some sort or might also offer proof that nothing paranormal was occurring. Yet without diligent and excruciatingly painstaking inspection, they could not be sure that they had made the best use of their evidence.

Two days after the initial investigation of the Murray residence, Roosevelt, Jeremy and Sam gathered at Jeremy's home to go over everything they had amassed. They had agreed to spend the day between the investigation and the evidence review resting. Since they had been in the Murray house until almost dawn, they needed to rest as much as possible, because the task they faced was daunting and likely to be exhausting. Both Roosevelt and Jeremy had been anxious to jump immediately into looking at the evidence, but Sam's experience with the effort involved in stakeouts won out.

"Look fellows, I want to know as much as you do what's going on, but I gotta tell you—I'm beat. I know if I don't get some serious sleep, I won't be worth a good God-damn in looking over our stuff. And you know it too, you won't be either"

"Samuel, I will admit that you are correct."

"Rosy, really? That easy? Man, mark this day down as a victory for Sammie!" He gave his deep belly laugh.

So when they did meet, they were now refreshed and ready to go. They would take turns making food runs and commit to a long job ahead of them.

Since they had over eight hours of recordings on each piece of equipment, it would take at least two days to cover everything. They started in the morning, worked for two hours, took a small break for coffee or tea or food, and then returned to the table for more examination. Each tape, each recording, each photograph, or video recording was analyzed and noted.

"Record keeping, man, it's essential to be thorough. It can make or break a case." Sam had been referring to his time as a detective and how important all evidence was recorded, because any discrepancy in evidence could change the course of a trial. "You never wanted some scumbag to go free because you screwed up the evidence chain. I've seen it happen too many times."

"Well, at least we don't have to worry about any incompetent or corrupt attorneys affecting our investigation, Samuel," Jeremy added.

"You got that right."

Whenever they did think that they found something that might be significant, they always noted from what source and when, and then they had the others check it immediately. They agreed that if at least two of them did not concur that a find was significant, they would discount it.

They didn't discover anything of interest on any of the cameras, still or dvd cameras, but what they found on the digital voice recordings was both interesting and disturbing.

Jeremy had been listening to one of the recordings when his eyes grew large, and he paused it. "Guys, guys. I think I have something here. Listen to this."

He removed his earphones so the others could hear what he had found. "Sam, when you and Ralph were in the living room and you asked if anyone was there, I think you got an answer."

Jeremy hit the play button. They listened to Sam ask the question and pause. Then a sibilant voice seemed to hiss out a slow *"Yessss."*

"Jeremy, play that again, if you would," Roosevelt said.

"Certainly."

He went to it again, and they listened once more. *"Yessss."*

"Shit, that's clear," Sam said.

On the second day of review, they found two more EVPs. Sam was listening to the EVP session that Roosevelt had conducted in Ms. Murray's office when the room had gone cold. "Damn, Rosy, Jerry, you gotta hear this."

They both paused in their reviews and turned to him.

"Man, I gotta tell you both. I've dealt with some of the worst scum of the earth as a cop. People that make you happy you have a gun when you have to face them. I saw one guy, a murderer, with dead eyes—he had the coldest eyes I have ever seen, and a quiet, but fuckin scary voice—and you two know me, not much scares me, but that guy, he makes me shiver just to think of him. I'm tellin' you that because his voice sounded like what we got on this recording. I'm not shittin' you.

"Here it is: when you were in the office Rosy, and you asked who it was." Sam played the EVP recording. First they heard Roosevelt ask, "Who are you?" Then there was a few seconds pause, and a distinct voice spoke, one that suggested quiet menace, *"Maledicus."*

"No way guys, it's so clear, and I don't like it," Jeremy said to them.

Roosevelt visibly shuddered. "Neither do I."

"I can't believe we got something this distinct, guys. That sounds like some kind of name." Jeremy shuddered and then grabbed a coffee cup and took a swallow.

A few hours later, Sam found another EVP. "Yo, listen to this! Damn, damn. This, man, this is something."

Roosevelt quietly said, "Please play it for us, Samuel."

"Man, this is almost crazy, but I'm sure it's the same voice. Rosy, you asked why it would frighten Ms. Murray and the little girl. Listen."

Sam played the recording. They heard Roosevelt ask this question and then a few seconds pause.

Then a response: *"Because I like it."*

They all sat in silence for a while. Then Sam looked at them. "We gotta do something here. This ain't right."

"I agree," said Jeremy.

"Would you both agree that this sounds like an intelligent haunting, that whatever is there has consciousness and motive?" Roosevelt was deeply concerned about Ms. Murray and her niece, as were the other two men.

"Guys, if that really said what we heard, then this thing said that it likes scaring them. It sounds like a bully."

"Jerry, it sounds like more than a bully…it sounds like a fucking twisted freak to me. What do you think Rosy?"

"I would probably not use your colorful language, but otherwise, I agree with you Samuel. I hope it is just some kind of mischievous spirit, but I think not. And we need to eliminate its presence as soon as possible."

"Fuckin' right."

"Yes, we do." Jeremy's face was set in a grim look. He hated bullies and those who preyed on the weak.

Roosevelt finished his coffee and looked at his friends. "We need to bless the house first and then do another night of investigation to see if that worked in ridding Ms. Murray's home of whatever this entity is."

"Is our buddy around?" Sam was referring to their friend from the Vietnam War, then private George Bruno, now Father Bruno.

"Unfortunately, he is not, Samuel. He is out of town on a trip to Rome."

"Rome, wow, Georgie, has really gone up in the world…man, the next thing you know, we'll have to bow before him and call him Your Eminence."

Jeremy laughed.

Roosevelt frowned and added, "He will be back next week, Samuel, and I do not think you have to worry about bowing before him. Yet, I think we need to do something before then. I do know a local gentleman who might be able to help. I will find out."

NINETEEN

DECEMBER 12

Patrick sat in the barely lit room, the only illumination by the small brass banker's lamp with a green shade on the desk. The green tinged light did little to brighten the deep darkness of the room. Patrick's head ached. The pain was like that of an extreme toothache, with a vise that seemed to compress and release on his temples attuned perfectly to his heartbeat, and no medicine did anything to abate the agony. Additionally, he desperately needed to get some real sleep—he hadn't sleep in over 24 hours, but his desire to read what was on the tablet in front of him outweighed his body's needs.

Patrick had again made contact with Michael, and once again, it came at a price. His head felt like a blacksmith were using it for an anvil, and drops of blood slowly feel from his nose.

Patrick had again used the meditation technique to achieve the state of not being and being. To anyone watching, he would have seemed merely to be a man in a deep sleep, one who is troubled by bad dreams and who moved his right arm in a very odd way while he slept, as if he were writing. The observer would have noticed that the sleeping man never looked at the pad on which he was writing erratically. If the observer were astute, he might also have noticed that a very slow nosebleed developed during the course of the "sleep". As Patrick's head lolled to one side, several drops of blood fell from his right nostril onto his desk and pooled there, looking like a spill of red ink.

Several hours later, Patrick slowly emerged from his deep stasis. He opened his eyes into mere slits, recoiling from the dim light of his desk lamp. It seemed as if someone was shining a glaring flashlight into his eyes. He was groggy, and his head hurt badly, pounding to the point that he felt nauseous. Patrick knew that he had not fully achieved the desired meditative state and that he had instead slipped into a kind of trance, some unknown condition. It was in that state that his brother could communicate with him via automatic writing. The physical hand holding the pen and marking the page was Patrick's, but the force behind the writing and the handwriting itself belonged to Michaels.

Patrick shielded his eyes with one hand and reached for his tablet with the other. He began to read . . .

Hello, once again little brother. I am more certain than ever that we both have a part to play in this. There is a growing darkness . . . what had been visible is now murky—but I think we will both soon know

Those were the only words on the page. Patrick dropped the tablet and rested his hand on the desk. He felt something sticky and looked at the small puddle of drying blood. He became aware of the dripping from his nose, and with great effort, he rose from his chair and made his way to his bathroom where he staunched the flow of the blood.

TWENTY

DECEMBER 12

"No! No! Nooooooooooooooooo!"

Helen's eyes opened fully. She was on her feet, out of bed, and running to her niece's bedroom.

As she ran in, she saw the little girl thrashing in bed, moving her arms in front of her as if she were trying to keep some invisible attacker away.

Helen rocketed to her, and began trying to hold her in her arms, but the child kept screaming, hitting and kicking.

"It's me, sweetie. It's Aunt Helen. It's ok. No one can hurt you. I'm here."

The little girl's eyes opened in fear, not seeing her aunt, but staring straight past her at something that wasn't there.

Helen held her arms down gently but securely. She continued to talk to the girl in a very soft and calm voice, all the while, her own heart racing like an antelope chased by a cheetah.

It took a while, but eventually, Helena stopped looking into the distance and through teary eyes, looked at her Aunt Helen. "Aunt Helen?"

"It's me, honey. I'm here. No one can hurt you." Helen gently brushed the girl's tears away and kept looking straight into her eyes.

"The monster was here. The Bad Man again. He wants to hurt me." Helen was chilled by the solemn and calm way the girl said it.

"There's no monster here, honey. I will make sure no one can ever hurt you. But it's still late. Would you like to sleep with me tonight, Helena?"

The child nodded her head up and down, making her unruly mop of brown hair bounce as if it had a life of its own. She threw her arms around Helen's neck and held tight. Helen scooped the child into her arms and carried her to her bedroom, all the time thinking, *this is getting worse.* Helena fell asleep after two hours of soft crying and Helen rocking her in her arms.

TWENTY-ONE

DECEMBER 12

When Roosevelt woke in the morning, he no longer saw his Sarah's eyes first thing, and that absence renewed his grief. She had been dead for four years, but every day, especially in the morning, the pain in his soul was as great as it had been on that terrible day when she died.

Time heals all wounds. What nonsense. What infernal garbage! Roosevelt despised that cliché, no matter how intentioned it was by anyone who tried to comfort him. Roosevelt's wife was gone, and he missed her as much every single day since the time of her death. He knew the pain would never decrease. He would feel her loss keenly as long as he lived. *Part of me is gone. I lost the better part of myself.* He compared the psychic torment of her loss with the phantom pain some amputees feel from their lost limb. Nevertheless, Roosevelt had learned to move forward with life. He was a strong, determined man; after all, he had promised Sarah he would live. *I never break my promises.*

Many who knew him assumed Roosevelt had recovered from his sorrow since he appeared strong and well-adjusted in public. He conversed with those he met, and he was always polite and engaged. They did not know, however, of his continuing grief. Because he was a very private man, he disliked displaying weakness. Roosevelt hated the victim's mentality he had seen creep into the mindset of many Americans. He understood, better than many, how victims of oppression and atrocity existed, but he also believed it was crucial to muster personal strength and to face life directly.

Despite his outward façade, his best friends knew better. Samuel, Jeremy, and Roosevelt all knew the grief that bound them together.

Almost every night, Roosevelt's sleep was filled with dreams, some of which he remembered. Two were the most prevalent.

In one dream, Sarah and he were flying, one of their favorite ways to travel: she loved the exhilaration of the takeoffs and landings, while Roosevelt enjoyed looking at the vistas as they soared like eagles. They flew in a private jet and cruised at 35,000 feet in completely calm air. As they sat and enjoyed the flight, a flight attendant brought them champagne, one of Sarah's favorite beverages.

Roosevelt held the open bottle and poured into two long delicately fluted crystal glasses. He raised his glass and looked into his wife's sparkling eyes, "To my beloved wife, may we be together forever."

Sarah looked into his eyes with her intense gaze, so strong that many flinched from it, and she smiled. Roosevelt adored that powerful look. He felt they were joined when their eyes locked. She said, "To us. Forever."

They clinked glasses and drank.

They set their glasses on a small metal table at an outside café in Paris near the Jar din Luxembourg. It was late spring, and the Paris colors were vibrant; the sky was blue and shimmering in the warmth of the late May day. Roosevelt and Sarah had just visited the Musee D'Orsay, their preferred museum in Paris, and they spoke of their love for the Impressionists. Roosevelt found them to be the most compelling school of painters.

"When I was a teenager, and I had just begun to enjoy looking at paintings, the first school of art that attracted my attention was the Impressionists." This preference remained with him to the present. So many of the other boys at the private academy, the youngsters who considered themselves hip, followed the Abstract Expressionists. They considered Monet, Renoir, and the like to be passé and beneath them in their would-be rebel posing. Roosevelt ignored his peers, thinking them silly. The Impressionists showed a concept of beauty and a stand for idealism, which never left him.

"At first I thought the painters were creating a world more beautiful that it was," Roosevelt said to Sarah, who listened indulgently and patiently to her husband, since she recognized that he had slipped into his professor's mode. "But when I first came to Paris, I realized I had been mistaken in my boyish innocence. They were idealizing nothing. They were painting the world they saw, the beautiful light of Paris."

The couple walked along the banks of the Seine at sunset. They strolled arm in arm, with no one else around. The world was just for them. They stopped and kissed, that kind of kiss that eliminated the existence of the rest of the world.

Then, they woke in the bed of their honeymoon cabin with coffee waiting for them. Their lives were ahead of them, a magnificent canvas, waiting to be painted in beauty.

In another recurring dream, Roosevelt stood alone in McConnell's Funeral Parlor, a place he now detested. He was looking at Sarah in her coffin. The funeral director had done a fine job in preparing her for the viewing; he had restored the color she had lost to her face, and the wasting from the disease appeared to be gone. She was dressed in a simple, white gown, with a wedding photograph placed in her hands.

Many bouquets of flowers and cards, filling the calling room with expressions of grief and love, showing how many people had cared for her. There were photographs of her life, on stands, each on either side of the casket. Images of Sarah as a gap toothed child grinning into a camera. One of her siblings' and Sarah were playing with an adored golden retriever; a gangly young teenager in a cheerleading outfit; her high school graduation portrait; as a young intern hard at work in a hospital; with her elderly parents; with the children she taught at the Boys' and Girls' clubs; and many with Roosevelt. He treasured all the images.

Roosevelt looked at his wife, reached out, gently took one of her hands in his. He leaned over and kissed her softly, and his tears fell on her face.

Her eyes opened, full or love and worry. Always, it was Sarah who was most concerned for everyone else. She was the nurturer. She spoke with a quiet voice. "Roosevelt, how are you, my husband?"

"Sarah, I cannot let you go. Please, do not die."

"You know I am already gone, my love. I can't do anything about it, but you must listen to me."

He looked at her and, without being able to speak, nodded his head.

"I want you to be well, my love." She gripped his hands with a gentle insistence.

He managed a whisper. "I do not know if I can be without you."

"You must be strong, my beloved Roosevelt. I loved you since the day I met you, and I will always love you. I'm not leaving you, my husband. I'm simply waiting for you."

Roosevelt tried to speak but couldn't. He felt like his throat was turning to stone.

Sarah reached up and stroked his cheek. She looked at him with great compassion and filled him with her love, as she had done all those past years.

"You must believe I will be waiting for you, but you must also be strong. Try to be happy."

Roosevelt nodded grimly. "I will try to be strong my Sarah, but happy? That is impossible. I do not know how I can do that."

"But it's what I'm asking of you, my husband."

She placed her hands back folded on her chest as they had been.

"Sarah, I need you. Please stay with me."

"Roosevelt, my love. I have already gone. You must be strong."

Then she was simply still, her hands ice cold in his. He knew the corpse in the coffin was no longer his wife. She had moved on.

Just as he always did when he had this dream, Roosevelt awakened suddenly. Neither the dream nor his emergence from it ever varied. When he felt her frigid hands, he awakened immediately. His eyes snapped open, not with fear; this was not a nightmare, but from sorrow, emptiness, and the knowledge that he had to face another day without Sarah.

TWENTY-TWO

MARCH 1927

A curious feature of the Maledicus statue was it continued to find its way from collector to collector. Mr. Remington, a dealer in antiques in London, found the little figure when examining the estate purchase he had made from an unfortunate man who had died in terrible and mysterious circumstances. The executors had simply offered many of his belongings as a bulk purchase, which Remington considered he was fortunate to buy at an almost unbelievably low cost.

Mr. Remington was a fussy little man who kept his antiques stores in excellent condition. Nothing was ever out of place, and the premises were always immaculate and impeccably arranged. He despised going into shops and finding any traces of grime or disarray. Remington felt a store that was not in completely correct arrangement was an indication of the lower class of the owner, regardless of any claim otherwise. "I am a dealer in fine historical items, artwork if you will, NOT refuse or worthless junk." He prided himself on the fact most of his customers were people whom he considered to be "of quality." It had been Remington's hope in life to discover that he was descended from nobility, but his extensive genealogical research had shown otherwise. He had come from non-descript commoners, but no one else need know of his shame. If he were not of noble birth, he could at least project and handle himself as if he were

Mr. Remington had an excellent eye for value. When he saw the odd-looking little Roman statue, he recognized that it might be worth considerable money in the circle of those who collected arcane of the more mystical sort. He sent word out to several people, including one Mr. J. R. Harris, a railroad magnate from Pennsylvania who was currently visiting London that he had an item of interest. Remington had sold various objects to Harris in the past and thought he might be able to interest the American in this unusual Roman idol.

An extraordinary man, Harris was highly intelligent, monied, ambitious, deeply curious about the unusual, and also cunning and vicious. He fit the description of the American robber baron, so while not noble by birth, he was, in essence, an American of the titled and privileged class. In business it was known, he would have great success in any endeavor, and that he would crush any opposition that might stand in front of him, be it another captain of industry or a budding union. All fell before him. Harris was willing to do whatever was necessary to achieve his ends. Some would-be opponents feared that even ordering killings was within Harris' capabilities.

As it were, there was talk back in the United States that Harris was considering a run for a major political office, perhaps for the Senate. He had the public exposure, the connections, and the money to make a successful campaign. As a senator, his power would increase beyond that of a business magnate, and he loved the idea of more influence. At times, he mused, "I might be invincible." If he were able to become a senator, why couldn't the Presidency be within his reach? He could be the most powerful man in the United States of America. He knew that this idea was not an idle dream—he had yet to fail to achieve any goal he had set for himself.

His London trip was almost over, so Harris was in a hurry—his normal pace of life. When he came bursting into Remington's store accompanied by two large and imposing male secretaries, everyone else gasped and stepped out of their path.

Remington had been speaking to an elderly man who was looking at a gold watch fob, but Harris shoved in front of the man.

"Remington, I'm in a hurry here. I have no time to waste."

"Of course, of course, sir." Remington tried to soothe over the old man's very ruffled feathers but without any success. The storeowner watched as the old man left in a huff.

"Don't worry about him, Remington. You know that my business is far more valuable to you than that old coot."

Remington nodded and said nothing even though he was shocked by the American's rude behavior. But what else, he wondered, could be expected from someone on the other side of the pond? They all were, by their very nature, uncivilized compared to the British. That old coot, as Harris had called him, was Sir Geoffrey Reynnalds, a Knighted old colonel of the Royal Army. Not to worry; he would find a way to make it up to Sir Geoffrey another day. For today, it was business considerations first, and Harris always spent well.

"Mr. Remington, I received word that you have an interesting item."

"Mr. Harris, what a pleasure it is to see you again." Remington had recovered his calm and showing apparent obsequiousness, bowed before this man.

"Oh stop that!" Harris waved off the show of fawning. "I'm not one of your lazy Brit nobles. I earned my money, didn't have it handed down to me. And I'm in a rush, so show me this piece! Get to it, man!"

Remington jumped with a start and went into his back storage room to retrieve the statue. He brought it out and placed it on the counter in front of Harris. Compared to the glitter of the brass, silver, and gold items, it was dull. Many pieces of furniture in the store were made of rich dark wood and appeared to be far more substantial than this seemingly delicate and, at once, crude piece of sculpture. It was the kind of work that many buyers would overlook. This figurine, however, caught Harris' eye.

"Yes, yes," Harris murmured in a soft tone that neither of his secretaries had ever heard him use before. He held it up and turned it around. Then he looked at it under the light of a desk lamp.

"This is magnificent." The American looked up at Remington. "What are you asking for this piece?"

"Well, Sir, this is a very rare item from ancient Rome, so it has an unusual valuation." Remington was used to justifying his often ridiculously high prices to his clients.

Harris put the idol on the counter and calmly reached across to grab Remington by the lapels of his jacket. "I said," he spoke in a calm, low voice that reverberated with implied threat. "How much do you want for it? I won't haggle with you. I want it, but remember, if I don't get it, you have lost my business for good. If I leave this store without this statue, I'll never be back, you little British snob. Additionally, I will spread the word that you run a dishonest establishment. Certain authorities will then be looking into your business affairs. Do you understand me?"

Remington had no fears from visits from the Office of Revenue. He was impeccable in his bookkeeping, and he never cheated on his taxes. In that regard, there was little that Harris could do to him. But the look in Harris' eyes, which resembled the glare of a predator as it stalked its hapless prey, frightened him. Remington understood implicitly that the American was making a much deeper threat and did not doubt that Harris would carry through on it.

Remington managed to squeak out a "Yes, Sir" and shook his head up and down rapidly like a broken jack-in-the-box.

"Remember, I never threaten. What I say is what I do. Now, one more time—how much do you want for it?"

Harris realized that the statue would probably be of great interest to certain reclusive, but fascinating, circles of devotees. He was one of these people, and he would not let them have the statue. He was expecting a price of at least one hundred pounds and was willing to pay much more for this prize.

"Sir," Remington said in a soft tone. He wanted to get rid of the statue as soon as he could, and he wanted Harris away from him, far away. He felt the physical threat the man exuded. He saw the looks that his "secretaries" had in their eyes and the bulges from under their coats. He knew that they were carrying firearms. Remington did not doubt that if he failed to sell the statue now to Harris, something terrible might happen to him. He made up his mind.

"Ten pounds."

Harris smiled and released him. As the small man stood before him trembling despite his best efforts not to, Harris took out his billfold and placed a ten-pound note on the counter.

"Pack it in a box for me now."

"Certainly, Sir," Remington stammered.

A few minutes later, Remington handed the box containing the idol to Harris, who handed it to one of his men to carry. Harris looked at his secretary and said, "Be careful with that. Your employment depends on your care."

The young man nodded. He held it, as if it were his own baby he was protecting.

Harris turned to Remington, who was now sweating profusely even though the air was chilly and damp. "It was a pleasure doing business with you, Remington. I will see you on my next trip to London." He laughed and exited the store, followed by his men.

With that incident behind him, Remington decided to sell his business, take his proceeds and retire to a quiet country village in Scotland, far away from such items and such men as Harris. He thought that if he had stayed in business, he might lose his life or worse.

Harris immediately became obsessed with the idol. He kept it in his stateroom on his voyage back to the United States. Usually a gregarious man, known for his long nights of drinking, dancing, and womanizing, he remained in his cabin and watched over the idol. Even his normally trusted bodyguard, Harry Smith, a man who had been in his service for over 15 years and knew most of his employer's secrets, from his illegal business deals to purchasing of bootleg whiskey to funding of several mistresses, was not allowed to be alone with the idol. Harris trusted no one with it. The figure was his, and no one would ever have it. The idol whispered to Harris and promised him greatness. It seemed the most natural thing in the world. *Of course it came to me,* he thought. *I am destined for fame and power, the ultimate power, and the statue will guide me. I will kill them, any of them, if they try to take it away from me. It's mine.*

In the United States, Harris was considered to be one of the most important and active members of high society. He was invited to every major function, even to Presidential balls, even to those of Presidents whom he did not support; such was his power and influence. He always attended these affairs accompanied by his beautiful young wife. He had had his first wife, the mother of his three children, and a mousy and timid woman who was unsuited to the intricacies of high society, involuntarily committed to an insane asylum, a prison of an institution, which he, of course, funded. It was a place of no return for those patients admitted there. This place was for wealthy men to hide embarrassing members of their families or wives they wanted to be rid of. At this time, involuntary commitment was easy for those with the kind of money and influence that Harris had. Since he was the primary benefactor of the Everton Asylum, the attending doctors had no difficulty in finding a diagnosis of incurable insanity for the unfortunate woman. She was declared incompetent, and his lawyers were easily able to gain a divorce for Harris. The former Mrs. Harris then suffered the indignity of an early form of lobotomy, which left her a veritable cipher. She no longer had any will or independent thoughts. She simply existed in a grimy room and waited to die, which she would do twenty terrible years later. This left him free to marry the beautiful young woman whom he displayed on his arms like a piece of valued art.

For two months after his return to the United States, Harris completely vanished from the parties and balls he was so used to attending and in which he would make himself the center of attention. His absence was noted and whispers about him began to circulate. Was he ill? Was something wrong with his wife? Had something terrible happened in his travels? No one had any real idea, because he had given his staff strict orders, under pain of immediate dismissal, never to let any word of his situation out to the world.

At home, he had deteriorated badly but not from any physical illness contracted. Nor was he truly insane; rather, he was obsessed with the idol. He kept it on his desk in his office and looked at it constantly. No one else was ever again allowed in that room, not his bodyguard nor his wife. When his wife pressed him about what was happening, he grabbed her by the throat and told her that he would kill her if she did not let him alone.

She was so afraid of him that she quickly threw together a bag of clothes, took some jewelry and left. Ordinarily Harris would have had his men track her down and bring her back to dispense his own brand of justice on her, but now he did not even notice, nor would he have cared if he had realized that his pretty display piece was gone. She no longer mattered to him. All he saw was the statue and its importance.

After two months, his hair had grown wild, and he had grown a shaggy beard. Normally a man who prided himself on his immaculate appearance, he now resembled a bum who should be on skid row and not living in a palatial mansion on the Main Line in Philadelphia. He hadn't changed clothes in three weeks, and he stunk. His odor had become so bad that anyone could smell him outside of the door that he kept closed. He had food delivered to his door, and then he waited for the frightened servant to leave before opening it and pulling the meal into the room.

In the last three days, however, he had not even bothered to eat. He was beginning to starve, but he didn't notice. That Saturday, he wrote out a hurried note that he wanted the staff to come to his room precisely at one o'clock in the afternoon. He slid the note under the door into the hallway, and he heard his bodyguard stop and pick it up. When the time came for the butler, cook, maids, secretaries, and bodyguard to arrive, he was waiting for them behind his desk. He had not cleaned up at all, but he had unlocked the door. The room stank like an uncovered sewer. His body stench, the refuse of the food he had eaten, and the deposits in his makeshift toilet in a corner of the room combined to create a hellish bouquet. Regardless, Harris was sure that they would come. He still was the one who signed their paychecks. *I still control them. I have the power.*

"*Yes, you do control them, and you know what you must do,*" the statue said to him. Harris heard the words clearly.

Yes, yes, I do. I understand. I will follow your directions.

The staff didn't know he had hidden directly behind his desk two double barrel 10 gauge Winchester shotguns, a Winchester repeating rifle, and two pearl handled Colt 45 revolvers, all loaded. He had a virtual arsenal that could hold off a small army.

The staff came as he expected—precisely on time. They entered slowly, gasping at the condition of the room—its appearance and its stench. They tried to pretend that everything was normal, but they were deeply frightened. Some cowered behind the others, and some tried to stand straight as if nothing was unusual.

"Come in here, now!" he screamed at them. "Come in and sit on the floor in front of me. All of you."

He was delighted to see they obeyed him. He watched as they looked at each other, then slowly moved forward and sat on the floor. Harris smiled. It was amazing to see the power of his money in action. "I want to show you now, how much I appreciate your service to me."

He grabbed one shotgun and fired twice, instantly killing the butler and one maid. As he did, turmoil ensued. Some screamed and held out their hands. Others stood and began to run out of the room.

Harris dropped the first shotgun, grabbed the other and killed two more servants. Then he put the pistols in his belt and grabbed the rifle. Using the repeating action on the rifle and holding it out from his hip, Harris began to shoot quickly and stepped over the dead and bleeding bodies on his floor. In the hallway, he saw the cook running to the stairway. With one shot to the back of his head, Harris killed him.

"I always knew you all were terrible as help! Time to be fired!"

He sighted the rifle to see one of the last maids, a newly hired Irish girl of 15 recently arrived in the country, huddled at the bottom of the staircase in front of him. "You never could clean worth a damn, bitch."

Before he could pull the trigger, he heard a voice. "Stop now, Mr. Harris."

It was Smith, his bodyguard, standing bent over and bleeding like a flowing fountain of burgundy from an abdominal wound.

"Well now, Harry, I thought for sure you would be obedient. Why don't you just be a good boy and die?"

The bodyguard was holding a small pistol, and he pulled the trigger three times quickly. Harris felt the impact of the well-placed bullets tearing into his chest, and he slid down, dropping his rifle and rolling partly onto the top of the stairwell.

As he died, he heard the statue calling to him. *"Harris, you are now mine. Come to me."*

TWENTY-THREE

DECEMBER 13

After reviewing the evidence of their initial investigation, Roosevelt, Sam, and Jeremy agreed something very serious and potentially dangerous was haunting the Murray house; they all agreed they needed to do something to help ease Helen Murray's fears and to rid her of this haunting.

In a situation where a blessing is needed, Roosevelt typically would have turned to his friend Father Bruno, but since he was just back from his trip to Rome and it was the time of year when the end of the semester was at hand, Roosevelt knew how busy his friend would be. Because this should be merely a simple blessing of the house, Roosevelt suggested that they contact someone else. In this case, they turned to Martin Gerard, a local bookstore owner, whom they knew well. In addition to being a merchant, Gerard was also a practitioner of Wicca and Druidism and a medium. While many in Bethberg were quick to dismiss such beliefs as either far out, dangerous, or just silly, Roosevelt had seen much in his life. He was far too knowledgeable of the Renaissance and its heavy interest in the study of the occult, to be narrow-minded. He was open to using whatever techniques he needed to help a client. Roosevelt knew that Gerard was a good and kind man. He also knew he took his approach to spirituality very seriously, but he also had a light touch about it.

"I have no desire to preach to anyone or try to convert anyone. Life's journey to spirituality is a very personal thing, and I reject proselytizing to anyone. Each person must explore life on his or her own," he said recently to Roosevelt when having dinner one night.

Roosevelt agreed with this sentiment completely. He had long ago abandoned the Episcopal Church of which his family had been members for generations. "There are still many current Franklins in the Church," he said

112

to Gerard. "I think they will continue to be well represented without me. Many of my family are more comfortable with my absence than they are with my presence. I have rarely held myself back from disagreeing with many of my family's …uh…rather extreme beliefs."

During the meal, Roosevelt explained the situation to Gerard. When they were relaxing after dinner with cigars and whiskey, he asked Gerard's opinion.

"Well, you know Roosevelt, given my religious views, I do believe in the existence of the spiritual realm and its interconnectedness with our earthly existence. I suppose you could argue that, in that sense, the views of my religion are similar to that of the Catholic Church, which does recognize the existence of spirits, especially when they speak of the Holy Ghost. The Catholic Church is not being metaphoric."

"True, at least for the most traditional of them."

"And as a very involved member of society, I do believe that evil does exist. It is not an illusion, Roosevelt."

Roosevelt gave a tight smile and nodded. "You are preaching to the choir, Gerard. I have seen evil. I know that it is not a relative concept or mere consequence of human behavior. Certainly some human behavior can be explained in that way, but true evil does exist."

Gerard sipped his whiskey. "And I do really like Ms. Murray, and I adore Helena. She is a delightful little girl. I love to talk with her when they come into my bookstore. She loves to read and to talk about the stories—she is a huge fan of Dr. Seuss." Gerard took a long, slow puff on his Rocky Patel cigar. After letting out the smoke in a long stream, he said, "I'll do it. I'll bless the house, and, I hope, it'll get rid of this problem."

"Thank you, Gerard."

"Do you object to my bringing Branwyn with me? I am not psychic at all, and she might be able to detect something. When she has accompanied me in the past on blessings, she has proven to be valuable, and she is very level-headed under stress."

Roosevelt rarely used psychics in their investigations, and he knew many were frauds and many were simply self-delusional. Roosevelt, however, did not discount psychic abilities, and he did know that some psychics were legitimate. Additionally, he respected Gerard, and he knew Branwyn, whose real name was Karen Miller, a local bartender who was also a priestess of a local Wicca coven. Karen had helped in a previous investigation. She was a bit flighty but a good person, and he knew she was honest. If she were able to help Gerard in his blessing, then he had no objection. "Certainly," Roosevelt said, clinking glasses with Gerard.

Gerard, Branwyn, Roosevelt, Sam, and Jeremy met at the Murray's house the following day. It was early afternoon, and Ms. Murray was still at school, as was her niece. Helen had given Jeremy a key to the house and told them that she would take her niece for ice cream after school so they would have plenty of time for the blessing. The day was bright, and the sky had the kind of clarity that made it seem a person could see forever through the crystal blue. It was an unusually warm, but comfortable, December day, and a slight breeze gently moved through the town. It was the kind of day that made ideas like the supernatural haunting of anything, seem almost impossible.

They entered the home together, Roosevelt leading the way. While the air had seemed heavy upon immediately entering the home in their last visit, now everything felt fresh and light. Roosevelt wondered if they were wrong about their analysis. Perhaps nothing evil was in this house.

"I don't like this, Rosy," Sam said to him as he leaned over to whisper. Sam frowned as he looked around the home.

"What do you not like?"

"It feels too good, like a stakeout where the perps know we're watching, so they cleaned up and cleared out."

"Or guys," added Jeremy. "Like they're hiding, so they can't be seen, but are still there."

"Yeah, good point, Jerry." Sam held an unlit cigar in his mouth, a habit from his stakeout days.

"We're going to wander a bit while you set up your equipment." Gerard and Branwyn moved throughout the rooms as the IPS quickly set up cameras and recorders.

A little while later, the two explorers returned, ready to begin. Roosevelt noticed that both looked a little nervous.

"Are you both all right?"

"I'm fine and a just a little anxious to begin," answered Gerard.

Sam watched Branwyn as she kept looking around with darting little glances.

"Karen, I mean Branwyn," Sam corrected himself as she glanced up at him in irritation. She always wanted her Wiccan name used. Sam felt she was being pretentious, and while he was willing to go along with her wishes for the sake of the blessing, he was wondering about her readiness. "Are you up for this? You okay?"

"I...am....fine," she said almost in a whisper. "But I am detecting...something in here."

"What is it? Can you tell?" Jeremy was intently watching over the monitors on the control table. He liked both Gerard and Branwyn, especially because they, like Roosevelt and Sarah, had been among the first to accept him fully for whom he was in this sometimes-insular town. He did not like seeing either of them uncomfortable, so he wanted to make certain that he missed nothing on his control table. If he could help in any way, he would.

"I can't really tell, dear. It seems to be here, but then gone. And I can't see anyone, so I don't know who or what it is. But I don't like it. I do think this house needs this blessing."

They began in the living room.

"Then everyone, let's begin." Gerard spoke with a clear and strong voice.

"I want to let you all know that what we will be doing is an amalgam, a combination of purification rites from both the Druidic and the Wiccan traditions. We also invoke Christian prayers," he added.

Roosevelt raised his eyebrow. "Does this matter?"

"Well, it does to some people. It depends on their religious convictions and attitudes, but I think that it is best to use what you think will work in the given circumstances, because I do believe in the eclectic Druidic idea that all the Gods and Goddesses are one, that the disparate names of these deities are simply human interpretations and distinctions for the same force."

I am going to have everyone hold something, except for Jeremy, who will be recording this. Is that ok?" Gerard asked.

They all assented.

Branwyn and Gerard gave sage to Roosevelt, a vial of salt water to Sam, and Branwyn and Gerard kept a feather, a broom, sage, and a candle.

First, they lit the sage, which immediately filled the living room with a pungent scent. They slowly circled the room, moving around the coffee table in a counter-clockwise direction, and then they proceeded to each room of the house and did the same, always moving counter-clockwise around whichever room they were in at the time. They even did this in the cellar and the tiny attic, which resembled a crawl space more than an actual room. They ignored no area, no place that an entity or negative energy might inhabit. None of the closets were big enough to hold them all, so either Gerard or Branwyn entered each closet and turned counter clockwise. When they were finished, they returned to the living room, and the entire house was filled with the smoke and scent of sage.

"Sage is a purifier and cleanser. I always begin a blessing with the burning of sage. Because of what you told me about the circumstances, I wanted to be sure to cover every part of the house."

Gerard turned to Branwyn, who had become uncharacteristically quiet. He watched her carefully and whispered to her. "Branwyn?"

"Something is here." She seemed puzzled. "I'm feeling something stronger than before we burnt the sage. Very odd."

Roosevelt looked over to Jeremy. "Anything unusual?"

Jeremy simply shook his head, but he seemed to be a bit worried, and Sam was also tense.

"Please hold the objects we gave you as I offer various prayers," Gerard instructed.

Gerard reached into a bag resembling that of a certain fictional archeologist of filmic fame and pulled out an old Bible. He ran his hand over the cover respectfully and opened the book. Gerard began with the Lord's Prayer, a definite surprise for the IPS, which elicited a wry smile from Branwyn.

"Our Father, who art in heaven,

Hallowed be Thy name.

Thy Kingdom come,

Thy will be done,

On earth as it is in heaven

Give us this day our daily bread.

And forgive us our trespasses,

As we forgive those who trespass against us.

And lead us not into temptation,

But deliver us from evil.

For Thine is the kingdom, the power and the glory, for ever and ever.

Amen"

The rest of the group echoed, "Amen."

"As I said before," Gerard explained to the perplexed members of the IPS, "all the gods and goddesses are one, so I use what I think are the most effective statements of goodness, regardless of origin, and I happen to like the Lord's Prayer immensely."

Gerard turned to a page that he had designated with a cloth bookmark. He next recited the 23rd Psalm:

"The Lord is my shepherd;

I shall not want.

He maketh me to lie down in green pastures;

He leadeth me beside the still waters.

He restoreth my soul;

He leadeth me in the paths of righteousness for his name's sake.

Yea, though I walk through the valley of the shadow of death,

I will fear no evil. . ."

As Gerard reached this point in the Psalm, they all felt the air in the room becoming heavy, as though it were filled with a deepening humidity. Gerard felt his pulse begin to speed up with adrenalin, but he calmed himself and continued. The IPS members felt the change in atmosphere, but they refrained from commenting or interrupting the blessing.

Gerard continued:

"I will fear no EVIL: for thou art with me; thy rod and thy staff they comfort me.

Thou preparest a table before me in the presence of mine enemies;

Thou annointest my head with oil; my cup runneth over.

Surely goodness and mercy shall follow me all the days of my life

And I will dwell in the house of the Lord forever."

Gerard gently closed the Bible and replaced it solemnly in his carry bag. As Gerard finished stowing the book, they all heard the sound of a distant, but audible tinkling, almost like a far off laugh.

"Did you hear that?" Roosevelt asked.

"What the hell was that?" Sam added.

"I hope we got it on the audio," Jeremy said as he focused on the equipment. Then, he looked up at the others. "Guys, do you smell that?" Jeremy had the keenest sense of smell of the group, and he knew that he had detected something new, an odor distinctively different from the sage that was burnt for cleansing the rooms.

"Sorry, I cannot." Roosevelt's sense of smell was not good these days.

"Yeah, I do, but what the fuck it is, I don't know." Sam seemed to be getting angrier by the minute.

Gerard and Branwyn both could smell it. They looked at each other and then back at the group. "It's very slight," Branwyn said softly. "I believe it's sulfur."

"Yeah, it smells like there were fucking gunshots." Sam looked at Roosevelt. "It smells like we are somewhere where a gunfight had happened several days ago."

Roosevelt still could not smell anything, but he saw the looks of concern on their faces. "I think it would be best if we would continue."

Gerard shook his head in agreement. "Next, I am going to use a combined Wiccan and Druidic blessing:

"I pray to the Goddess and God, to all the spirits of good,

Bless this dwelling and those who abide here,

Give protection to your servants,

Lend us your power so that we may dispel anything negative or evil herein.

Spirits of the Wood,
Spirits of the Wind
Spirits of the Earth,
Spirits of the Air,
Spirits of the Water
Bless us with your power and bless this house with your power, protect all who live here.
Spirits of evil, begone!
Spirits and unnatural creatures, begone!
Leave this place, and let the good in!
Leave this place and let the Goddess and the Horned God in!
We compel you in their names to leave!
You are unwelcome here!
Begone! Begone! Begone!"

They moved from room to room, and Gerard repeated the prayers and incantations in each room, including the basement, attics, and all closets. When the group had completed the last room, Gerard again handed each person sage and had them burn it once more.

Gerard then walked a circuit of the home once again and repeated all of the prayers and incantations. Finally, he was finished.

"I hope that will do."

Branwyn frowned and shook her head. "I don't think it worked."

"What do you mean, dear?" Jeremy asked as he joined the rest of them in the living room.

Branwyn screwed her face into a misshapen knot. She shook her head like she was trying to deny what she felt. "I'm not sure how to describe it."

Gerard asked, "What are you feeling?"

"Well," she said. "Like you know Gerard, it usually feels light, airy, after a blessing, like when you've had a head cold and it finally lifts. Yet I still feel something in here. It isn't right. I want to leave, now. I don't want to stay in this house a moment longer."

TWENTY-FOUR

A change was imminent. Even though the air seemed more like a mild spring day than late fall, a storm was coming. A winter storm was approaching. For those who were sensitive to the smell of approaching snow or who could feel the chill deep in their bones, the signs were there.

A blizzard was coming.

TWENTY-FIVE

DECEMBER 13

After they left the blessing of the Murray house, Gerard and Branwyn climbed into Gerard's 1975 bright yellow Volkswagen Super beetle that he carefully and lovingly restored. When he first bought it, it was barely functioning, with more body putty apparent than paint, and with a floor rotted through in places so that someone sitting in the passenger seat could see the road going by beneath them as they drove. Gerard took several years in its repair, complete with a refurbished body, including a welded replacement of sections of the floor and a reconditioned motor, which he had worked on and personally installed. It was a secret joy to Gerard that he was a talented mechanic. Now instead of the bright yellow vehicle shaking around like an old beat up car that threatened to fall apart at any moment, it shook around like a new version of an old beat up car. Yet it held together and was now a dependable, if neither fancy nor fast, automobile.

They drove in silence for a while. Instead of taking Branwyn directly home, Gerard simply drove out of town north into the Pocono Mountains. When he aimed the little car out of town, he asked, "Do you mind taking a ride?"

"Let's do that," was all she said.

Simply staring ahead through the tiny windshield, they continued the drive. Soon they had passed Stroudsburg and were moving into the wilderness along route 402 North.

They entered a stretch of road bordered by a dense myriad of trees, the majority of which had lost their leaves and looming like skeletal specters, intermingled with occasional evergreens. There was almost no traffic and very few homes along the way. They drove to a place where state forests had hunting and fishing places that ruled the land. It was quiet and dark.

After they were a good distance away from Bethberg, Gerard glanced over at his friend and asked, "Do you mind if I smoke?"

He pulled over along the side of the road so they could sit and talk.

"No, in fact, I'll have one."

Gerard was startled. Branwyn was a former two pack a day smoker, for over 15 years. It had been five years since she had stopped, courtesy of a scare from a deep cough she had developed and her doctor being concerned that she might have developed lung cancer. Thankfully, she had not, but Branwyn decided that the scare was a warning from the universe, one that she should pay attention to, because there might not be another warning. Next time, it might be the real thing.

Since she had quit, she had become one of the most rabid anti-smokers he knew. When she spoke of the evils of cigarettes, it was with the light of the newly converted in their eyes when they were preaching the word of whatever God they believed in. When she got on a roll about the evils of tobacco, she sounded to him like a televangelist exhorting the flock sitting at home in front of their televisions to send in whatever money they had—"to help build God's new themed playground!" or "because GOD! don't want his preachers riding around in no little hatchbacks! No Sir! GOD! wants his prophets to be driving in a new Mercedes-Benz!"

Gerard started to laugh at the image of Branwyn whipping up a crowd to a frenzy of money donating.

"What's so funny?" She always thought that he had an odd sense of humor.

"Oh nothing. Just thinking of you as a televangelist," he snorted.

She shook her head in disbelief. "You can be so stupid sometimes. Like an eighth-grader."

"Yeah, I know," and he laughed again, a long series of bellows and snorts, making him sound like a dysfunctional steam train engine. Finally, he gained control of himself and turned to her. His face was red from the laughing. "You sure you want one?"

"Yeah," Branwyn looked more serious than he had seen her in a very long time. "I really need one."

"Ok, hold on a minute. There's a better place up the road."

Gerard pulled back onto the road and in only about five minutes found his destination. He pulled into the parking lot of a diner/fishing store located on a popular local fishing spot known for its abundance of pickerel and bass. The place was closed for the night, but Gerard was sure that the owners wouldn't mind them stopping.

He turned off the little car and reached into his shirt pocket. He took out a pack of non-filter Camels, took one for himself, and then held out another for Branwyn. Then he flicked open his gunmetal colored Zippo, a prized possession that reminded him of his beloved tough guy detective novels and lit her cigarette and then his own. Then he closed the lighter with a solid clank. "There you go, doll."

"Give it a rest, Gerard. You don't sound like a detective, nor do you look like one, dear heart."

Gerard smiled, and he inhaled deeply and then let the smoke out slowly through his nostrils.

Gerard had never tried to quit. He enjoyed the calming effect of the nicotine, and he felt since something would kill him, sooner or later anyway, he might as well enjoy this one bad habit, well, that and one of several bad habits. He did like to indulge in one or three beers a night. He liked to think of himself as a connoisseur of good beer, not a drunk.

"So, what did you think of the blessing?" he asked her.

She took a deep drag and slowly let out the smoke. "Well, I suppose I'm back in the saddle again. Damn, that tastes good."

"I meant. . ."

"I know what you meant, dear heart. Don't be impatient."

She took another drag and savored the feel of the soothing smoke in her lungs. It was as if she had never stopped. She looked out the small car window for a few seconds then said, "I don't ever want to go back in that house again."

Branwyn startled Gerard for the second time since they left the Murray house. First she was smoking again, and now she seemed frightened by what she had experienced as a psychic. And Branwyn was one of the gutsiest people he knew. Despite her appearance as an aging hippy, one of the crunchy-granola crowd with her long gray hair, her beaded jewelry, and the bright sundresses she wore, he knew that she was capable of facing down drunks in her job as a bartender. He had seen her stand up to those in the community who thought that being Wiccan somehow meant that she was evil. The Bethberg area, as a whole, was welcoming to people of most religions and races, but it still housed its share of ignorance and bigotry. Some of these bigots were people who, quite-frankly scared the piss out of Gerard. He would always rather face any kind of a ghost than a quasi-militia nut packing too many guns. Branwyn was not intimidated, even by that ilk, so now, if she were truly frightened, he knew he had to pay attention.

She looked out the window at the lake. "I don't know. I just don't know. You know? I've never felt like that before."

"Well, I gotta say Branwyn, I didn't like it either."

"I've known that I have had these abilities – to perceive the presence of spirits and sometimes to communicate with them for years, since I was a little kid. Once I began to understand that I was not crazy. . ."

Gerard began to smile.

"DO NOT go there!" She grinned at her friend. "Once I knew that I wasn't nuts, I began to learn about what I could do. I eventually found a good teacher and learned how to use my skills so I would no longer be afraid of what I could see and, more importantly, to be able to help others, to understand, what they were experiencing. Sometimes, I have been able to help lost spirits go into the light. That has been the most rewarding for me. But this, Gerard, I am completely serious. I have never felt anything like this before."

"Yeah, it was very strange, Branwyn. I had blessed houses before. I have even felt some bad stuff before, but. . . "

"Yeah, BUT. That's it exactly." She flicked the remainder of his cigarette out of the window. "May I have another?"

"You sure? You can consider one just a very minor falling off the wagon."

"Fuck the wagon. The wheels came off that damned cart back at the Murray house. Give me the cigarette."

"Okay, never refuse a lady."

"Or me." She said and laughed. "Gerard, on my life and the spirit of the Goddess, there is something very bad in that house. I felt it. I know it is there, but I'm not sure what it is, and I'm scared of it." When she said this, she sounded like a little girl who was afraid of lightning and thunder. Her normally strong and resonant voice had collapsed into a tinny squeak. That frightened Gerard.

She took another deep drag. "Ok, Gerard. What do you think?"

He hesitated before answering, because while he was accepted as a part of the Pagan community, he did not hold with some of their beliefs. He was not a vegetarian, nor was he a pacifist, as many were in the neo-pagan world of Bethberg. He believed in fighting when needed but hoped that he never had to. He did not like to think of himself as a coward.

Finally, he said, "I have to agree with you. I'm frightened also."

"It's very definitely not a human spirit." Branwyn was completely serious now. "I've seen too many ghosts, spirits of people, to mistake this abomination for human. And I've seen other things in the past, what some might call nonhuman entities, and even then, I felt discomfort, but I always felt like I was in charge of the situation—you know? That if confronted by a nonhuman entity, I could deal with it. I was always sure about that."

She flicked the butt of his cigarette out the window, held out her hand and arched her left eyebrow. Gerard was amazed. He had just finished his first. But he knew better than disagreeing with a lady, especially this lady. He held out another for her and flicked open the Zippo.

The cherry of the cigarette glowed bright red as she inhaled deeply. In a moment, she continued. "But this, this is the darkest, most evil thing, that's all I can call it now, a thing."

"And you don't think that we helped with the blessing?"

"No." She took a long drag, held it, and slowly let it out. "I'm afraid that we may have made it worse, like pissing off a hungry bear."

"That's not a good thing." He shuddered and looked around the parking lot. "Hope there are no bears around now."

"You have a gift for understatement. I think it is as if we went hunting for a grizzly bear with a .22 popgun, and all we did was upset it and let it know that we are there. And soon, we were facing a mean, growling, huge destructive beast that was seriously pissed at us."

"You certainly do know how to ease a man's fears."

"Anytime, dear heart."

"Branwyn, do you think it's confined to that house?" This point was something that had been bothering Gerard since they had left the Murray residence.

"I hope so." She took another deep drag and then slowly let out the smoke. She looked as if she were staring into a fog, trying to see what was ahead. "If not...and I think, I think it is strong enough to go past that house. If not, we might have one hell of a nasty bear coming for us."

TWENTY-SIX

MAY 1958

Maledicus was pleased. In his existence with THEY in the In-Between, it was an unusual experience. After the joining into THEY, Maledicus had expected an eternity of infernal joy, at experiencing the pain and anguish of others, but for what seemed to be near eternities, he felt only boredom and lethargy. That to him was a kind of purgatory. He needed the stimulation he was used to.

Unlike many of the other spirits that had joined with THEY, Maledicus had never truly lost his self-awareness. Most were simply absorbed, conjoined and digested into the maws of the larger demon, making them only morsels of what they had been. They became true gibbering idiots, former souls with no individuation, feeling only the simple pleasure of their belonging to the larger obscenity of THEY.

Maledicus, however, never forgot who he had been or who he was. He had been procurer and spy for the Emperor, and if fate had not intervened, he would have become Emperor of Rome himself. Not for him was the abandonment of consciousness, of identity. While he was nowhere near as ancient or powerful as the original core of THEY, he felt that eventually he could become a separate Demon, as strong, if not more powerful, than his present host. As always, he had plans for his power. This time, unlike the unfortunate discovery by Caligula of Maledicus' plans in Rome, he would bide his time and build his strength. He was aware that he was able to keep his thoughts separate from THEY. This was the demon's weakness and his strength. He had joined with THEY to gain power, and he had. But he had also established separateness, which would serve him in the future.

When the joining had occurred, some part of his being, some invisible spiritual strand was connected to Earth. THEY had communicated to him

125

that the strong ones are reconnected to a visceral, tangible thing in the place the people had inhabited as corporeal beings. This allowed THEY to grow even stronger by causing havoc, evil, and destruction on the realm of the living.

When he had been absorbed into THEY, Maledicus' opportunity for rebirth on Earth had been lost forever, but through the extension that was created, he would not lose influence on the pitiable creatures he had left behind. That spiritual arm was an implant of him. It was a small non-descript Roman statue, a household idol that he had commissioned of himself. It was not spectacular by Roman standards, but it held the force of his evil. Anyone who owned this statue or who were near those who did, he could influence— he could corrupt them, drive them insane, sicken them physically, or even kill them. Maledicus had to be patient; these occurrences were rare, but when they did happen, they served a twin purpose: they infused him with perverted joy, and they increased his power; thus, he would continue to grow stronger, in preparation to become his own demon.

In the In-Between Maledicus was suffering from ennui. When the dull ache from not being able to inflict pain stultified him for too long, he felt at risk of losing himself, something that he deeply feared. THEY delighted in his agony—THEY knew that he had accepted union with THEY, but that he had resisted complete subservience. THEY even knew of his plans, but THEY never let Maledicus be aware of this knowledge.

This one would be separate from THEY one day, so let THEY find the proper time for his punishment. In the meantime, his agony is nourishing to THEY. THEY punished him, making him suffer near eternities of non-stimulation, only relieved when someone on Earth would take possession of the statue.

Maledicus suddenly rejoiced. He felt the statue held and taken. He could see what was happening through the eyes of the idol, almost as if he lived inside it. The place it was taken to was very different from what he had known on Earth, but that was expected. Maledicus had long ago realized that human accoutrements, their clothing, their items, their buildings, their superficialities that they used to define their empty lives, constantly changed, but he also understood that people themselves remained the same: he reveled in their avarices, greed, sadism, lust and corruption. He also delighted in finding weakness, naiveté, and innocence—qualities upon which he could feed and then corrupt.

In his using of the statue as an extension of him, Maledicus was able to identify weaknesses in the owners that he could exploit. It was a weakness of the mind that he coaxed into violence or insanity; it was sometimes a need that could be developed into a life-destroying addiction; or it could be a physical weakness that could be amplified—a favorite was to sicken children, even killing them, in order to destroy their parents.

Maledicus watched in amusement at his latest target.

Professor John McGuigan was pleased with his discovery. He was sitting in his study at his Victorian era, oak roll top desk that his wife had bought for him as a 40th birthday present. He had a pad in front of him and was taking preliminary notes on what, he thought, might be an important, but definitely not earth-shaking, find in the area of Ancient Roman archeology. As a historian of the American Revolution, he was not an expert in the era of the Roman Empire, but he knew enough to recognize a find of potential importance. It was a small statue, not particularly distinguished, and a little battered with chips missing from the hands and head. It had certainly not been stored well or carefully handled. Why should that surprise him? After all, he had come across the little idol during one of his yard sale excursions.

McGuigan delighted in keeping artifacts from various time-periods around his office. Human skulls, like the Memento Mori, were kept on the desks of scholars during the medieval period that served as reminders of human mortality: "to this end we all come." McGuigan liked to have such objects as a reminder of how little he knew about history that was outside of his area of expertise, to retain a scholarly humility in the face of discovered knowledge. All new information simply opens doors to a great expansion of further possible study. Knowledge is never an ending but a beginning of exploration he would tell his students during his lectures.

Quite by accident, while spending a quiet Saturday morning in late May, digging around the local flea markets and yard sales, while his wife and their two children went visiting a friend of hers, he found something unusual. This had become a hobby, a way to relax, while still indulging his need to explore. You never know what you might find at such places. People sell things that they have no idea about what they are or are worth.

He loved bringing home little treasures, especially antique toys, for his eight-year-old son and ten-year-old daughter. Even though these playthings were not as cool as the toys advertised on their new television set, an infernal contraption that he wished he had not purchased, but he could not deny his wife anything she wanted, and the children were always delighted when their Daddy brought them something from his "hunts," as he called them.

He had already found a small red haired doll for his daughter and an old metal steam train engine for his son. McGuigan was at the last flea market on his itinerary, because it was almost time to return home and meet his family for lunch. He was looking over a table of clustered bric-a-brac run by an elderly man he had never seen before. The old man was sitting back, chomping loudly on tobacco and spitting long streams onto the grass. McGuigan almost passed the table by, but a small piece in the clutter caught his attention. He wasn't sure how he managed to see it, since it was almost covered by other junk on one side and a pile of magazines, resembling a rotted paper Leaning Tower of Pisa, had nearly fallen onto the other side of the piece.

McGuigan gently extracted the small statue and looked at it.

"Interesting thing, ain't it?" The old man spoke with a twinkle in his eye.

"Yes, it certainly is. Do you happen to know anything about it?"

"Nah, just picked it up with a pile of junk I got at a auction—some old guy died. His kin was sellin' his stuff. I figured—might as well buy a box…never know what treasure you might git. Never did find nothin' worth a damn. Just tryin' to get rid of the lot."

"Mmhuh." McGuigan looked at the statue carefully. He was reasonably sure it was old, maybe an authentic Roman piece, or perhaps only a replica. It certainly did not project being valuable or impressive, especially since its authenticity was in doubt, nevertheless, he wanted it. Its uncertainty was perfect. It would serve in his collection dedicated to his scholar's humility.

"How much for this?" McGuigan was expecting the fellow to try to gouge him with a ridiculously high price, but he didn't know that the old man would be happy to just be rid of it. The odd-looking statue had made him uneasy since he had found it, wrapped in a foul-smelling rag in a rotten cardboard box that had little critters nesting in it. Nathan Smith had been a junkman for over 65 years; he had started helping his daddy with his own junk business, and normally he liked what he did. It was always amazing to him the stuff that people would throw out, especially rich folks. He liked the talking, the give and take of the sales, but occasionally something just didn't feel right. And Nathan did not like the ugly little statue. "Just as soon destroy it, but you never know, I could make some money on it," he mumbled to himself.

"You can have it for two bucks."

McGuigan almost blurted out "Really?" in astonishment, but he forced himself simply to say, "Okay." He handed over two folded one-dollar bills and happily took his newly purchased statue home.

The boy, William, and the girl, Susan, were McGuigan's pride and joy. He was a good professor, but more than that, he was a devoted husband and father. With his wife Andrea, and his beloved children, he felt that his life was as close to perfect as possible.

Then he brought the statue into his life.

Less than a week later, both children became ill. Both John and Andrea McGuigan thought that the children were suffering from one of the many colds they brought home with them from school. Then several nights later, both children quickly developed very high fevers – John watched with a forced calm on his face as Andrea held the thermometer up to the light, first for the boy, then the girl.

"John, my God, they both are running fevers of 105."

"Okay, let's get them to the hospital. Now!"

They quickly bundled their sleeping and feverish children in blankets, loaded them into their station wagon, and drove way past the speed limit to the hospital.

The emergency room physician admitted the children to the hospital, but he was unable to provide a clear diagnosis, other than "It is probably just a bad case of the flu, but we better keep an eye on them anyway."

John and Andrea went home thinking that the children were in "good hands". The next day, neither showed any improvement.

A few days later, both children slipped into comas. With the distraught parents at their bedsides, the doctors told them that they really had no idea what was happening. All of their tests indicated that there should be nothing wrong with the boy and girl, other than the fever, and they had done everything they knew to bring it down, even subjecting the children to ice baths. Nothing had worked. The fevers had grown to 107.

The McGuigans slept next to their unconscious children, and they refused to return home.

It seemed as if the nightmare would never end. After a week, the children seemed to be recovering slowly. Their fevers abated slightly, and they began to murmur unintelligibly, which was fortunate for their parents, because the children could see the demon laughing at them.

Then after their fevers almost broke, they once again took a turn for the worse. Both children had opened their eyes wide with terror, coming out of their comas for a few seconds, but emerged screaming, like the shrieks of the damned. Then their eyes closed, and they quickly relapsed back into their comas. Their fevers grew slowly, much more slowly.

The up and down roller coaster ride for the McGuigan's continued for three more weeks. Every day that passed, they saw the physical condition of their son and daughter deteriorate. At the end of the third week, their small bodies could stand no more, and both children died in agony, screaming, as their helpless parents watched.

The children's parents were not the only spectators. Maledicus had become a connoisseur. He had learned to the pleasures of prolonging his victims' pains, and he felt his power growing. Soon, he realized, he would be able to extend his influence past the immediate surroundings of the statue.

Maledicus rejoiced. He was once again invigorated from the sweet pleasure of the children's deaths and the even more delightful taste of the agony of their parents, truly delicious. He felt like he was, once again, regaining himself, and reinvigorating with intense strength. He still had room for dessert.

Soon after the funerals, after the last of the mourners had departed, Maledicus began to enjoy his sweet ending to the feast.

He projected himself through the statue and saw the crying father, alone at his desk, with his head held in his hands. The man was questioning why God would do such a thing. Maledicus laughed. *God has nothing to do with it.*

Maledicus saw the wife enter the room and simultaneously infected both of them with suspicion and blame for the children's death on each other. From that moment, the basis of their relationship was argument with vicious, hateful accusations hurled on each other.

"Stupid bitch. You're a useless excuse for a mother – why didn't you know how sick they were?"

She sneered at him, "You call yourself a man. What kind of man would have waited until the kids got so sick to take them to the hospital. Pathetic hopeless bastard."

Their arguments seemed to be nonstop. They ended each day with both drinking themselves into oblivion and falling asleep wherever they happened to be. They reached a point in which they could consume a fifth of whiskey or vodka in a day. Soon, the arguments ended in violence, with McGuigan punching his wife or Andrea hurling plates and pans at him, both intending to inflict serious injury on the other.

A month later, McGuigan was fired for coming to his lecture completely drunk. He had been warned—the College was not unsympathetic to the man's situation, but screaming at his students and hurling a bottle of rotgut whiskey at them was a bit too far.

After going to his car and sleeping off the drunk, he started to drive home. He made a single stop on the way, at a local gun and tackle store.

That's it. Feed me. Maledicus could taste the oncoming dessert.

McGuigan entered his house. "Honey, I'm home."

Andrea, having just finished a half a fifth of vodka, staggered into the hallway.

"Stop yelling, you useless fucker." He aimed the .38 caliber pistol he had just purchased and loaded at her face. He fired twice, ripping her face apart and killing her instantly. Then he went to his study, looked at the little statue, put the barrel of the gun in his mouth, and he pulled the trigger.

Absolutely delicious. Simply divine. I must have more soon.

Maledicus was delighted.

TWENTY-SEVEN

APRIL 2004

The battle erupted. After the initial bombardment of the city, the Marines began the first battle of Fallujah. It was a difficult operation, intended to gain control of the city and fought in two different times. Ultimately, the Allied forces were victorious, but the entire campaign was difficult and bloody.

Riding in a troop carrier, Patrick was satisfied to be going into combat with his men. He never wanted to be the kind of officer who stayed behind in safety in a fortified encampment while his soldiers engaged the enemy in combat. He believed that true leaders faced the same dangers as the regular Marines who went into battle and had to face the enemy's fire. Both Patrick and Michael held as their heroes, examples of leaders who had entered the fray along with the men whom they commanded: Theodore Roosevelt in the battle of San Juan Hill during the Spanish-American War and Henry V of Britain in the Battle of Agincourt during the Hundred Years War. The brothers, who had faced the same perils in combat, as did the soldiers they commanded. The brothers despised as cowards those who chose to conduct a battle from the relative safety of a command post.

Patrick, before leading his men into battle, recited a portion of the St. Crispin's speech from Shakespeare's *Henry V*:
"We few, we happy few, we band of brothers
For he today that sheds his blood with me
Shall be my brother."

He believed in the sentiment that all soldiers who fight next to each other develop the closest of bonds, that they truly were united as brothers.

Even though Patrick and Michael were twin brothers, both officers in the Marines, and were serving in active combat in this war, they were not in the same unit. U.S. Military policy was to separate family members in combat. That way, unlike in World War II, when some families lost several siblings at the same time in the same land battle or on board a Navy ship, there was more of a chance of survival and less of a chance of one of the siblings losing objectivity under duress. They would not be looking out for each other and making mistakes. So, as Patrick commanded his men, Michael was leading another unit on a similar attack on the other side of the city.

As the Marines first made their way into the outskirts of the city, an odd silence had hung in the air. The initial aerial bombardment of the targets had ceased to allow the Marines to begin their assault. Where before they had heard the droning screams of the jets as they roared through the air unleashing fiery carnage on the city, now only a silence, like that of a tomb, pervaded.

As Patrick's unit progressed into the city, his Marines were tense with the expectation of combat—this was what they all had trained for, but also what they all were secretly dreading. Some tried to project a complete lack of fear, but underneath their bravado, it was there. As it should be—Patrick believed that the soldier who did not fear battle was probably insane and certainly more likely to die from impulsive and careless action than the Marine who had fear but controlled and used it. Both brothers believed fear was natural and could be used in a positive way. Courage was not doing what came without fright, but facing overwhelming terror and proceeding in spite of it.

As they made their way down the city's streets, the Marines dismounted their vehicles and progressed on foot. As Patrick's men entered an area with tight streets and alleys, the shooting began. Enemy combatants were firing from different places inside of houses, often homes with civilians in them, so that they could try to protect themselves from return fire. They assumed the Americans would be unlikely to shoot on targets with innocent civilians. In battle, however, self-preservation often overcame moral inhibitions. When fired on, they returned the fire. Bombs, improvised explosives, went off inside some buildings and also in the streets. A cacophony filled with the discordant jumbling of shooting and explosions filled the air.

Loud. Overwhelming. Confusing. Terrifying.

Screams filled the streets as civilians inside some of the homes were wounded both by the exploding bombs and by gunfire.

Patrick's men followed him and moved into their places. They spread out into offensive positions and opened fire. As they did, another troop transport vehicle exploded in the next block. They could see the flames and hear the screams of their fellow Marines.

They tried to focus on the battle at hand and to continue with what they had to do.

Patrick led his men forward. They moved slowly but with certainty. As they did, in the ensuing hours, they took pieces of the city under their control, killing the enemy as they progressed. In the initial surge, only one of Patrick's men was hit.

"Medic! Man down! Over here now!"

A Marine Corps Medic ran to the fallen soldier, who was shot through the stomach and Patrick, satisfied that the wounded soldier was receiving care, led his men forward.

Then chaos erupted, like a sudden volcano exploding over an unsuspecting village, pouring molten death and fiery ash down on unprepared civilians. The battle expanded rapidly. There were sudden flashes, followed by darkness. And noise everywhere, followed by brief sudden silences. Patrick's men were performing well, firing on the enemy and maintaining some sense of discipline.

Three Iraqi soldiers stood to fire, and his men quickly eliminated them. Patrick waved the marines forward where they crouched down against a wall of a building. His men were moving quickly and efficiently, as they were trained to do. He was proud of their courage and focus. They continued to move towards the center of the city. They laid down covering fire and advanced.

As they saw enemy soldiers retreating, Patrick's men split into groups and went down various streets and alleys. Shooting as they advanced, Patrick led several of his men down one alley. They moved quickly and fired in well-planned bursts. Four Iraqi soldiers emerged from a building and prepared to throw grenades at them. Patrick's men spotted them. They fired and killed them before they could toss the grenades. As the dead Iraqis fell, they dropped the grenades, which soon exploded, obliterating their corpses. Patrick watched the enemy soldiers go farther down the main street as his men continued their advance. When the shooting halted for a brief time, they began to move into the next block. Patrick allowed himself to glance momentarily at the dead Iraqis. He saw one, not more than a teenager, and shook his head. Then, Patrick forced himself to look away…right now they were simply the enemy; there would be plenty of time later to consider these dead men and to mourn their passing.

The Marines moved quickly down the next street. By this time, the battle had been under way for hours and the sun was beginning to set. Patrick was amazed at how quickly time had passed. As twilight began to set in, he and a few of his men branched off from the others and entered a narrow alley from which they had heard what sounded like enemy soldiers. As they moved halfway down the alley, Patrick realized this was a cul-de-sac. He understood the potential danger they were in. He signaled to his men to stop. He looked around and saw no one where he had expected to see crouched men. He waved his men to go back out, to retreat the way they had come.

Too late.

Iraqi soldiers had positioned themselves at the entrance of the alley, effectively forcing the Marines into a trap. Patrick realized he had miscalculated badly. The alley had no exit except the way they had entered, and now the enemy was blocking their exit.

Motherfucker! I fucked up big time.

Patrick led his men against the enemy at the opening of the alley. The Marines began firing at the enemy and receiving fire back. As debris began to fly, dust filled the air. Vision was obstructed. *We're not going to die like rats in a fucking cage.* There were only eight Marines, and they faced a seeming swarm of the enemy.

The Iraqis soon discovered that the Marines would not be easy prey. They thought the Americans would panic and fall easily, but these were U.S. Marines, the finest soldiers in the world.

Guns flashed. Men screamed and fell. Dead Iraqis littered the entrance, and Patrick's men were falling around him. The man to his right took a round that removed half of his face. Soon, only Patrick and three other men were left alive. Patrick flashed back to a memory during advanced Martial Arts training…. "Sensei," he had asked, during a session with many opponents against him. "What happens if there are simply too many assailants?"

His teacher had answered, "Then faced with overwhelming odds, you will lose. Yet, always remember what I tell you. Never lose your honor."

The Iraqis, seeing their advantage began to advance down the long alley. They fired as they went, taking casualties, but they were determined to finish this group of Marines. The man nearest to Patrick fell. He was hit several times. Patrick shot one of the advancing Iraqis, who were now down to eight soldiers. Patrick began to fire, but a searing hot flash burst through his right leg and upper chest. He fell slowly.

As Patrick collapsed, he saw all of his men were dead. The remaining four Iraqis advanced forward to see if any of their enemy was still alive. They were satisfied that the others were dead and smiled at the wounded Marine officer. This would be a major victory for them. Patrick tried to raise his rifle, but he had no strength left in his body. He could only wait and watch.

From the ground, with his mind going in and out of consciousness, Patrick saw a gun flashing from behind the enemy – at the beginning of the alley. He heard a familiar voice call out, "Semper Fi, you sons of bitches!" In a few seconds, all of the remaining Iraqis were dead.

Patrick lay on his side on the ground. The pain had passed. He felt little except a deep cold enveloping him. He tried to look at what was around him, but his vision was fading into a dim fog. As the darkness began to close in, he was jolted awake by the pain of a pressure on his chest. It was as if he had been sliding down a ramp and suddenly grabbed off the slide by sharp hands of steel. The blackness abated a bit, and Patrick felt a hand put a compress on the wound on his chest. He felt strength in the man's arm and his head was cradled against a soldier's chest. He looked up at the man holding him. Though his vision was still cloudy, he could see that it was his brother Michael, who was both very pale and deeply worried.

"Hey baby brother, it looks like I had to get you out of another mess." Michael smiled a wan grin at his twin. "You're going to be ok, Patrick. You hear me?"

Then Patrick passed out.

Patrick, airlifted to a hospital in Germany, remembered nothing more until he regained consciousness several days later. He was attended to by battlefield Medics, then moved to a MASH unit, and then airlifted to the hospital where he underwent major surgery to his chest and leg. His massively damaged leg would leave him with a limp for the rest of his life, and the chest wound with an extensive scar for decoration and a diminished lung capacity as a constant reminder of what he had experienced. The base doctor smiled and told Patrick that he should not have any more cigars.

When Patrick first awakened, the immediate thing he did was ask about his men. The doctor told him that he was the only survivor from the alley. Then, Patrick asked where Michael was.

"I need to talk to him. C'mon doc, you have to be able to find him."

The doctor said that he had no idea, but that he would try to find out. "I'll let you know what I'm able to learn. In the meantime, get as much rest as you can. That's an order, Marine."

The following few days were a haze as Patrick slipped in and out of sleep.

But a few days later, Patrick's commanding officer, Colonel Hernandez, a tall regal looking man with very short graying hair came to visit Patrick. After exchanging pleasantries, the colonel became solemn.

"Major Franklin, I have something very unfortunate to tell you. I didn't want anyone else to deliver the news."

"Colonel?" Before the officer spoke, Patrick knew what was going to be said.

"Patrick, your brother Michael was killed. He fought bravely and inflicted great harm on the enemy. He died saving one of his men. I am sorry."

Tears began to flow down Patrick's cheeks. Maybe tough Marines were not supposed to cry, but he didn't care. He had lost his twin brother.

"At least, Sir, I got a chance to see him once before he died."

A puzzled look came over the colonel's face. He knew that combat and casualties could disorient anyone, even as fine a soldier as Patrick. "What do you mean, Major?"

"He was the one who saved me. I was close to being finished. The Iraqis had me down and were ready to finish me, but then Michael was there. I couldn't move, but I saw him kill the Iraqis. And he stopped my bleeding."

The colonel said nothing. He respected Patrick enormously, and he knew the trauma the major had suffered. He knew what Patrick was saying was impossible; Michael had been killed clear on the other side of the city, long before the time Patrick had come under fire. War was certainly unpredictable, and odd things were known to happen, but this? It defied logic. And Colonel Hernandez was a man who used logic to run his life. He was sure that Patrick was mistaken, driven to this belief by having his life nearly ripped from him, but what harm did it do? If Patrick held a vision of his brother saving him, and that image comforted him, who was he, a man who had ordered both men into combat, to take that away from this Marine who had fought so bravely? Delusion could be better than reality, he reasoned. He knew, however, that Michael had been dead for at least two hours before Patrick had been wounded. What Patrick said was impossible.

After his long recovery, Patrick retired from the military. He had already served 20 years, and he no longer wished to continue. While he had planned to stay on for life, with the death of his brother, Patrick no longer felt the desire or the passion for the armed forces. That part of his life was over forever. He could no longer be where he could not speak to anyone about what had happened. Regardless, of what anyone told him. Michael saved him that day. Patrick intended to explore the implications of this event, during the rest of his life.

TWENTY-EIGHT

THE IN-BETWEEN – DECEMBER 13

Ohhhh, this is delightful! These old fools and their meddling friends will add to the dish of the woman and child. I will taste each of them separately, and it will be a delicious feast! The old men and their helpers will be the appetizer, and the woman and child the main course!

Maledicus' form undulated in the murky darkness, his shape ever changing and growing, as he looked more and more like THEY. After all, he was formed in THEY's image. The image of his victims' faces pulsed against his form, all showing their torment, trapped in the hell of his being.

Each will feed me with their pain and fear.

I will have their souls.

I will continue to grow stronger!

TWENTY-NINE

2:00 P.M. DECEMBER 14

The cemetery was comfortable. Sam had come immediately after finishing his shift. He was working a murder case, had spent too much time on it, and needed to relax. There was no better place to unwind than the cemetery.

It was evening, so no one else was around. Sam knew he didn't have to worry, because he was, after all, a cop. *Who was going to say anything to him? If I want to go there, then, to hell with what anyone else thinks.*

He knew the path to the gravesite well. He had been there many times before. The cemetery itself was old; it dated to the Revolutionary War, it spread over hundreds of acres. With many hills, it was almost like a town until itself, divided into many sections – there was an old section for converted Native Americans, a Jewish section, and a black section. It was the way things were done in the past. Today, the entire populations of the new gravesites were integrated, like the rest of Bethberg, well integrated.

Still, the area where he searched, was in the hills towards the northeastern corner, with the most foliage and trees, something he found to be beautiful. Even though it was night, he could clearly see the large elms, oaks, maples and pine trees that formed a protective cocoon around the gravesites.

Light cascaded upon him.

He looked at the way the leaves of the trees had changed colors, hanging against the air in their shimmering palette like a painting from an American Impressionist artist in the bright sunlight. This was one of Sam's guilty pleasures as a cop. No one knew how much he loved art.

The day was now cool and the sun was bright. He stood at the headstone he wanted. "Joshua Sadlowski Beloved Son".

He swept the area to keep it clean and tidy.

Sam unfolded a fishing seat and sat down.

He opened a soda and began to talk, "How are you, son?"

"Good, Pop. How was your day?"

Sam was happy to hear his son's voice so clear and happy. It always filled him with pride.

"Long and hard. Let me tell you, Josh. Don't be a cop…I want you to be an educated man…a lawyer, a doctor, an architect, whatever makes you happy, but have an education."

"When I was little, I didn't imagine being anything but a cop."

Sam laughed at the memory. "Yeah, you used to run around with my badge and pretend to arrest the bad guys."

"I loved to do that. When you got me my toy pistol, I was so happy."

"Yeah, you loved it, but, boy did I catch hell from your Mom. She wasn't thrilled with you having a toy gun to play with. But you were a boy, so I thought it wouldn't hurt."

Sam finished his soda and put the can aside.

"Pop, can I get you another?" Josh asked and walked over to the refrigerator in their former house.

"Sure. Do we have any root beer?" Sam watched as his boy walked over to hand him a soda and then sat at the kitchen table. He was already taller than his dad.

"Thanks, Josh. You having one? Root beer was always your favorite."

Josh gave Sam a long look. "You know I can't have any soda anymore."

Sam blinked. "Oh yeah, of course."

"It's ok, Pop. I don't really miss it, and besides, I can still remember what it tastes like."

Sam nodded at him and sipped his soda.

"Can I ask you something, Pop?"

"Sure, you know that we can talk about anything."

"How is Mom these days?"

Sam took a long swig from the bottle of cold root beer. He wiped his mouth with his hand. "She is doing the best she can I guess."

"C'mon, Pop. I know better than that. She and you aren't married anymore, are you?"

"Josh, you can't imagine how tough it's been, on both of us."

"Really, you think you have it tough? I mean, c'mon, Pop. Let's be real, ok?"

Sam closed his eyes and felt a headache coming on. He knew from the way it was gathering in the front of his head over his eyes, it was going to be a bad one. He rubbed his eyes, slowly opened them. Seated in lawn chairs on either side of Josh's grave, Sam and Josh were wearing the Eagles sweatshirt that he had given him as a Christmas present. Josh had loved that shirt almost as much as he loved his Philadelphia Eagles.

"I mean, at least you get to go home. This…" He pointed at the open grave. "This is where I get to stay. I thought that my first apartment when I grew up and moved out would be small, but this isn't even a tiny efficiency." Sam took a drink of soda, and Josh laughed.

Josh looked different now. His skin was gray, his eyes were dull; it was the look Sam had seen too often when he viewed a homicide victim.

"Josh?"

"Yeah, Pop?"

"I'm sorry."

"Really? Are you?" Josh looked directly into Sam's eyes. "I don't think you're sorry."

"Don't say that, Josh. I think about you, every day."

"Well, at least you get to do what you want. You're not trapped in this nasty hole in the ground. Do you have any idea what it's like living, well, sorry, having to reside with the things in that ground? There are worms, rats, you fucking name it. It's shitty here, let me tell you."

"Josh, if I could have done anything to save you, I would have. You have to understand that. I love you."

"Do you, old man? I don't think so. I don't think you ever tried to understand me at all. You thought you knew everything about me. But you…knew…nothing."

Sam stared at his son's face, now showing signs of decay, like a corpse beginning to rot away. Long strips of skin began to hang from Josh's face.

"Why, Josh?"

"Why what, Pop?"

"Why did you do it?" Sam whispered the question that had been slowly consuming him from the moment of his knowledge of Josh's death.

Josh smiled a wide grin that stretched his rotten flesh and showed the workings of his jaw muscles. "Because I hated you, dear father."

"No, I loved you. Don't say that."

"Some detective you were. Couldn't tell that your wife was cheating on you and your son hated you." Josh burst out into laughter.

Sam tried to say something, but it felt like his entire body had turned into a block of stone and he was incapable of any kind of movement.

"I hate you, old man, because you never showed me any kind of real love. Never."

Sam started to shake. He looked at Josh and began to cry.

"You're a pathetic old fool. I'll give you one chance to prove your love to me. Will you take it, Pop?"

Sam could talk again. "What is it?" He asked softly.

"You know old man. Take the traditional cop's way out. Show me that you are willing to join me."

"What?"

"You always said that you would take a bullet for me. Well, that's what you can do to prove that you love me. If you don't, then don't ever come back here to talk to me again. Understand, old man?"

Sam looked at his right hand. He held his service weapon in it. He slowly raised it to the right side of his head.

"That's it, you old fool. Come and join me." Josh's face was now not much more than a skull with eyes that seemed to glow.

Sam closed his eyes and prepared to pull the trigger, when a loud noise startled him.

Sam woke. He found his hand in the position of holding a gun to his head. The sound of the alarm clock crashed through his aching head, and he reached over and thumped it off.

Sam realized he had been dreaming and wrapped his arms around himself and curled into a fetal position and began to cry, sobbing in loud wailing bursts, like the sound of an emergency alarm blaring for help.

A couple of hours later, Sam's phone rang.

THIRTY

2:00 P.M. DECEMBER 14

The sky was dark, just beginning to gain the smallest touch of dim pink as dawn approached. The fighting had halted for a few hours. They were all alert and wide-awake with adrenalin still running through them, even though few of the Marines and soldiers had been able to get any sleep in the prior 24 hours. Roosevelt was manning one of the key positions on the northwestern ridge, with one of the best views of the hill that led to their camp. With him were several other Marines, including a man on an automatic machine gun. Spread out along the ridge to his left and right at a distance of about 20 yards each were Bruno and Sadlowski. Directly to his left, the closest man to him was a private James Barrie, a recent arrival in Vietnam. He had the look of a corn-fed Midwestern farm boy, with tan, freckled skin and blond, cropped hair. He did, in fact, come from Iowa, and planned to return to run his father's farm when his enlistment was over. He told Roosevelt earlier that when he realized that he would be drafted, that he wanted to decide what branch of the service he would be in rather than have the government make that choice for him, so he enlisted in the Marines. "My Daddy and Granddaddy were both in the Corps, so it was an easy pick for me."

Roosevelt was nearly soaked from the hot, humid air that had blown down on them with the force of an invading army. He often thought he would have had an easier time dealing with the frigid conditions many of the Marines had faced in Korea. He was accustomed to frosty winter conditions from his many skiing trips, and he was a man who always preferred cold weather over heat. Nothing in his life had prepared him for the intense mind-numbing heat and humidity of Vietnam. The twin meteorological characteristics made him feel as if he were an ancient man long before his time. He used to laugh at the idea of retiring in 30-40 years to somewhere hot like Florida. That was for people who would be ready to give up on life—to settle down for shuffleboard and canasta, not for him. Roosevelt saw the irony. Now Florida probably would seem cool next to this soaking inferno. Roosevelt's father had suffered from arthritis, but he had refused to leave the Catskills where he had grown up. He thought of his father and the way he tried to hide the fact that his joints were troubled by intense pain. "Always make sure you keep using your body son. That way you can keep this motherfucker of a disease at bay." The first time he had heard his father swear like that, Roosevelt had been shocked. His father had always seemed to be a man who was deeply aware of propriety and proper behavior. It wasn't so much the look of discomfort on his father's face that informed Roosevelt of how much pain the older man was in, but the very fact he swore in a manner that he knew his father detested. He wondered, as he watched for movement by the VC, if the way he was feeling now was a harbinger of how he would feel later in life. That is, if he lived through this war.

"They are coming," Roosevelt whispered to the men to his left and right. He sent the signal. His man Barrie, on the communications radio, notify the rest of the unit.

"How can you tell?" Barrie whispered to Roosevelt. "I can't see anything. There's no one out there."

There was no visible sign of the enemy. The sunlight was beginning to break through the last vestiges of the night onto what seemed to be an idyllic setting of bucolic peace: A long sloping hill that connected to another forming a valley between lovely heavily forested mountains.

"I can hear them, and I can feel them"

Barrie looked at his commanding officer with disbelief.

"It is true. You spend enough time in this place, and you become accustomed to it, in tune to the sounds and the feel of it. And I am certain that they are advancing now."

"I guess I just ain't been here long enough to tell."

"That is not a problem, Marine. Just be ready, because they are coming. And remember, keep your head down when firing. We have an excellent position here, with adequate coverage and a fine visual field for fire."

"Yes, sir."

The attack began suddenly. First there was no enemy on the hill, then it seemed as if a horde of VC were racing up the hill at them, sounding like a swarm of very pissed off hornets looking to sting anyone they could over and over. Anything resembling standard battlefield activity was rare in this war, this type of fighting was highly unusual, but it was happening. The Tet Offensive, in many ways, resembled old-fashioned military tactics, rather than the guerilla methods more often employed by the Viet Cong.

From along the entire length of the ridge, fire rang out, breaking up the emerging day like a sudden hailstorm on a summer's picnic.

To Roosevelt, who was an excellent marksman, it seemed as if he did not have to aim his weapon. So many enemy were advancing all he had to do was point his rifle and fire. He was certain to bring down an opponent with every round. The Marine rifles and machine guns were blazing at their strategic points and creating a killing field on the hill that the V.C. soldiers were attempting to move forward in order to capture the ridge. If the enemy took the ridge, then advancement and eventual overrunning of the entire U.S. camp seemed likely.

There were so many V.C. that they seemed to be swarming up the hill by the sheer enormity of their number. They seemed to be a force of nature, moving like a wind sweeping over a plain more than an organized group of ordinary men. As the fighting continued in the early hours of the morning, some of the V.C. soldiers came so close to the top of the ridge that Roosevelt could see their faces before he fired on them. Ordinarily he would have wondered about the lives of the men he was facing in combat, but today there was no time for any kind of reflection, only enough to reload and continue shooting. The one thought that did begin to creep into his mind was they might run out of ammunition before the enemy ran out of soldiers. He hoped, at some later point, he could forgive himself for the number of lives he had taken.

This wave of the battle they had been fighting for several days finally dwindled to a stop. They had once again repelled the enemy, but Roosevelt knew the extraordinary army they were facing, many battle hardened from their time, serving against the French, and they were brave almost beyond human capacity for courage. While he killed them because it was his duty, Roosevelt felt a deep respect for the men he had faced in battle.

The fighting had ceased, and the only sounds coming from the field, littered with stacks of dead and dying men, were the soft moans of those critically wounded soldiers. The Marines, who were in serious need of ammunition, were awaiting a supply convoy. Yet, they had no way of knowing when it would come because their communications man was dead and his equipment destroyed by an enemy grenade. They did what soldiers have done since the beginning of organized warfare – they went onto the battlefield to find more weapons, ammunition, and supplies.

145

No order from higher command was forth coming about what to do with the wounded enemy, but many Marines simply administered a coup-de-grace as the dying enemy soldiers lay on the field.

"I can't stand to hear them making those sounds," one Marine said to another as he passed by Roosevelt.

Roosevelt had decided to remain in his position and keep watch. He understood the men's desire to find more supplies, but he distrusted the field. It was too wide open, and the men who went out onto it were extraordinarily vulnerable to enemy fire. They were used to fighting in the jungle, moving in small units, not in this open field type of combat.

About fifty yards behind the ridge, an impromptu campfire had been constructed, complete with coffee brewing. Roosevelt indulged in sending Private Barrie to bring him a cup of Joe. It was morning, and if Roosevelt could not enjoy anything else, at least he would have a cup of what passed for coffee in the field.

He watched as the huge youngster lumbered back up the hill towards the top of the ridge. He seemed to Roosevelt, who was only in his early twenties himself, like a child. In that moment, Roosevelt realized that he was determined to make sure that Private Barrie made it back to his farm in Iowa.

"Here you are, sir," the private said as he sat down next to his Lieutenant.

"You know, Private, you might have brought a cup for yourself."

"Aw, it's all right, sir."

Roosevelt realized that this huge kid, who had the size to be a professional football player, did not drink coffee, and they did not have any cocoa on the battlefield.

"Have you had any food in a while?"

"It's ok, sir."

"Marine, that was not an answer to my question. I repeat, have you had any food in a while?"

"Sir, no sir." He had snapped to attention, like a new recruit, in boot camp on Parris Island. Roosevelt almost smiled at the incongruity of this huge youngster's innocence in the face of such carnage.

"At Ease, Private, and sit down." Roosevelt took out of his backpack a chocolate bar he had been saving. He broke it in half and handed it to Barrie.

"Have some breakfast with me. I know that officers and enlisted men are not supposed to fraternize, but I am sure it will be okay." Roosevelt smiled and winked conspiratorially. Then he whispered, "Just do not tell anyone." Roosevelt watched Barrie nod his agreement with a solemn and serious face that nearly broke Roosevelt's heart to see. It was wrong that someone like this kid was fighting in this war.

Roosevelt heard footsteps and looked quickly to see some of the Marines returning from their scavenger's hunt. Bruno and Sadlowski slid down on the ridge next to Roosevelt. Bruno was carrying several rifles, grenades, and a mortar launcher. Sadlowski was grinning. In his cache were three rifles, a knife, two grenades, and a pistol, along with several bags filled with ammunition.

"It's Christmas, sir. Let's see what Santa brought you. Ho ho ho!" Sadlowski tossed one of the rifles to Roosevelt who caught it and smiled. It was in excellent shape. Sadlowski then tossed a bag filled with ammunition to Roosevelt.

"Now, I feel bad, Sadlowski. I did not get you any gift in return."

"It's not a problem, sir. When we get out of here, and go on R & R, I can think of several presents you can get me." Sadlowski grinned at Bruno, who only shook his head. Next to them Barrie sat blushing furiously, his face as red as blistered skin.

"Is that all you think of?" Roosevelt said and smiled.

"Pretty much. Well, that and staying the hell alive."

A shot rang out to interrupt them. They looked and saw one of the returning Marines fall forward screaming in pain. He was shot in the right leg and was doubled over, holding his wound, trying to keep the blood from flowing out of his body. Several other Marines still hid in the field, opened fire and quickly disposed of the shooter. As they ran to aid their fallen comrade, more shooting rang out, and they fell over.

"Son of a bitch! They are using that Marine as bait. He was shot in the leg intentionally." Roosevelt whispered to Bruno. The Marines along the ridge returned fire for a brief period and then stopped. They could all hear the moaning of their three wounded comrades.

"What're we going to do?" Bruno looked up at Roosevelt.

"I do not know. Anyone who goes out there is likely not coming back. I will not order any of my men out on a suicide mission."

"Fuck it," Sadlowski said. "They don't call us the Suicide Squad for no reason. I can't let those poor sons of bitches out there."

"I can't either," Bruno added.

Roosevelt gave the order along the ridge that he wanted suppressing fire while the Marines went out to recover the wounded. It was the best cover he could think of.

"All right, this is how it goes, so listen up. Sadlowski, Bruno, and I, along with those three men" he pointed to three Marines crouched next to Sadlowski ". . . are going out to get those men. You, Sergeant Bonner, are to stay with your machine gun. If I do not return, you are in command. The rest of you give the suppressing cover. Ok, ready? Let us do this."

The Marines sprinted out of their positions on the ridge and ran quickly towards their fallen comrades. As they did, the other Marines on the ridge opened fire beyond them, towards any place that was likely to have an enemy soldier. They moved quickly and in zigzag motions, hoping to create a more difficult target. On his right Roosevelt heard a sound and looked to see one of the Marines who went out fall with half his face gone.

He saw Bruno lifting one downed man and carrying him back up the hill. Bruno was so fast and graceful he seemed to be moving almost as if he was not carrying any weight at all.

Roosevelt found the first man who was hit and kneeling by him, looked at his ashen face, the open and staring eyes. He was too late. The Marine died from massive blood loss.

Roosevelt felt two bullets miss him by no more than the width of a fishing line, and he dove to the ground. Then he bolted up to a crouch and scurried to another downed Marine. Even though the field boomed with the sound of guns firing from both sides, when Roosevelt reached the next fallen man, he seemed to hear nothing. Everything appeared was covered with a blanket of white noise. He saw the Marine, who was still alive and holding the wound in his chest. Roosevelt picked him up with two arms, holding him the way a father would hold a child and moved quickly up the hill.

He felt gunfire around him and bullets nicking him but not doing any serious damage, more like the annoying sting of a bee than the vicious piercing of a wasp. He saw Sadlowski and one of the other Marines had made it back with their men, and he was within ten feet of the top of the hill when a bullet went through his calf. He lurched forward and dropped the man he was carrying. He heard the sound of other men jumping over the top of the ridge and pulling the wounded man to safety. He began to rise and hobble back up the hill when a giant seemed to appear and scoop him up and carry Roosevelt just as he had carried the other man.

Roosevelt felt himself being handed over to other men and then looked back at Private Barrie, who was filled with pride. He began to say something to Roosevelt when Barrie's head exploded from behind from an enemy shot.

Roosevelt watched as the Marine tumbled forward, his large body collapsing in front of where Roosevelt crouching as the medic tended him. Barrie was dead, but he turned his head, what remained of it and looked directly at Roosevelt.

"I did this for you," the voice came out of Barrie's mouth but had none of the sweetness that it had before. The tone was deep and ugly. "If you hadn't gone out to be brave, I would be alive. It's your fault. It's your fault! YOUR FAULT!"

Roosevelt jackknifed up in bed and gasped for air. He could still hear the sound of that voice as he realized that he had been dreaming. His nightshirt was soaked in sweat, and his bed. He looked down and saw his groin was soaked. *My god*, he thought…*I lost control and urinated on myself.*

As he stood very unsteadily, his wet nightclothes sticking to his shaking body, he could feel his mouth becoming dry, and the familiar pain begin under his tongue and along his arm. His chest began to pound.

He reached for his pills on the night table and quickly placed one under his tongue. As the pill dissolved, he felt his body begin to reclaim its equilibrium. The pain began to subside and his chest relaxed.

Disgusted, Roosevelt stripped off his clothing and bed sheets. The last thing he wanted to be was an incontinent, old man who needed someone to take care of him. He would rather die than be reduced to that indignity.

He went to his bathroom and showered. As the water cascaded over him, the images from the dream filled him again, especially that of the dead boy, and he cried, a long slow, cry that built to an explosive wail, but one that no one could hear. *At least, I can have that dignity.*

After the shower, he dressed and went to his study. It was three in the morning, but he knew he would not be able to go back to sleep that night. He sat with a crystal glass of 18 year old Macallan and thought.

His heart had recovered, and he felt almost normal now. *I have had something close to that dream many times, but not like that. I know that I am at fault for his death. I never specifically ordered him to stay undercover no matter what happened. He hero-worshipped me. I caused his death as much as if I had ordered him on a suicide mission. I know it. I have tried to accept it for too many years now, and I have dreamt about it too many times. Yet, never like that. The dream always ended with his death. What was that voice?*

Roosevelt was determined not to go back to sleep that night. He did not want to take a chance on having that dream recur, so he picked up the first volume of Morris' excellent biography of Teddy Roosevelt and began to read.

About 30 minutes later, his phone rang.

THIRTY-ONE

4:30 P.M. December 13

Jeremy sat on his Victorian Era yellow and green embroidered sofa in his immaculate living room. He knew he should be going over evidence that was recorded during the attempted blessing of the house, but his spirit was simply not ready. After they had finished and stowed the equipment, he had walked home, slowly and alone. David was on his mind. It was not as if the memory of his beloved partner was ever far from his thoughts, but recently and especially this afternoon, it was almost as if David had been there with Jeremy, and the sadness he felt was intense.

Jeremy gazed at the living room they had carefully restored and decorated. David and Jeremy had loved renovating and decorating the old Victorian style house they had purchased for what was then a song. David had told Jeremy that compared to the prices in New York City and its surrounding communities, the real estate market in Bethberg, now undervalued would be a steal. "Especially with what I have to spend," he had told David.

He was correct. It was then 1970, and what would cost a million dollars in some surrounding areas of New York, such as Long Island or Connecticut, would only be 50-70 thousand in this area of Pennsylvania. They found an old house in serious need of repair on the edge of the small downtown area, listed as "needing TLC". The advertisement was correct. The house was in extremely bad shape with the entire roof needing replacing. Almost all of the windows needed repairing or upgraded, and the condition of the walls and the floors was terrible. The wallpaper was peeling away from most of the walls, and various critters, ranging from roaches to chipmunks and squirrels, had established the old place as their palatial residence. "It's a veritable Waldorf Astoria for the local fauna," David had observed. They even encountered a deer in the kitchen when they were inspecting the house one day. The back door to the place had fallen off, and the doe had simply wandered into the room searching for food.

While the house was in near shambles, both men saw great potential in the building. They were able to visualize what it would look like when carefully and lovingly restored to its former glory. Neither David nor Jeremy was given to waffling about major decisions, especially those concerning their lives or business. After carefully checking the structural integrity of the house's foundation and of its walls, which they determined to be sound and solid, and after an evening of discussion over a fine meal at The Hotel Bethberg, then considered the finest restaurant in town, they made a decision to purchase and renovate the building.

"To the restoration of 359 W. Nesquehoning Ave. May she soon be once more a fine painted lady!" David smiled widely at his toast and held up his wine glass. Clinking their glasses, both smiled. At this point, due to his recognition of his alcoholism, Jeremy was drinking white grape juice in his wine glass. David had broached the subject of his drinking wine when they were together much earlier. He had been concerned that he might be a bad influence on Jeremy.

"I love you too much to be an influence that might cause you to drink again," he had told Jeremy. But Jeremy had assured him that it was no problem.

"Just because I can't drink doesn't mean that anyone else around me, especially you, cannot imbibe. I'm no child, and I'm not so weak that I can't control myself when around alcohol."

"Are you sure?"

"David, I've known that I have been an alcoholic for many years now, and I have my disease under control. I go to AA meetings once a week, but I'm not dependent on them, unlike some of the other members. I don't wish to disparage them, but they are truly weak. I have made a decision to control my situation, and I go to those meetings to remind myself of what could be if I ever decide to be foolish. I have no desire to be a drunk ever again."

Jeremy smiled and finished his grape juice, then ordered a refill from the server.

"I told you before how bad I had become. I used to wake up in rooms I didn't know, not being sure what I was doing there or how I even got there. I was close to destruction, and one day, when I was walking down an alley— can you imagine me sleeping in a garbage and rat infested alley?—I was walking down when I saw someone I knew there. He was also sleeping it off, and I recognized him. He had been one of my professors in college, a brilliant art historian, whose career had suddenly veered off course, and he dropped out of sight. Something happened, I never knew what, but soon after I graduated, I learned that he had lost his tenured position, and you know how hard that is to do. He must have been in his early 50s when I saw him, but I swear that he looked like he was in his late 70s. I considered waking him, but I decided that he had chosen his life and had to live it. It's what we all have to do."

David reached out and gave Jeremy's hand a subtle, but reassuring squeeze.

Jeremy managed a little, sad smile and continued. "That might sound cold, but I knew that if I didn't immediately stop drinking, I would end up like him, dying in an alley somewhere, alone and forgotten. So, the upshot of all this is that I decided to go cold turkey, then and there. I have not had another drink since then, and it's been several decades. Please don't misunderstand me. I am not heroic, nor am I very strong, but what I was then and still am is a man terrified of what I might have been and could still be if I don't watch myself carefully."

"I'm proud of you, Jeremy," David said. "I want you to know that. I'm proud of you, and I love you."

"I love you too."

Those days were filled with work. They had purchased the old house and spent several years working on it. They did much of the work themselves, and for the rest that they could not do, they hired the best contractors they could find. When they were finished, the house was a showpiece, with the kind of beauty featured in magazines devoted to architecture and home renovation. In fact, they both celebrated when their home was chosen for a spread in one of the magazines.

In addition, to making the house into their beloved home, they created a storefront for what would become their highly successful antiques business, the place that would draw many people and lead to their friendship with Sarah and Roosevelt.

Jeremy thought about David's smile and his touch, and he missed him, as if a hole in his spirit was cutout when David had died. Jeremy wished that David was somehow there. David had died 7 years earlier, but the pain of his loss was still as strong as ever. Jeremy still slept on the same side of their bed, continuing to leave the other for David. He still went to the same places that they used to go together. And despite others gently suggesting that he try to find a new partner, he was adamant that he would never do that. It was not that he was against others finding new lovers, but he had finally found his soul mate, his life's true partner, his one love, and he knew that he would never be able to find that with anyone else. Jeremy had committed to remaining a widower, as he called himself, and faithful forever to his partner. He still wore the ring, the one they called their wedding ring that they had given to each other in a very private, and not legal, ceremony, long before the days when sanctioned marriage for gays had arisen in the country's consciousness. They had both felt that their commitment to each other was as solid and binding as any legal marriage that some of their straight friends had.

When he had been at one of his worst moments after David's death, Sarah had visited him often. She had become a confidant and trusted friend, like the sister he had always wished he had; indeed, he felt that Roosevelt also had become his brother. Sarah had spoken to him about the subject of dating because he had mentioned to her that others had suggested he do it. When he told her that he could not, that he would love only David, she had said she understood completely. "That is the way I feel about Roosevelt. If I should outlive him, I would never consider anyone ever again."

Sarah had held him and comforted him when he broke down and cried, as he said, like a child.

"David, I do miss you so much," he said to the air. He began to cry softly, and he turned to rest his head on the arm of the overstuffed sofa and fell asleep.

8:00 P.M.

It was early evening when he walked into the bar. It was a place he hadn't seen in many years, McElroy's, a little dump in The Ruins, the Bowery-like section of Bethberg, as it was not so affectionately called by the locals. McElroy's faced an alley just off Lincoln Avenue, the rutted road that was the central street of The Ruins. All that remained here were a few bodegas, an adult bookstore, and many shuttered buildings.

The bar's lights were on, but it seemed like the dust and dinginess of the place kept much of the light from producing any illumination. A murky fog of dust hung in the air. He looked around and saw that most of the seats at the old bar were still open. Jeremy walked past one old man who was asleep, head down on the counter. Another fellow, two seats down, was muttering softly and incoherently as he sipped from his beer. At the corner table two men of indeterminate age sat fading away into their drinks.

Jeremy went halfway down the bar and slowly climbed onto one of the old and rickety wooden chairs. He glanced at the clock that hung over the center of the cash register at the center of the wall across from the bar: 8:15. He sat down, and the bartender, someone Jeremy vaguely remembered seeing in the past, came over to him.

"Yeah?" the fat man asked as he wiped the counter in front of Jeremy with an old, filthy bar towel.

"Vodka and tonic, over ice." Jeremy really needed a drink, so he might as well skip the beer and go straight for the good stuff. No sense in wasting any time and the bartender mixed the drink, set it in front of Jeremy, and took one of the bills Jeremy had set on the counter.

"Keep the change from that one, and keep them coming." Jeremy unceremoniously downed the drink in one shot. He felt the alcohol move quickly through his system, and he began to relax. *I needed that for too long.*

He set the glass down carefully – he always hated those guys who pounded their glass down noisily when finished, as if they had accomplished some great feat by drinking their drink.

What idiots. Jeremy signaled the bartender for another. This one he downed a little more slowly. As he drank, he looked around the room. At the end of the bar, a small black and white television played—a baseball game was on, but the volume was down, so he couldn't tell who the teams where. Not that it really mattered to Jeremy, because he never followed sports, except when he was in a bar. Then he wanted to watch the Yankees if he could. Then it seemed to be important.

When the bartender came over for another round, Jeremy asked, "What game is on?"

"Mets and Braves."

"No Yankees on?"

"Nope, not tonight. Now we gotta suffer through these assholes tryin' to imitate playin' the game."

Jeremy sat and watched the silent innings go by. It seemed like a perfect thing to do – watch an unimportant contest in silence while he kept pace with each half inning with his drinks.

Jeremy glanced over at the clock. It was 9:30, and he was definitely feeling better. Whatever was bothering him, seemed to have vanished, and he was feeling like he could sit in this seat and watch game after game for as long as he wanted. *This was life. This is what I need.*

The bartender placed another vodka and tonic and a shot glass of whiskey in front of Jeremy. "Well done, sir. Well done! You must have read my mind." Jeremy raised the shot glass and looked at the amber liquid in it. He swirled it around as if it were the finest single malt scotch and not the cheapest bar hooch available.

He nosed it and sighed. "A truly fine bouquet." Then he shot it. He shuddered at the burning feeling as the whiskey went down. Warmth spread through his body. The Water of Life – Uisce Bahu. He set the glass down and reached for the vodka and tonic. It was time for the chaser. That, too, went down in one swallow.

I have to make up for lost time.

The next time Jeremy looked up at the television, he realized that a different game was on. A perplexed look came over his face. What was going on?

"Bartender, is this the same game?"

The bartender looked at him and shook his head. "It's the Yankees and White Sox, 3rd inning."

Jeremy smiled. This was better. He glanced at the clock – 10:00.

Another vodka and tonic appeared before him on the counter, along with another shot of whiskey. They kept coming in pairs.

1:30 A.M. DECEMBER 14

Later, the game was over, and Jeremy was very happy. The Yankees won. That always makes it a great day.

"One more for the road Sir, and a very good tip for you. Actually, make it two more." He placed several large bills on the counter and saw, as if by magic, two vodka and tonics and two shots of whiskey appear before him.

He stood and looked at the drinks. *Let's see if I can still do it, four in a row!* He began with a vodka and tonic and downed it, then a whiskey, then the other two drinks in the same order. He wiped a stray bit of drink from his mouth with his sleeve.

"I am afraid, sir that I must depart, but I am sure that I will see you again."

The bartender turned and looked at him and smiled. But his eyes were different. Before they looked like they belonged to the old man who used to work in here, but now, they were very different, clearer, and dark, very dark.

The bartender grinned showing a mouth of perfect white teeth, gleaming in the murk of the bar. "I'm sure you will. We can plan on spending a great deal of time together," he said as he wiped the counter and collected the very large tip that Jeremy had left for him.

Jeremy shuddered and felt cold. He didn't want to look at the bartender anymore, and he wanted to be out of the bar quickly. He stumbled forward as fast as he could, but walking was suddenly very difficult, as if he were trying to move through a pond of mud. With every step he seemed to drag his feet through unseen muck, and he staggered with the effort.

He pushed the door to the bar open and stepped out into the night. The air was cold and harsh, with wind howling. He couldn't see properly, and stepped off the curb clumsily and twisted his ankle. He tumbled into the grimy and wet alley. As he fell, Jeremy heard the terrible snap of bones breaking in his ankle.

His ankle throbbed with pain, and as he grabbed it, he awoke suddenly.

Jeremy was in his living room, but he was on the floor next to the sofa. He must have been sleepwalking and fell while he moved around. Yet, as in the dream, he had hurt his ankle. He lay grimacing in pain.

Slowly, he gathered his strength and used his ever-present cell phone to call for an ambulance. He hobbled to the front door to open it and waited for the ambulance to arrive. Tears ran down his face as he felt the injured ankle swelling.

Damn, I could use a drink, he thought, and he was horrified at his reaction to the dream. He realized that the urge to drink was now as strong as when he had first quit. He wasn't as strong as he thought he was.

Several hours later, at the Bethberg Medical Center Sam and Roosevelt waited for their friend to finish being treated. At the hospital, Jeremy had called Roosevelt. He didn't want to, but he knew that Roosevelt would have been deeply offended if he didn't, and Jeremy agreed with Roosevelt. This is what real friends do. Jeremy sighed and called Sam too. While Roosevelt could handle any assistance that Jeremy would need, he didn't want Sam to think he was not needed or wanted. Even though the big man pretended to be such a tough guy, Jeremy knew a very sensitive soul was hidden under the gruff exterior.

It was around 4 A.M., and the doctors had taken x-rays and confirmed that there were no broken bones. This was simply a very bad sprain. They wrapped his ankle, gave Jeremy a cane and sent him on his way with orders to stay off his feet for a couple of weeks. Roosevelt and Sam smiled, knowing their friend attempt to walk around tomorrow.

"That's true guys, but I at least will be using a much better and much more fashionable cane than this monstrosity." He held up the standard issue hospital cane with a look of disgust on his face. "If I do have to use a cane, I know which one it will be. The wolf-head oak cane that was David's. It's a thing of beauty."

"Yes, it certainly is," Roosevelt said. "Now, shall we take you home?"

"Absolutely not, guys," Jeremy replied with a weak smile. "While we're up, why don't we all go to the diner and have some breakfast? I don't know about you guys, but I really could use. . . a couple of cups of coffee."

As they helped their friend out of the hospital, Roosevelt and Sam glanced at each other. They both caught the possible hidden meaning in what Jeremy had said.

THIRTY-TWO

1:00 A.M. DECEMBER 14

Helen Murray woke with a start. She heard something wrong, and her emergency hearing was as keen and refined about anything concerning her niece as was any mother's towards her own child. She was instantly awake, unlike the years before she had Helena under her care when fully coming around took the work of a long shower and five or six cups of strong black coffee. As she jumped out of bed, she heard a soft moan and a whimper from her niece's bedroom.

Helen sprinted out of her room, down the hallway, and into Helena's room.

Inside the room was a faint, soft glow from the little girl's pink fairy night-light. The comforting light showed the pictures on the walls that Helen had painted to create a delightful pixie and forest paradise of smiling animals, flying fairies, and rainbows. Around the room, surrounding the child's bed, were laughing chipmunks and squirrels and grasshoppers perched on mushrooms, happy field mice with smiling faces and magical dragonflies with bright, glowing wings. The room was over crowded with stuffed animals of myriad variety. Helena lay in bed clutching tightly her favorite, an old-worn out giant teddy bear. Helen had tried to give the little girl as happy and normal a life as she possibly could. She knew that the child would always have to deal with the loss of her parents, but she wanted her niece to know that she was beloved. Until this trouble had begun, Helen had believed that she had succeeded in wrapping the little girl in the arms of her protective love and care, and that she had insulated her from harm and peril.

As she looked at her niece with her tiny arms clutching the large stuffed animal, Helen was frightened. Normally a peaceful sleeper who could stay in a deep, comfortable slumber no matter what commotion might be occurring

158

around her, Helena had clearly been thrashing in bed. Her covers, tossed aside, as she turned so that her head was at the foot of her bed. Helen bent over the little girl and put her hand on the child's forehead. Helen gasped. The little girl was soaked in sweat, her auburn hair was matted to her face. Her forehead felt as if it was being heated from within by a portable stove.

"My god," she whispered. Helen didn't need a thermometer to know the child had a terrible fever. She could feel the internal heat radiating through the skin of the tiny forehead onto her fingers. Helena, except for a few colds, had been an exceptionally healthy child. This fever was very unusual.

Helen was not a worrier by nature. An even-tempered and logical person, she did not run to the doctor every time her niece had a sniffle or took a tumble. She knew these experiences were part of growing, and she knew she was perfectly capable of dealing with such negligible problems herself. This fever, however, was not minor. Just to be sure, she ran to the bathroom, grabbed one of the forehead strips, and came back and checked Helena's temperature—105 degrees, definitely serious.

Helen, without hesitation, decided what to do. She ran to her room, slipped on a pair of sneakers and the old clothes she was wearing, she wasn't concerned if anyone saw her in the Bethberg College sweats she wore to sleep in—then bolted back to Helena's room. She wrapped the sleeping child in a blanket, picked her up, ran downstairs and grabbed her purse and keys.

As she carried her niece, Helen was startled to realize that she could feel the girl's fever even through the blanket. She took a moment and kissed the child's forehead. Helena opened her eyes just a bit and gazed up at her aunt with nearly glassy eyes.

"Aunt Helen?" The child's voice was more of a croak than a whisper.

"Sh…sh…go back to sleep, honey."

"Aunt Helen, is the bad man still there?"

Helen's heart seemed to freeze at these words. There had been no one in the room. She was sure of that. If a man had been there and tried to hurt her niece, she was certain she would have killed the intruder—she was no pacifist and would not hesitate to do anything to protect her niece—but no one was there.

"It's ok. Go to sleep, honey."

The girl's eyes closed, and she was quickly back asleep. Helen hustled out of the house to the old Volvo she drove, which was parked directly in front of her property. She efficiently placed and buckled Helena into her child safety seat. The car might be old, but it was strong and safe, and the car seat was brand new.

Then, driving like an experienced NASCAR racer, she barreled through the almost empty streets of the city, and in a few minutes, the car came screeching to a halt in the parking lot of the Bethberg Medical Center Emergency Room.

Luckily, on this particular weeknight, the emergency room was almost empty—there had been no fights, no arrests, and no accidents, so when Helen came in carrying her niece in a bundle of blankets, almost at a run, she immediately caught the admittance clerk's attention.

The clerk, Patricia, by her name tag, was a very large, indeed, obese woman, who was irritated immediately that her nice, quiet evening had been disturbed. *Why is it I can't even get one lousy night of peace in this godforsaken place? Don't I do enough here?* She had a celebrity magazine to read, her nails to paint, and her chocolate cupcakes to eat. *Can't this crazy bitch see I'm busy? Been waiting all week to read this.* She needed to catch up on the latest celebrity breakups and the awful state of TV singing competitions. What she didn't need, and she was sure of this from the look of the woman, was another welfare mother to deal with.

"Hey!" Helen barked at the woman when she refused to look up from her magazine. "My niece is burning up with a fever. I need her seen by a doctor—now!"

Patricia reluctantly looked up and thought, *real flippin great. Just what I need, another nutty mother. I got better things to do with my time than deal with this and nursemaid your over-active imagination. If you can't take care of your kid, why did you have it? Be real…The kid has a cold…go the hell home.* "Ok. Just a minute. Before anything else happens though, you need to fill out these forms, and I need to see your insurance info." She gave Helen a smile. "Or your welfare information." She pushed the papers towards Helen and turned her bulk back to her magazine.

What Helen did next surprised both the clerk and herself. She was not normally a violent person, and she often told her students, while fighting was sometimes necessary, it should always be a last resort to settling a problem. Now, when she saw this fat bitch ignoring Helena's illness, she felt herself go cold, and she saw a red haze spread in front of her eyes.

She reached across the counter and grabbed the clerk by the front of her shirt and when she spoke, she hit every word with such emphasis, that if felt like she was slapping the clerk with her voice.

"LISTEN-TO-ME-YOU-STUPID-BITCH!!"

Patricia's eyes widened in shock—a tiny squeak slipped through her now tightly closed lips. It sounded like "Erp."

"This is NOT JUST A COLD. My niece is seriously ill, and SHE NEEDS A DOCTOR!—NOW!"

A doctor was walking nearby when he heard the yelling. He hurried towards the two women. "Is there a problem here?" He looked around for the security guard, but as always, the temporary rent-a-cop was nowhere. It wasn't likely that he would have been of any help anyway. He spent most of his time on break, outside smoking.

The doctor hurried out of the Emergency Room area and to the admittance desk. "Ma'am, you have to . . . "

He had begun to address Helen when he stopped and stood with his mouth hanging open as he looked at the furious face of the woman who had been his favorite teacher in Bethberg High School. The same teacher, whose recommendations helped him gain entrance to and several scholarships from prestigious Lafayette College, located to the south of Bethberg in Easton, Pennsylvania.

Jonathon Wilson had been a very bright but very unhappy boy. He came from a family seen in town as "bad". His father and two brothers had all been in trouble with the law for various offenses, ranging from petty theft to dealing drugs. His mother was a heroin addict who was arrested numerous times on a wide variety of charges. When no one else seemed to believe in his dreams of going to college and becoming a doctor, Ms. Murray had seen something in the boy and had given him the support he needed. She had even confronted his father during a parent-teacher conference, in which the elder Wilson's attendance was almost as rare as an appearance of Haley's Comet, when he, obviously drunk, started saying he hadn't gone to college, he had turned out all right. Why should any of his kids try to show him up by going to college? The man made the mistake of saying this directly to Ms. Murray, whom he assumed he could easily intimidate. He was accustomed to using his 6'5" and 250lb frame to bully men and women, but when Ms. Murray was finished with him, he seemed to shrink by about one foot, and he continued to slouch in his chair at her onslaught.

Jonathon had watched all of this in awe. His mother, now only a shell of a person, had always quaked in fright whenever his father went on a rampage. Even his older brothers, both huge men themselves, stayed clear of their father's anger. Jonathon had once seen his oldest brother stand up to his father, and it ended with his father dropping him with a left hook to the belly. The sibling who terrified Jonathon the most was writhing on the floor, holding his stomach. When he saw Ms. Murray facing his father down, although he did not remember the words she said, he would always remember that lightning had flashed in her eyes and thunder had roared from her mouth. Soon after that meeting, the elder Wilson seemed to avoid any mention of college and let the boy study in peace, at least for a while, until his alcohol-riddled brain forgot her message. Jonathon remembered after Ms. Murray's initial storm of passion had subsided, she had quietly taken his father aside and made him bend down so she could whisper in his ear. He saw his father grow pale and mumble, "Sure, sure. Ok."

Since that time, his life had improved enough that he could focus on his studies, at least for a few months. Then the yelling and the beatings came back, worse than ever. He, like his brothers, had been a big youngster, over 6'2" and 210 pounds at the age of 16, but he had also learned from many years of violence directed at him to be timid. When he came to school one day in the winter wearing sunglasses to hide his two black eyes, Ms. Murray made him stay after school, and she reached up and took off the shades. He remembered the look in her eyes as she sent him away. It was about one week later when Lieutenant Sadlowski had intervened and Jonathon was put in foster care. He was grateful to the police officer, but he knew that this help had begun with Ms. Murray. He was convinced she was a guardian angel sent to save his life.

"Ms. Murray?"

Helen looked up at the towering doctor who had interrupted her fury. Then she smiled. "Hello, Jonathon. It is wonderful to see you, but I seem to have a problem here." Helen shot a look at the admitting clerk that reminded him of the way she had looked at his father. "Maybe you can help, since NO ONE else seems to be inclined to!"

As she heard those words, Patricia shrunk into her bulk, just as his father had years ago.

"Do you know this woman?" The clerk's voice was a mere squeak.

"Yes, I do, Patricia. I am sure everything is fine. Why don't you go take a break now, and I'll take care of everything. I'm sure that Ms. Murray is simply worried."

The clerk backed off her chair and exited in a huff as fast as her huge form could waddle.

"Don't worry about Patricia. It'll be fine."

"I'm not worried about her at all. It's Helena I'm concerned about."

"Ms. Murray, I haven't seen you in years, and I would love to catch up." He looked over at Helena, who, amazingly, was still sleeping. "But first I think there is something more important to attend to. Let me take a look at your daughter."

"Thanks, Jonathon. Helena is my niece, not my daughter. But she is mine."

He looked confused.

"I am her legal guardian. I'll explain later."

"Well, bring her in here." He led Helen through a pair of swinging doors into the main section of the E.R. and to one of the examination cubicles. He closed the curtain behind them for privacy, and Helen placed the girl gently on the table.

A nurse came over and slipped into their area. "Doctor?"

"This child is ill. Let's see what we can do to help. If you don't mind, Barbara, can you get the insurance information from Ms. Murray later and enter it? There was a little problem with…"

"With Patricia." The tall African-American nurse shook her head and sighed. "That woman is useless." The face of the nurse tightened as she thought of the clerk. "Don't worry, Ma'am. Everything will be taken care of." Barbara was a woman who took her work seriously, even when others around her did not, and she was devoted to her vocation of helping others in need of medical care. She did not suffer fools easily and especially incompetents like the huge woman who wasted time behind the admittance desk and who only retained her job because she was a niece of someone higher up in the chain of command. Patricia often created more problems for the people who came seeking help than they had when they originally arrived in the ER. As she took the insurance card from Ms. Murray, Barbara looked straight at her. "Your little girl is in good hands now. I will take care of this, and we will make sure that your child is taken care of."

"Thank you." Helen felt such relief from this expression of caring that she felt tears begin to well up. Yet, then she tamped them down as her father used to push down the tobacco in his briar pipe so it would compact and give a good, manageable smoke. There was time enough later for crying; now Helena needed her to be strong.

The doctor did a quick but efficient examination of the sleeping child, and he pulled his brow tight into furrows, which made him seem older than his thirty years. "Whatever has caused this is not clear, but this child has a very high fever, and it seems to be rising. Did you check it before bringing her in?"

"105."

"Of course you did. Well, it is almost 106 now. That is beginning to enter dangerous territory, so it is the very first thing we are doing to deal with. We have to bring the fever down, then, get fluids into her, because she might be dehydrating. This may not be pleasant, Ms. Murray. I am going to have her wrapped in special chilled blankets. I hope it will be enough. If not, and her temperature keeps rising, we might need an ice bath. We have to stop this fever. Then we can determine what caused it, which might be as important as the fever itself. Do you want to stay for the procedure Ms. Murray, or would you rather wait outside?"

"I'm not leaving her."

The nurse returned and handed the insurance card back to Helen. The doctor then informed the nurse of what they would do. She hurried out and returned shortly with the chilled blankets. They quickly undressed the little girl and got her into a small robe. Then as the doctor wrapped her in the chilled blankets, the nurse hooked up the IV with a water drip and connected it to a small needle in the child's right arm. Helena whimpered a little and shivered, but she did not wake up until after the fever had broken. When she did, Helen hugged her and gave her a small cup with a straw to sip water from.

The doctor took care of having Helena admitted for observation. Often the medical staff would simply send a child home with a prescription after breaking the fever, but he wanted to be sure that the little girl was truly healthy before she left. He owed at least that much and, in reality, much more to Ms. Murray.

Later, after Helena had gone back to sleep, Jonathon sat and talked with Ms. Murray. "It was the right thing you did bringing her in."

Helen looked at him with exhaustion in her eyes and nodded.

"This could have become very dangerous very quickly."

She reached over and took his hand. "Thank you, Jonathon. I see you have justified my faith in you."

He looked at her and beamed, pleased that he was able to give something back to the one person who believed in him when no one else did.

He began to speak, but his voice caught, and he stopped. She looked at him and smiled. Then he continued. "I do want to keep her in for observation. I have already arranged for it, providing that you agree. I think, it would be a good idea, because we don't know what caused the fever, nor do we know what it made it rise so quickly. It might simply be a bad cold, but I want to be sure."

Helen shook her head in agreement. "Will there be a chair in her room?"

"Of course, and you may certainly stay with her. I will make sure that a cot is brought put in the room for you. I am here all night, so I will check in when I can, Ms. Murray."

"Thank you and Jonathon . . ."

"Yes, Ma'am?" He sounded like he was, once again, the very respectful and shy student in her 10th grade world literature class.

"Call me Helen."

He looked at her with a startled look on his face.

"You are no longer a child, nor are you any longer my student. You are a grown man, and you have proven yourself to be a fine doctor and a good man."

"Thank you," he said softly. "I…uh…have to go and do my rounds. I will check back later, Ms…I mean, Helen."

He went on his way, and she smiled at his discomfort in seeing himself on the same level as his former teacher. His embarrassment was cute, but she was very proud of the man he had become.

THIRTY-THREE

DECEMBER 14 – THE IN-BETWEEN

Oh no, it will not be so easy, my little aunt and niece. This is entirely too much fun. I am going to enjoy stretching this out. I will savor your torment. This is like a delightful feast, and I intend to savor the sheer taste of the girl's pain and the aunt's fear. It is like a banquet of palates.

Maledicus' form undulated in ecstasy. Like the form of THEY, his spiritual body pulsed with extrusions and appendages, appearing and receding, like obscene demonic lampreys.

This was delicious—such delicate pain to inflict and savor. He would gradually up the ante on the game, such larger stakes to devour.

Slowly, I will do it slowly and enjoy the flavor of each morsel of pain and despair. I have not felt this level of stimulation for too long. I will make it last.

The girl and the woman are the main dishes, but those three old fools will serve as delectable appetizers, each with their own distinctive flavor. While none of the ancient cretins has very long to live, I can still make what remains of their time excruciating. They all have such lovely guilt; I will beat that lingering pain like a chef making an omelet into a feast of torment for the old men.

These fools—they think they can help you, stupid woman, but they will all be mine. My power is ever expanding—none of you can stand against me. I am already beginning to inflict pain on the others. It is soooo lovely to see you all writhe in pain and frustration.

Maledicus was deeply impressed with himself. As time passed, he felt his form growing and his mass seemingly increasing, even though he could not truly feel anything physical or corporeal, but he was increasing in size and strength. He was sure of it.

Soon, very soon, I will be my own demon. Soon, I will be free of THEY. THEY have no idea of my plans. Even THEY are insignificant compared to me.

THIRTY-FOUR

5:00 A.M. DECEMBER 14

After having spent much of the early hours of the morning driving north of Bethberg, Gerard finally had turned his VW Beetle south and headed home. Branwyn and he were both exhausted. By spending many hours driving and talking, Branwyn and Gerard had avoided the inevitable drive to Bethberg. Neither felt comfortable after what they had experienced.

"Well, we've gone through my entire pack of smokes. Maybe it's time to get our butts back home." Gerard shrugged. He wished they could stay out longer, but his eyes were drooping. It wouldn't be safe to drive much longer.

Branwyn sighed. "Yeah, I suppose so. But if we do pass a C store on the way, be sure to stop. I want to get a couple of packs."

"You know hon, you can just think of tonight as a major slide off the saddle. You can always get back on again."

"Dear heart, this was a slide off the saddle like Hiroshima was the dropping of a firecracker."

Gerard grunted and kept driving.

"I'm not just back in the saddle—my butt is glued there. And I don't care."

"Yeah, well, it's a very nice butt."

She laughed. "Don't you forget it."

About an hour later, they pulled up before her small house. Branwyn had another cigarette lit, from the two packs she bought in a local 7-11. Gerard stopped the car and turned to her. "I just want to be clear about this. Do you think we should try another blessing, or do we just let it alone?"

"Gerard, I don't think that we accomplished anything. Whatever is there has some powerful Mojo, and I don't mind telling you that we are seriously out of our league here. Maybe I can come up with someone who might be able to help, but I really don't think so."

He nodded again. "I don't know, but damnit, I don't like leaving those people alone. I feel like a fucking coward."

"I know. I feel the same way, and it doesn't feel good. I keep thinking about the pictures of that little girl I saw in the house." She lit up another cigarette. "Shit," she mumbled.

"What is it, Branwyn?" He reached over and lit one for himself.

"I can't do it. You know. I can't just let them go. I think we gotta help them. We do."

As she spoke, she felt a shiver pass through her. "Damn, it must be getting cold."

"Yeah, I think it is." He had felt the same chill, but the heater was on in the little car, the custom heater he had installed to be sure that the car would be toasty in the winter. *Dammit Branwyn, why do you have to be so fucking brave?*

They smoke their cigarettes in silence then ground them out in the little ashtray.

She reached over and patted the side of his face. "Look, dear heart. Go home. Get some sleep. I'll come by tomorrow, and we'll talk again over coffee. Okay?"

"Sure, Branwyn. I'm beat. Talk to you then."

She got out of the car and watched the little yellow bug chug down the street. She would not see him again.

THIRTY-FIVE

DECEMBER 14

Helen sat on one of the chairs in the room and watched over her sleeping niece. She tried to stay wake but occasionally drifted off into a shallow slumber for a few minutes; then she would wake and look at Helena, making sure that she was there and ok.

When Jonathon stopped in a few hours later, Helen was sitting up and watching Helena. The doctor felt the little girl's forehead and smiled. "There is no fever."

"She's been sleeping quietly the entire time."

"Well, the medicine I prescribed for her has probably helped her sleep. The poor little thing needs rest. As do you."

Helen smiled wanly. "I'll get rest later."

"Then I'll be back in a few minutes," he said and exited the room. Helen looked at him as he left with a bit of confusion. *Probably needs to check on someone,* she thought.

A few minutes later, he returned with a tray. On it were two cups of coffee, some creamer, sugar, and some pastries. "If you are going to stay up anyway, I thought you could use something. These are from the doctor's lounge, not that coffee from the machines. I never trust it."

"You're a life saver, in many ways."

He set the tray down on the dresser in the room. "How do you take your coffee?"

"Black, no sugar. Thanks." He handed her a cup of steaming coffee and placed a plate with a pastry near her. "Be sure to eat that. Doctor's orders."

She laughed a bit. "Thank you, Jonathon."

"No problem, Ms…..uh…Helen." He remembered to use her first name when she looked at him with her eyebrow arched.

"That's better."

He took a cup and poured in a healthy shot of cream along with four sugars. "I like a little coffee with my cream and sugar." He sipped it. "I'm sure your niece will be fine. Children get sick all the time. And with the blood work I've ordered, just to be sure, if it's anything else, we'll find it. I promise. I don't think it is anything serious. I certainly don't want to alarm you, but I also don't want to ignore any possibilities. I want to know. I'm sure you do also."

She put her hand on his arm as if she were a proud mother. "Indeed, I don't like not knowing. And if there is anything else, I am sure you'll find it. I have faith in you." She smiled as he blushed. "You've done well for yourself. I always knew that you would."

"Well, you had confidence in me long before I ever did."

"I was lucky as a teacher to have a student like you. I saw something in you. I saw your potential."

He gave a sad, wistful smile. He started to speak, then he paused. Helen waited. She knew, after many years of teaching, sometimes people must give others time to speak in their own time on their own terms.

Finally, he began. "I wish my parents had given me the same support that you did."

"I know you do. All children want that, but unfortunately, you didn't receive it. It's a shame what so many children have to face. Even my niece. She has lost her parents. She has me, but what a terrible thing to have to face for the rest of her life." Helen paused, then continued, "And you, Jonathon. You faced more at home than most teenagers could ever dream of. But you survived that hell. No, you did more than that. You emerged triumphant. And look at you now – you are a fine man and an excellent doctor. I can't think of anyone I would rather have looking after Helena than you."

As he reddened and slightly lowered his head, he once more appeared to be the frightened and shy boy he had been in high school. Helen knew how much he had suffered at home with a drug-addicted mother, an alcoholic and abusive father, and two older brothers, both of whom were already convicted criminals. Much of Bethberg thought the family was simply no good, that no one who came from it would ever amount to anything. White trash, garbage, good for nothing losers: these were some of the gentler and more refined names some of the townspeople used for the Wilson family.

At first when she had Jonathon in her class, she had also wondered if he were destined to be like his older brothers, who had caused her many problems before they both dropped out of school. She hated to admit to herself that she was on her guard toward the boy. Soon she realized that he was not like the rest of his family. She saw a shy but inquisitive, respectful, and intelligent boy, one who was frightened despite his already formidable size. He had been over 6 feet tall and two hundred pounds in tenth grade, but he walked with a slouch, not from a teenage attitude but from trying to be invisible.

Helen worked hard at supporting him and encouraging him. He was a natural student, and she wanted to help him find his own abilities. Yet, when she saw the unmistakable signs of abuse, the black eyes, bruises, wearing of long shirts in the warm spring months, she decided to intervene. Certainly, others must have reported some suspicions, she thought, but she soon found out no one had, perhaps out of fear of repercussions from the family. Others simply turned their eyes away from the boy's situation, because to many, things like that occurred in other towns, the places more like big cities, maybe Allentown, and Scranton, but certainly not in idyllic Bethberg.

Helen had gone straight to the police when no one seemed to respond to her notifications. For some reason, the local social workers avoided going to his house. She had had enough. She marched into the police station with photographs she had taken of the boy's injuries. She brushed by the main desk, past a startled officer who finally got up to go after her.

"Ma'am…Ma'am! You just can't go back there."

She ignored him and walked right into the office of the one officer she knew reasonably well because his son was also in one of her classes, Sergeant Sadlowski.

Sam looked up to see Ms. Murray, looking at him with an expression of exasperation mixed with anger, and old Officer Warren, huffing into his office.

"I tried to stop her, but she just went by," the old man said with his ample belly shaking from his gasping for air.

"It's ok. I'll take care of this." Warren left, and Helen approached Sam.

"Is something wrong with Josh?"

"No, Sergeant, nothing is wrong with Joshua. He is doing just fine as always."

"So, why this visit?"

"There is a problem with another boy in my class, and no one seems to be willing to deal with it. Not the school, not the social workers. And I'm sure it's because they're all too frightened to do anything."

Helen went on to detail all of her suspicions and showed him the photographs of her student's injuries. As he listened to the story and looked at the boy's marks, Sam's face turned stony.

"Don't worry about this anymore, Ms. Murray. I'll take care of it."

"Sergeant Sadlowski, don't tell me that if you don't mean it. Don't say you'll do something and then just stuff the papers away somewhere." Helen's face reddened as she went on a verbal roll down a large hill that she couldn't stop. "If you don't intend to do anything, then have the fucking decency to tell me, and I'll try to find someone in this god-damned-oh-so-perfect-town with a big enough set of balls to do something!"

First, he was shocked at this language from his son's teacher, then he laughed. "Ma'am, if any of your students talked like that…"

"They would get detentions. Of course, and I am sorry if I offended you. But right now the boy needs help. Will you help him?"

He put the papers on the desk in front of him and looked straight at her. "Ms. Murray, I give you my word that this has become my priority. I will look into it immediately, and I'll get him out of that hellhole of a house he's been living in. Don't you worry."

Sam was true to his word. He lit a proverbial fire under the social workers, threw his considerable official weight around, and had the boy removed to a foster home with a good, caring couple. Soon, the boy was seeing an excellent youth counselor and had some stability restored to his life. Sam then imposed his will further, and both of the boy's parents were soon in a detox and rehab unit. The brothers, well, they were soon serving several years in a state penitentiary for drug dealing.

Ms. Murray helped Jonathon with entrance to college, where he excelled. He then went on to Medical School at the University of Pennsylvania, and unknown to her, took a position at the Bethberg Medical Center.

She told him that she had assumed he would have chosen to be a doctor in a major hospital like Johns Hopkins.

"Well, I could have done that. Sure," he said, finishing his coffee with a big slurp. "I received several very flattering offers, but I wanted to come back here, at least for a few years."

She stayed quiet as he paused.

"My father died several years ago, and my mother is not well. And maybe it doesn't make any sense, after everything that happened with them, but I need to be here for her. She doesn't have much time left, and I'm all she has. She's dying of throat cancer, and she hasn't used drugs in years, so if I have any shot at a semi-normal relationship with her, well, I have to try. I have plenty of time to go somewhere else."

Helen smiled and nodded her head. "Look at me, Jonathon. You made a decision that was important for you to make. No one has the right to judge it or you. You did it for yourself and your mother—there is nothing wrong with that. You're right, you can go anywhere you want to. You are a young man with your entire life ahead of you. Whether you are here in Bethberg or New York City, you will be an excellent doctor."

She gave a wide smile. "And I'm being selfish now. It is serendipitous that you were here. I did sort of lose my cool tonight." She laughed. "I might have slugged that …woman…at the desk. We, Helena and I, needed you."

He smiled, stood, and hugged her. Then he got control of himself and went back to his rounds. Helen sat back down to watch over her sleeping niece.

THIRTY-SIX

5:30 A.M. DECEMBER 14

Helen sat at her dining room table alone. She was having a cup of Earl Grey tea with lemon and reading Gibbon's *The Decline and Fall of the Roman Empire*. She had read this book several times before, but she was rereading the text in preparation for a unit on Roman History that she was going to teach in her 12th grade honors history class. It was going to be a two-week unit, and Helen was determined to recover as much material as possible so that she would have the resources she needed to bring the ancient time alive for her students.

"Helen."

The familiar voice startled her from deep concentration. Helen looked up to see her sister standing across from her in the kitchen. Jessica was frowning and shaking her head slightly, a gesture that Helen knew meant her little sister was extremely displeased. It was a motion Jessica had used several times in the past, especially to punctuate her disapproval of her elder sister's actions. At times like those, they seemed to switch places, with the younger having control over the elder. Further accentuating this impression, Jessica's mouth was drawn tightly, and her brow, normally very smooth, was lined. When she had that expression, she looked just like their mother did when she was displeased with one or both of them. Such a look usually preceded a very long lecture and some kind of punishment. That look instinctively filled Helen with anxiety.

"What is it, Jessy?"

"I think you know, Big Sister." Ouch, that was another stinger. Jessica only called Helen big sister when she was upset with her.

"Jessy, I really don't know what's wrong. I do have to get through this reading. I have a ton of prep work to do for my classes. Can't we talk about this tomorrow night?"

174

"Of course, you have soooo much work to do. You never have time for me," Jessica said and sat down at the table. She was holding a cup of coffee in her hands. "You always have time for yourself don't you, but you never have time for your sister!"

As she listened, Helen saw Jessica's mouth moving, but the words were in her mother's voice, the voice of disapproval, the sound of You're-Not-A-Good-Enough-Daughter.

"Oh Jessy, please don't talk like that."

"I will talk to you any way I wish, young lady. And it would do you well to remember who's in charge here!"

Helen started and nearly dropped her cup. Sitting across from her now was her mother, the same age as Helen was now. She was in her formal black dress and smoking a cigarette with a holder. "Look at you. You're a disappointment to the family. You're a disgrace, young lady. Nothing but a bookworm. With the way you keep yourself, with the way you look, what man would ever want you anyway?"

"Mother, please don't say that."

"MOTHER please," she mocked. "You are PATHETIC! You know that, don't you? Can't have your own man, can't have your own kids…what good are you?"

"Stop! I don't want to hear this!"

"Well, you have to hear it, Big Sister. I'm not going anywhere." Now it was Jessica who looked at her but dressed in her mother's clothes and smoking from the cigarette in the holder.

"It's your fault. This whole thing is all your fault."

"What is, Jessy?" Helen asked in a now tiny voice as she sat and trembled, spilling her tea.

"You know exactly what I mean. Don't be a stupid bitch. It's because of you that Andy and I are dead."

"What?" Now all Helen could manage was a raspy whisper.

"Think about it, Big Sister. You're supposed to be so smart. Use that thick skull of yours." She took a long draw from the cigarette just as her mother did. "We only went to the bed and breakfast because we knew you couldn't watch Helena for longer than a couple of days. If you could have spared even a few more days, then we would have gone to Europe, as we wanted. AND NOW WE WOULD BE ALIVE!"

Helen reached out to her sister. "Jessy."

"Don't touch me you bitch! You selfish! Stupid! Bitch! IT'S ALL YOUR FAULT!"

Helen recoiled from the words as if they had been punches hitting her.

"I'm sorry. Sorry." Helen tried to get up, but she felt like she was moving in slow motion, as though she was trapped in quicksand.

Helen was pulled back into her chair. The wood from the slats on the back of the chair separated and wrapped around her, holding her in place. The room went black. All she could see was Jessica's face looming above her, only now it was much larger, and the voice coming out of her mouth was loud and deep.

"Fucking stupid whore!" The voice amplified in tone and volume. "Do you think you can be rid of me?" Helen watched in horror as Jessy morphed into a dark form, indistinct, but resembling a man in some sort of a robe. *I'm here, and there's nothing you can do to remove me. Those men who are trying to help you are weak and stupid! They are nothing! You and the whelp belong to me!*

Helen jerked up suddenly. She was sitting in a chair in Helena's hospital room, and she had been dreaming. Now completely awake, Helen was shaking, her body nearly in convulsions. Drenched in sweat, she looked at Helena.

The little girl was sleeping but tossing and turning. She was murmuring almost inaudibly and whimpering.

Helen calmed herself as much as possible and went to her niece. She climbed into bed and held the little girl in a tight but gentle embrace. She lay on her bed, held the girl's head to her chest and stroked her hair.

"I'm here, I'm here, princess. I've got you. Nothing can hurt you."

The little girl eventually stopped crying. She did not go back to a deep sleep. Helen kept stroking her hair, and the child eventually awoke and looked up at her aunt. "Where is the bad man, Aunt Helen?"

"What bad man, honey?"

"The scary man that was standing by my bed and said he was going to hurt you and me."

"There is nobody here, sweetie. And don't you worry no one is going to hurt you."

"Promise?" The little girl looked up at her aunt with frightened eyes, like those of a small rabbit quaking in fear from the presence of a large predator.

"I promise you, baby girl. Cross my heart." Helen rocked the little girl in her arms, and eventually Helena feel back asleep. The child had seen the same thing she had. This had to end. There had to be a way.

She would not let anything harm her niece. She would die to protect her.

THIRTY-SEVEN

THE IN-BETWEEN DECEMBER 14

You will die, bitch, and I will have your soul. Delicious, simply delicious! Maledicus absorbed the delightful pain he was causing and shuddered in delight. Since the woman had purchased the idol, he had managed to establish a connection to her and those fools around her. They mistakenly thought that the house itself was haunted. The thought of this misinformation made Maledicus happy indeed. *These tiny idiots would not only suffer, but also they would never understand the reason for their pain. All they would comprehend was their slow and inevitable destruction.*

The infusion of the humans' psychic distress spread through his spiritual form and made him feel as if he had indulged in a Roman feast. Each new bit of pain they felt came to him like a delicacy served to him by slaves—smelled, bitten into, swallowed, and savored in its digestion.

Just as he had at the earthly Roman feasts, he seemed to be able to partake incessantly. Only here there was no need to vomit between courses so he could clear space for more food. Here his capacity increased along with his consumption. With each intake of pain, in addition to his capacity, his desire and need for more grew concurrently. Like an addict whose brain craved more and more stimulation with each new fix, Maledicus desired more and more pleasure from each influx of pain from his victims. And this time, he felt that the potential for pain was enormous, more than he had taken before, more than he had ever expected.

Typically, his victims were confused and frightened. Sometimes they went insane; occasionally they became violent. Never before had someone resisted him. This fighting back was a new element to the feast, but like a recently discovered spice, it amplified the taste of this pleasure. Their futile resistance colored his dining with the delicious dashed hope that the victims would

177

inevitably experience. He knew they would believe they could fight him, and their recognition of their defeat would make them inconsolable. *How wonderful that would taste.*

Maledicus laughed. *This stupid human bitch and her allies were determined to oppose him—to match their puny human strength against his power. To make it more humorous, what the woman had for an army was a few pathetic old men. What a laughable force!* He would toy with them and then sweep them from his path like a Roman Legion crushing the uprising of an undisciplined and untrained group of rabble. No one could stand against the power of the Roman Empire on Earth, and no human could stand before his power. He was Maledicus. And he was going to relish every morsel of agony that he would cause and then suck those delightful tidbits into his very being and digest them fully. He had grown; he had felt his ability develop from only being able to influence the owner of the idol to being capable of affecting those around the owner, an enormous increase in strength. He would continue to grow. Soon he would be separate from the spirit he knew as THEY. *Soon I would be my own demon.*

He smiled.

He would begin with one of this woman's so-called helpers.

THIRTY-EIGHT

DECEMBER 14

For Patrick, the communication with his brother was becoming clearer, more coherent. Previously mostly jumbled, now the writing had become more focused and more comprehensible. The previous few sessions over that last couple of days had produced results with the most clarity of communication. At first, noticeable phrases had appeared, but then sentences and entire paragraphs began to show. Most importantly for Patrick, it was clear that the voice of the writing was his brother's. As the messages improved, the psychological and physical impact of the sessions correspondingly decreased. The time he needed to recover from each session was also lessening. The headaches and nosebleeds, however, did not diminish. In fact, they had increased.

The most recent session had also produced the most disturbing communication. Patrick read from the yellow tablet; specifically one passage was the most crucial.

Patty, (this was the nickname Michael had often called him, even though he knew that Patrick hated it. He claimed it was the prerogative of an older brother: older by a few minutes, but older nonetheless.) … *the time to act is coming…I can't protect you, although I wish I could. I can't be with you to fight this battle, but it must be fought…you must help them…will contact you.*

Patrick ran his hand over his closely cropped hair, still in the style he had worn in his 20 years in the Marines. *Protect whom? From what?* Patrick had never been afraid of danger, nor was he terrified by death—after all, he knew from his contact with Michael that there was more to life than simply this earthly existence. He also conceded to himself that he might simply be losing his mind, but Patrick didn't believe that.

Yet, if he were going to protect someone, he needed much more information: Who was the person in distress? Who was the threat? Why was he the one who should act? How was it that Michael would know of this danger? It was extremely frustrating for Patrick that he did not know more. Action without the pertinent knowledge was fruitless. It would be like going into a battle without any reconnaissance of the enemy's position.

And what did that brief clause mean "will contact you"? *Who will contact me? Did Michael mean that he would or someone else would?* Patrick hated to wait to find out. He could feel the call to battle and was ready to proceed, but he did not know where.

Patrick loved the early tough guy detective novels, especially those of Mickey Spillane and Dashiell Hammett. They had served as a diversion from the very serious business of the military, but now he felt like he was one of the detectives from the forties or fifties, wearing an overcoat and a fedora and on a tough case. He was investigating without information, not even of the victims. So he could not tell from where or from whom threats could arise. *What do I do now? How do I proceed?* Patrick did not doubt the importance or veracity of what Michael was trying to tell him. He simply wished for much more to go on. *Michael, I need more information.*

Patrick stood slowly and went into his kitchen. Using an old grinder, he formed an espresso grind from dark African coffee beans. He filled the machine, turned it on, and waited for the brew to emerge. Several cups of strong, black coffee might help him to think. He grinned…it felt like he was back in college and staying up all night cramming for exams.

With a large mug of steaming coffee, he returned to his study and began to pore over his notes, trying to find patterns in the messages, anything that could help him determine what kind of mission his brother was intent on assigning him.

After several hours of thinking and many more cups of coffee, he decided to try to achieve better focus.

He changed into loose fitting sweat clothes, but he went without anything on his feet. Patrick then bowed and entered the dojo in the basement. Whenever he stepped through the archway, it signified that he had entered a world in which nothing else existed. All cares, concerns, worries about the outside world were to be left behind. They could be dealt with when he left the dojo. He began his training with 20 minutes of meditation and Taoist breathing. He went through 15 minutes of stretching, an activity he disliked but remained consistent in performing. When he was young, he loved the stretching, but even to a man who had kept himself in prime condition as an athlete, he could not escape the fact that he was now in his mid-forties, and his body was not as supple as when he was a youngster. So he engaged in difficult stretching, making blood flow through his muscles and preparing himself for extremely strenuous activity.

Next, he did 30 minutes of forms of unarmed combat. He focused carefully and always varied the techniques, incorporating forms from the various disciplines he had studied. He moved from forms from Karate to Kung Fu to McMap. To an outsider the exercise might have seemed to be somewhat slow and relaxing, but the reality was that it was intense both physically and mentally. After the forms, if he had maintained proper concentration and breathing, he would be completely focused.

He then picked up a bokken and practiced Chinese and Japanese sword techniques. This intense workout was followed by European saber exercises that he had learned in the Marines. The final weapons work was on subtle knife-fighting techniques. In all of the work with the blades, he felt as if the blade had become an extension of his body, fitting the McMap axiom: One Mind, Any Weapon. To Patrick the weapons he held were as much a part of his body as the hands that gripped them.

His body was aching, and his head had begun to pound, but he pushed himself through the difficult workout. Patrick executed a straight 20 minutes of shadow-boxing, followed by an intense 30 minutes of work with punches and kicks to his fortified heavy bag. When he was finished, he was drenched in sweat. He stretched for a few minutes, then bowed as he exited the dojo.

His mind was now clear and focused.

He would attempt another communication with Michael immediately.

Back in his study, he again rested and began his deep breathing exercises. This was an unusual situation—he had not before attempted two sessions with Michael in the same day, but he felt that it was crucially important that he get answers as soon as possible. A battle was brewing. He could feel that. He had to know more.

An hour later, he was still sitting in the chair, but now he was reading a simple line of writing, just three words, around which were large splatters of blood from a fresh nosebleed: *contact Uncle Roosevelt.*

Patrick would do that, but first he had an appointment in New York City.

THIRTY-NINE

DECEMBER 14

After Gerard had dropped her at home, Branwyn immediately made herself a cup of green tea and sat at her kitchen table to think. She had not been very forceful in asserting to Gerard that they should pursue this case any further. After all, it was she, who had been able to see this thing, this horrible entity, not him. She knew the level of evil they would face. And she was terrified. *We did our best. What more could we do? Damnit! I sound like a fucking coward.*

Now, in the comfort of her home, surrounded by the books and artwork that she loved and drinking a steaming hot cup of tea, she began to focus on the situation, on the problem at hand. She was not the kind of person who usually ran from anything or anyone. She had always been proud of her ability to stand up to even the rowdiest of drunks at her job as bartender at McClanahan's Irish Pub. Even though its name suggested an upscale Irish tavern, McClanahan's was just a leftover neighborhood joint, now struggling to stay afloat, and not given to attracting the best clientele.

Branwyn had worked there for years, and even though she could easily have moved to a better kind of place, there was something about the shopworn appearance of the bar and its lack of pretension that made her feel comfortable. She occasionally was the butt of jokes about being the local witch, but she simply shrugged them off and gave as good as she got. She was not a wuss.

So why was she acting that way now? She knew that many people simply dismissed her ability to see the dead and to sense things, but she also knew this gift, or curse, was real. She hadn't asked for this ability, but she had learned to accept it, live with it, and use it in the most positive way she could. She had never charged anyone for her help, and she never would. That would be a kind of evil in itself.

She put the tea down and went to a bottle cabinet in the kitchen, where she kept her alcohol. Time for something serious—she pulled out a bottle of Smirnoff and poured two shots into her tea. Not quite a toddy, but it would do. The tea was cooling, so she belted it down quickly and poured a couple of more shots into the cup.

Now she sipped it slowly and savored the warm feel of the alcohol in her chest. *I'm glad at least I convinced Gerard to stay out of this fight. He's a good man, but I don't think he's strong enough to face this thing. I don't think any of them realize what they are up against. I will simply have to meet with the old guys and tell them. They are sweet old men, and plenty tough, but still, it isn't right for them to go into this battle unaware of their enemy. They also need to know that they have me as an ally.*

Branwyn picked up the cup and took a sip.

And it certainly wasn't right to walk away from a child in peril. That thing wanted both the aunt and the niece. It would, if unopposed, kill them and try to claim their souls. Well, fuck that. It will have to deal with me first.

She raised the cup in a toast. *To beating this thing!*

In the In-Between Maledicus smiled. *"This silly little human who thinks that she can stand against me will be my next morsel. A little bite to whet my appetite for the feast to come."* Maledicus delighted in his extending his power past simply affecting those in the vicinity of the statue to those who had been near it. Previously he could only affect those who were near it, but now with his increasing strength, he could extend his influence to those mortals who had been near it recently. He was indeed growing stronger.

Much stronger.

Years ago, Branwyn had suffered from asthma, to the point where she was hospitalized several times from severe attacks that almost killed her. Since she had become a practitioner of Wicca and an adept of Yoga, along with her knowledge of herbs and of advanced breathing techniques, she had conquered the condition. At least ten years had gone by since her last incident, and she was convinced that she never again would have to face the disease.

She put down her teacup and began to stand. With a shock she sat back down. Her breathing was becoming constricted. As if her last attack had been only days ago, she remembered immediately and completely the horror of this feeling, when it seemed as if her neck and chest were conspiring to shut off her air passages. *But it's impossible! I have beaten this.*

She no longer owned an asthma inhaler—she had deemed it a waste of money.

But with growing fear, she recognized the symptoms. She could feel her air supply shutting down. Her breathing was coming in loud gasps, and she had broken out in a cold sweat. Branwyn tried to control her breathing with Yoga techniques, but nothing was working.

Have to call 911.

She reached for her purse sitting on the table near her. Her arms were sluggish. Every movement was difficult and made her breathing even harder. Branwyn fished the little cell phone out of her purse and desperately hit the numbers, 911.

"Hello this is 911 emergency. How may I assist you?" The voice on the other end of the phone was clear and competent, but no reply came from Branwyn. The deep retching sound of her labored breathing had stopped, and she had moved into the silent chest phase. She was unable, however, to produce any words as her lips began to turn blue, and her eyes widened in panic.

"Is anyone there?" The operator realized that this might be a serious situation and put a trace on the call. She would send police to the address to investigate as soon as that information became available.

The phone slid from Branwyn's hand and landed on the table. Almost no air was getting through now, and she had entered cyanosis. The situation had become critical.

As Branwyn began to lose consciousness, she again saw the thing that she had perceived before in the Murray house. It seemed to be laughing, gloating. It was doing this to her.

Goddess, I come. She lost consciousness.

Police were dispatched to Branwyn's house. When they arrived, she was dead.

Delicious! Delightful! Maledicus was overjoyed at his message sent to this preposterous pack of his opponents. His form undulated and grew.

FORTY

Marcelo's was a small Italian restaurant located approximately halfway between Bethberg and St. Bernard's College. Since both Father Bruno and Roosevelt enjoyed Italian food, it was a natural meeting place for the two men. They had been coming here since Bruno had begun his position as Professor of Religion, and the owners knew them well. Marcelo's was an old business, started over 60 years ago by the current owners' grandfather. The grandsons had maintained their beloved grandfather's insistence on good basic food everyone could enjoy, reasonable prices, and a friendly, unassuming atmosphere. The grandfather had emphasized his beliefs to his grandsons. "Remember, that we are immigrants, not from the wealthy society. We serve food so hard working people can enjoy it." Many customers did over many years. The place was considered a local treasure. A small establishment, Marcelo's had two rooms for dining: a large main room and a small side room with only three tables. It was in that room where the two men were sitting.

They had finished their main courses: Bruno ate Scungilli Alla Marinara, and Roosevelt had Shrimp Scampi. They were sharing a bottle of Chianti. Roosevelt poured another glass for both of them.

"It could present difficulties for you, my friend." Roosevelt held his hand up to silence Bruno before he could reply. Roosevelt was very aware of Bruno's willingness to help anyone. "I know your abilities and your knowledge. I am very aware of your deep compassion for those in trouble."

Bruno blushed a bit, making the elderly priest seem reminiscently as young man.

Roosevelt continued, "But I know that this might go past the standard work of a priest. This might go past the simple blessing of a house."

185

"You certainly have my attention." Bruno sipped his wine and listened to his long time friend.

When Roosevelt had told Bruno about the situation at the Kaufmann house, he had immediately volunteered his assistance. Bruno had come to their home and blessed it. He had been thorough and had blessed every room, including the crawl space and cellar. When he was finished, the spirit that had been acting like a grumpy, old man had left. When Roosevelt last checked in with the family, everything was fine. Their home was once again a place of comfort and quiet.

"You know how much I appreciated your help with that case, George." Even though he was a priest, Roosevelt still referred to him by his given name, as he always had.

"You know, Roosevelt, that there's nothing I wouldn't do to help you."

Roosevelt understood. Their connection solidly formed in the fiery flames of battle. Both men had saved each other's life several times in combat. Their mutual distaste of war had not dampened the reality of their having been warriors together.

Both men had lived long and complex lives.

George Bruno had an odd and circuitous route to the priesthood. A son of second-generation Italian parents, there had been an expectation that he would attend college and enter one of the professions; his parents had hoped he would become a doctor or a lawyer. As a youngster in high school, he had demonstrated strong intellectual potential, while also exhibiting a decidedly headstrong teenage attitude. He was at the age when he knew everything, and adults, specifically his parents, knew nothing. He wondered how they had ever managed to survive without his teenage wisdom.

Bruno blazed his way through high school, winning academic awards; he was a National Honor Society member and salutatorian of his high school, achieving athletic fame among his peers—he was a three sport lettered athlete, breaking girls' hearts with his charming smile and good looks, and indulging in teenage pranks without getting in trouble. However, he did come close to serious disaster a few times. Because he had two uncles who were police officers, when he was caught at a party with pot and alcohol, he was not charged; regardless, he was not let off completely. He suffered his punishment first from his uncles, who made him stay overnight in the drunk tank and then told him he would be "volunteering" to do community service, then at home. His mother's tears nearly broke his heart. It had never occurred to him that anything he did might ever have caused her heartache. His father preferred to yell and curse at him, then give him the silent treatment. Additionally, his parents grounded him for six months.

The punishment bothered the boy, but it was not enough to change him. He thought he could still charm and talk his way through anything. So, when he was caught a second time, his uncles threw him into the drunk tank and arranged for him to spend a week in jail. Unknown to the young Bruno, he was not officially charged, but it was agreed that this treatment might help him see the difficulties he was setting up for himself with his reckless behavior. The place that was used was the local jail, and Bruno was put into his own cell away from other inmates where he had plenty of time to think about what he had done. His parents had reported that he was ill, so the time missed from school was not an issue. His uncles kept a close watch on him so he would be safe. Safe, he was, but not comfortable.

After a week in the small cell, which stank of urine, and the nights of sleeping on a rock hard cot, and eating food that could charitably be described as not very good, he emerged with a changed attitude. At first, he had been furious, but slowly the anger died. Then boredom set in along with frustration. Finally, he began to consider his situation about what he had done. He was a bright kid, so it was hoped that he might finally begin to think about his actions. Towards the end of the week, he began to see himself for what he had been, foolish and self-centered. At that point, the boy started to become a young man.

After that week, George Bruno focused on his schoolwork and went to college on a full scholarship. This was in the middle of the Vietnam War, and Bruno had a deep discomfort with his ability to avoid the draft as a college student when other, less fortunate or less academically inclined young men were forced to go to war. He was a philosophy major at Brown University, and he deeply immersed in the writings of Plato. He felt that if Socrates was able to go to war, then perhaps, he should also. He did not like the idea that he should somehow be exempt from this service. To the great dismay of his parents, he left school after one year and enlisted in the United States Marine Corps.

Bruno served in the same unit as Roosevelt Franklin, and he proved himself to be a very capable fighter. Bruno was brave but not stupid or foolhardy. He was willing to do what was necessary, but he did not like taking ridiculous chances. He was dedicated to his unit and grew to think of them as his brothers. When he was in high school, the football coach often said that the boys were going to war with the opposing team. He now understood how superficial and demeaning a claim that was to true soldiers. Boys should never be told they were going to war when they were simply playing a game. It was fun, and they cared about it, but it was nothing more than a simple diversion from life. Unlike the game of football, with tackles and touchdowns, war encompassed killing, blood, screams from the wounded, and horror.

Bruno was a good Marine, but the realities of war shook him to his very core. He had been ambivalent about the politics of the war before entering, but by experiencing it, he knew that the American public had not understood the circumstances of it. How could they? They weren't in country. The debates over the war, the political arguments waged by people who, for the most part, had not engaged in battle missed the practical realities of its horror: the uncertainty about the enemy. A woman or child might be carrying grenades under their clothing, and the enemy did not wear a uniform that marked them as the opposition. There were few planned battles; much of the fighting involved small search and destroy missions. The mission of the war itself was uncertain. Were the soldiers there to win or to simply fight a losing battle? No one seemed to know what was going on.

Eventually the killing began to turn him against the war and his part in it. Seeing the faces of the dead VC, the mutilated corpses of innocent civilians, and destroyed villages made him question everything he was doing. But he held together and finished his tours of duty.

When Bruno came back home, the man who had returned from the war was not the boy who had enlisted. He had changed. He was no longer carefree or impetuous. He no longer indulged in parties and seeking out fun. He had become a serious man. Even though he was only 23 years old, Bruno projected the temperament of a man in his mid-thirties. Rather than returning immediately to the University, he took a job at a local supermarket and spent much of his time reading the Bible. He was raised as a Roman Catholic, but he had not previously put much thought into the religion. It had simply been something he did with his family on Sundays and holidays.

His self-disgust with his actions in the war and his guilt at having killed drove him further into his religious studies. After the year of working at the supermarket, he returned to the University and earned a Bachelor's Degree in Religious Studies. He then entered the seminary and earned first his Master of Arts, then his Doctor of Divinity Degrees. Soon afterwards, he was ordained as a Catholic priest.

His research for his doctoral degree focused on esoterica in The Renaissance. As an advanced graduate student, George discovered a talent for conducting painstaking investigations into unusual topics. He soon became an expert on magic, the occult, alchemy, and some branches of Humanism in the Renaissance. Among the focus of some of his studies were such thinkers as Marsilio Ficino, Count Giovanni Pico della Mirandola, John Dee, and Paracelsus. He was drawn to the ideas of the eclectic and syncretic thinkers, those who saw possibilities in philosophies outside of their normal range of study and those who attempted to combine a myriad of ways of thought. Even though he was a committed and serious Catholic, he believed that being knowledgeable about a wide and disparate range of ideas, religions, and philosophies would certainly serve to increase his understanding of the workings of God.

He served for a number of years in a variety of assignments for the Church. He spent time in Africa and Asia, working among the poorest people. He could have tried to climb the hierarchy of the Church, but he had preferred to remain an unnoticed man, someone who could study as he wished while still serving people who needed help, while atoning for his killing in combat.

Eventually, in his fifties, despite his attempts at anonymity, after he distinguished himself in his decades of working with the poor, and his continued academic research, including the publication of two books on the Renaissance, he was rewarded with the position of Professor of Religious Studies at St. Bernard's College, a small Catholic liberal arts college situated about 20 miles northwest of Bethberg.

As much as he had appreciated his previous work, he now felt completely at home as a teacher and researcher. The life of the college professor fit him completely. He was able to teach young men and women about the Renaissance and its influence on contemporary society. When his student advisees complained about the courses they had to take to meet the school's liberal arts requirements, he would give them a small lecture on the origins of the liberal arts from the Humanists, the Studia Humanitatis. It rarely satisfied the impatient youngsters, but he delighted, nevertheless, in delivering that lesson.

During the course of his travels, serving, and teaching, Father Bruno had maintained contact with Roosevelt. Their communications were of the old-fashioned kind: snail mail, as it is called now. Both men were both prolific letter writers, and they would compose long epistles to each other several times a year. In that way, they were able to follow each other's lives. They did see each other on occasion. If Bruno had reason to be in the United States, or if Roosevelt was traveling near were the Father was ministering, they would arrange a visit. And when Roosevelt married, Bruno proudly served as one of the groomsmen in the wedding party.

It was with great delight that Father Bruno had told Roosevelt of his position as a professor at St. Bernard's. The two men now lived very close to each other and were able to visit over a meal about twice a month.

Roosevelt sipped the wine and let the fruity, deep flavor linger over his tongue before swallowing. "I mean that this particular case has more depth and is potentially dangerous. Unlike the one at the Kaufmann house, I do not believe this is simply a disgruntled spirit who delights in being cantankerous. I think there is something truly evil there."

Father Bruno raised his head. Roosevelt had his full attention now. "Evil is not a word that I would use lightly, Roosevelt."

"Nor would I." Roosevelt looked directly at his friend. "We have both seen evil, George. We know it exists, that it is not a mere reflection of society, as some would have it today. We both know that the social relativists are incorrect in their beliefs that there are no truths. Of course, the tricky part is the search for truth."

"Of course."

"So, this particular case could become a, um…delicate situation for you, especially because it goes beyond blessing a house, especially for you as an official member of the Church."

Father Bruno set his glass on the table, folded his hands in front of him, and looked Roosevelt in the eyes. "Go on."

"We have already tried a blessing of the house, but it was not, um, altogether successful. In fact, it was a complete failure. Whatever is there simply became more angry. It felt like we had upset a lion by trying to hunt it with a .22 pistol. We only made it more enraged….and dangerous."

"Why, Roosevelt, may I ask, didn't you have me do the blessing?"

"I am very sorry about not contacting you George, but I knew that it was a busy time of the semester for you. Remember, I am a retired professor, and I know how busy it can be grading final papers and exams. So, for a simple blessing, I went to a local minister. It was a mistake."

"You're forgiven, my son," Bruno said seriously before breaking into his wide grin. "Say two Hail Mary's, and pour me some more of that fine wine."

Roosevelt smiled. "I also have two Opus X cigars for later."

"Now, my son, you really are forgiven!"

Roosevelt took another swallow of wine and became serious. "I believe there is some kind of entity, probably inhuman, possibly even demonic, in this house. I think it is dangerous, and that it has chosen to focus there because it is preying on a woman and a child, her niece, living there."

Father Bruno's hands tightened, and his eyes narrowed a bit. He hated bullies of any kind. He had, even as a priest saved the weak and innocent from bullies and predators by physical means. "If God punishes me for beating a thug who was threatening a child, then so be it," he had once confessed. "I will accept my punishment. However, I will not sit by and watch any bully torment a helpless victim."

Father Bruno listened carefully to his friend. He knew and respected Roosevelt as he did very few other people. Their time together in country had enabled him to get to know his friend intimately and completely as someone who was strong, courageous, levelheaded, and intelligent. Roosevelt had an open-mind but was not impressionable, nor was he given to flights of fancy. If he said there might be a demon in that house, then Bruno believed that it could be so. The Father had never yet seen a demon himself, but he certainly acknowledged the possibility of their existence.

"I am not certain, George, if what I think is necessary is even possible. I am not sure if such a procedure even exists, but I think I am asking you to do . . .ah. . .an exorcism on a house, not a person."

Father Bruno raised an eyebrow. This situation was becoming far more interesting than he had suspected it might be. He was certainly familiar with the rite of exorcism: he had studied it from an historical perspective as well as from the understanding that any kind of weapon in the battle against evil might be useful. At the very least, it fit into his study of the esoteric. He also knew, however, that receiving permission from his Bishop to perform any exorcism was difficult, if not nearly impossible, in the 21st Century. A full medical and psychiatric examination of the supposedly possessed person was required. In these times, medical doctors and psychiatrists treated almost all cases that were previously handled by exorcists. Very few priests today even acknowledged in personal discussion the existence of demons. In the few cases with which Father Bruno was familiar, the subjects of the exorcisms were people, human beings, not a domicile. These issues did nothing to deter Bruno's interest; rather, they piqued his fascination with this problem.

"Please fill me in on the specifics of your investigations thus far, Roosevelt."

Roosevelt did just that in close detail, and one hour later, he finished. Father Bruno leaned back in his chair. This situation intrigued him, as a priest, as an intellectual, as a soldier, and as a man. "My dear Roosevelt, I believe that the idiosyncrasies of this investigation provide me with a bit of theological wiggle room." He smiled his wide grin. Roosevelt knew how much his friend enjoyed tweaking the figurative noses of any bureaucratic network, including that of the Holy Church.

"This is what I propose to you. First, I will perform the official blessing of the house. Now, I know that this has been done, but I want to do it again. I mean no offense to whomever conducted it, but perhaps I will have more impact. This will present no official problems for me."

"And if that does not work?"

"If it does not work, or if during the blessing itself, another situation arises which demands a different approach, then I might be forced, for the sake of these people, to take other actions. I shall be prepared if the necessity arises. When we were in country, we learned quickly that very few plans go as expected, and that the Marines who can think on their feet and change course if needed are the ones most likely to survive and to prevail. Improvise, adapt, and overcome. For the sake of this woman and child, we must prevail."

Roosevelt nodded in agreement. "And I will continue another avenue of investigation. I may have found a source that will give us some background of the cause of this problem. Any information that we find might be of use to us and to the Murray family."

"Very true, Roosevelt. Then it is decided. I will help."

"Thank you, George. And I hope this effort does not cause you any difficulties with your superiors in the Church."

Bruno waved his hand as if brushing aside an annoying insect. "Remember, my dear Roosevelt, as we used to say in the Corps, what the generals don't know…"

"Won't hurt them."

FORTY-ONE

DECEMBER 15

The weather was beginning to change. The unusual warmth was gone, and the day was cold, feeling more like the beginning of winter than the end of autumn. All of the leaves had fallen, and the air felt like an early winter storm was imminent.

Patrick entered the office located on the 34th floor of a skyscraper in midtown Manhattan. He had dressed lightly, only a light black leather coat over a black sweater and blue jeans. Generally, he loved the cooler weather, but now it was bothering him—he felt a chill that seemed to permeate into his bones, and he wished he had worn a heavier coat. He had taken a bus from the Bethberg Bus Depot and then picked up the connecting train to New York at Clinton, New Jersey. The ride had been smooth and on time. From Grand Central Terminal, he had grabbed a cab to the doctor's office.

Patrick sat in a corner seat in the ultra-modern waiting room. Unlike many physicians' waiting rooms, this one was spacious, gleaming, and decorated with paintings purchased directly from galleries in Soho and with streamlined, but unfortunately not very comfortable, furniture. The room seemed to exude a sense of wealth and power. It felt like the kind of huge corner office a high-level corporate executive might have. Patrick half expected to be ushered into a large room with a huge desk and a man in a suit waiting in a leather chair. He knew, however, that despite his initial impression, it would be a standard doctor's office.

Only a few other patients were in the waiting room, and they obviously had come from upper-class families. Patrick felt uncomfortable. He preferred dealing with people of middle and working classes; he mused if he were being hypocritical, since he, too, was born into wealth. But where did the not-so-moneyed people who needed such specialized help go? What facilities were available to

193

them? He was not naive; those with money received far better medical care than those without. The fact that he could easily pay anything that insurance did not cover certainly helped him get this appointment with one of the pre-eminent neurologists in the United States. That this doctor was also a veteran helped. When the doctor heard that Patrick was a Marine, he was ushered to the front of the line. Patrick couldn't help but wonder why weren't there any other soldiers here who certainly needed help also? If he hadn't the money he did, would this doctor still have seen him, veteran or not? Patrick suspected most vets would have to make do with the doctors provided by the Veteran's Administration, most of who were dedicated professionals, but who were also overwhelmed by the sheer numbers of cases they had to try to help.

In spite of being from the upper class, Patrick had immediately taken to life in the Marine Corps, in which he was judged on what he could do, not on who his parents were. In fact, he had made a point of never making his background clear. Instead, he would give vague and uncertain answers that could be taken many ways whenever some other Marine asked him about home. The strongest he gave was that his brother was also in the Corps.

Patrick relished belonging to a group that was tight knit and focused on goals and actions, not on politics and status. He had been an officer, but he treated all the Marines, all the men and women under his command, with respect. He believed that all people considered by their actions, not their backgrounds. Patrick was hard and demanding but no more on his Marines than he was on himself. He saw that most of the Marines had come from poverty or the working class. He understood and respected them.

Patrick shook himself out of his reverie. He reached down to pick up a magazine to page through, even though he knew he would not remember anything he was looking at, especially the fashion magazines that dominated the holding rack. He scanned them aimlessly, ignoring ads for the latest looks and how-to-be-your-best articles. His head was beginning to hurt again, a slow ache that seemed to start deep inside his brain and spread over his entire skull. He put down the magazine, leaned back in the chair and closed his eyes. He reached into his jacket took out a set of darkly tinted sunglasses and put them on. Sometimes masking the light helped. Sometimes it did not. This seemed to be one of the times when the latter was the case.

"Mr. Franklin?" He looked up at the voice that belonged to an overly perky clerk. "The doctor will see you now."

He stood and walked through the door the young woman held open. He followed her even although he had been here before several times and knew his way to the office.

"Come in, Patrick, and have a seat." The neurologist, Dr. Peyton, was also in his mid-forties, but unlike Patrick, he was the image of carefully maintained good health and appearance. This man appeared to value the way he looked and the way his status was perceived. He worked out five days a week at the gym in his Condo building, and he was impeccably dressed, always in hand-tailored Italian suits and shoes. He was not concerned that his haircuts usually cost around 300 dollars. Peyton worked very hard, and he believed in rewarding himself with the finest things in life. This doctor was excellent in his field, and he wanted that recognition. Around his office were numerous degrees, citations, awards, and memberships in medical associations. Additionally decorating the room were photographs of the doctor with major political figures, including the last two Presidents of the United States. He didn't care about their political party affiliation as long as he could be seen with them. If vanity were truly a mortal sin, he would sometimes tell his friends, he was in deep trouble.

Patrick sat on the slightly reclining seat facing the doctor's desk. It felt more like a visit to a therapist's office than to a medical doctor's. He half expected to be asked about how he was dealing with the trauma or how he had related to his parents.

"Let's go over the findings, shall we?" Dr. Peyton knew that Patrick disliked small talk and did not need or desire sugar-coating, and he respected that. Even though he was now primarily a doctor to the wealthy, Peyton still remembered his time in the service, and he saw the officer's bearing and mien in Patrick. This was a man who wanted the truth, not a mealy mouthed euphemism, or an insincere expression of hope.

"It is bad, Patrick. I have had sufficient time to go over the MRI and consider your history, and I don't like what I see."

Patrick nodded. He had expected as much. After his last communication with Michael, he had contacted the doctor, who had called him in for examination at the New York-Presbyterian University Hospital of Columbia and Cornell Hospital in Manhattan. They had conducted a full battery of tests including MRIs, blood work and x-rays. Of course, he had not told the doctor about what had precipitated the problem. He did not need this doctor thinking that he was delusional and then referring him to a shrink. He knew he was perfectly sane, or at least, he hoped he was. Yet, he was going to continue to operate on the assumption of his mental well-being. If he was sane, then he had choices to make about his future, a plan of action; if he were insane, then it would not really matter.

"I do have to ask you, Patrick, if you have been keeping something from me?"

Patrick simply looked at him.

"For example, why the shades? Do you have a headache now?"

"Yes, I do."

"Then take them off and let me see your eyes."

Patrick hesitated for a moment then acquiesced. This was what he was here for, "to be examined." The doctor watched Patrick's eyes. He was surprised because he had expected bruising or a black eye. He went over to Patrick and used a small penlight to look into his eyes.

"Are you still practicing martial arts, Patrick?"

"Yes, I am. I always will."

"I see. Well, then let me ask you this—are you sparring, you know, are you engaging in full contact sessions?"

This question startled Patrick. He hadn't participated in full contact sparring sessions for years. "No, I haven't, Dr. Peyton. What makes you ask?"

The neurologist returned to his seat and looked Patrick directly in the eyes. "You have several subdural hematomas, bruises on the brain, one that looks like there was a very small amount of bleeding involved. These injuries are the kind often found in athletes who engage in high contact sports, such as boxing, football, or martial arts. Especially in those who continued such contact for far too long. That is why I asked." He sat back in his chair and watched Patrick.

"I can put your mind at ease, Doctor. I only practice with bags and forms, no sparring."

"That's good to hear. I can't keep you from doing anything, but as your doctor, I highly recommend that you do not engage in any kind of high level contact such as sparring."

"You have my word. No sparring."

"Good. However, we are not done. There are also indications of what might have been several small strokes, although the evidence is not clear. Have you experienced any times of lack of clarity, dizziness, or confusion?"

Those were exactly some of the characteristics of the after effects of his sessions with Michael, but he wasn't going to say anything about them.

"No, no. I haven't."

"Again, that is surprising. If you are holding out on me for some reason, I highly advise you not to. It will be very hard to diagnose your condition and treat you properly if you keep back any information. Do you understand?" The doctor was frustrated. He admired Patrick, but he was sure that Patrick was not being honest, although he had no idea why he would dissemble. Patrick showed himself to be a man of honor. Had they still been in the military, it would have been easy. He would have invoked a medical order for full disclosure, but now all he could do was to give Patrick his best advice.

"Do you have a prognosis, Doctor?"

"Just this. I believe that you have brain injuries, the extent of which is definitely not clear, and I don't know why. I believe that the subdoral hematomas are not the main problem; rather, they are symptomatic of a potentially more serious underlying condition. As the hematomas present, they have the potential to become serious, even possessing the possibility to develop into a critical condition, especially given your past medical history. And I am speaking only of what I believe to be the symptom. I am fairly sure that there is more. Do you understand, Patrick?"

Patrick simply nodded. It was as he had suspected.

"And the headaches are becoming worse, aren't they? That is why you are wearing the shades during the day, correct?"

"Yes. They are back, and they are motherfuckers."

The doctor smiled. Few of his patients ever used that kind of language here. It would have shocked many of them, but he knew Patrick's background, both family and military, and it made him happy to hear the words but not their message.

"Your brain has had too much trauma already, Patrick. Many would not have lived through your war injuries, let alone recover the way you did. But I am concerned that what is occurring presently either might be some residue of those traumas or could be the onset of a new, but as yet, undetermined neurological condition."

Dr. Peyton waved his hand as if dismissing a bad idea. "But that is speculation, and I am deeply averse to such conjecturing. I will be completely honest with you, because you deserve that respect. I really do not know why your brain is having new injuries. If I did, I would do everything to stop their occurrences. All I can do now is to caution you to be very careful in your life. Do not sustain any head contact. Nothing! Stop drinking, no smoking, and I want to see you once a week, to be able to monitor your situation."

"Well, Doctor, I can certainly make the trip into New York as you said. It is never wasted time for me, and I will try to avoid contact so that nothing hits my skull, but give up my bourbon? I don't think so, doctor. Jack and I have a special relationship."

Doctor Peyton sighed. He expected that response, and it worried him. Was this man becoming an alcoholic also? "Well, at the least, keep the consumption to a minimum. No more than a small drink every day. Can you do that much at least?"

197

Patrick smiled widely. "Of course I can. I was busting on you. That is all I have anyway. I make a fifth stretch for at least one month. Sampling new small batch bourbons is one of the pleasures of my life, and I am giving it up. I am not, however, stupid about it."

Peyton shook his head. "Okay. Remember what I said though. Your brain is in serious jeopardy. Don't do anything to cause it further trauma. The results could be paralysis or even death."

FORTY-TWO

DECEMBER 15

Around 9 in the morning the IPS met for breakfast at the Bethberg Diner. It was a very subdued affair. They had all dressed warmly because they could feel the change in the air. The unusual warmth that had been hanging over Bethberg was being replaced by a serious chill, a potential Clipper coming down from Canada.

Sam was the first to arrive and Roosevelt came in helping Jeremy, who was now walking with a crutch.

"Quite a war wound you got there, Jerry." Sam had tried to make a joke to lighten the mood, but nothing seemed to help.

"Don't joke about it, alright? We all know how I got this, so there's no point in pretending any different. I got drunk."

They ordered their breakfasts and ate in silence. Finally, Roosevelt spoke up. "You had not been drinking, Jeremy. They found no alcohol in your blood at all."

"You don't understand, Roosevelt. I dreamt about it, in a dream so real that I may as well have been drinking. I feel now like I'm hung over. That feels worse than the God damned ankle."

"Language, Jerry. Watch your language. This is a G rated place." Sam smiled. Jeremy was fastidious about being civil and well-mannered in speech and conduct. Those were the coarsest words that Sam had ever heard Jeremy use.

"The important thing, Jeremy, is that you did not drink." Roosevelt could feel his friend's anguish and wished he could do more to help.

"No, that's not the important thing," Jeremy snapped. "The point is that I wanted to."

After a few minutes of silent eating, Jeremy looked up at his two friends. "There is more"

They waited for him to speak.

"I want to drink now. It hasn't left me. The urge is stronger now than it has been in years. After we finish, I'm going to go to an afternoon meeting. I have to, or I think I'll drink again. I don't think I can be at Father Bruno's house blessing."

"That is ok, Jeremy. He does not want any more witnesses than necessary."

Sam finished his coffee and added, "Well, from what you said, this ain't exactly officially okayed, so I understand. But, I gotta tell you guys, this thing has me shook up too. I don't know. I might need to take a break from it. I had some seriously weird dreams last night."

Roosevelt simply nodded. He did not intend to tell anyone about his dream. "Well, I think we all might need a break after this. I am starting to feel worn down from all this."

"Guys, I am not talking about any break…I just have to get to a meeting. But take a break? This lady and the kid need us. We can't be cowards."

Roosevelt and Sam both colored in embarrassment and focused on their plates. They lapsed into silence and ate their food. They were all thinking about the news that had traveled quickly around the small town.

"Guys, we need to check in on Gerard and see how he is doing." Jeremy glanced up at his friends. He knew that they had to talk about this.

"Shit, man. I can't believe that she's dead. I mean, an asthma attack? Who knew they could be that dangerous?" Sam shook his head. He didn't really know Branwyn well, but still, they had all just seen her.

"Gentlemen," Roosevelt said quietly. "Asthma can be brought on suddenly by great stress, and she was very anxious at the blessing."

"Roosevelt, do you really think that is what caused it? I mean she might simply have gotten ill."

"Yes, Jeremy, I do. I think she became so frightened that an attack was inevitable."

More silence at their table.

Finally, "Rosy, listen to me. This isn't your fault. You hear me? None of us even knew that she had asthma, or that there might be a problem. You gotta remember that."

"Yes, I hear you, Samuel." But he did not believe his friend. He knew it was his responsibility. It felt like he was back in Vietnam again.

FORTY-THREE

Roosevelt and Father Bruno entered the Murray house. In daylight during mid-afternoon, on this tree-lined street, nothing seemed threatening. Ms. Murray had given Roosevelt a key to the house and had stayed away as per their arrangement. It was unusual that Roosevelt was the only member of the IPS present with the good father, but given the circumstances of what they were attempting, and of the delicate and tense situation with the nerves of the IPS, Roosevelt had insisted that only he be present for this unofficial action, and that the group completely respect Father Bruno's wishes about how he wanted to proceed.

"You need to understand, Roosevelt, that what I am doing is completely without official sanction. I fully understand the possible consequences of performing this rite without my Bishop's permission, but I also believe that the official process will take too long. And there is no certainty that I would be granted permission. In fact, I think it is more likely that I hit the jackpot on the lottery than be given permission to do what we plan."

"My dear George, I had no idea that you played the lottery. You, a man of the cloth."

Bruno smiled. "Roosevelt, I don't play the lottery. That's the point, but that is extraneous. The Bishop would not give permission, and I do think this is the right thing to do. Sometimes, the ethics of a situation is in complete conflict with the dictates of the organization. So, I make this decision outside of the confines of the Church. Still, the fewer involved the better."

They had decided that Roosevelt would act as Father Bruno's assistant, not only because they were old friends, but also because they had been soldiers together. They had faced death before in the jungles of Vietnam, and if need be, they would do so again in this pretty-little-house in the quiet town of Bethberg.

The two men stood in the foyer of the house and silently looked around them. There was no indication of anything wrong. For the moment, the house simply seemed to be a peaceful domicile. They had decided to perform the rite of exorcism during the daylight. They were not going to use any recording devices, and they would conduct no ghost investigations, so they may as well see as fully as they could.

Dressed in his full regalia, Father Bruno was an impressive figure. He stood six foot three inches, with a very broad chest. He looked like an older version of a powerful athlete. With his graying hair combed straight back, and his broad forehead, he looked like an old but still physically imposing scholar. His array was a full vestment: black Cossack, white surplice, stole, and collar. In his hands, he carried a copy of *De Exorcismis et Supplicationibus Quibusdam*, the official rite of exorcism. Roosevelt carried another old leather satchel and stood next to his friend.

"Roosevelt, you said that the activity seems to spread throughout most of the house, that there doesn't seem to be any one central location?"

"That is right. I wish there were some specific place. I think it would make things a great deal easier for us. This almost feels like being out on the battlefield but not knowing where the enemy is."

"Or even who the enemy is."

"I am not sure who this spirit is, but I am investigating a possible name we found."

"Can you tell me who it is?"

"I am hesitant to do that. If I am wrong, then would it not weaken your exorcism if the incorrect name is given?"

"That is a distinct possibility. Still when you know for certain, be sure to tell me."

"I will. What do we do now?"

Father Bruno looked at his friend and nodded. "Well, we begin. Let's go to war against this particular enemy, whatever its name is, shall we?"

They moved to the living room and set their material on the coffee table. Father Bruno removed a crucifix from the leather satchel, kissed it, and then handed it to Roosevelt. "This might be the best weapon I can hand you, old friend."

Roosevelt took the cross and held it, but he did not tell Father Bruno that although he deeply respected his friend's faith, he had long ago lost his own belief in Christianity. He believed in a God, but he no longer believed that any religion had the absolute answer. He had become a Deist, but he still thought that Father Bruno's faith would be a powerful weapon against this thing.

Father Bruno took a small metal flask out of the satchel. Roosevelt looked at him and raised an eyebrow.

Bruno laughed. "It's holy water, not whiskey. I think that particular drink is what we will need later. For now, this blessed water is our liquid of choice."

"As a reward for our efforts, George, I have a bottle of 18 year old Macallan at home waiting for us."

"Then by all means, let's do this. Shall we get to work?"

"Let us."

Father Bruno picked up the holy water and sprinkled some around the room. Then he picked up the text and began to speak. First he prayed.

"Our Father,
Who art in Heaven,
Hallowed be Thy name.
Thy kingdom come;
Thy will be done on earth as it is in Heaven.
Give us this day our daily bread,
And forgive us our trespass,
As we forgive our trespassers.
And lead us not into temptation."

They both added, "Amen."

As soon as they finished the prayer, the quality of the air in the room began to change. Even though the day outside was bright and sunny, the house seemed to be enveloped slowly in clouds. The light dimmed as if thunderheads had gathered directly overhead.

Father Bruno picked up the book and stood straight. He began to read in a deep, clear and commanding voice:

"I command you unclean spirit, whoever you are, along with all your minions now attacking this servant of God, by the mysteries of the incarnation, passion, and resurrection, and ascension of our Lord Jesus Christ, by the descent of His Holy Spirit, by the coming of our Lord for judgment, that you tell me some sign of your name, and the day and hour of your departure. I command you, moreover, to obey me to the letter, I who am a minister of God despite my unworthiness; nor shall you be emboldened to harm in any way this creature of God, or the bystanders or any of their possessions."

As soon as Father Bruno finished speaking, a gust of wind thrust through the room. Hot, damp, sticky, and fetid, it felt like the decay of corpse in a stinking swamp in the middle of August in the deep South. As it stopped, a terrible stench settled around them and seemed to graft onto their bodies.

Father Bruno crossed himself and then made the sign of the cross over Roosevelt.

"A nasty smell, but we have both smelled worse in Vietnam. Are you all right, Roosevelt?"

"Yes, I am."

Father Bruno looked at his friend carefully then continued with the rite. He prayed again, and spoke the words of several psalms and cast more holy water about the room. Then he spoke the Apostle's Creed.

"I believe in God,

the Father Almighty,

Creator of Heaven and earth;

and in Jesus Christ, His only Son, Our Lord,

Who was conceived by the Holy Spirit,

born of the Virgin Mary,

suffered under Pontius Pilate,

was crucified, died, and was buried.

He descended into Hell.

The third day He arose again from the dead;

He ascended into Heaven,

Sitteth at the right hand of God, the Father Almighty;

from thence He shall come to judge the living and the dead.

I believe in the Holy Spirit,

the holy Catholic Church,

the communion of saints,

the forgiveness of sins,

the resurrection of the body,

and the life everlasting. Amen."

Even though Father Bruno was not trying to exorcise a demon from a possessed person, he still spoke the rite as if he were doing so. He reasoned that the house itself could be possessed.

As Father Bruno prepared to continue with the rite, a voice exploded in his mind.

PRIEST! You think you can come here and defeat Me? You think you have any power here? You are nothing—less even than the bitch and the whelp I now own.

Father Bruno ignored the voice and began to read; "I adjure you ancient serpent, by the judge of the living and the dead, by your Creator, by the Creator of the whole universe, by Him who has the power to consign you to hell..."

Priest, you fool, I embrace your hell. It carries no fear for me.

Father Bruno felt his head begin to constrict, the way it always did when he was beginning to have a migraine headache. *Not now,* he thought.

"I cast you out, unclean spirit, along with every Satanic power, every demon from hell, in the name of our Lord Jesus Christ! Be gone and stay away! For it is He who commands you!" As Father Bruno spoke, his voice deepened in register and increased in power until the full range of his distinguished baritone soared through the room.

Roosevelt watched in awe and fear. The light in the room dimmed, and the malodorous smell permeated the room. In the corner of the room, he caught a quick image, and then shut his eyes…he had seen the dead bodies of VC soldiers he had killed in combat. He saw a trio of men whom he had once surprised on a night patrol mission. They had prepared to shoot at him, but he had fired first and managed to kill all three. They now stood before him, their bodies bleeding from their wounds. Their eyes accused him of murder.

"Roosevelt, are you all right?" Bruno asked him in a near whisper. "Roosevelt! Stay with me!"

"It is ok. I am here," Roosevelt whispered. "Keep going, get rid of this bastard." As he closed his eyes and opened them, the VC soldiers vanished.

"Begone you enemy of faith, you foe and betrayer of the human race, you begetter of death, you corrupter of innocence and justice, begone in the name of the Father, the Son, and the Holy Spirit! Begone!"

A near whirlwind encircled them both. Papers spun as if in the grip of a mini-cyclone, and pictures flew off the wall. It sounded as if a jet were preparing to take off from a nearby airstrip.

Father Bruno's head began to pound like a sledgehammer was beating it. A flashing jagged light appeared in his peripheral vision. *NO! Not now, not now…hold on, I have to keep going. I'm needed here. I must complete this.*

"Begone in the name of our Lord Jesus Christ!"

Roosevelt saw another image appearing in the room, directly in front of him. It was Sarah, and she was pleading with him to stop. He could hear her voice, *make it stop Roosevelt. It hurts so bad. Make it stop.*

"Sarah?" he whispered.

Even through the tumult, Father Bruno saw his friend and the look on his face.

"Roosevelt, what is it? What's wrong?"

"It's Sarah. I can see her. She wants us to stop."

"No, Roosevelt! It's not her. This thing is a liar, and it will use anything it can to stop us. We must be hurting it."

"But I can see her."

"Then leave and I'll continue. If you have to, get the fuck out of here, but I must continue."

Roosevelt was crying and bent over, sagging like an old and diseased tree that was about to collapse. He had dreamt of Sarah many times since her death, but this was the first time he saw her, and he couldn't hurt her, no matter what.

He heard her again. *Please Roosevelt, I can't stand it.*

"Sarah, I want you to know, my love, that I was doing this to help a child."

I don't care, Roosevelt. What does the little bitch matter to me? How can you possibly put a child above me? I need you to go.

Roosevelt looked straight at the vision of Sarah. He straightened his posture and said to Bruno, "Keep going. I am staying."

"Are you sure?"

"Yes, this is not Sarah. She would never tell me to abandon a child. I am seeing what this thing wants me to see. And she is not a servant of this fucking abomination! Continue!"

Roosevelt! Don't abandon me. Don't do this to me!

Her voice echoed through his mind, but he tried to ignore it, because he knew it was not truly that of his wife.

Father Bruno rang out, "I command you demon to get out. Depart then transgressor! Depart, seducer, full of lies and cunning foe of virtue and tormentor of the innocent. Give place, abominable creature, give way, you monster, give way to Christ, in whom you found none of your works. For he has already stripped you of your powers and laid waste your kingdom, bound you prisoner and plundered your weapons. He has cast you forth into the outer darkness, where everlasting ruin awaits you and your abettors."

The smell in the room intensified.

Father Bruno screamed and dropped his book. He doubled over and grabbed his head in his hands.

"George! George! Let's get out of here. Now!" Roosevelt stood next to him and tried to coax his friend to leave.

Bruno held up one hand as he sat. "Just let me rest for a moment, and I'll be fine."

Priest, I cast you out! I know your secrets. I know that you did not receive official sanction for your puny attempt at exorcism. You think that you are enough to deal with me. You commit the sin of arrogance.

Father Bruno stood again.

"George, we need to go," Roosevelt said through clenched teeth.

"No, I will not leave. God damn this thing to hell!"

As he stood to confront the entity, flashes of lightning cracked across his field of vision, and he felt half his head encased by an iron vise, squeezing as if it were trying to pop his head open like an old, overripe melon.

Father Bruno's voice was cracking now. "It is the word of Christ who commands that you leave, demon. It is the power of our Lord who compels you!"

As he spoke, the fetid smell and the wind spread like the stench of a na-palm bombing. Neither man noticed that blood began to seep from Father Bruno's left nostril and from his left ear.

"It is God who casts you out! Nothing is hidden to Him. It is He who repels you! It is He who expels you and prevents you from bringing harm to the innocent. It is He who casts you out, and it is He from whose mouth shall come a sharp sword, wielded by one of His angels, one of His heavenly warriors to smite you and cast you out! Begone from this place and these people!"

Priest! Nothing, no one can harm me! Nothing can cast me out! I reject your puny attempts. I laugh at your god! I laugh at you! Now feel my power!

"I command you unclean spirit…" Father Bruno's voice faltered, then a strange look of calm came over his features. "Demon, one with a sharp sword will destroy you!" Bruno shouted. He then looked over at his friend, gri-maced, and dropped the book.

"George?"

Without saying another word, Father Bruno's eyes bulged and blood poured from his nose. As Roosevelt reached for him, the priest fell to the floor.

Roosevelt held his friend and heard laughter shaking the house.

Roosevelt dialed 911 on his overlarge cell phone, designed for senior citi-zens, and tried to carry Father Bruno out of the house. As he did, he heard a voice that he did not recognize call out to him.

It is too late. The stupid, arrogant priest is mine, old man. All of you are mine!

FORTY-FOUR

DECEMBER 17

The phone call came in the afternoon. "Roosevelt, you need to get here as soon as possible."

About 30 minutes later, Roosevelt pulled into the parking garage at Bethberg Medical Center to visit Father Bruno. Even though he was not an immediate family member, Roosevelt had been able to use his connections both with the board of the hospital and as a close friend of Sister Anna, one of the oldest nuns of Father Bruno's order, to gain access to the ICU. Sister Anna was there when Bruno arrived, so Roosevelt knew what it meant when he received her phone call.

She was officially retired from duty but maintained as many functions as she could, including visiting at hospitals. It was natural that she was there, but she also knew of Father Bruno's very serious medical condition.

"Father Bruno is one of the best men I have ever known," she told Roosevelt with a sparkle in her eyes during his previous visit. "No, I do NOT mean in the Biblical sense!" she said and playfully slapped Roosevelt's hand. "But, truthfully, even if considering it were a sin, if I were not a Sister and he not a Priest, well then. . . "

Roosevelt raised one eyebrow.

"Don't you be shocked. I was quite the hellion when I was younger. I didn't take my vows and enter the service of God until I was in my 30s. So, I know what I left behind. And I am very aware of what I felt, what I still feel for Father Bruno. God help me, I have confessed it often enough."

Anna smiled playfully at Roosevelt. "You should have seen me then. I was quite the looker. But you wouldn't know that now." She waved her hand at her now corpulent body and lined face.

"Sister Anna, you are one of the most beautiful women I have ever known."

"You are a gallant gentleman, and I thank you for the flattery."

Roosevelt smiled softly. "After my Sarah, of course."

She patted his hand. She knew how much Roosevelt had loved his wife, and she knew how close the two men had been as friends. Even though it was unclear how the Church was going to proceed, considering what had happened, she wanted to make sure that Roosevelt would be able to see his friend. She knew Father Bruno did not have much time left.

"But I do know this," she had said while looking at Father Bruno in a coma on his bed. "He is one of God's men. I know that he doesn't often follows orders. In fact, he dislikes rules intensely. He has always been a kind of rebel. I know that he has been in trouble with the hierarchy before, but I also know this—what he does, no matter the circumstances, is to help others. He is incapable of seeing someone in trouble without trying to do something about it."

"At what price though, Sister? What did I drag him into? He did not need this kind of trouble." Roosevelt lowered his head into his hands. He could feel his eyes tearing.

"Don't you dare blame yourself!" she snapped with the kind of authority that made many middle school children who were being disruptive in her class come immediately to order. She reached over and took his face into her two calm and strong hands. She fixed her eyes on Roosevelt with a gaze that was as steely as any soldier he had ever known. "Father Bruno is a grown man. He understood the chances he took and the choices he made. No one has ever forced him to do anything since I have known him, and no one could keep him from doing something if he thought it were necessary and right. If he has to make amends with anyone, it is with God, not anyone on earth. You have nothing to feel guilty about. If you were Catholic, I would drag you to the confessional for the good of your soul and your mind."

"But even if he does get through this, what will the Church say?"

"I am a devout Catholic, and I love the Church with my entire being, but I don't love its bureaucracy. Whatever anyone official may say, regardless of their worldly statements, I am completely certain that God will not punish that good man for trying to help a woman and a child in need. If a priest does not respond to that kind of need, then what kind of priest is he?"

This conversation ran through Roosevelt's mind as he hurried through the long halls of the hospital. Even though he had been coming every day to visit, he still hated the place because it always brought back memories of Sarah's illness and her painful stays in the medical center.

Roosevelt rounded the corner to the ICU. There he found Sister Anna waiting for him. With tears cascading down her winkled face, she held her arms out to him. He wrapped her in a hug and looked over at Father Bruno. Another priest, an old man, whom Roosevelt did not know, was administering, in a very soft voice, the last rites. Roosevelt could not hear what was being said, but he knew that the elderly priest was praying for Father Bruno's soul.

The priest finished with a sign of the cross and stood.

He slowly, almost in a shuffle, walked the few feet to Roosevelt and Sister Anna, who was now standing next to him. The elderly priest took her hand and smiled sadly. "At least now," he said to her. "At least, he will still be in the Church's good graces."

"May I ask you something?" Roosevelt said in a near whisper as he gently touched the old priest's arm.

"Yes, please do," the elderly gentleman replied.

"Is the Church dropping the matter now?"

The priest was startled by the question. Not knowing who Roosevelt was, he was uncertain if he should answer.

Sister Anna reached out to the priest. "It is all right, Father Tompkins. Roosevelt is a very dear friend of Father Bruno, and he knows the situation. You can be assured that he is discreet."

Father Tompkins hesitated for a bit then made his decision. "They are not going to pursue it. Given the circumstances, they thought it better for all involved for it to simply be dropped."

Father Tompkins smiled briefly. "If you will excuse me, I have to see other patients." He moved out of the room with the slow gait of the very old.

Sister Anna and Roosevelt went to Father Bruno's bed and sat on either side of their friend. They waited quietly, each deeply involved in their own thoughts.

In what may have been ten minutes or ten hours to Roosevelt, since he had lost track of time, he heard a change in Father Bruno's breathing. He was still comatose, but now his respiration was deeply labored. No breathing apparatus was attached to Father Bruno; he had made it clear in his living will that he wanted no extraordinary medical attempts to keep his body alive. "When I am dead, I want my organs to be there to help someone else if they are still have any use," he had told Roosevelt during one of their lunches.

Sister Anna and Roosevelt both took one of his hands and held it. A few minutes later, Father Bruno took one last breath and exhaled.

He was gone.

FORTY-FIVE

THE IN-BETWEEN

*Y*essssssssssssssssssss! Maledicus sung with the glory of what he had done. *A priest! A priest! I have killed a priest!*

I can feel my power growing. Soon nothing, nothing will be able to stop me. Not those fools with their impotent powers. Not even their priests can stop me on Earth.

I feel my power growing and rising beyond even what I imagined I could do. Soon even THEY will not be able to hold me. Soon I will be free of THEY! Soon I will be a demon to be feared by all, even by THEY.

THEY rejoiced. This was far better than THEY had originally planned.

FORTY-SIX

DECEMBER 17

Helen Murray looked up at the clock in the hospital room—it was 7 P.M. She had been there all day with her niece, whose condition had been deteriorating. The doctors had not been able to discover any physical cause for Helena's sickness, and she had seemed to be improving, so she was released from the hospital. This period of remission, however, was short lived. Dr. Wilson was sure to check in every day with Helen to monitor the little girl's progress, but nothing had changed. She had taken personal time from school for the days prior to the holiday, something that would not be a problem, because she had amassed a great deal of unused sick days and personal days, but she would have taken this time off even if it meant being fired. Her niece mattered more than any job.

On his most recent checkup on Helena, Dr. Wilson had clearly been unable to keep the concern from showing on his face. He had spoken with Helen earlier about the little girl's condition.

"I truly don't understand what is causing this, Helen. I have to admit that I am stumped. I don't know what Helena's illness is. I've run every test that I can think of, even some that would not seem to have any bearing on her condition. I have drawn more blood from that tiny body than I would think possible, but I still come back with no answers. According to every medical criterion I can find, she is healthy, but, Helen, she is definitely one very ill child."

"What do you think we can do? Or should do?" she asked him with a sound of desperation in her voice. "We need to find some answers, so we can find a way to help her."

"I think we need to admit her to Children's Hospital in Philadelphia. They have more facilities and experts who might be able to shed some light on her case. I have already contacted the hospital and a few doctors in case you agreed."

"Jonathan, I'll do anything to help her."

"I'd like to move her tonight, Helen, but with the forecast of a major storm, I think taking her on the road now would be dangerous, so I suggest that we readmit her. Then as soon as the weather permits, we will transfer her."

"That sounds like a good plan to me."

Later that evening, Dr. Wilson came into their hospital room. "Helena is sleeping now, and you need a rest. Why don't you come with me and have a cup of coffee? You need to try to relax, and we'll be back with her shortly. I'll make sure that the nurses look in on her constantly."

Helen agreed and stood wearily. She had been sitting in the chair next to her niece for over five hours and was stiff. As they walked down the hallway, Helen stopped to look out of a large window. The sky was dark, clouded over.

"I wonder if that storm they are predicting is coming?"

"The ski slopes will love it if it does," he replied.

As they were sitting down to a small meal of sandwiches and coffee in the cafeteria, Dr. Wilson was paged. He sighed, excused himself, and stood to return the call.

"It's Helena. Come with me, now!"

They ran through the halls back to the child's room. As they rounded the entrance to the hall, a nurse came out of Helena's room and called, "Dr. Wilson! Come quickly!"

They both sprinted to Helena's room. Both knew, without being told, that something was seriously wrong with the child.

"What is it, Nurse?"

"Her heart rate and blood pressure have dropped dramatically, Doctor."

"Oh my god, oh no, no, no." Helen stood over the little girl.

"Helen, wait in the chair please."

The doctor treated the little girl and brought her heart and blood pressure under control.

As he held her eyes open to shine his light in, he grew very concerned. "She is not responding. I want her moved into ICU now."

Dr. Wilson was certain that Helena had slipped into a coma.

FORTY-SEVEN

DECEMBER 17

After leaving the hospital, Roosevelt walked slowly to his car in the Medical Center Parking Garage. Normally the simple act of sitting in his 1967 Porsche, a car he had owned and maintained from new, would have given him a sense of joy. He loved that car, not simply because it was a high performance machine of the highest German automotive engineering that could handle any road condition, be it highway or curvy back roads, but because Sarah had also loved it. She had delighted in riding in it with him, from a simple errand to the many road trips they had taken, with only the sparsest of luggage packed in the small trunk. Usually whenever he sat in the car, he could feel her presence.

This day, however, was different. He stood by the driver's door of the gray car and held the key with a trembling hand. In order to make his hand stop shaking so he could get the key into the lock, he had to grab his right hand with his left. He was able to steady himself enough to open the door and sit in the driver's seat. He held the wheel tightly with both hands but did not turn the ignition.

What have I done? Roosevelt looked out the window but saw nothing. Anyone walking by would have seen an old man lost in his thoughts, and they might have wondered if he was in need of assistance. George Bruno and he had been through so much together. After facing combat together in Viet Nam, several times in which he thought they might die, Roosevelt thought that Bruno and he could face any foe together and emerge victorious. They seemed to be impervious to any threat. After all, what was the peril posed by a ghost or spirit compared to the life threatening danger given by highly trained Viet Cong soldiers? He had become arrogant about his own strengths.

Roosevelt realized that he had made the worst mistake any warrior could make; he had underestimated his opponent. He had seriously miscalculated the strength and viciousness of this entity, and that mistake had cost his longtime friend his life.

Roosevelt felt his eyes begin to moisten and build with tears. *No! I will not cry, not here—not where I can be seen.* He pounded the steering wheel three times with his hands, and his entire body shook, with a near convulsion.

A young woman walking hand in hand with a small child saw him and considered asking if he needed any help. Something about the situation frightened her though, and she hurried on her way. She hoped the old gentleman was going to be all right.

I continue to make mistakes. I continue to fuck up. His mind flashed back to the young Marine who had been killed while helping him to safety. *That bullet was meant for me. What did that boy lose? His chance for a wife? For children? To have a family? And why? To save my miserable life. He should have lived. I should have died that day.*

Roosevelt sobbed hard. Then he wailed. Inside the little car, the sound amplified like discordant bursts of trumpets played loudly and out of key. But Roosevelt gripped his grief with what was left of his self-control. He stifled his crying when he heard the sounds of footsteps in the garage nearby. He heard other visitors returning to their own vehicles. Roosevelt forced himself to sit straight. He wiped his eyes and attempted to look as if everything was fine.

I will be calm. I will start this car and I will drive out of here. His hand, now trembling with only a slight tremor, turned the key. He pressed the gas pedal, and the old, but still powerful, engine roared to life.

With great care, Roosevelt backed out of his parking space and, with equal caution, drove out of the garage. The movement of the shifting and the feel of the precision vehicle responding to his touch offered a small bit of calm but absolutely no solace.

Roosevelt could not face going back to the house Sarah and he had shared as their home. He had always been completely honest with her and she with him. Some people believed that complete honesty was not healthy in a marriage, but he knew that she was the only person whom he trusted enough to be totally open with. He had shared everything with her, good and bad, successful and unsuccessful, his hopes and his fears. His love for her was the most complete he had ever had for anyone, and she was the one who had known him better than anyone else. She would never have let him lie to himself, ever. And now, if he went home, he knew that he would feel her presence there, and right now, more than anything, he deeply wanted to lie to himself and to forget.

Instead, he drove into town and pulled into the parking lot of The Slainte, a local bar that had been a dive for decades, a place for those only one step up from being winos and bums on the street, but which had recently been purchased and remodeled into an Irish Pub, complete with Guinness and Harp on tap, a full range of Irish whiskey, and a wide assortment of pub grub, from fish and chips to bangers and mash. *Guinness and Bushmill's. That should do the trick.*

Usually Roosevelt patronized The Slainte for a meal, often Shepherd's Pie and a pint of Guinness. Then he would have conversation with anyone he might know or meet over a cup of coffee, and soon he would leave.

This day he went straight to the bar. A young bartender, or at least in comparison to Roosevelt, one whom he had seen only a few times previously, was behind the counter. Jimmy, the bartender, was recently hired to work a few shifts. He had seen Roosevelt before, but he had never waited on him. He had noticed, though, that the elderly gentleman had always been respectful and never a problem. When he asked the other bartenders and wait-staff about him, two waitresses said that he was polite and a good tipper.

"Afternoon, sir. What can I get you?"

"I believe I will begin with a pint of Guinness and a double of Bushmills—neat, if you please."

The bartender was surprised at this heavy duty order from a man he would have expected to order white wine followed by tea; after all, in his tweed suit, the gentleman looked like a retired college professor. "Sure thing, coming right up."

Typically, whenever Roosevelt went into a restaurant or a pub to eat and he was alone, he always had a book with him for company. He believed no one was ever truly alone while reading, that communication with the author through his or her words was a very real, if somewhat one-sided, conversation. This time, however, he had no book, no magazine, nor a newspaper. He simply sat and looked directly forward, at nothing in particular.

Roosevelt tried to think of nothing.

And he drank.

It had been many years since Roosevelt had been drunk. He was a man who prided himself on his strong will and his self-discipline. Whenever he saw anyone over the age of 21 inebriated, he felt disgusted, especially by public drunkenness. He felt if someone must be intoxicated they should have the common decency not to inflict their sloppy condition on other people. This should have been established courtesy.

Roosevelt knew he was being hypocritical, but he did not care.

Fuck common decency, he thought as he shot down the double of Bushmills and quickly chased it with the pint of Guinness.

Roosevelt signaled for the bartender to bring him another. He then fanned out several twenty dollar bills on the counter.

"Young man, when I leave I would very much appreciate if you would you call the local cab company and arrange a ride home for me. I am sure that I should not be driving home, do you not agree?"

"Uh…sure."

"Also, please let Mr. Doyle know that I will leave my vehicle in the parking lot overnight. I will be here tomorrow to retrieve it."

"Uh, who do I say you are?"

"Roosevelt."

"Just Roosevelt?" The bartender was fairly sure now that this old guy was losing his marbles or already had, but he seemed nice enough, and he sure had enough money to cover the drinks and a ride home.

"Simply Roosevelt. Mr. Doyle knows me, son. He will understand, and trust me, if you do as I request, you will earn a large gratuity for your services."

The bartender began to go for the phone, but Roosevelt stopped him.

"But first, young man, another double of Bushmills. Then please make your call to Mr. Doyle."

The bartender replaced the drink and made the phone call to the owner of Slainte. After hanging up the phone, he looked over at Roosevelt and gave him a thumbs-up. Roosevelt simply nodded and sipped his whiskey. This one he would take a bit slower than the previous drink. *What was the hurry? After all, I have all evening.*

Several hours later, Roosevelt was still sitting at the bar and looking into space. Except for a few trips to the men's room, he had been quiet and still the whole time he was in the pub. He had ignored any attempts by other customers to have conversation, and everyone left him alone. Only the bartender came over to give him another drink. Jimmy had been worried about the amount of alcohol the elderly man had consumed, but Roosevelt did not appear to be visibly drunk, and the bartender saw no reason to cut him off. *What the hell, he isn't causing any trouble, and he isn't falling off the chair. As long he wants another drink, until we have to close, he can stay. And Mr. Doyle made it very clear that I am to take care of the old fellow.*

No one other than Jimmy could tell how much Roosevelt had drunk, nor could anyone see the turmoil raging inside him. His face was vacant, but images of Bruno at the hospital played over and over in his head. It was like an unending movie loop; he kept seeing Bruno die.

It was nearly one in the morning, and Roosevelt realized he was near the end of his ability to control himself. He slowly raised his hand to catch the bartender's attention.

"Another?"

"One more please, and then I believe that I will be finished. If you do not mind, I will need that cab."

The only difference that Jimmy noticed in the elderly man's demeanor was the he was now speaking a little more slowly. His words were still distinct, with no slurring, but he could hear Roosevelt's forced clarity, like a drunk's forced careful walking.

"Certainly, sir. I'll let you know when it's here."

The bartender placed one last glass of whiskey in front of Roosevelt.

"Thank you, young man."

Approximately twenty minutes later, Jimmy told Roosevelt his cab was waiting.

Roosevelt left a fifty-dollar tip and slowly, very carefully, with only a minimum of teetering, made his way out of the pub. When he stepped outside, the cold December air shocked him, but it was not enough to sober him. For that, he was grateful. Jimmy had watched Roosevelt's progress inside the bar, but he had stayed back, not wanting to insult the old fellow. Then Jimmy went to the window and watched him, making sure that he was able to get into the cab without falling.

FORTY-EIGHT

DECEMBER 18

One half hour later, Roosevelt was sitting in his office at home with a crystal decanter half full with Macallan 12 year old Scotch Whisky next to him on a side table and four fingers of the excellent single malt scotch in a crystal glass. No one around and with his mind sufficiently numb, his iron discipline collapsed, and he began to cry. He was not loud, nor did he wail. Instead, a stream of tears poured out of his eyes and ran down his wrinkled face.

"George…" he whispered. "George, what have I done?"

He quickly drank a large swallow of the whiskey and sat back in the chair. His eyes began to close, and he faded in and out of sleep, in and out of dreams.

"Jesus Christ, save me, sir!" the young Marine screamed as a Viet Cong bullet hit him from behind. Roosevelt reached out for the soldier who had helped him back to safety. As he did, the young man's head exploded from behind.

Roosevelt stood over the man's body, crumpled on the hill. The air had grown quiet; there was no more shooting. The dead Marine turned his head and looked up at Roosevelt, gazing up with only half a face. He pointed at Roosevelt.

"You did this. It's your fault."

Roosevelt screamed and woke up suddenly.

"No, no, no, no…I am sorry, I am so sorry." He still had the glass in his hand, with about two fingers of whiskey remaining, and he drank it in one swallow.

As he looked into the quiet room, Roosevelt could still hear the soldier's voice, and he broke into sobs. Roosevelt whimpered and poured more whisky into the glass. No matter how hard he tried or how much he drank, he could not get drunk enough to forget or go into oblivion.

I failed them. I failed that Marine. I failed Sarah. I failed George. And now I cannot even make myself drunk enough to pass out or to forget. I am a fucking failure.

My god. I thought it would be easy. We would just do a little exorcism. The blessing did not work? No problem, we will just have a little exorcism. What could go wrong? Easy? I am such a supercilious ass.

Roosevelt violently slugged back the rest of the whisky in the glass. Nothing. He did not even feel the burn as the liquid went down.

What a fucking failure. Hamlet was right. What an ass am I!

Oh god, Sarah, you would be so ashamed of me. I am ashamed. I thought I had everything under control. I thought this would be a simple problem to solve.

Fuck, George is dead. I might as well have killed him myself. Roosevelt poured more Scotch and took another drink.

Might as well have put a gun to George's head and pulled the trigger myself.

"Fuck me!" Roosevelt roared and threw the glass across the room. The heavy crystal hit a bookshelf, bounced unbroken, and rolled on the floor.

Roosevelt laughed with a bitter sound. *I cannot even break a goddamned glass. I am just an old fool, a useless old fool. Fucking useless.*

A useless old man who has no purpose.

Roosevelt heard a sibilant voice. *You know what to do, old man.*

He rose on severely unsteady legs and walked with slow and highly guarded steps to a long cabinet in the far corner of the room. He looked at the keypad that guarded its lock. For a few moments, he could not remember the code, suddenly his right index finger shot out and tapped the combination. The lock disengaged, and the gun safe opened.

Roosevelt swayed slightly as he stood and looked at the guns. All of his weapons were well-maintained and of the highest quality, two Sieger rifles, a double barreled engraved Winchester .10 gauge shotgun and two pistols, a Beretta semi-automatic, and his favorite weapon, a Colt .45 peacemaker, a beautifully crafted revolver, a single action antique that still worked as well as the day it was made. Here was a genuine functional antique weapon for a worthless decrepit failure.

Yessss...that's the one to use. The voice spoke to him again.

He picked up the Colt, bullets from a box, and he and slowly walked back to his chair. He sat down, loaded, the gun, and placed the gun's barrel to his right temple.

I'm coming to you, Sarah. I'll be with you soon, my beloved.

He cocked the hammer and prepared to pull the trigger. This would be very fast.

Yesssss...now...do it! It spoke again and Roosevelt began to put pressure on the trigger.

"ROOSEVELT THEODORE FRANKLIN! PUT THAT GUN DOWN!"

His rheumy eyes blinked, and he looked around the room. Did he truly hear that?

Ignore the bitch! Do what you have to do! The voice was still there, but now it sounded desperate.

He listened carefully for a full minute. There was only silence. His eyes moistened again, and he began to cry. Yet, he still held the gun to his head.

"I SAID PUT THAT GUN DOWN!"

Roosevelt blinked to clear his eyes of tears and looked around. No one was there. He gently replaced the hammer, but still held the gun against his head

Nooooo....don't listen to her! The voice insisted.

Only two people in his life had ever addressed him like that, his long dead mother and his beloved Sarah, and then only when she was exasperated with him. He had recognized the voice immediately, but he had not believed what he had heard. Her voice, however, had been clear. Roosevelt had heard his wife, or he was going insane.

"ROOSEVELT, YOU WILL LISTEN TO ME. PUT THAT GUN DOWN!"

Tears rolled down his cheeks, and he placed the gun on the table beside him. The other voice faded.

"Forgive me, please, forgive me," Roosevelt said in a tiny voice, and he curled up his long frame sideways into the chair; he looked like a little boy trapped in the body of an old man. He softly cried himself to sleep.

As Roosevelt slept, Sarah was talking to him. She looked as she had before the illness had taken hold of her. Her face was lined with age, but he had told her that she continued to grow more beautiful every day. Her hair was gray, and her eyes were shining with love for him. She was holding Roosevelt in her arms as they leaned together on an old loveseat. His head was resting on her breast, and she was gently stroking his hair.

"My poor Roosevelt," she said softly. She took his head in her hands and made him face her. "My poor husband, you have to stop blaming yourself. You didn't cause George's death. He chose to go into battle with you, just as he did those many years ago. It was his choice, and he knows it. He also knows it was the right thing to do."

"But, Sarah." Roosevelt spoke to her as he slept. "I asked him to help."

"Yes, my beloved, you did. That was the right thing to do, because you can't fight this thing alone. George agreed to help. That was his choice. You are not responsible for what happened, only for your own choices."

She kissed him and spoke to him almost lip to lip. "I want you to think of this and remember this, my husband. I am proud of you, deeply proud."

He smiled a weak smile. "Thank you, my wife.

"But, Roosevelt. . ."

He looked into her beautiful eyes.

She took his face again in her hands, as gently as the sigh of a soft early autumn breeze. "It isn't over."

"No, it is not."

"My beloved, you must stop blaming yourself, and you must return to the battle. That little girl is dying. Worse than that, her very soul is threatened, and you are the one who can help her, along with the others. If you do not, this child is forever lost."

"I am so tired, Sarah."

"I understand, Roosevelt. I love you, and I always will. But you must face this choice: either to help the little girl or know you abandoned her. I know you couldn't face yourself if you gave up on this child.

"And my beloved, never consider doing again what you almost did tonight. It's not your way. I have known for a long time you were worried that you were following in your father's footsteps. He was a troubled and ill man, a good, but weak man. You're not weak my love. You are neither fated to follow his example nor to do what he did. Your life is your own. Just because he killed himself doesn't mean you must also.

"Remember, my beloved husband, You Are Not Your Father! You are the good, kind, and strong man I married. You are the man I love."

She leaned forward and kissed him, not a light kiss, but a full passionate kiss like the kind they shared. He felt her against him and in the fullness of her being. Then she was slowly enveloped by a bright light into which she faded. As Sarah slowly disappeared, he heard her say, "I am always with you, my husband."

The next morning when he awoke, Roosevelt was cramped and extremely stiff from a night of sleeping in the chair. He had a nearly blinding headache that pounded around his temples, but he also was filled with resolve.

Soon after he woke, his telephone rang.

FORTY-NINE

The In-Between, December 18

In the In-Between Maledicus howled with frustration. *Nooooooooooooooooooooo. I had him! He was mine! That bitch! That bitch took him from me!*

As he screeched, his form undulated in an arrhythmic pulse accompanied by a discordant cacophony of screams. His massive size very slowly, almost imperceptibly to anyone or anything except THEY, reduced.

THEY laughed.

THEY were pleased. It was fitting punishment for their new pet.

Maledicus wasn't giving them proper obeisance.

FIFTY

Patrick couldn't sleep. He was extremely restless and wished he could go to his dojo and perform an intensely strong workout. That kind of exertion would usually exhaust and relax him so he could sleep, but he knew even more than the doctor did he was losing the ability to perform physically the way he used to. Additionally, he knew the toll it took on him these days. Since returning from the last visit to the Neurologist, whenever he tried to workout, his headaches hit almost immediately. The last time he had tried to use the dojo, he had to drop to the floor and lay motionless for thirty minutes before even attempting to get back up. Instead of trying again, he simply went into his study, poured himself two fingers of Maker's Mark, and opened a book to read.

He had been sitting for an hour at his desk trying to be absorbed into Theodore Roosevelt's account of his expedition into the Amazon River Basin after his unsuccessful campaign for the Presidency as a Third Party Bull Moose ticket. Patrick loved reading about his hero, but this early morning, he had a difficult time focusing on the words.

He had also been unsuccessful recently in trying to make contact with Michael. And he had no idea why. Either something was simply going wrong, or something was trying to block their communication. But with the way he was feeling this early morning, he was going to give it another try.

Patrick marked his place in the book with the leather bookmark that Michael had given him as a 30th birthday present. It was a fine handcrafted piece Michael had found on one of his journeys in Italy. The leather was a deep and rich brown etched in an ancient Roman design.

Patrick set the book aside, put a yellow legal pad in front of him, and held a ballpoint pen in his right hand. Then he turned the light to low, and he began to perform measured Taoist breathing. In a few minutes, he had cleared his mind. Either something would happen, or he would be asleep soon.

Patrick started, as if he had been dozing. He felt his head jerk and the pen fly from his hand. A headache had already begun, and he felt vaguely nauseated. He looked at the clock on the desk. 4:00 P.M. Two hours had gone by.

As he looked down at the writing tablet, he saw two distinct things: a pool of blood, which was still forming from the blood dripping from his nose, and a single sentence.

Call Uncle Rosy.

He grabbed a few tissues and leaned back, squeezing his nose tightly. It hurt like hell, but he needed to stop the flow. When it reduced to a trickle, he reached for the phone and punched in Roosevelt's number.

FIFTY-ONE

Roosevelt checked his pocket watch. It was almost time for his punctual nephew Patrick to be here. Even as a child, when most kids would completely lose track of time in the course of their play, Patrick had been aware of time and when he was supposed to be where. He later said that he had been born with an internal clock that was always correct. He was one of those people who could tell himself at night what time he should awaken in the morning, and he always did, at least until his wounds from the war. They had severely affected Patrick's internal timepiece.

The doorbell chimed. There he was. Roosevelt made his way to the door and opened it. Standing there, dressed in black, was the remaining twin, one of the two nephews and only members of his family with whom Roosevelt had kept real contact. Roosevelt and the twins, Patrick and Michael, had shared a bond of dislike for the snobbery and materialism so many members of their family exhibited. The three had long ago decided to disassociate themselves from most of the family. Roosevelt had maintained a perfunctory contact with some, but not many of the clan, but he was close only to the twins. Before the war, Patrick had done the same, with Michael being the first to extricate himself from the family's clutches fully. After the war, with Michael's death, Patrick had completely cut himself from any family ties, with the exception of his Uncle Roosevelt. Even their contact, however, had been sporadic and usually over the phone or by hand written letters.

They rarely saw each other in person, only meeting for a rare meal. The last had been several years ago. After Patrick's call, he anticipated their meeting

The two men embraced at the door. They hugged tightly, and then Roosevelt stepped back and held his nephew out to look at him.

"My god, Patrick, it has been too long."

"Yes, it has been, Uncle Rosy." The two boys had had a difficult time saying his full name when they were toddlers, so they had called him Uncle Rosy, and the name had stuck with them. They were the only two people who called Roosevelt that without it bothering him.

"Come in, come in, Patrick."

Roosevelt led his nephew into his study and had him sit in one of the leather chairs so they could talk.

"Would you like something to drink? Whiskey? Beer? Coffee? Water? Anything?"

"Yes, actually I would. Please some of your single malt Scotch. You choose the brand, uncle."

Roosevelt arched an eyebrow. Patrick had been a beer drinker since he was a young man. He had seen the drinking of fine whisky as a kind of snobbery, so he had resisted it. Roosevelt did not find the drinking or consumption of fine liquor or food to be inherently snobby, only if it was done to impress others, or in the case of some whisky connoisseurs, collecting the stuff and putting it on display rather than drinking and appreciating it. Roosevelt happily poured two fingers of 18-year-old Macallan into a crystal class and handed it to his nephew. He then decanted one for himself.

"To my nephew, the one member of the family, who is not a snob." He held up his glass, and Patrick clinked it, and then they both took a swallow of the extraordinarily smooth and rich liquor.

"I have to admit, Uncle Rosy, this is damned good." He smiled widely at his uncle. "You always did have good taste."

"I took the liberty of cooking a meal for us. Indulge an old man and let me tell you that you need some meat on your bones, boy."

Patrick looked at him and smiled. "Certainly we can eat, although I did tell you that my appetite is not what it used to be. And…"

"Yes?"

"Please tell me you didn't prepare something that our family would serve. I can't stand haute cuisine."

"Now do not insult me, young man!" Roosevelt was stern and glowered at his nephew. "You should know me much better than that! I am not a goddamned snob! I am NOT like the rest of this god forsaken family!"

"It's ok. It's ok. I'm sorry." Patrick held up his hands palms out to Roosevelt. "I didn't mean to upset you, but I had to tease you a little." Patrick did not remember his uncle ever reacting like that before. He started to become concerned about his elderly uncle's state of mind.

Roosevelt continued to glare for a few seconds, then he broke into a wide grin and laughed a deep belly laugh. When he stopped and caught his breath, he said, "It is still easy to tease you, Patrick."

"Why you old bastard, you got me!"

Roosevelt laughed and rose from his seat. "Yes, I did. Now do you think our family would ever deign to eat old-fashioned beef stew, because that is what I made for us."

The thought of the stew instantly brought back memories of sitting at his uncle's and aunt's dining room table eating Aunt Sarah's hearty stew, full of tender beef, carrots, onions and potatoes in a thick broth. Michael and he were teenagers then and would sit at their table and enjoy a long meal filled with conversation, laughter and debate. Their uncle and aunt always listened to them and respected what they had to say. This was not something that they experienced in the ancestral family home. In that place, decorum was always observed, and in their family, children, even teenagers, were meant to be seen and not heard. Their meals were consumed in excruciating silence. The food prepared by the finest chefs that money could buy, but both boys swore that it was for appearance, not taste. They used to snicker at their parents when they said that you had to learn to eat first with your eyes. Both twins already, even in their teenage years, had a strong appreciation of art, and they did not consider the presentation of food on a dish to be anything other than a way to distract from the lack of portion and taste, simply effete pretentiousness.

"I've missed you, Uncle Rosy," Patrick said as he put down his fork after finishing his second bowl of stew. "And I miss Aunt Sarah."

"I know, Patrick. I, too, have missed you, and I miss my Sarah. Always." His voice choked a bit, but he sipped some water to cover it.

They ate the hearty meal and spoke of literature and philosophy.

After dinner was done, and Patrick helped Roosevelt wash the dishes, and they went back to the study.

Roosevelt offered Patrick another drink and a cigar, both of which he accepted.

"So, Patrick, I have to ask you something."

Patrick looked at his uncle as he puffed on the Opus X. "Go on, uncle."

"Why did you call? You have helped on occasion with our investigations, in strictly a research capacity, but you have not recently."

Patrick puffed and then blew out a perfect ring of smoke. "Because I was told to."

Roosevelt arched his right eyebrow and looked a bit like Mr. Spock from *Star Trek*. "Did Sam or Jeremy call you?"

"No, it was nothing quite as….normal…as that. Are you prepared to hear something extraordinary, Uncle Rosy?"

"Certainly, I am." Roosevelt leaned back in his chair and sipped his whisky.

Patrick recounted much of the experiences he had in communicating with Michael. He told his uncle about the numerous times his brother had contacted him, but he did omit the issue of the nosebleeds, headaches, and the visits to the neurologist. He saw no need to burden his uncle with those details. Patrick did not want to cause his uncle to worry about him. It was enough that Patrick knew the risks and potential consequences. If his uncle knew more, then he might not be willing to include him in whatever was needed.

Roosevelt listened in fascination. If anyone else had told him these events and if he had not been enveloped by almost unbelievable circumstances, then he might not have accepted the narrative as true or he might have thought that the teller of the fantastic story believed its veracity but was, in fact, insane. Roosevelt, however, believed his nephew.

"Uncle Rosy, it was Michael's last message that told me what to do. Yesterday, I experienced another incident, and this, to make the gist of it brief, had three very important words: 'Call Uncle Rosy.'"

Roosevelt nodded. "That is …ah…unusual."

"So, I knew what I had to do. And either I'm completely crazy or something very much outside of the realm of the normal is happening here."

"If you are irrational, my boy, then I am too. I believe very much in my sanity. So, either we are two lunatics compounding our mutual delusions, or we are two sane men facing nearly insane circumstances. It is my turn to tell you a story." Roosevelt then recounted everything that had happened up to that point. When he was finished, they both had smoked their Churchill sized cigars down to a nub and dropped them into the hand-made clay cigar ashtrays.

"So that is what we are facing, Patrick. We need your help."

"Uncle, you have it." As Patrick was leaving and he stepped into the frigid air, he stopped and turned to his uncle. "Semper Fi, Uncle Rosy."

FIFTY-TWO

THE IN-BETWEEN DECEMBER 19

Maledicus seethed. *I will have the two females…and I will destroy the others. No one opposes me.* His form moved like a mass of sludge in a sewage treatment plant. Slowly a tentacle like appendage formed and moved out. *Ah yes, it will be done slowly. I will enjoy it.*

In the hospital, Helena whimpered, "the bad man is here." And her fever grew higher, and she fell into unconsciousness.

Yessss. The little sow will soon be mine.

FIFTY-THREE

DECEMBER 19

Jeremy and Roosevelt sat in the window booth at the far end of the Bethberg Diner and watched Sam shivering as he smoked his cigarette. The sky was full of clouds, and the forecasters had predicted a major storm, perhaps even a blizzard. This part of Northeastern Pennsylvania was used to hard winters, but a storm of this magnitude as predicted, was still unusual for mid-December. Jeremy had watched the local TV forecast that claimed as much as three feet might fall starting anytime in the morning to the end of the next day. They were also calling for winds of 40-50 M.P.H. It now looked like winter had awakened and was preparing to deliver an incredible reminder of its power.

The temperature had dropped to a very cold 15 degrees with forecasts of only 5 degrees in the night. With the wind chill, it would feel like 20 below zero. This was indeed a cold spell, especially after having been in the upper sixties only a week earlier.

Sam steadfastly refused to believe in weather forecasts. He reasoned that they were wrong so often that the best bet was to assume the opposite of what they called for, so if they were predicting a blizzard, then we should expect unseasonably warm temperatures, maybe even in the 60s. He was dressed in a light windbreaker and huddled near the door as he smoked his Marlboro. It was already in the low 20s and dropping.

"You'd think," Jeremy, said with a soft laugh, "Sam would know he was going to have a smoke or two outside as he always does, and he'd be prepared for this storm and wear something warm. I mean, come on, you don't have to be a meteorologist to know a major weather event is coming."

"I agree, Jeremy. I can feel it in my bones. I used to scoff at anyone who made such claims when I was a young man, but I understand them now. In the last few years, whenever a major storm was coming, my back would ache. It is odd, because I never injured my back in any way, but I suppose it is simply part of becoming an old man."

"Roosevelt, I'm with you on that. My knees are aching."

"Just your knees, Jeremy? How is your ankle feeling?" Roosevelt was concerned about his friend, because he knew that Jeremy's pain tolerance was not very high, and a damaged ankle, well that had to be causing him serious problems.

"With the pain medication they gave me, it isn't too bad. But I'm trying to take them only when I have to. It's serious stuff. Oxycontin."

"Indeed, it is."

"You know, Roosevelt, I'm an alcoholic, not a drug addict, but I see no reason in taking chances."

"I understand completely. I am proud of you, Jeremy."

Jeremy blushed at the compliment from his friend, whom he considered to be one of the toughest and bravest people he had ever known. "It's just what I have to do."

"Now our Samuel, though, he is nothing if not stubborn. He insists on smoking those evil smelling cigarettes during the day, when he could simply wait and share a fine cigar in the evening. So he stands out there, looking like an adolescent sneaking a puff in back of the school."

"And he's freezing his nuts off." Jeremy laughed heartily. It was a sound that made Roosevelt smile.

Janine, a waitress, always worked Thursday mornings when the IPS made their semi-regular weekly pilgrimages to the diner, walked over holding a pot of freshly brewed coffee.

"A refill, guys?"

"Yeah," Jeremy answered. "Keep it coming."

"I will have more, and please refill Samuel's cup. I am sure he will be in need of some warmth, "Roosevelt said and smiled.

"Is that damned fool outside in this cold having a smoke?"

"Yes, he is, and we are all worried that the nicotine will eventually stunt his growth."

She laughed and walked away shaking her head. She liked having these guys as customers. She had waited tables at many places before. As a single mother with two kids, she had always worked hard to support them, even if it meant working two or more jobs. Sometimes the people she waited on seemed to forget that she was human, and some were just mean. She had dealt with guys who were not gentleman, not by any length, so she appreciated the old guys. After all, she thought, *they were nice, never got over-friendly, if you know what I mean, and they always tipped well, more than most of the customers in this dump. I wish the rest that came in here were more like them.*

"Is Sam done yet?" Jeremy was beginning to be worried about his friend. It was seriously cold out there.

"I think he is." Roosevelt watched as Samuel cupped the cigarette in his hand, the sign that he was a combat veteran who knew that the glowing end of a cigarette was a convenient target for a sniper. A soldier learned to hold a cigarette that way or faced the risk of dying by a sniper's bullet.

Sam took a last drag on the cigarette and dropped it to the sidewalk. He stepped on the glowing ember and crushed it out. Then he quickly turned and reentered the diner.

As he slid shaking into the booth next to Jeremy, Roosevelt pointed out the fresh coffee. "We both thought you might need some warmth."

"Ah, such good friends." He worked out a large shiver, looking like a large mutt shaking water off its body, then took a gulp of the hot liquid.

"Jerry," Sam said as he put down his cup.

"What is it, Sam?"

"Look, it just started snowing. Son of a bitch, but you were right. I gotta' give you that."

"Are you really surprised, Sam?" Jeremy smiled a satisfied Cheshire Cat grin. "After all, I'm usually correct, you know."

Sam smiled and drank more coffee.

"I'll let you in on something though. This time, I wish I were wrong. After all, I do despise snow."

"No, no...Jerry, snow is great! I feel like a little boy when I see it begin to snow. I just never expect those morons on TV to get the weather right."

"Well, Sam," Roosevelt added. "You love it because you really are a very large little boy."

"Maybe," Sam said with a twinkle in his eye. "But if I am, then at least I am not an old fart like the two of you."

Roosevelt smiled. He knew Sam enjoyed being the youngest of the group, even if it was only by three weeks to Jeremy and two months to Roosevelt. "Indeed, you are the veritable youngster here, my dear Samuel, but I submit that being the oldest here is still better than the alternative."

"Yeah, Rosy, I can go with that."

"So, guys," Jeremy said. "Are we ready to talk seriously here?"

"Gentleman, I suggest that we finish our meal, because a guest will be arriving very soon."

An hour later, the snow had metamorphosed from a slight dusting to a serious storm. It was falling fast and heavily, and it was blanketing the town. Throughout the town many were cursing the early blizzard because of the shoveling they knew would be coming, while many children were celebrating and already outside playing, making snow angels and having snowball battles.

As Sam, Jeremy, and Roosevelt finished their food, a black Range Rover drove around to a parking place down the street from the diner. They watched a figure get out of the truck and make his way towards the diner. They could not see who it was, but Roosevelt knew.

"The cavalry has arrived," Roosevelt said.

FIFTY-FOUR

Wind howled around Patrick as he walked toward the Bethberg Diner. The wild air was increasing almost by the minute, and snow was falling rapidly. The frigid Arctic air cut through the winter service coat Patrick thought would protect him, but it didn't. He had begun to feel the cold much more these days, yet Patrick was grateful for the change in the weather. It had been very warm only a few days ago, and for a man who had spent too much time in Iraq in 120° temperatures, he had developed an intense dislike for heat. Still, this wind was like a sharp katana cutting into his very being.

As he turned the corner, the old Diner, with its 1930's style Pullman design, recently repainted, refurbished and shining like polished silver, struck Patrick, and he stopped.

Not yet, he thought.

He turned and went into Harold's Newspapers, an old store that sold newspapers, magazines of all sorts, cigars and tobacco, and now, of course, lottery tickets. Harold Jr., the owner who stood behind the battered wooden cigar display case, was now in his mid-80s. He was the grandson of the original proprietor, who had opened this store in the late 1800s.

A dim light from an old overhead fixture gave a green tint to the dusty room, and a hint of mildew clung to the inside of the store. It was as if all the cigarette, pipe and cigar smoke, the smell of stored old papers, and the odor of hair tonic had infused the atmosphere of the store with an aroma made from old memories.

"Yeah, can I get somethin' for you?" Harold asked without looking up from his Daily Racing Form.

"Yes, you can, Harold. And I see you still run a first rate place here."

Annoyed at the perceived insult, Harold looked up at the man standing

235

across the counter, opened his mouth, which still had a few teeth in it, to tell the wise guy to get the hell out of his store, and he stopped.

The old man squinted and leaned over the counter to be able to see the person he was looking at.

Patrick held a somber poker face for a few seconds, then he broke into a wide smile.

"I'll be a son-of-a-whore! Patrick, you sneaky bastard! Is it really you?" Harold moved as quickly as his ancient, thin legs would take him around the counter and shook the younger man's hand.

"It's me."

Harold was a bit shaken. He shook his head slightly and sighed. "It's a damned shame about your brother. Him and you was both pains in the asses when you was little, always tryin' to sneak looks at the girlie books. Had to keep chasing you away. But you both turned into damned fine men."

"Thanks, Harold. I appreciate that."

"I want you to know, Patrick, I put up the paper about your commendations, both you and Michael, at the V.F.W. post. It ain't much to see, just the clipping, but it's important. What he did, what you did, well, lots of people here appreciate it, son."

Patrick was embarrassed. He didn't like to talk about himself like this.

"Did I tell you, Patrick, I am an old war horse myself?"

"No, no you didn't, Harold. Where were you?" Patrick had heard this store many times before, but he wouldn't deny the old man the pleasure of retelling it.

"Korea. Chosin Reservoir. Like you, a Devil Dog, the Corps."

Patrick whistled. "Chosin Reservoir. Son-of-a-bitch, Harold. That was serious fighting."

"Yep, it was. Got me a Purple Heart to show for it." Harold laughed. "But I gotta tell you, it's pretty damned stupid the way I got it."

"I want to hear."

"Well, we was fightin' just to try to keep our position above the Reservoir. Never seen so many Chinese soldiers. Didn't seem like they'd ever stop comin'. It was cold, Jesus Christ—after that winter, I hate cold weather now. If I had the money, I'd move to Arizona. Well, anyways, it was at the end of the battle, and I was just happy to be alive and in one piece, when a Chinese grenade, them old potato mashers. You know the kind?"

"Yes, I do."

"Well, one got thrown over the hill and landed near me. I got crazy and used my rifle like a gold club, not that I knew anything about golfing, and just lobbed it away from me. Damn, I was amazed that it worked. Son-of-a-whore, I was so impressed with myself, musta thought I was Sam Snead, so I turned to say something to the guy next to me. Now I was still standing, like a fuckin' jackass, and I got hit, shot right in the left asscheek. Ain't that somethin? Lemme tell you. I still don't sit right sometimes."

Patrick laughed with Harold, then he stopped and said to the old man, "It was pretty stupid, but Harold, you deserve that Purple Heart. I know about that battle. You were a hell of a Marine."

This time, it was the elderly man who was embarrassed and whose eyes began to moisten.

"Anyway, Harold, can I get a pack of Camels, non-filters?"

Harold handed him a pack. "They're on me, Patrick."

"Thanks."

As Patrick opened the door to leave the store, he stopped, turned and called out, "Harold! Semper Fi!"

The old man smiled. "Semper Fi!"

Patrick stepped outside into the tundra-like air and tapped the cigarette pack several times, then opened it, and lit one, carefully cupping the cherry in his hands.

He smoked it the same way, in the habit of veterans, always keeping the glowing cherry hidden by his fingers. As he smoked, snow swirled around him and began to accumulate on his coat and hair. When he finished, he dropped the cigarette to the pavement, crushed it out with his boot, and headed for the diner.

Patrick entered the diner, brushed off the snow, and walked to the end booth where Roosevelt stood smiling and embraced him. Patrick wasn't used to such displays of affection, and he stiffened slightly at first when the older man hugged him. Then he slowly relaxed.

"Patrick, it is so good to see you."

"It's good to see you too, Uncle Rosy. But I'm afraid that I'm not so young anymore."

Roosevelt laughed. "In comparison to us, you indeed are a youngster, Patrick. Otherwise, I am afraid to think of what that makes me then."

"One of a group of old farts," Sam said as he rose. He reached out and grabbed Patrick in a bearhug. "It's great to see you."

"Whoa, let me breathe there." Patrick shook Sam's hand and then Jeremy's, who remained sitting because of his ankle.

"Please forgive me, Patrick, for not standing to greet you."

"No worries, Jeremy. I heard what happened. And besides, it's always good to see you guys." Even though it had been years since he had seen either Jeremy or Sam, he respected his uncle's view of the two men, and he had a deep esteem and affection for them.

As they sat back down in the booth, Patrick joined them by sliding in next to his uncle.

"Do you want anything to eat, Patrick?" Jeremy began to signal to the waitress, but Patrick stopped him.

"No, Jeremy, I'm fine. I'll just get some coffee when the waitress comes by."

Over the next hour, Patrick recounted to the three men what he had experienced in his contacts with Michael. He omitted nothing except for the nosebleeds, headaches, and the visits to the neurologist. As with his uncle, he didn't want these fellows to worry about him. His fate was in his own hands.

"You realize that you're the only people I can tell this to." Patrick's face was even, but his eyes revealed anxiety. "Anyone else would think I was insane."

Sam was tempted to make a wisecrack, but he held back. He saw the seriousness and deep doubt in the younger man's face, and Patrick was someone whom he admired and respected deeply.

"Well, Patrick," Jeremy said in a quiet and even tone. "If you're crazy, then we are also inmates in that particular asylum." Jeremy had only met Patrick a few times, but he had followed the twins' careers in the military through his friendship with Roosevelt and Sarah and their infectious pride in their nephews had flowed into him. "I, for one, am proud to be your fellow inmate."

"Patrick, you know that I believe you." Roosevelt looked at him squarely.

"So do I, youngster," Sam added.

"And I, too." They all understood that they were deep in a realm beyond any normal comprehension.

"And now it is our turn, Patrick. I gave you a full report in person, but I want Samuel and Jeremy also to tell the events in case I missed anything." Roosevelt signaled to the waitress to bring more coffee. "We will need the caffeine."

When the men had finished telling the events, they sat back and watched Patrick. He had listened calmly and carefully to their stories, which might have seemed to an outside observer to be as fantastic as his own.

"That is everything that has happened thus far," Roosevelt said. "There is one additional piece of information that I am investigating and of which I should have an answer later today. If I am successful in my research, then I will tell all of you what I have learned. It could be of great importance to us."

Jeremy and Sam simply nodded at Roosevelt. Even though they were eager to know what he was hinting at, they knew that they should not push their friend. He would tell them when he was sure of his facts.

"So, what do you think, St. Patrick?" Sam had called Patrick this when he was a boy. It was an odd nickname for a youngster, but Patrick tolerated it because he could always tell that Sam was not mocking him. For his part, Sam had always believed there was something deeply good about the boy, so the name was a natural for him.

"Well, as you said, gentlemen, either we are four sane men facing something truly terrible, or we are all insane together."

"This point is very important to agree on," Roosevelt said. "I believe completely that we are rational, and that this is a very real manifestation of true evil that we face."

They all shook their heads in agreement.

"Guys, we are not crazy," Sam insisted. "We may be old farts, but we're lucid old farts. Except for you, St. Patrick. I think you're with it, but you're not old enough to be an old fart yet. Gotta work on that for a few decades before you can claim that title."

Patrick smiled. "Well, sometimes, I feel like I am. Old that is. But I think we're all sane."

He became serious. "Gentlemen, I believe that Michael directed me to be here with you, and I believe that we must fight this combat as a two front war."

As Patrick began to outline his approach, Jeremy's phone rang with its distinctive Judy Garland version of the song "Get Happy".

"I need to take this, guys. Hold on." They all sat quietly while he answered the call.

"Yes, Helen?" The others watched silently as he spoke to Ms. Murray.

Jeremy's face darkened as he listened. "Yes, Helen, I understand. Can you hold on a second please?"

He turned to them. "Helena has gone into a coma. And the doctors don't know why, but it doesn't look good, guys."

"Please tell her, Jeremy, that we are going to try to deal with this tonight and that she and Helena will be in our prayers."

Jeremy spoke with her a little longer. "Sure, uh-huh. Hold on."

He pressed the mute button. "Guys, Helen wants to meet with us. What do you think?"

Roosevelt nodded slightly. "I think that she has every right to be a part of our group. Please ask her if she can meet tonight at my house around 7 P.M. for planning. We need to be sure that we are prepared and have a specific plan of action."

Jeremy hit the mute button again and asked Helen. "It's set guys. She said she'll be there. She said she feels helpless right now at the hospital, but she will only be able to meet with us for a couple of hours and then she'll return to the hospital."

"Of course," Roosevelt said. Jeremy grew quiet as he saw Sam almost retreat into himself in thinking about the child's danger. Jeremy glanced over at Roosevelt. They both knew that Sam would carry deep undeserved guilt over the death of his son for the rest of his life.

Patrick broke through the silence. "Gentlemen, I need your attention." He spoke the words quietly but with assured authority. "We must be ready. It is time for battle."

FIFTY-FIVE

DECEMBER 19

The IPS, along with Patrick and Helen, had gathered around Roosevelt's large table in his study. Rather than sitting in the comfortable leather chairs in one end of the large library and having a relaxed conversation about their studies, they were sitting in old oak chairs pulled up to the table. Roosevelt looked around at his colleagues. "Gentlemen and Ms. Murray, thank you for coming to this, ah, unusual meeting of the IPS."

The others nodded and waited for him to continue. Roosevelt folded his hands neatly in front of him and spoke in an even, calm, and subdued voice.

"You are all certainly aware of the progress, or shall I say, the lack of progress, in our case. Please understand gentlemen. I am not saying anything in recrimination, because there is none. Any criticism that should be leveled is aimed at me, not you. I think that I have made certain serious mistakes in planning our actions."

"C'mon Rosy, don't you go there. No one here is blaming you for anything." Sam wasn't joking now. He pointed at Roosevelt and held his gaze. "All of us are in this by his own choice. No one is being forced to be here."

Roosevelt continued. "I do think, however, given the serious of what has happened, that a review of …ah …certain aspects of the case that have recently been discovered need to be shared with you."

Sam sat back and watched. He knew everything Roosevelt was going to say, but he did not reveal this to Jeremy, Patrick, or Helen. He knew that what Roosevelt was going to propose was not going to be easy to accept.

"As you know, gentlemen, Ms. Murray came to us several weeks ago with what, at the time, seemed to be an unusual and interesting case for us. Because of her circumstances, specifically of the child being involved, we decided that we needed to begin an immediate investigation.

241

"We began in earnest. I commend everyone here with his professionalism, on this case as well as the others we have investigated. As we soon discovered, and I am sure that you remember from the events of that night, this was going to be a very, ah, unusual situation."

Roosevelt looked at Jeremy, who was staring down at his lap with his head shaking slightly. He knew that Jeremy was frightened and ashamed that he had been afraid on previous cases. "Jeremy," Roosevelt said gently. "Look at me."

Jeremy raised his eyes slightly. They had tears in them. "Jeremy, no one blames you for ever being frightened."

"Yeah, Jer," Sam added. "I've been scared shitless. Especially at the Kaufmann house, so buddy, you got nothing to be sorry about. "

"But I do, guys. I am a coward."

"No, sir!" Roosevelt snapped. "You are not a coward. You have been certainly frightened, as have we all. Some of us simply know how to mask our fear better than others do. You, sir, were not and are not a coward."

"That's easy for you guys to say. You were both soldiers. What have I ever been?"

Roosevelt looked straight at Jeremy's tear-filled eyes. "Jeremy, you are my good friend, and you know that I do not lie to my friends. You know that. Am I correct?"

"Yes, I do."

"Then listen to me. You are not a coward. Being frightened in such circumstances is a normal response to them. And fear is a needed element of survival." Roosevelt looked over at Sam, who was nodding in agreement.

"I served in combat, and I can tell you that if there are soldiers facing combat who are not frightened, then they are foolish. You, Jeremy, at the Kaufmann house, you were terrified as were the rest of us, but you remained at your post. Only when I gave the order to leave did you leave your position. You showed bravery. Remember that true courage is not doing that which you do not fear…that is nothing. True courage is doing that which terrifies you. You are a good man. And you are a brave man to face this with us. Now I do want to ask you a serious question, and I want an honest answer. Will you give me one?"

"Of course, I will."

"Do you want to proceed with this investigation? If you do not, we will all understand."

Jeremy's face reddened. "Goddamnit, Roosevelt! How can you ask me that? I'm sticking with this no matter what!"

Roosevelt smiled. "It is good to see you get your anger up."

"Thanks," Jeremy barely whispered.

Roosevelt paused for about ten seconds and then continued. "Even that initial investigation of Helen's house was not a failure. We did gain valuable evidence. We captured audio and visual records of the …ah …thing in that house. As you know, we soon came to understand that it was some kind of malevolent spirit or entity. My suggestion was that we move forward in a standard manner. I should have thought about it more."

"Roosevelt, stop it!" This time it was Jeremy, whose stern voice scolded his friend. "You will not feel guilty for what we all agreed on."

This time, Jeremy locked his gaze on Roosevelt.

"Thanks, Jeremy." Roosevelt said. "We, therefore, recommended a cleansing of the house. We asked our friend Martin Gerard, an adept of Wicca to do this. Gerard performed the ceremony, but he cautioned us that he was unsure of the results.

"He proved to be prescient. Nothing was gained by the attempted cleansing, except a negative result. It seemed the entity was too negative and powerful for the gentle Wiccan ways. The haunting increased in power and effect. And Branwyn, well, we all know what happened."

"But we don't know for sure," Sam interjected. "if it was connected to the investigation, but it sure looks that way."

"So, the next step…we decided to up the ante, so to speak. I contacted Father Bruno, who has assisted us before. As you know, he was a very good man, and he recognized that Helen and Helena were in potential peril. He then decided to…ah…overlook the issue that they are not Catholic. They were souls in need of help. He believed those who can give aid must assist those in need." Roosevelt stopped to regain control of his voice as it began to catch when he spoke of his recently deceased friend.

"Father Bruno was also a man after my own heart in other ways. We both believed that bureaucracies must be ignored at times and that rules must be broken when they are counter-productive or when morality dictates it. The rules of man do not supersede the rules of honor, morality, and for Bruno, God. So, he acted without official sanction of the Church.

"You all know what happened when Father Bruno attempted to perform an exorcism of the house itself. After the …ah…unfortunate events of that evening, Father Bruno was hospitalized in intensive care at the Bethberg Medical Center. He suffered a massive stroke and went in and out of consciousness. He was unable to speak, so we were not been able to communicate with him. And he was apparently, from what I have gathered from my sources, in trouble with the Church itself and faced potential disciplinary action if he recovered. Now that he has passed, those issues have been forgotten by the Church."

Roosevelt stopped to sip water and wipe tears from his eyes with his handkerchief. "But we will not forget our friend nor what he did and his sacrifice. Our friends and associates, Father Bruno and Branwyn are the first casualties in this war."

The room was silent as Roosevelt let the full impact of his words sink in to everyone.

"Yes," he continued shortly. "I said war. Gentlemen and lady, I believe that we are moving far past what was simply an investigation into the paranormal. I believe that we are now preparing for active engagement with something very evil, that we are beginning a combat against a foe that wishes to destroy Ms. Murray and her niece. We are going to war."

"War?" Jeremy shifted nervously in his chair. "I hate fighting. I don't think it serves any good purpose. And Roosevelt, thank you for your kind words earlier, but guys, I'm scared out of my mind right now."

"Jer, I'm scared too, scared out of my wits." It was the first Sam had spoken in a while.

"You, Sam? You scared? Mister-I-can-handle-anyone?"

"Jer. I am not afraid of any living person. I know I can't defeat everyone…shit, I am an old man now, but I know how to take care of myself in a fight. What do I have to lose anyway? So, I ain't afraid of no man, but…"

"But?"

"But I'm scared shitless here, folks. How do we fight something we can't see? If it was a man, I could punch him, or I could shoot him, but what do I do against this…thing?"

Silence encompassed the gathering at the implications of Sam's question. Then Helen spoke, "I have to thank you all for helping us, but I'm terrified also. Not for myself, but for Helena. The doctors can't seem to find out why her condition is deteriorating, and I'm worried out of my mind about where this is heading. But I'll do anything to help her."

Patrick spoke. "There is good reason for all of us to be afraid. We must all be afraid in battle, but we must control our fear."

Roosevelt looked at all of them. "That is well said, Patrick. That is why I, too, am terrified. I will not lie to you about that. The only thing that has scared me more than this was when I realized that Sarah was going to die. So let us be clear. We are all frightened. Let us accept that fact and move on."

Roosevelt opened his old, brown leather briefcase and took out a yellow, legal pad. "I have done some research on the evidence we gathered, and I told you before that I might have some important information. I have been successful and will share it with you now. Despite the outcome of that night we investigated, we have learned some very interesting details. Just to recap: we had thermal hits of an entity, we had infrared photographs of something with us, and we had several audio EVP recordings, one of which I think is the most important, the one that said... 'I am Maledicus.' I was somewhat familiar with that name, but my expertise was in Renaissance history, and I was quite sure this was a name from Ancient Rome. I, therefore, contacted an old colleague of mine, Professor Guisseppe Mirandola from the University of Milan. He is an expert in the period of Ancient Rome under the Caesars. Additionally, I had wondered about the interesting collection of antiquities that Ms. Murray had, so I photographed as many of them as I could."

Roosevelt turned to Helen and smiled. "I hope you take no offense. I was not prying into your personal life. I simply had a thought that they might prove to be useful."

"It's okay. I want to know what you found," Helen said and looked at him with her teacher's glare. "But you might have asked permission, before you did that, as a courtesy."

"I do apologize, Ms. Murray," Roosevelt offered with a small bow to her. "You are correct, but I must continue. You might wonder why I did this? Well, I learned long ago to pay attention to my feelings, hunches if you will. Samuel, as a police detective, I am sure you will agree how important this is."

Sam nodded. "You gotta' follow your gut."

"So, following my hunch, I emailed the photographs to my friend in Italy, thanks to Jeremy teaching me how to do that" Roosevelt nodded his appreciation to Jeremy's knowledge of technology.

"Ms. Murray . . ." Roosevelt continued.

"Please call me Helen. You gentlemen are helping me, and I don't want you calling me by a name reserved for my students." She looked at Roosevelt to let him know there was no issue between them.

"Certainly, as you are aware gentlemen and ...ah...Helen, entities have been known to attach themselves to objects and infest a house into which that item has been brought. I wondered if such a thing might have happened here."

Roosevelt looked directly at Helen. "The information I am going to give might be disturbing. Are you sure you want to hear it?"

"Don't treat me like some helpless damsel in distress! I'm here to be a part of this, and if there is information that can aid us in helping my niece, then I want to know it!"

"Your point is taken, and my dear Sarah would have scolded me for speaking that way to you. I apologize."

She brushed it off and motioned for him to continue.

"After reviewing the pictures and doing some research, Professor Mirandola identified one object that might be the cause of the difficulties. He said the one small statue was a figure from the time of the Emperor Caligula and that the item itself has a sordid and fascinating history. It was initially found and later 'lost' at a dig at Roman ruins in the lowland area of Britain. Its history seems to encompass one appalling event to another. Pulling from extra academic, ah ....somewhat esoteric....sources, Professor Mirandola was able to identify at least four accounts over the years in which several people who possessed it met with disastrous consequences. In all four cases, insanity and death, often homicide and suicide, occurred. Professor Mirandola also suggested that there were likely more incidents, but that these were the only ones of which he was able to gain a level of verification. In addition to Professor Mirandola's research, I recruited Samuel to enlist his colleagues in the law enforcement world to try to substantiate these claims."

Jeremy noted that Sam had been included in the research but said nothing.

"The first case involved the man, a Mr. Taylor, who found the statue inadvertently and sold it for profit. He had been trying apparently to raise money to fund his son's university education. The man who sold it died the next day of an apparent stroke, and his son sunk into an unknown form of insanity, from which he never recovered. He died in an institution for the insane.

"The second incident was of a Mr. Ross, a wealthy British gentleman who fancied himself an intellectual of the obscure and the occult. He purchased the item from a black market salesman, and he soon died of a massive cerebral hemorrhage.

"The third incident of which there is some level of evidence shows the idol being purchased and brought to the Unites States by a Mr. Harris, one of the robber baron industrialists of the late 1800s and early 1900s. He was in industry and in life a ruthless man. The records show that he withdrew from a very active social life, finally going insane and killing many people and he was killed in a gunfight.

"The last, and perhaps most disturbing case for us, is that of a Mr. McGuigan, a family man in the United States who found the statue at a flea market and purchased it. He was married with two young children, who soon were afflicted with ...ah ....an undisclosed illness." Roosevelt hesitated and looked at Helen, who signaled him to continue.

"The children died in a few weeks, and then there was a murder-suicide of the couple."

Helen's face hardened.

"Well, gentlemen and lady, another possible connection is of an American antiques dealer who may have owned the statue. We cannot be sure, but his case certainly fits the pattern. After perhaps owning the statue, again we are not sure, he used a very sharp and very old Samurai Katana that he owned to kill his family: he beheaded his wife and two young children, and then he committed ritual Seppuku. He killed himself with the traditional double cut across the stomach and then up through the body. It is a very difficult feat to accomplish, especially without an assistant, even for a skilled warrior. It is important to note, he ….ah….had no training in the Martial Arts. He had the sword as a prized artifact, not a weapon, nor did he know how to use it. But we have no way of knowing if this is definitely connected."

"So," Sam added. "It looks like everyone who had this statue died in some bad fucking way."

"A succinct way of phrasing it Samuel, but you are correct."

"Guys, this is just terrible, horrible." Jeremy was clearly shaken.

Helen's face had grown stern as she listened. She knew that she had purchased the little statue simply as an historical curiosity, and it appeared as though it had directly brought this evil upon them.

Patrick stayed silent and watched.

Roosevelt paused to sip his water.

"This is the same statue that we now find Ms. Murray's…Helen's…home. As we know Helen, you are an historian and, apparently, an amateur archeologist with a specific interest in things of Ancient Rome."

"How did you find it, Helen?" Jeremy asked

Helen explained that she found it at an estate auction in the Catskills and she was able to buy for a very reasonable price. "I have to admit that I was delighted to be able to purchase it so reasonably. The fellow didn't even haggle a bit. I thought I had quite a bit of luck going there. Some luck."

"This is not all that my good friend Professor Mirandola was able to find out. He said it was one of the many Lares, or household gods, often minor deities that many prominent families had in their homes. This one he was able to identify the likely household in which it originally was placed. It was made for one Senator Lucius, who went by the nickname Maledicus, because he was known to make some of the vilest speeches in addressing the Senate, and his voice was reported to sound like the hissing of a snake." Roosevelt stopped in the middle of his account when he realized this was what the other voice in the night urging him to commit suicide sounded like. It was coming after all of them.

"Uncle Rosy? Are you all right?"

"Yes, sorry. I just had a bad moment there. Well, let me continue. This Maledicus lived during the reign of Caligula, and he was one of the Emperor's distant cousins. He amassed a fortune in a somewhat cloudy business, which suggests that he was, by today's standards, a criminal or a gangster. Mirandola said that there were reports of Maledicus taking part in some of the orgies and bloodbaths arranged by Caligula. He may also have served as a procurer of victims for the Emperor's entertainment."

"He was a fucking pimp," Sam added. "Excuse my language, Helen."

"No problem. I hear worse every day in the high school."

"Yes, he was that, Samuel. And perhaps much worse. Now whether or not this Maledicus has any direct correlation with the statue is unclear, but it seems likely that with the evil history associated with the statue and with the Roman pimp, it seems likely."

"I don't think it is much of a stretch for us to operate on that assumption," Jeremy said.

"Regardless of whether it is Maledicus or some other malevolent spirit connected with the statue, I believe that the haunting is based on the statue. I think it brought something into that house, something that is trying to harm Helena, and perhaps you, Helen, and that is what we are facing."

"This is, I believe," Patrick said, "A very real and very dangerous opponent."

"Yes, I am very sorry to say that this is, in no way, a simple investigation," Roosevelt said. "And I do believe that it is imperative, gentlemen, that all of us understand the danger that we face, that is if we choose to continue with the case."

"Go on, Rosy. This is getting more interesting."

Roosevelt glared at Sam. "Samuel," he said with a slow emphasis on the full name. "Unlike any of our previous investigations, this case involves both physical and psychological peril. I believe, gentlemen, and Helen, that if we continue to investigate this case, we are putting our bodies, minds, and perhaps souls at risk. I do not think I am overstating the danger at all."

"Son of a bitch," came from Sam.

"Oh my..." muttered Jeremy.

"Therefore, I suggest, no, I insist, that each one of us decides individually if he wants to continue on this case. This is essential. I will prod no one to move forward with this, nor will I think any less of anyone who decides not to continue."

"Well," Sam said in a slow voice, "I've been with the IPS since the beginning, not that it was that long ago. But you know what I mean. And I've known both of you a lot longer. I gotta tell you, this thing scares the piss out of me, but. . .but I'm in. Whatever that thing is, man, it's trying to hurt a woman and a little girl. That just ain't right. It ain't right. So, whatever happens, I'm in."

Roosevelt nodded at Sam. "Jeremy?"

"Roosevelt, Sam, this situation is really, really crazy. I mean, I'm just a retired antiques dealer, who loves new technology…that's it. I don't know how to fight. In fact, I hate violence. I've never punched anyone, never been in a fight….not even as a kid. I was the one who used to run or give up my lunch money to the school bullies. I hate to admit it, but it's true."

"It's ok," Sam said. "We understand."

"Yes we do, Jeremy."

"NO!" Jeremy snapped, and the vehemence of his tone startled them. They rarely heard their friend raise his voice. "You don't understand. All my life I've been the scared one, the one to get picked on, the one to hide away, to avoid conflict. I'm the one who always backed down…my whole life. And I'm tired of it. In fact, I'm sick of it."

Ignoring the pain that shot through his ankle, Jeremy put his hands on the table and stood. At that moment, he looked like a general. "Plus I hate the idea of a child being threatened. So, I can't tell you guys how I'll do. I can't claim that I will hold up, but my friends, I'm with you. Count me in."

Roosevelt looked Jeremy in the eyes. "Good man."

"Good fucking man," Sam added.

Patrick simply said, "I am with you."

Roosevelt shifted in his chair. "I suppose that it is my turn. Now gentlemen, you know that with the exception of my few close friends and my wife, I have never cared what anyone thought about me. But I do care what you think, and I do care what my wife would have thought about this. I know, absolutely, that she could not countenance any evil or harm towards children. I know what she thought about child molesters and abusers. I know what she considered the priests who abused those children we all read of. To my Sarah, those men were monsters. I know what she would expect me to do in this case. I know that if it were in her power, that she would have faced this thing. I can do no less. I know that she would expect me to defend this child and her aunt. I will not disappoint my wife. So, gentlemen, I am in."

Helen stood up. "Thank you all. I want you to know how much I appreciate your help. And I want you to know that I will stand with you against this thing, no matter what we have to do." She sat as they took in her words.

Roosevelt stood and walked to his liquor cabinet. He returned with a decanter of 18 year old Macallan single malt scotch, which he considered to be the best single malt Scotch whiskey. He also carried four crystal glasses. He then turned and walked out of the room. Both Jeremy and Sam glanced at each other.

Roosevelt returned with a carafe of black coffee. He poured some into one of the glasses and Macallan into the others. He handed the coffee to Jeremy; Sam, Patrick, Helen, and he took the whisky.

"To our battle against evil. To our fellowship and friendship. And if the worst should happen, I want to tell you that I am proud to have fought with such fine, brave men and women."

They clinked glasses.

"To our battle," said Sam.

"To our fellowship," answered Jeremy.

"To all of you and saving Helena." Helen looked at the others.

"To fighting alongside the brave."

They sat and drank the whiskey and coffee without speaking.

After about five very quiet minutes, Roosevelt looked at his comrades in arms. "We need to get some rest now. Tomorrow we will act."

FIFTY-SIX

DECEMBER 19

The snow storm had become a blizzard. Traffic came to a near halt on the major highways, and whiteout conditions had made any travel a dangerous adventure. The police, ambulance, and fire departments of Bethberg and the surrounding communities were on alert and very busy trying to deal with the various emergencies that were occurring.

Chaos Theory had proved to be accurate once again. None of the sophisticated computer models used by contemporary meteorologists had correctly predicted the "winter storm event" would metamorphose into a massive Nor'easter. The storm had combined a huge Arctic air mass settling over the northeastern United States and a large storm moving up the Atlantic coastline. When it reached just east of New York City, the storm settled in place and began to produce what might be one of the largest blizzards, in the history of modern meteorology.

No one knew how long the storm would last or how much snow would fall. Some were predicting as much as four to six feet throughout most of Pennsylvania.

Almost all flights were cancelled over the entire Northeast. People were being advised to stay inside and off the roads, if at all possible.

FIFTY-SEVEN

DECEMBER 19

Helen sat in a chair next to her comatose niece. The little girl, who was physically delicate, almost ethereal normally, seemed to have shrunken in her illness. She seemed to be disappearing before Helen's eyes. The snow outside the room was swirling, and the wind was buffeting the room's windows, but Helen didn't notice. All she could think about was her niece might die. *Not you too. I can't lose you. You have to live.*

"Helen?" She started at the voice. Dr. Wilson had entered the room and sat next to her.

"Oh, hello. I didn't hear you come in."

"I have run out of ideas. I hate to admit it, but I don't know what to do for her anymore." The young man looked stricken. He didn't care that the answers had eluded him, but he did care that the little girl was clearly in danger of dying.

"Are you giving up?"

"No, no. I am not, but I don't think Bethberg Medical Center is the place for her anymore. As I mentioned before, I arranged for Helena to be admitted into Children's Hospital in Philadelphia."

"What is it? I can feel a 'but' coming."

"It's this storm. I already arranged a special medical transportation for her, but now the flights have stopped, so we can't use a Medevac helicopter for her, nor can we use a transport ambulance, because the roads are too bad already. She would be at a greater risk on the road than staying here."

Helen leaned over and took her head between her hands. It felt like it was going to explode. Wasn't there anything that could be done? She held back tears and looked up at the doctor. "Do whatever you can for her now. God damn this storm!"

He shook his head and started to stand. Helen reached out and held his arm, keeping him seated. She looked at him. "I have to go somewhere tonight. Promise me you'll watch after her. I want her transferred as soon as possible, and I want you to continue to monitor her progress at Children's Hospital. Will you do that?"

"Certainly, Helen. Of course, I will. But go somewhere tonight? In this mess?"

"It's very important, and I can't tell you where I am going, but it concerns Helena. It's something I have to do."

He started to ask more, but she held her hand up, like she used to do in class to shut down any interruption. "Please don't ask me anymore. Jonathon, I need you to trust me and to follow my wishes. Will you do that? Please?"

"Yes, I will."

"Be sure to watch her carefully tonight. Are you on duty tonight?"

"No, it's my time off."

"Then I have a very big favor to ask you. I know how hard you work and how much you need to rest, and I wouldn't ask if it were not very important."

"Please, Helen, just ask me. I owe you more than I can possibly ever repay."

"No, you don't, Jonathon, but thank you. Can you personally stay with her tonight? I don't want anyone else to be here with her except you or me. Can you stay with her?"

"Yes, I can." He smiled at Helen, but it was a very worried and forced smile.

"Can you tell me what this is about?"

"Not now, but I promise you that I will."

FIFTY-EIGHT

Maledicus felt pain—THEY were inflicting it on him, trying to punish him, but he ignored it. Whatever THEY did, he would withstand their attempts at controlling him.

Maledicus knew THEY were trying to thwart him as well as the impotent little group of humans who were attempting to battle him. But he had plans. He would crush the humans and then their souls would be added to his, and soon, he would be even more powerful a demon than THEY.

Maledicus could feel his power growing. It was no different here than on earth. Those in power depended on such as he but had no idea of his strength. He was ever growing, always amassing more influence.

Soon, I will be able to use it. Very shortly I will break free. Then THEY would learn to serve me. And I will not make the same mistake with THEY that I did with Caligula. This time, I will emerge supreme. I will be Emperor, not of Rome, but of the In-Between.

First, to finish the tiny issue of dealing with the humans...

FIFTY-NINE

DECEMBER 19

Patrick drove the IPS first to the Medical Center where they picked up Helen Murray and then to her house. Inside his Range Rover, the raging nor'easter was kept at bay. An excellent driver, and using the four-wheel-drive, Patrick was able to maneuver them efficiently and carefully through the rapidly accumulating snow. Helen was in the front seat, and Roosevelt, Sam, and Jeremy were in the back.

"I never would have believed we could get a storm like this so early in the season." Jeremy shook his head as he watched the snow billowing towards them as if mythical giants, maybe Paul Bunyan himself, had been shoveling great clumps of snow towards their vehicle. "Especially after how warm it was just a few days ago."

Jeremy had received Helen's call shortly after speaking with Dr. Wilson. She had made it clear she was ready and wanted to be picked up. "Either you come and get me or I'll walk to my place. We're doing this together. I want to get this thing, this bastard that's hurting my Helena."

Jeremy had tried to talk her out of it. Of all of them, he was the one who was the most concerned for her safety. He had told her that it was bad enough that they were facing this thing. Why not stay there and watch over Helena?

"Goddamnit, Jeremy! I can't lose her. Don't you understand? That little girl is the last bit of my sister that I have left, the last of my family. I had to bury my parents, my sister, and my brother-in-law. I am NOT going to see Helena die. She will outlive me. There isn't anything else I can do here, and I'm going to fight this with you. Understand? I don't want to hear any bullshit chivalry from you. I don't want to hear that a woman shouldn't fight. I am more capable of fighting than the rest of you old men, so are you coming with me or not?"

255

Jeremy was hurt by her words, but he reluctantly said yes, and they made their way to the front of the hospital. When Helen saw the Range Rover idling out front, she hurried to it and got in the front seat, which they had opened for her.

"It's one of the biggest fucking blizzards I've seen around here," Sam said.

"At this point, I think that nothing else that happens will surprise me." Roosevelt was thinking about dreams he had and the visitation from Sarah. Whatever happened next, at least they were all together, and, hopefully, prepared.

Patrick suddenly pulled the SUV over and looked at the sky. "Gentlemen and lady, look at that if you will." He leaned forward and gazed up at the sky.

"Oh my God," Helen muttered softly as she too looked forward. The others leaned forward to see what had happened. It was as if a summer thunderstorm intertwined with a blizzard. Snow was swirling down dramatically, but the clouds were lit up from the inside. They watched as ball lightning appeared from the clouds, and the air shook with sudden fierce claps of thunder, sounding like the firing of nearby cannon. The ground shook from the sound, and a lightning bolt struck the ground up the street from them.

Both Sam and Roosevelt cringed a bit and ducked for cover.

"Are you okay back there?" Patrick didn't laugh at them. He knew that this thunder sounded more like the explosion of artillery than a phenomenon of nature. He would never laugh at fellow veterans.

"Yeah, Patty, we are ok." Sam's words were meant to be confident, but he could not mask the tremor in his voice. He was scared, as were they all.

Jeremy, who was sitting between Roosevelt and Sam and could feel them trembling, spoke up, "Patrick, everyone is fine back here." Patrick caught Jeremy's eyes in the rearview mirror, and he quickly and almost imperceptibly, nodded to him.

Helen turned to say something, but she stopped when a long sudden strike of lightning stretched from the sky to the road about one block away. They all saw it hit the ground and then heard an immediate boom of thunder. At the same time, for an instant, the sky was as bright as the most intense summer day.

They were all silent.

Patrick pulled the Range Rover back onto the street and carefully drove the rest of the way to the Murray house. Even though their journey was only a few blocks, it seemed to last for hours as the car moved slowly along the streets. They were the only car on this road, but, with visibility nearly nonexistent, Patrick was driving as prudently as he could. Finally, they reached Helen's house. As the rest slowly got out of his car, Patrick stayed behind the wheel.

"Aren't you coming in?" Jeremy looked at Patrick with a bit of confusion. He thought Roosevelt's nephew was in this battle with them. Was he chickening out now?

It didn't seem likely for a man with his background.

"No, I'm not, Jeremy. But don't think I'm abandoning you. This battle is going to be fought on two fronts, and I have to take another position. But trust me, all of you, I am fighting with you. Uncle Roosevelt understands."

They nodded at him and prepared to slog up the sidewalk to the house.

"Gentlemen, please wait for a moment, and lady also. No offense meant, Ma'am."

Helen smiled. "None taken. Believe me, Patrick, I know whatever you are doing, it's to help."

Patrick stepped out of the vehicle and went to each of them. He shook hands with Jeremy, Sam, and Helen. Then he embraced his uncle in a massive bear hug.

Without another word, he stepped back into his Range Rover.

They stood and watched as the big black SUV pulled away and vanished into the blinding white.

"Let's do it." Sam looked at them and started to walk towards the door of the house.

SIXTY

If an uninformed observer had happened to enter Patrick's study, they would have found him sitting back in his easy chair, with his eyes wide open, but unseeing. They might easily have assumed that he was either dead or in a coma, because his eyes were glassy and non-responsive to any physical stimuli. His pulse, had they been able to check, would have seemed to be almost nonexistent. This man, however the situation might have dictated, was not dead, nor was he in a coma.

Patrick was for all outward appearances gone from this world, but his mind and spirit were very much alive. After nearly deadening efforts to achieve direct communication with Michael, all with great physical and mental consequences, Patrick had finally achieved the state of mind he needed, and he had made connection.

After dropping the others at Ms. Murray's house, he drove through the blizzard and returned home. Even though he was both an excellent driver and used to dealing with bad winter conditions and driving the nearly perfect vehicle for such extreme circumstances, he almost skidded off the road twice when near whiteouts occurred. Patrick kept his cool—he was never one to panic. It took longer than he expected, but he finally pulled into his driveway.

Once inside his home, he quickly doffed his winter hat and coat and went directly to his study.

Rather than sit at his desk with his pen in hand, he sat comfortably in his easy chair, not reclining, but still in a position of comfort. He held in his hands Michael's Marine Corps officer's sword, one of his twin's most cherished possessions, and he emptied his mind through careful meditation. He first used the Taoist breathing technique that he had learned many years ago, centering his breathing at his diaphragm and filling his belly with air on each breath and pulling it all the way in on each exhalation. The process was slow, producing four full breaths each minute. He continued this for about twenty minutes, until he felt his mind and body calming. Then he went into a more esoteric meditation taught to him by a Kung Fu Sifu with whom he had studied for many years. As he approached this desired state, he felt movement, not physical either external or internal, but spiritual. He felt himself separate from his body, and he wondered briefly if this was what dying was like, but he knew that he was still very much alive.

He couldn't see anything, but he didn't feel as if he were blind. His normal senses seemed to have lost all meaning; instead, he simply knew he had moved to somewhere important. This was what he had tried to do.

Slowly, he began to be able to see, only with what eyes, he was not sure. He perceived that he had a body, and he was dressed in his combat uniform. He had not put on since the day of his wounding. In his right hand, he carried the Michael's sword—he held it up and saw a very gentle glow seem to emanate from the ceremonial weapon.

Then a voice came clearly to him. *"Baby brother."*

The sound was soft, almost inaudible, but he knew he had heard the voice of his brother.

He heard another voice call out, "Michael!" He realized it was the sound of his own voice, but it didn't sound like anything he had ever heard before either in his own head or in a recording. It was light and seemed to transmit without the need of airwaves. It seemed to be sound, but it was different.

Patrick heard his name once more and then another noise, like what he would have assumed the devils of hell sounded like. He had experienced terrible combat, had killed men, had held dying men in his arms while they cried for their mothers, and he was nearly killed as well. In all of those instances, Patrick had been deeply frightened. It would have been nonhuman not to be afraid, but this voice filled him with a terror beyond anything that he had ever experienced. It wasn't his life for which he feared when he heard that terrible sound, but it was for his essence, his very soul.

Patrick heard a terrible roar, a loud guttural exhalation like the sound of bomb exploding nearby. It jarred him as if it were a physical explosion. The sound reverberated in him, as if he were wearing a helmet again. He was terrified. He wanted to duck for cover and find a place to hide. He wanted to be back in bed as a child cowering from the unseen monsters in the dark. It seemed as if he was a five-year-old boy shaking in his bed and trying not to let his feet hang over because the monster under the bed would get him. Only this time, he was not a five-year-old boy, and he was certain that this thing was the equivalent of the monster under the bed, only it was real, whatever that meant in this realm.

He didn't want to face it. What was he doing here? He didn't belong here. He didn't want to be here. This was insanity. As his mind raced, filled with fear, he felt himself starting to recede, to return to his place of origin, although at this point, he wasn't sure where that was. He looked at his hand holding the sword, and he saw that it had begun to grow dim. The sword no longer had any glow, and he could begin to see through his arm, as if he were as insubstantial as a soft spring breeze.

Going back. To safety.

SIXTY-ONE

DECEMBER 19

Roosevelt, Jeremy, Sam, and Helen Murray, who now seemed to be much older than her years, had gathered at Helen's house. She no longer looked like the vibrant and powerful middle-aged woman whom they all had come to know. Now she seemed to have shrunken a bit and aged to the beginning of being elderly. Her hair had begun to go white.

We are all aging more, Roosevelt thought grimly.

They stood outside in the bitter cold and the near blinding snow. Even though they knew they needed to enter, they were all afraid and hesitant. As much as he had grown to dislike the bone-aching cold, Roosevelt preferred the deep cold in his bones to the fear in his heart. He knew the others felt the same.

"Where is Helena?" Roosevelt asked hoping she was far away but knowing that distance did not seem to matter. The child was in jeopardy no matter the location.

"I left her at the hospital with Dr. Wilson and Sister Anna. She said that she would do anything she could to help her." Helen's face indicated that she didn't know if the good sister would be able to help. There was nowhere else that was as safe. If not in the care of a Sister of the Church and a good-hearted doctor, then where was safety against such evil?

They leaned close to each other so they could hear despite the howling wind.

Jeremy touched her arm gently. "How is she?"

"Worse and the doctors don't seem to be able to do anything." She screwed her face up into a tight knit ball. She wanted to cry and scream and hit out at the same time.

"God damn this thing! I won't let it take Helena!"

"Maybe God had already damned it." Roosevelt and Jeremy were startled to hear that come from Sam, who had stopped speaking of God since the death of his son.

Jeremy was the next to startle Roosevelt. "Let's get in there and see if we can finish this motherfucker and send him to wherever this asshole belongs. It's time to kick some supernatural ass!"

Helen started laughing at the look on Roosevelt's face. "Why Roosevelt, you look like you've never heard that kind of language before. I thought you had been in the military."

"I was, but I have never heard that kind of language from our Jeremy before."

"Damned straight, Jerry," Sam added and gripped his shoulder. "Let's go put a butt whuppin' on this lowlife scumbag." Sam clapped Jeremy on the back, and they all started walking towards the door. Roosevelt led the way and tried to keep a straight face, but he felt the too familiar pain in his arm and chest begin. *Not now. I will not have a heart attack now.*

Roosevelt stepped back and turned from the others. With the dexterity of a stage magician, he pulled his nitro pills from one of his coat pockets and slipped one under his tongue. Then he turned and put his hand in his breast pocket. It was there, his personal talisman. Since the dream the other night when Sarah appeared to him, he decided to keep one of his favorite pictures of her with him at all times. She had said in the dream, "I will always be with you, my love." He was not sure if that were even possible, if what he dreamt was a true visitation from his beloved dead wife, or if he had simply been giving into his unending grief and now accentuated stress, but he would carry the picture of her beaming and wearing jeans and a sweatshirt as she stood at their honeymoon lodge in Canada, with the smile that always pierced his heart with joy.

Sam looked at him and nodded. He understood. He, too, carried his own amulet with him. It was not a photograph; rather, it was a simple, battered Topps Baseball Card of Derek Jeter, who had been Josh's favorite player. Taking Josh to Yankee Stadium to see his beloved team play and sharing the joy that Josh had felt was one of the best memories that Sam had. He had never felt closer to his son than that day. After the game, they had stopped at a diner and eaten a huge meal, a guy's meal, as Josh said smiling, of cheeseburgers, fries and soda, followed by a CMP sundae. Sam felt like he was going to explode from all the food, but he wanted that moment to live forever. When they got home and were still in the car, Josh had turned to him and said, "Pop, that was the best day ever. Thanks. I love you." After Josh had died, Sam had found that card in his room. He had placed it in his top dresser drawer, but yesterday, he took it out and put it in his wallet, in one of the photo holders, next to his son's picture.

Jeremy, likewise, held his own talisman, the walking stick that he used since he hurt his ankle. It had been a favored artifact of David's, and he felt David's presence merely by using it. Like Roosevelt, he had dreamt of David. That dream had filled him with wonder and courage. After waking, he had stopped wanting to drink again. *I will be strong. I want to be clean and sober when I next see my beloved David.*

Helen became a warrior, as much as a mother bear, protecting her cubs. She had decided that she would face anything to help Helena, and she wore a necklace that the little girl had made for her from a bead kit. It wasn't well balanced, and it had all the colors of the rainbow scattered in it in random patterns, but Helen felt the child's essence and love in it. *You can't have her, you son of a bitch. I'll die to protect her.*

They walked in the door and felt the air temperature drop by around 20 degrees.

Sam pulled the entrance door shut, and they heard laughter. Then, in a sibilant hiss, *"So, my little lambs have come back for the slaughter. And by the way, the smallest lamb is mine already."*

SIXTY-TWO

DECEMBER 19 THE IN-BETWEEN

"Patrick! I need your help!" Michael's clear call pulled Patrick back from the abyss of surrender and running. In that moment, Patrick heard the voice of his brother, the person with whom he was the closest, the person on whom he had counted so many times, the man whom he had admired and idolized, and he heard fear in his brother's voice.

I can't be too afraid to help Michael.

"Michael!!" Patrick screamed with what passed for a voice in this place. "Where are you?"

Patrick looked down and saw that he was substantial, as fully formed and whole as he had been in his office. Once again, he was wearing his combat uniform, and once again he was carrying the sword, which now had begun to glow with an inner light of its own, as if it were alive.

Again he heard the terrible and strange roar, and its vibrations shook him as if a grenade had exploded only a few feet away, but this time instead of being frightened, he was angry.

You're not getting rid of me that easily, you son of a bitch.

"Michael! Talk to me, big brother. Where are you?"

He heard Michael call to him again, and he began to cross a field of battle. It was somewhat familiar to him, taking the form of some of the landscape he had seen in Iraq, but it was also unfamiliar, looking like vistas from other times and places. As he moved across, he saw corpses of dead soldiers, some American Marines whom he had known, some Iraqi soldiers, but others were scattered from history: Japanese soldiers from the Pacific Theater in World War II, laying strewn in the heat of Tarawa, British soldiers with their faces contorted from gassed trenches in France in World War I. There were others whom he could not identify, some holding Renaissance weapons, others older still. Then he came across the moldering remains of ancient Celts and Roman Warriors, hacked to death by their own weapons.

"This is a battlefield of death, a place for lost soldiers to lie for eternity." Maledicus hissed the words. *"You, puny man, you will soon join them. You think you can oppose me? First I will destroy your brother, I will then make you gaze on his form, while I slowly destroy you, and I will rejoice!"*

Patrick realized that the voice sounded different. The change was slight, but he noticed it. It had lost some of the booming timbre it had before; some of the arrogant confidence had left it.

"I'm coming for you, Motherfucker. You have to face both of us now!"

Patrick kept moving forward, slogging through mud and blood. Since his realization about the voice, the intensity of the visions of carnage had increased. He was literally walking across a sea of dead bodies. With each step, he could feel his feet step into rotting corpses, but he didn't care. He could hear the moans and cries of the dead soldiers as he waded through them as if he were moving through a sea of fetid and noxious muck.

As he moved forward, Patrick felts hands reaching for him. Impossibly old, some with only the fingers of skeletons, all reaching for him, trying to grab him and pull him down with them. As he felt the hands getting purchase on his uniform, Michael used the sword like a scythe and cut through the fields of the dead, opening a pathway through the gore of battles past.

He had to continue.

He had to get through this morass of death.

Michael needed him.

SIXTY-THREE

DECEMBER 19

"Code Blue!" the nurse yelled, and the alarm sounded in the children's section of the hospital.

Dr. Wilson ran to Helena's room faster than he had ever run in his life. *No, no, no. We are not going to lose her. I am not going to fail them.*

Sister Anna stood next to the little girl praying as the nurses held an oxygen mask over Helena's tiny face.

The nurse holding the apparatus shouted to Wilson as he ran up to the small bed, "She isn't breathing, and there is barely a heartbeat."

SIXTY-FOUR

DECEMBER 19

"**F**ools!*" the voice boomed. *"You should not have come. You are nothing but three impotent old men and one defenseless woman. You are nothing to me."* They huddled in the foyer and winced at the power of the sound. It was as if someone had put in a new set of amplifiers and speakers and cranked up the volume.

"Ignore it. It is trying to frighten us." Roosevelt tried to sound calmer than he was. He could still feel his heart pounding against the inside of his chest.

"Hey! Listen to me, scumbag!" Sam said and smiled. "You sound just like a bully who's about to get his ass kicked."

"Damn straight!" Jeremy added and this time, he slapped Sam on the back. "Let's go get this bastard."

"We're coming for you, asshole. You can't have my niece." Helen's eyes had grown grim and cold, like the look on a sniper's face as they took aim on an unsuspecting target.

They moved through the foyer and into the living room. As they did, images of horror poured into their minds.

Sam saw his son Josh sitting in his running car in the garage, inhaling the poison fumes deeply, say *"It's because of you, Pop. You made me do this. I hate you! I hate you!"* Josh slumped to the floor and blood gushed out of his eyes and mouth, forming a river of blood flowing around Sam's feet. Sam thought he was prepared for anything, but he wasn't ready for this. He screamed and collapsed into a fetal position and started murmuring, "No.no.no.no.no."

"Samuel! Ignore it. This is all a lie!" Yet, Sam couldn't hear Roosevelt from the sound of his mind screaming. He stayed in a fetal ball, staring at the vision of his dead son.

267

"We have to find it. It's in the house somewhere, somewhere central probably." Jeremy spoke to them with a voice of quiet authority. Then Jeremy saw David standing before him and laughing. "What do you think you are going to do? You're nothing but a small town hick, a little fairy who is afraid to come out of the closet. You were a terrible lover, Jerry, you never pleased me. Not once." Jeremy tightened his grip on the walking stick and then held it up in front of him. Jeremy knew that this was just a lie, this thing's attempt to divide them, to dispel them. He held the cane tightly and shouted into the room, "You're a liar, you son of a bitch, and we know it. Guys, ignore whatever you see or think you see. This thing is a liar, and it's afraid of us. These lies are its weapons."

Jeremy crouched next to Sam. "It's a lie, big guy, a lie. Whatever it's telling you." Jeremy sat and cradled Sam's head in his lap. "It's just a lie."

Sam looked up at Jeremy. Sam was crying, with huge tears pouring down his cheeks. "My boy hates me. Josh hates me." Sam broke into an enormous wail that almost made the walls shake.

Roosevelt leaned over to reach into Sam's back pocket and pulled out his wallet. He opened it and said, "Of course, it had to be here."

He opened the wallet to a picture of Josh, happy and smiling and to the baseball card. "Look at this, Samuel." Roosevelt held the picture and the card directly in his friend's face. "Look at this, marine! That is an order!" Roosevelt had taken on the voice of command from his days in the Vietnam War. The sound cut through the screaming in Sam's mind, and he looked at Roosevelt.

"Not at me, at this!" He held the opened picture section of the wallet to Sam. Sam slowly stopped rocking. "That is right, Samuel. It is all lies. This is the truth. I know how much pain you are in, but I also know this. Your son loved you. That is the truth."

Sam, with a spasm that shook his large frame, reached out and took the wallet. He looked at the picture and the card and shook his head. He slowly began to stand.

"I'm ok. I'm still here," he said in a shaky voice.

"Good man." Jeremy helped him up and stood next to him.

Helen stood, almost rooted in one place with a look of horror on her face. Maledicus had shown her what he intended for her niece, how he intended to absorb her soul into the many that he inhabited, to become a part of the demon itself.

"It's worse than murder or rape," she said. "He wants her soul. Oh my god, can he do that?"

"No, Ms. Murray, he cannot do that. That is what he wants you to think, to frighten you. He may be powerful," Roosevelt said directly to her, "but he is neither God nor the Devil. He is a demon, and he can be defeated." Roosevelt prayed that he was correct, but he was not certain.

She stopped and looked at Roosevelt. She thought of who this thing had been. A monster, but a human monster, a sociopath, one who had been destroyed in his own life, but who now continued doing as a spirit the same abominations he had performed as a human. With that thought, she touched the necklace that Helena had made for her, and she smiled a tight, even smile. Her eyes glittered with an anticipation of action. The warrior was back. "Yes, he can be defeated. He will be."

SIXTY-FIVE

DECEMBER 19 THE IN-BETWEEN

I t was like the kind of dream when he seemed to be stuck running in place. No matter how many dead warriors Patrick moved through, there were always more to replace them. Their bodies seemed to merge to form a kind of rotted gelatinous mass, clinging to him, and threatening to suck him down. His legs were growing tired, and he was becoming frustrated and impatient. *I have to stop,* he thought.

Fuck stopping. That's what it wants. It wants to frustrate me and make me act foolishly and with distraction. This was, he knew, a classic type of combat maneuver, to frighten and upset the enemy, to make them wonder about themselves and their abilities. When in this state of mind, they lost some of their capacity for efficient battle. Patrick remembered one of his original Martial Arts teachers, a very old man, one Sensei Mikadu, who had told him that if your enemy succeeds in enraging you and knows how to take advantage of your mental state, then you lose the combat.

He closed his eyes and calmed himself, breathing to center himself. It did not take long to achieve balance. *I will not listen to your lies. They mean nothing to me.* His body felt real and whole. When he opened his eyes, the corpses were gone.

You're a liar. I know what you are. We're going to destroy you, motherfucker.

Patrick entered a field, the kind on which ancient armies might have contested a battle. The kind when the phrase "winning the day" had great meaning. In the center of the field, was a monstrous murky cloudlike thing undulating with an obscene movement and stinking as if a million rotting corpses were inside it. It seemed to grow as he watched it. It was trying to take something into itself, to pull it in with an amoeba-like embrace.

Patrick looked carefully and saw the victim was Michael.

"Michael, I'm here!"

"It's about time, baby brother. I could use a little help here." As he spoke, he was able to leap back from the mass, but tendrils of gray slime clung to him like rotting vegetation from a forgotten primordial swamp.

Michael looked as he had the day he had saved Patrick. He was in his combat uniform but without a helmet. They looked at each other from across the field. They were unable to join together, because Maledicus' form continued to undulate and threaten to absorb them.

"Try not to let it touch you, Patrick. It grows by absorption."

"Absorption? Of what?"

"Of souls, baby brother, of souls."

They heard another enormous roar, and the mass began moving towards Michael.

"Patrick, I could use a weapon here."

SIXTY-SIX

DECEMBER 19

"My office. We have to get to my office." Helen Murray realized that while the living room would have been central to the entire house, the office was where she kept other artifacts, and even if it had somehow hidden itself, it was likely to stay near the other Roman pieces; it was likely to feel comfortable near something from its own time. Helen quickly turned and sprinted up the steps with a speed that suggested she were once again an athletic teenager. She bounded up the stairs two at a time.

"Follow me!"

The IPS moved after her as quickly as they could but still considerably slower.

"Here comes the geriatric fucking cavalry," gasped Sam as he lumbered up the steps. "I really have to work on losing some weight."

Roosevelt was next, moving as quickly as his once again pounding heart would allow, and Jeremy struggled up the staircase, wincing with each step. His injured ankle was flaring with excruciating pain. At the next to the top step, he felt a snap, and he screamed and collapsed.

"Jerry, what is it, man?" Sam knelt next to his stricken friend.

"It's my ankle. It's broken." Jeremy held his ankle tightly with both hands as if he were trying to push the brittle bones back together.

"Damn, Jer. I'll stay with you."

"No! You have to go on. I'll be fine."

"Pop. He's right," Josh said to Samuel in a voice only he could hear, *"They need you, and I know you can do this. Pop, I love you."*

Sam swelled as he heard Josh's voice. He knew that this time, this was really his son speaking to him.

"I'll be back for you, Jerry." Sam stood, left Jeremy and followed the others into Helen's studio.

After he heard the door to the office shut, Jeremy offered a silent prayer that he would be able to stand. *Please let me do this, please! They need me. I can't stay behind. The guys need me, and that little girl needs me.* Jeremy grabbed the banister and pulled himself up, trying not to scream with the pain of the exertion. He stood and held onto the banister for balance as his head swam from the lancing knives that seemed to cut through his broken ankle. *I'm getting too old for this kind of thing.* He tried to move, but the most intense pain he ever felt shot through his body. Jeremy stifled a scream. With tears streaming down his face, he tried to move forward.

"Jeremy, my love. You aren't getting old. You will always be my youngster, and you can do this. I know you can." Jeremy heard the sound of his David's voice next to him and felt his lover's firm grip around his shoulders, helping to support him. Jeremy wiped the tears away. Then, he leaned heavily on his cane and moved slowly down the hallway towards the office. Each step, even though he tried very hard not to put any weight on his damaged ankle, caused excruciating jolts of agony to shoot up his leg, as if blades were cutting into him from behind.

Jeremy heard noises coming from the office. *Hold on,* he thought. *I'm almost there.*

SIXTY-SEVEN

DECEMBER 19 THE IN-BETWEEN

Patrick looked at his brother, and love and admiration swelled inside him. He knew he was where he needed to be. The sound emanating from the demon was nearly overwhelming, like the sound of the war in Iraq. Patrick, despite not being able to maneuver behind that thing, had an idea of a way to keep it at bay. This thing was not the only one who could fight with sound. Their voices would join as a unified, powerful weapon.

"Michael! Listen to me! It's important!"

"What is it? I don't think we have much time here."

"Do you remember our favorite section of Shakespeare?"

"Shakespeare? Are you serious, baby brother?"

"Yes, *Henry V*, when he addresses the troops before the battle of Agincourt."

"That's right," Michael said and smiled.

"We have to use what we know and care about," Patrick shouted.

Michael began the speech as if he were addressing a whole squadron of Marines:

"This story shall the good man teach his son;
And Crispin, Crispin shall ne'er go by,
From this day to the ending of the world,
But we in it shall be remembered. . ."

As he spoke, his voice began to ring with a mighty tone, and the sound of Maledicus' roar began to subside, to become muddled.

Patrick picked up the speech:

"We few, we happy few, we band of brothers.
For he today that sheds his blood with me
Shall be my brother; be he ne'er so vile,

274

This day shall gentle his condition."

The brothers heard the roar try to increase in volume but subside again as they joined their voices, almost singing out the words.

"And gentlemen in England now a-bed
Shall think themselves accurs'd they were not here,
And hold their manhoods cheap whiles any speaks
That fought with us upon Saint Crispin's day."

The effect of their voices was clearly stinging the demon, causing it pain and confusion. It was writing and sounds like painful screams cascaded out of its ever-changing form.

"More, baby brother, we need more. We've hurt it, but I don't think we've stopped it," Michael said. "Do you have any more ideas?"

Patrick smiled and said, "Yes, I do, but I need you to try to stay on key, big brother."

They both knew what was coming, their most beloved song, the anthem that carried the meaning of their lives. Now the mass had receded a bit, and they were standing side by side looking directly at it as they raised their voices together. They were loud, clear, and definitely on key as they broke into song.

SIXTY-EIGHT

DECEMBER 19

Jeremy reached the office door and tried to open it, but it wouldn't move. He heard screaming coming from the office. *Please,* David, he thought. *I need your strength. Help me with this.* He braced with his good foot, and he threw himself against the door. It opened with a crack, including the sound of his right shoulder dislocating. As the door flung open, he fell into the office and landed on the floor with a thud. He looked up with his eyes tearing from more suffering than he thought a human being could possibly feel. Roosevelt, Helen, and Sam were trying to get at the statuette, but it was guarded by a gray, ugly mist that seemed to have mass. Whenever they tried to move towards the statue, it touched them, and they screamed as their skin blistered.

Not now. Please not now. Roosevelt felt a horrible taste in his mouth. His chest felt like it was encased in a steel vise, and he could barely breathe.

"Not yet, my husband. You must hold on. We will be together shortly, but now stay in the battle." Roosevelt looked up and could see Sarah watching him. She smiled, reached out and touched his chest.

Jeremy saw Roosevelt clutch his chest and slump to the floor. Sam was screaming in pain, holding his hands in front of him. They were blistered with third degree burns as if he had put them on a burning surface. He had tried to grab the statue, but the mist had scalded him.

Helen was still yelling at it, almost incoherent in her anger.

"Helen," Jeremy yelled to her. "Be careful."

"Fuck that. I need a weapon, Jeremy. I can't do it like this. I can't get to it!"

SIXTY-NINE

DECEMBER 19 THE IN-BETWEEN

The two brothers stood shoulder to shoulder and faced Maledicus. They held their heads high, and they sang the anthem, the music whose creed they had lived by and that had defined their careers:

"From the halls of Montezuma
To the shores of Tripoli;
We fight our country's battles
In the air, on land and sea;
First to fight for right and freedom
And to keep our honor clean;
We are proud to claim the title
Of United States Marine."

After this verse, the demon was undulating rapidly almost as if the various spirits and souls that made it up were battling inside. They could hear voices from within begging them to continue and others begging them to stop. Michael and Patrick now stood next to each other, directly in front of Maledicus, and they increased their volume and power, sounding almost as if it were an entire unit of Marines singing:

"Our flag's unfurled to every breeze
From dawn to setting sun;
We have fought in ev'ry clime and place
Where we could take a gun;
In the snow of far-off Northern lands
And in sunny tropic scenes;
You will find us always on the job –
The United States Marines!"

Their diaphragms were strong, from many years of Martial Arts training, and their conviction was clear. Their voices supported their beliefs and the power of their spirits.

"Here's health to you and to our Corps
Which we are proud to serve
In many a strife we've fought for life
And never lost our nerve."

The very last part of the hymn was the strongest. They belted out the words as if their very lives made the song reverberate with power. Their voices seemed to envelope Maledicus with their music.

"If the Army and the Navy
Ever look on Heaven's scenes;
They will find the streets are guarded
By United States Marines!

Michael turned to his brother. "I need my weapon so I can guard Heaven's scenes."

Patrick smiled and handed the Marine Corps Officer Sword to his brother.

SEVENTY

DECEMBER 19 – BETHBERG AND THE IN-BETWEEN

"Helen," Jeremy said in a tremulous voice. He could feel sobs hitching in him as he forced the words to leave his mouth. "Here is your weapon." David's cane had begun to glow with an unearthly golden light. Jeremy rolled over and tossed the cane to Helen, then he screamed as his dislocated shoulder and broken ankle pulsed agony through him. Helen caught it with one hand and turned, brandishing it like the rebellious female Celtic leader Boudicea facing the occupying Roman legions. As she faced the statue, she heard and saw two figures standing by her. Her sister and brother-in-law were floating off to her left, shimmering as if being seen through a translucent curtain. *"Save our Helena, my sister. We love you, and we know you are her mother now. Save Helena."*

I love you both, and I'll save her. Helen faced the statue. "GO TO HELL, YOU EVIL BASTARD!" She waded through the mist, ignoring the scalding heat and raised the cane above her head.

Michael raised the sword behind him in a classic attacking position. He, along with the sword, was now glowing with an intense internal white light. Maledicus cowered before the light.

All Patrick heard before Michael struck was, "Semper Fi, you Mother-fucker!"

Michael swung the sword in a mighty arc and went through the mass of the demon. The sword moved through it like it was cutting through a poisoned acidic pile of excrement.

Simultaneously, Helen brought the handle of the cane crashing down onto the statuette. The impact shook her. It felt like she was smashing a pile of concrete with a sledgehammer, and the reverberations cascaded through her body, making her nauseous. The statue smashed into thousands of pieces. Immediately a great howl, like the sound of an ancient prehistoric beast being ripped apart by another creature with its viscera flowing from its body, filled the room. Simultaneously, a sulfuric-like stench emanated into the room.

A voice screamed, *"NOOOOOOOOOO!"*

Helen raised the cane and continued to pound the shards, over and over, pulverizing them. With each blow, she felt the power in the thing diminish. Then the mist in the room howled in pain, screaming like the sound of a thousand wounded banshees. The mist undulated horribly. The sound stopped, and the mist vanished.

Maledicus screamed. *"No! This can't happen! I am immortal! I can't be destroyed!"*

His mass burst apart. Souls whom had been captured by the demon flew away like doves released from their painful cages, and the mass of darkness slowly faded until there was only a pathetic looking Roman standing before Michael and Patrick. He was short, bald, with spindly legs and a pendulous gut. He looked at them terrified and held his hands up to protect himself.

Then a white flash of light surrounded him, and he screamed. The light was as brilliant as a supernova exploding in its death throes. It lasted only for an instant, then, it blinked out.

When the light vanished, Maledicus was gone.

SEVENTY-ONE

"Doctor," the nurse said. "She's fine. The little girl is breathing, and her heart rate is normal."

Dr. Wilson broke into tears, and Sister Anna hugged him.

Helena slept calmly and clutched a teddy bear.

SEVENTY-TWO

Michael and Patrick embraced. They hugged each other with all of their strength. Then Michael held Patrick by the shoulders and looked at his brother.

"Baby brother, it's so good to see you. I've been waiting a long time for you."

"I know, big brother."

Michael smiled and led Patrick forward.

"It's time for us to move on."

EPILOGUE (PART I)

JANUARY 28

The wind, cold, strong and powerful, whipped across the open fields at Arlington National Cemetery. The snow from the recent winter storm drifted against the lines of carefully tended white tombstones and solemn trees like the whispering ghosts of departed soldiers. The gentle sound of the moving snow was like the whispers of the dead carried in the winter wind, begging not to be forgotten. The sun was shining brightly on this late January day but brought little warmth on this frigid afternoon, and four people, three elderly men and one woman, stood by a recent burial.

Roosevelt, Sam, Jeremy and Helen were at the foot of Patrick's grave, which was immediately next to his brother, Michael's. Over a month had passed since the funeral, a full military burial complete with the honors bestowed a fallen Marine Corps Officer. Roosevelt and Helen had attended the ceremony, but Sam and Jeremy had still been in the hospital recovering from their injuries. Members of Patrick's unit, along with an honor guard had been present, but no one, except for Roosevelt, was there from the family. That was exactly as Roosevelt had expected, and he wanted no one else from his detested family present.

Taps were played, a service read by a Marine Corps Chaplin, and Patrick's body had been committed to the ground. During the playing of Taps by a lone bugler, Roosevelt had broken into tears. Memories of the many fallen soldiers he had known, especially that of the young man who had died saving him, rushed into his mind. As he quietly sobbed, Helen rubbed his back.

Roosevelt, as Patrick's uncle, had been the executor of Patrick's will and had been the one to accept the folded American flag. Roosevelt had taken the steps to ensure that Patrick's wish to be buried next to his twin was honored: they were united in death. As a retired Marine Corps officer, and as a recipient of the Distinguished Service Medal, the Silver Star, and two Purple Hearts, Patrick had multiple eligibilities to rest next to his predeceased brother.

Sam and Jeremy had been deeply upset that they were not deemed fit enough to travel by their attending physicians, so it was agreed that as soon as possible, they would all make a special journey to visit Patrick's grave. The three men were all still battered, and the wind and cold made their bones and injuries ache, but they would not let that stop them from saying their goodbyes to a fallen friend.

Helen had left Helena behind with Dr. Wilson, who was delighted to babysit the little girl. Helen told Roosevelt that when the child was older, she would bring her to see the grave of one of the brave men who helped save her. But for now, it was too soon for the little girl to try to deal with this. Dr. Wilson had amassed a fair amount of vacation time, and he was happy to care for the now active and joyful little girl.

After visiting the grave, the small group left together in Helen's rented car and stopped at a restaurant in Georgetown where they ate and had their own wake for Patrick.

"To Patrick, a very brave man," Roosevelt offered as a toast. They were sitting at a corner table in a quiet restaurant. Roosevelt had a glass of Maker's Mark bourbon, as did Sam, in honor of Patrick. Helen and Jeremy both held up glasses of mineral water. "To Patrick," they said, and clinked glasses and sipped their drinks.

"Gentlemen, and lady, I wanted to share some information with you. I waited until now so that we could talk at ease."

They quieted and waited for Roosevelt to continue. "The medical examiner performed a full autopsy because of the …ah…unusual circumstances of Patrick's death. As you know, while we were confronting Maledicus in Ms. Murray's house, he had his own battle to fight.

Roosevelt sipped a tiny bit of the bourbon. Then, "As I was saying, Patrick went back to his house. He had already informed me that he was going to contact Michael once more and that he believed he would be able to face this monster Maledicus with his brother. At this point, with what we had all experienced, I was willing to go along with his plan, as extraordinary as it seemed. Besides, as we have recounted to each other, we have all experienced …ah….visitations from our loved ones."

The others simply nodded. They held those brief moments to be precious.

"Patrick told me that he would be facing that thing, but that he had to do it from his home. After the statue was destroyed, and it was clear that

Maledicus was gone, I called Patrick to check on him, but there was no answer. I then called 911 and had an ambulance dispatched to his home, where the EMTs found him already dead. He was sitting in his office and was holding his brother's Marine Corps Officers Sword.

"The Medical Examiner performed an autopsy and found that he had died of several severe brain hemorrhages. I had since learned that Patrick was under treatment from a neurosurgeon in New York City, and that his condition was precarious, at the most optimistic prognosis.

"I had a chance to examine the sword he was holding before the burial. I thought it best that he hold both his and his brother's swords in his coffin. I examined Michael's sword, and it had been marked, with chips in the blade and a dark mass on the edge discolored by something it had cut into. I have never seen anything like that, but I can safely say to the three of you that I think he used it against Maledicus.

"In any case, he died as he lived, as a warrior."

EPILOGUE (PART II)

BETHBERG, PA

In the abandoned steel mills on the outside of town, something was moving, something not alive.